THE HAUNTING OF MONROE MANSE

BOOK 1 OF THE DREAMIST SERIES

KIM POOVEY

This book is dedicated to God, my rock and my salvation.

ACKNOWLEDGMENTS

Each time I write, my heart is filled with love and admiration for the amazingly incredible people with whom the Lord has blessed me. It seems the list grows with each book. Please take the time to read these names, as they are some of the most supportive and loving people ever.

To my dearest husband, Darryl, who consistently supports all that I do, endures my incessant tantrums when the computer won't do what I want it to do, and loves me despite my eccentric ways. I love you!

To my mom, Karen Oates, who edits when I ask her, listens to my story ideas, and is my cheerleader when the book is released - thank you! Love you - you're the best!

To my "other mother" Millie Boyce - thank you for putting up with my crazy antics and sharing tea and conversation! Love you!

To my family who support my ideas and crazy endeavors - I love you all!

To Charlotte Rains Dixon - the best writing coach ever! Thank you for bringing this story to life and making me a better writer!

To my amazing Beta readers, Richard Norris and Doreen Plyler - Thank you, thank you, thank you! You guys are the best!

A special thanks to Mark and Allison Guilloud whose home was the setting for this story.

To Katherine Brown who lifted me up when I was down and ready to quit writing - thank you!

A special thanks to Alyssa Krob and Manny Floresca at Ghost Ink Editing - you guys are wonderful!

To my friends (many of whom inspired characters in this book) - thanks for making every day special and entertaining. I especially want to thank; Lynn Cook Bristow, Christine Lanning, Joan Jones, E. T. Harris, Anita Rivard, Alyssa Krob, Manny Floresca, Darlene Stokes, Jo Beaver, Cindy Valieant, Lorrie and Dave Anderson, Mark and Rose Cook, Darrin Devlin, Susan Palmer, Carol Hunter, Pauly Hesse, and Collin and Jane Bruce Booker.

Most importantly, thanks to God who gives me my stories and has blessed me with the opportunity to share them with the world. To God goes all the glory!

IN MEMORIAM

To those who have gone on to Heaven but are still alive in my heart:

Dr. Harvey Brown Oates, Catherine Oates, Michael Wiegel, Sam Poovey, Rachell Poovey Navratil, David Clark, Tom Boyce, Janet 'Dolly' Nash, Lisa and Paul Hesse, Pete McComas, Jess Commiskey, Ione Telech, Phyllis Sooy, Cathy Benson, Dottie McDaniel, Pat Conroy, and Daisy the dachshund. I will love you all forever.

1

———————

Sarah's heart pounded as she stared beyond the staircase into a dark abyss. She had nowhere to run. Turning back, she watched the formless figure gliding toward her, its translucent skin shimmering across a skeletal hand reaching from the shadows. A scream hovered at her lips; the sound suffocated as adrenaline rushed through her veins like white water rapids. Cadaverous fingers prickled her neck as the spectral form's decaying breath whispered, "*He's guilty.*"

Gasping, Sarah bolted upright, her hands clammy and her nightshirt soaked with sweat as she gripped the edge of the bed. In an effort to calm her quivering body, she pulled her knees to her chest and rocked.

Her mind drifted back to middle school when her parents sent her to a local shrink after an unfortunate episode at a slumber party. The therapist's office was located in an old house with spirits of its own. On more than one occasion, she'd noticed a woman wearing an apron holding a plate of cookies or a gentleman sitting by the hearth smoking a pipe. The apparitions never tried to harm her although their empty eyes were unsettling. By her fourth visit she was stuck between her own reality and the reality her parents and therapist wanted her to believe.

"Is this house haunted?" Sarah asked, staring at the shimmering woman by the door.

"Why do you ask?"

Chewing her lower lip, she considered her response. Although Dr. Schneider had always been kind, he'd dismissed her reports of haunted dreams. Would he believe her now when she said there were ghosts in the same room?

"I was wondering if you believed in spirits since we spend so much time talking about them."

Dr. Schneider grinned. "There are no such things as ghosts. It's nothing more than an overactive imagination or entertainment for slumber parties. Isn't that where all of this started?" he asked, his eyebrows arched.

No, they've been around a lot longer than that, she thought.

At that moment, Sarah realized neither her therapist nor her parents would ever accept her ghostly accounts. In subsequent sessions, she abandoned the topic of ghosts and haunted dreams, instead chattering about girl drama at school and having a crush on the cutest guy in class. This led Dr. Schneider to declare her cured, much to her parent's relief. Frustrated by the experience, Sarah vowed never to mention the dreams to another living soul again.

Unable to calm her frazzled nerves, she decided to go for an early morning run. If she couldn't wipe the images from her mind maybe she could outrun them. Slipping her hair into a ponytail, Sarah dressed in neon running shorts and a tank top, laced up her sneakers and headed out the door into the muggy Lowcountry morning. She jogged her usual route through the historic district known as The Point with its stately mansions and glorious gardens. The scent of jasmine and gardenia intermingled with the pungent marsh gas, filling her lungs with the comforting smell of home.

The marsh came into view as she rounded the corner, the sun peeking over the horizon in shades of mango and lavender. With each footfall, the dreadful vision from her dream seeped from her mind in ribbons of sweat taking flight with the great white heron as she ran past.

Reaching Bridge Street, she slowed to a walk as the town awakened to the hustle of delivery trucks and the delicate aromas of brewing coffee and baking bagels. Restaurateurs placed sandwich boards along the sidewalk advertising everything from a full breakfast menu to a simpler fare of pastries and muffins. Sarah sidled past her own storefront, a two-story mercantile she'd inherited from her grandfather and had transformed into an antiques appraisal and estate liquidation business.

As she strode past, a shudder rattled her body accompanied by a fleeting image that she quickly dismissed. A second look released the tension holding her muscles hostage when she realized the shadowy movement reflecting from her shop windows was nothing more than fluttering palm fronds and flags hanging on surrounding storefronts. Still, she felt a sense of discomfort as if something was watching her. In an effort to thwart the ominous feeling needling her nerves, she hurried home, showered, and prepared for the day.

Sarah followed her usual routine, stopping at *Antiques and Coffee Beans* for her morning hot tea latte. Lisa owned a lovely store on the ground floor of an antebellum mansion filled with vintage and antique treasures along with a coffee bar. The atmosphere was relaxed and the prices affordable. It was rare to see anyone leave without an antique trinket or a cup of freshly brewed java.

"Mornin' Lisa," Sarah declared as she stepped through the door, the robust aroma of coffee permeating the air. Although she loved the scent of coffee, she didn't much care for the flavor and had been a loyal tea drinker her entire life.

"Hey Sarah," Lisa replied placing a carafe of dark roasted coffee on the vintage buffet by the door. "Your usual?"

"Add a double shot of vanilla syrup and whipped cream too, please."

"You must've run this morning."

Sarah chuckled, "You know me too well."

Miss Jess, a lovely woman with snow-white hair entered. She wore her signature pearls and shuffled across the space with the help of a cane to her usual spot by the window. Miss Jess was one of the regulars and usually the first to arrive. She was a wise woman whose deep knowledge of silver was boundless. On more than one occasion, Sarah had consulted with her about items brought to her own shop.

"Good morning Sarah, Lisa," she said with a smile, lowering herself onto the bistro chair.

"Tea and a bagel Miss Jess?"

"Yes please," she replied, resting her cane against the wall. "Will Kayla be by with the receipts for last month?"

"She should be here any minute," Lisa said. "She's running a bit behind with taxes due in a couple of weeks."

Lisa walked to the counter picking up a rhinestone butterfly pin from the floor. "Resident ghost," she said, shaking her head as she set the brooch on the counter.

"You have a ghost?" Sarah asked.

"That's what the regulars say. Personally, I don't believe in ghosts. Yet every day I leave this in the jewelry case and every morning it's in a different spot."

The whir of the latte machine drowned out the thrumming of Sarah's heart as she walked over and fingered the glittering butterfly. A tingling sensation radiated up her fingers making the hair on her arm stand on end. Stunned, she withdrew her hand.

Lisa handed her a to-go cup with steam snaking from the hole in the lid.

"Thanks Lisa," Sarah said, placing a few dollars on the counter.

"See you tomorrow."

Lisa started on Miss Jess's breakfast as Sarah waved goodbye and stepped outside.

Sarah's antiques shop was only a block away but the humidity made it feel as if she'd traveled across the Amazon forest. Even though she was haunted by unknown entities, she was intrigued by things of the past. Something about the essence of a finely carved mantel or the mystery of an antique armoire brought comfort as if she could perceive the lives entwined in the piece's history. In her waking hours, Sarah was at peace with the idea of past lives being revealed in the things she handled yet the nightly visitations brought an entirely different reaction.

Unlocking the door, she sauntered over to the desk and noticed the blinking light on the answering machine. She took a sip of her latte and pressed the button.

"Hey Sarah, it's Danni. I wish you'd get a cell phone. No one uses these old machines anymore. Anyway, give me a call when you get a chance. I've got some amazing news that will blow your mind!"

Sarah exhaled at her best friend's message. It was too early for Danni drama. The clock showed eight, which meant she'd have to wait to return the call since Danni was probably in court.

Thankfully, the caffeine and sugar from her latte was

kicking in, adding to the wired energy from her early morning run and lack of sleep. Sarah's mind raced between Danni's mysterious message and all the things she had to accomplish before closing time. What she didn't realize was how her life was getting ready to change in ways that would haunt her forever.

2

———————

Sarah sat at her desk behind the counter paging through another reference book as Coltrane rambled from the classic jazz station. She was researching an item brought in by Mr. Boyce, a regular customer from Charleston who always unearthed an exceptional piece of china, art, or furniture. He'd consigned several antiquities with her over the years and purchased a few as well; however, his recent find was something of a mystery. She'd already discovered the maker of the porcelain vase but not the pattern. Skimming through another worn reference book, Sarah's head began to bob. While her early morning run seemed like a good idea at the time, by early afternoon she was regretting her choice. Her eyes began to blur as she rested her head on the desk, her eyelids fluttering shut.

The bell on the shop door jangled as Edie Monroe, one of the town's most notable characters, entered. Edie's reputation for hearing voices, drinking heavily, and blustering about the grand old days of sit-ins and protests still swirled about town like a tornado. Bathed in Chanel No. 5, she wore her usual flamboyant attire of a vibrantly colored formless dress and Birkenstocks with a hot pink bandana restraining her untamed hair now colored in shades of purple and pink. The Monroe ancestral home reportedly housed an extraordinary collection of rare and valuable pieces making Sarah's heart quicken at the idea that Edie might want to liquidate some of the inventory.

"Good afternoon. Welcome to Holden's Antiques," Sarah said, the suffocating scent of Edie's perfume making her cough.

Edie stumbled on the rug before catching her balance. Her bright red lipstick looked like it had been applied by a Kindergartener who failed to color inside the lines. One side of Edie's face was red as if she'd fallen which wasn't unusual when she'd been drinking.

"Are you alright?" Sarah asked, stepping from behind the counter.

"*We* need your help," she croaked.

Sarah tilted her head looking for the other person. "We?"

Edie moved closer, grabbing Sarah's shoulder to steady herself. Her icy fingers bit into Sarah's flesh sending a chill shimmering down her spine.

"You cannot escape what you are. Time is drawing near and you must accept the truth before all hope is lost," Edie muttered, her voice raspy.

Looking up, Sarah was stunned to see Edie's eyes were missing...

With a scream, Sarah bolted upright in her chair momentarily incoherent, her heart pounding against her ribcage. She shook her head trying to empty the horrifying image from her mind. She slumped over, burying her face in her hands.

Not again, she thought.

She'd never had one of her dreams during the day. Too rattled to do anything else, Sarah decided to lock up and go home. She scanned the room making sure nothing spectral lingered when her eyes rested on the answering machine reminding her of Danni's message. Blowing out a breath, she picked up the phone and dialed Danni's number. It went straight to voice mail.

"Hey Danni, it's Sarah. I'm returning your call. Try me at home later."

After making a few notations in the old leather-bound ledger she'd found when she cleaned out her grandfather's inventory, Sarah secured the black metal moneybox in the antique safe. With one more look around the room, Sarah turned out the lights, locked the door, and started for home.

She walked the few blocks to her 1890s-whitewashed cottage, taking in the sweet smells of spring as jasmine crawled across fences and roses began to unfurl, releasing their luscious perfume. Despite the lingering discomfort from the dream she'd just experienced, Sarah began to relax with each step, shifting her thoughts to other things. Her business was doing well although a bit slow at the moment. Hopefully, her monthly trip to the Atlanta Antiques Fair would improve her profit margin. Owning two historic buildings meant Sarah had to be prepared for leaking roofs or plumbing catastrophes. Her true desire was to pay off her home mortgage, and the equity line she'd used to renovate the business, so she could afford to travel outside of the Southeast region in search of inventory.

Reaching the front gate of her cottage, guarded by two fierce gargoyles, she snatched the paper from the brick walkway, hurried up the porch steps, and plopped down on the swing to read.

Reading the newspaper was Sarah's daily respite when she wasn't traveling for auctions or appraisals. There was something comforting in the rustle of each page and the scent of printing press ink that took her back to childhood when her parents read the paper every evening. It was another one of those old-fashioned pleasures she'd refused to forego. She skimmed over the day's events before flipping to the second section with the obituaries, a habit she'd developed the summer she worked at her uncle's funeral parlor.

A pang reverberated in her chest and her breath came in short puffs when a particular name caught her attention.

Obituary for Edith "Edie" Ann Monroe

EDITH ANN MONROE, *fondly known as Edie, died April 3^(rd), 2003 at her family home following an extended battle with health issues. Born on January 20, 1952, Edie was the last surviving descendant in the Monroe line.*

An accomplished gardener and environmentalist, Edie was often involved in local gatherings for the preservation of the town's natural landscape. Edie will be interred at the mausoleum in the private family cemetery on Church Street.

SARAH LET the paper crumple to her lap, her stomach knotting. Edie Monroe was dead. *It's only a coincidence,* she thought, trying to steady her breathing. She closed her eyes tightly and began using some of the calming techniques she'd learned years ago in therapy. *Take a deep breath, hold it for a count of five, and release slowly, then repeat.* She did this several times until her body settled and her legs were stable enough to stand.

She went inside, poured a glass of wine, and reread the obit. No doubt, the write-up would bring a great many snickers at the eloquent representation of Edie and her "health issues," which all knew to be "crazy" and "drunk." It was one of the things Sarah loved about southern small-town life, no matter how loony the person; someone could find a genteel manner of stating facts without being disrespectful or entirely dishonest.

Between the strange dream at the shop and the vague report of Edie's cause of death, Sarah pondered how the woman had perished. If her dream held any merit, Sarah concluded Edie must have been drunk, fallen down, and hit her head. But why would she have dreamt about Edie when she hadn't known about her death until now? Sarah took a long sip of wine and tossed the paper in the trash bin. Her appetite gone, she grabbed the bottle of wine and returned to the front porch where she rocked away the trepidation stirring in her soul as Edie's words echoed through her mind. *You cannot escape what you are. Time is drawing near and you must accept the truth before all hope is lost.*

3

Days later, Sara awoke, relieved, and somewhat refreshed after a night devoid of disturbing dreams. Maybe the previous day's vision was nothing more than a fluke. She sat on the porch with her teacup and newspaper as birds celebrated spring's glory in a harmony of trills and warbles. It was her only day off and she decided to spend it in the garden, another treasured pastime she'd inherited. The temperatures were still mild, allowing her to spend several hours working in the yard before the midday heat took hold. When her teacup ran dry, she went inside, changed into her gardening clothes, and headed to the shed.

Thudding and thumping reverberated as the trowel battled the hardened earth in the weed-worn flowerbeds of last season. Rays of mid-morning sun massaged Sarah's back, sending pearls of sweat trickling down her forehead from beneath a wide-brimmed straw hat, the same one her grandmother always wore when gardening. Sarah wiped a wave of perspiration from her face when the kitchen phone rang, summoning her from her garden stupor. Popping up, she jaunted through the back door into the kitchen, the wooden screen bouncing in its frame behind her.

A breathy "Hello" crossed her lips as she tried to slow her rapid breathing.

"Sarah? What's the matter? You sound like you've been running a marathon," Danni declared from the other end.

"I was working in the garden and rushed to answer the phone."

"If you'd step into this century and get a cell phone, you wouldn't have to go through all that."

"One of these days, I'll get around to it. I don't relish the idea of being on-call twenty-four-seven," she said, slumping into a ladder-back chair at the pine kitchen table. She was parched but the phone cord didn't reach as far as the fridge giving credence to Danni's prior statement about getting a cell phone.

"Girl, I'll never understand how you've been so successful without technology."

"Danni, did you call to discuss my lack of technological prowess or is there something more pressing?"

"Sorry I wasn't able to return your call yesterday but I got buried in a pile of paperwork."

"No worries. What's up?"

"Remember the Monroe estate?"

Sarah's heartbeat quickened at the sound of the Monroe name, unsure whether it was due to the valuable nature of the estate or the grisly image of Edie from her dream.

"Yeah, I know the one," she replied, steadying her voice.

"Frank Davidson, the attorney handling the estate is a friend of mine. He didn't want to deal with the complexities of hiring an out of state auction company and asked if I knew anyone locally who could liquidate the contents of the mansion. Of course, I put in a good word for you."

Flabbergasted, Sarah asked, "Do you think they'll consider me?"

"You start tomorrow. Does that answer your question?"

A squeal of delight crossed her lips, followed by a rush of thank-yous to her dearest friend although a twinge of apprehension poked her stomach.

"Come by my office tomorrow morning and I'll give you the keys to the place. Oh, and by the way, they need everything cleaned out by the end of the month so the real estate agent can list the house."

"That's only three weeks!"

"Take it or leave it. You know Sotheby's and Christies have been frothing at the mouth to get this listing.

"Fine, I'll start tomorrow. Thanks, Danni."

"See you in the morning."

With the dial tone buzzing in her ear, Sarah felt the need to pinch herself to make sure she wasn't dreaming. The Monroe estate was said to be valued in the millions. All of a sudden, the image of Edie's ghostly presence with its sightless stare resurfaced, dampening Sarah's enthusiasm.

Sarah's hand trembled as she opened the 1950s fridge and pulled out a pitcher of lemonade. Filling a glass, she stood at the farmhouse sink and sipped the tart drink. Despite her reservations, Sarah began the arduous task of convincing herself that the end result would far outweigh the dread percolating in her gut. Her life was about to change in ways she could only imagine. In essence, she'd hit the jackpot much like the folks she watched on *Antiques Roadshow* who found a $2 painting at a yard sale only to discover it was the missing Rembrandt worth millions.

If all went well, she'd be able to pay off both mortgages and maybe even travel someday. All Sarah had ever wanted was the proverbial 'normal life' free from ghostly images and debt. In spite of her thriftiness and business success, the renovation of her grandfather's mercantile had set her back substantially. But she was only thirty-three with plenty of time to recoup the money; or so she kept telling herself.

Thankfully, none of her friends or family had ever pressured her to marry, believing she was betrothed to her job. At least that's what she led them to believe. Sarah knew in her heart that the haunted dreams would hamper any serious relationships. Routine was the key to her sanity, the one thing in her life she could control in her crazy haunted world. Of course, working herself to exhaustion often helped her sleep.

Excitement bubbled in Sarah's chest over this opportunity. What she really needed right now were words of encouragement as she took on a defining moment in her career. Even though it wasn't the scheduled day to call her parents she couldn't wait to share the news with them. Hopefully she'd be able to catch them.

They'd been abroad since her father took early retirement from his law practice years before. She envied their freedom to visit faraway places all of which were documented in the weekly postcards that showed up in her mailbox. She dialed her father's cell number and listened to it ring.

"Hello" her mother said through the crackling connection.

"Hey Mom, where's Dad?"

"Right next to me. We're getting ready to board our flight and I left my cell phone in my luggage. Is everything alright?"

"Things couldn't be better. I got some great news today and had to call."

"Could you repeat that sweetheart? I'm only getting every other word."

"I said I got some great news and wanted to share it with you guys," Sarah was practically yelling.

Flight 728 is boarding for Rome echoed in the background.

"Oh my, that's our flight. Can we call you when we land?

Maybe we'll have a better connection when we get to our hotel. Ciao!"

The line went dead and Sarah's heart dropped. She'd hoped for some encouragement to get started on this endeavor. Alas, she'd have to settle for Danni's prodding and her own motivation to keep her focused on the monumental job looming before her.

You can do this, she thought, blowing out a breath as she headed back to the garden.

SUNRAYS TICKLED Sarah's eyelids as gauzy curtains danced on gentle breezes, waving good morning. She washed up, slipped on a pair of jeans, a floral cotton blouse, and sandals. She dabbed on some concealer, pulled her silky dark hair into a ponytail, grabbed a power bar, and ran out the door. Jumping into her old Chevy truck, fondly known as the Beast, she headed for Danni's office among a cacophony of coughs and sputters from the ramshackle engine.

Danni had been Sarah's closest friend since high school, the two having met in ninth grade when Danni moved to the area from overseas. Her father was commanding officer of the Marine base and her mother was a homemaker. Despite being raised by strict parents, Danni was something of a wild card, often challenging others to take chances, especially when injustice was at the core of the situation.

Although their personalities were quite different, they shared a love of preservation and quickly became close friends. Danni's outgoing personality gave Sarah the courage to venture from the confines of her self-imposed shell.

Sarah turned off of Queen Street onto the gravel parking lot at Danni's office. She switched off the ignition, the Chevy's engine continuing to rumble and sputter, as the skies darkened and thunder reverberated in the distance.

She entered the 1950s house-turned-law-office as the door blew shut behind her. Despite its humble brick exterior, the interior was decorated with silk curtains, Persian rugs, and an Empire sofa.

Across the room, Anita, paralegal extraordinaire, watered a hanging fern. She ran the office efficiently, doing everything from brewing coffee to researching cases. Danni referred to her as the "goddess" because Anita always knew exactly what was needed before being asked.

Without turning around, Anita spoke, "Good morning, Ms. Holden. Ms. Cook is expecting you."

Sarah returned the greeting when she noticed a cup of tea next to the coffee pot. These were the little things that made Anita so special. Sarah picked up the steaming brew and headed into Danni's office. "Thanks, Anita."

Anita smiled, acknowledging the thank you with a nod.

Despite her years as a lawyer, Danni hadn't changed much in her manner of organization, or lack thereof. Mountains of papers and files were stacked on every available surface including the desk, wooden file cabinet, and credenza. On the other side of the room, framed photos of family and friends sat atop a set of antique barrister bookcases.

Looking up from her paper-laden desk, Danni smiled.

"Good morning." A clap of thunder rattled the windows and shook the floor. "Sounds like a storm is brewing."

"Looks like it's coming up the river. It should hit soon."

Lowcountry residents were well versed in atmospheric transformations by simply studying the shade of the skies, the movement of cloud cover, and the direction of the wind and tide. They could determine whether the storm would remain on the river or make its way inland.

Sarah sat in the leather chair across from the desk, sipping her tea, while Danni rummaged through a file, removing a contract. In spite of her chaotic filing system, Danni could always put her hands on what she needed, as if the mess on her desk was an external view of how her mind worked. Putting on a pair of dollar store spectacles, one arm held on with a reconfigured paper clip, she scanned the pages before presenting them to Sarah.

"Look this over and see if it meets your approval." With eyebrows raised, Danni glanced over her glasses at the cup of tea. "How can you drink that scalding stuff when it's so muggy outside?"

"Because I like it and Anita had it waiting for me."

"There's something eerily psychic about that woman. She's always one step ahead."

Sarah read through the contract from the law office of Davidson and Davidson, astounded by the complexities of the estate and the short timeline in which she had to clear the house of its contents. Nevertheless, she wasn't going to let long hours, hard work, or cadaverous images of the late owner deter her.

"Danni, why does this have to be done so quickly? I need at least a month to catalogue, research, and appraise everything, not to mention setting up the auction house. Manny has agreed to run the store for me but I really need more time to do this properly."

"Sorry, but Davidson has consented to the timelines imposed by the realty company. They want the place listed as soon as possible."

"Who's the listing agent?"

"William Devereaux."

"Why didn't you tell me *he* was the one?" Sarah said, slumping back in the chair.

"Because I knew you'd whine about it. Don't worry; you won't have to deal with the arrogant twit except when he comes by to determine what repairs need to be done. Other than that, he won't be around."

"Repairs?" Sarah sat up ready to protest when Danni held up her hand.

"He's agreed to wait on the repairs until the place is cleared which is probably the reason for the short timeline. Just make sure you're finished by the thirtieth."

"Fine." A heavy sigh seeped from her lips as she scribbled her name on the contract and passed it back to Danni.

"Here's the key. You better get started if you want to meet the deadline." Danni reached into her top desk drawer and pulled out a cell phone. "You can use this while you're working."

"What do I need that for?"

"So I can reach you. There's no phone over there."

"You could call when I get home in the evening. I'll be too busy to talk while I'm working."

"Maybe you should stay at the mansion instead of going back and forth each day. It would save a lot of time."

"I don't think so," Sarah replied with a shiver.

"Don't tell me you're afraid to stay there."

"Of course not," Sarah shrugged. "I just sleep better in my own bed."

"Supposedly, Edie complained about ghosts in that place."

"Right. And there are zombies in the gardens and vampires in the attic," Sarah snickered, rolling her eyes trying to hide her unease.

"You never know, there's plenty of crazy stories about that place."

"What kind of stories?" Sarah's spine tensed at the thought of anything otherworldly stalking about.

"Aside from Edie seeing the undead and her father being a gambling drunk, there's the matter of her missing great-grandmother."

"What happened to her?"

"They say she ran off shortly after having Edie's grandmother."

"Perhaps I'll discover hidden letters or a secret diary that will reveal what really happened to her." A broad smile creased Sarah's cheeks at the thought of a history hunt. One of her favorite parts of clearing out estates was finding hints of the people who had lived with the pieces long before descendants decided to hock everything to the highest bidder.

"Don't get caught up in all that nostalgic stuff. It always throws you off task and then you stress about missing deadlines. Keep in mind, William will be the one coming after you, not me."

Disgust racked Sarah's body at the thought. "Thanks for the reality check. I suppose staying there would save a lot of time."

"Do you want me to stay with you? Haunted houses can be scary."

"No need. I'll string garlic cloves around the door frames and paint the window trims haint blue to keep the ghosts away." Sarah rolled her eyes at the idea that locals believed a paint color could repel *haints*, a common Lowcountry phrase for ghosts.

"That oughta piss William off. Go for it!"

"Maybe it'll repel him too."

"It'd take more than that to keep him away from a warm body," Danni huffed.

Staring at the phone in her hand, Sarah pressed the button. "I don't know how to use this thing."

Danni leaned across her desk. "For goodness sake, Sarah, it's not difficult. You use this to dial and press the green button to call. When you finish the call, press the red button. Got it?"

Sarah nodded.

"Here's the cord for it."

"Doesn't that ruin the whole point of having a *cordless phone*?" she smirked.

"You have to recharge it. Plug it in at night and it'll charge while you sleep."

Sarah stuffed the phone in her pocket and bid Danni goodbye. She jumped in her truck, cranked the blustering engine, and headed home to pack as storms brewed overhead much like the internal battle swirling within her.

4

Sarah hurried through her modest cottage gathering things she would need for her stay at the mansion. Turmoil churned her stomach over the prospects of the job versus the idea of sleepless nights and grisly images. Nevertheless, she was determined to see this thing through.

After packing her clothes and toiletries, she filled her knapsack with a tape recorder, legal pads, and pens along with tea bags, power bars, peanut butter, and a package of saltines. Snatching the portable CD player from the shelf, she grabbed a few of her favorite jazz CD's and shoved them in with the rest of her stuff. Music helped her focus when she was working, too bad it couldn't drown out the nightmares.

A chill rankled her spirits at the thought of being alone at Edie's place. *Why had she agreed to stay there?* For a moment, she reconsidered Danni's offer to join her but quickly squelched the idea. She loved Danni but wasn't ready to reveal her darkest secret, even to her closest friend. She'd learned a hard lesson at that slumber party in 5th grade reminding her that her secret must stay buried, at least for now.

Droplets of water began a rhythmic beat on the old tin roof, prompting her to grab a raincoat. Sarah ran to the truck, slinging her bags in the cab before climbing in. The rain drummed in cadence with the swishing of the windshield wipers as she drove away from her whitewashed bungalow. Sheets of water splashed between the screeching wipers, while the truck tires sent swells of roadside puddles in waves across the windshield. Lowcountry roads flooded quickly making for treacherous travel when the rain came hard and fast. Fortunately, Monroe Manse wasn't far.

Turning onto Walters Street, Sarah gazed at the tabby mansion looming beneath a canopy of storm clouds, giving it a foreboding appearance. The fact that the tabby exterior, comprised of oyster shells, lime, and water, had survived the elements for more than two hundred years astounded her. She remembered learning about the substance in elementary school and had always pondered how something so simple could endure for centuries.

A soaring brick wall encased the home, shielding it from onlookers like a medieval fortress. Oyster shells crackled beneath the wheels of the old Chevy, adding an extra beat to the symphony of raindrops as she drove between the iron gates and cruised down the drive. Sarah shifted the truck into park and readied herself for the waterfall of rain now spilling in torrents from ashen clouds.

The downpour flowing across the windshield distorted the image of the house with its unkempt maze of boxwoods and knee-high weeds. Taking a deep breath, Sarah pulled the rain jacket hood over her head, grabbed her bags, jumped from the truck, and stumbled across uneven stepping-stones to the front door. Once she reached the shelter of the portico, the rain was blowing sideways as she fumbled with the key.

With some aggressive jiggling, she clicked the key in the deadbolt, turned the antique brass knob, and gave the door a hard shove. Worn hinges screeched in protest, much like the ones in scary movies just before spectral visitants besieged the heroine.

"Home sweet home, at least for the next three weeks," she said, plunking her bags inside the door.

Sarah slipped off her rain jacket, draped it on the hall tree, and took in the grandeur of the place. An expansive entryway hosted multi-layered moldings and a crystal chandelier wreathed by a plaster medallion of acanthus leaves. Frayed rugs camouflaged lackluster heart pine floors that stretched all the way up a central staircase. On the wall to the right was a bow front Sheraton chest of drawers holding an old oil lamp that had been electrified as well as a bronze sculpture of the goddess Psyche. Portraits of Monroe ancestors lined the walls, soon to be peddled to the highest bidder.

Grabbing her overnight bag, she made her way to the second floor where she found bedrooms tastelessly clad in wallpaper and linens indicative of the 1960s. Thankfully, the value of the furnishings would make up for the worthless bed coverings and curtains. Sarah chose the master bedroom being it was in the best overall condition with an en suite bathroom sporting an old claw footed bathtub. There was nothing better than a long soak in an old tub after a day of moving furniture and inventorying household items. Add bubble bath along with some candles, a shot of bourbon, and a little Coltrane and you achieved euphoria. Her muscles relaxed at the thought of it.

Sarah walked down the hall and discovered a library with an extensive collection of reading material cloaked in layers of dust. She inhaled the distinct scent of old leather bound tomes as her heart palpitated at the prospect of digging through the volumes stacked on the floor and crowding shelves. Books had been Sarah's closest friends growing up, until she met Danni.

Wandering across the hall, she peeked into a ballroom, which was slightly larger than the other rooms and piled with stacks of old magazines, newspapers, and refolded wrapping paper. Aside from the disproportionate size, there was something odd about the room that she couldn't figure out. A sense of discomfort slithered across her skin as if something horrible inhabited the space. A bolt of lightning flashed outside the window followed by a rumbling burst of thunder that shook the floors. The image of a skeletal figure flashed through her mind as the faint sound of a piano whispered from the far corner sending Sarah bolting down the hall to the top of the staircase. Stopping at the landing, she caught her breath while admonishing herself for being so flighty.

Stop acting like a child. It's just your imagination playing tricks on you.

Rubbing her forehead, she stalked past the bedrooms to the end of the hall where she discovered a small linen closet with towels and fresh sheets she'd use to remake the bed later. Next to the closet was a narrow staircase leading to the attic door. Like a paperclip drawn to a magnet, Sarah was tempted to investigate. The first step wobbled beneath her weight followed by a roaring clang of thunder that nearly sent her tumbling backward.

"I'll check the attic later," she muttered, taking a deep breath to calm her racing pulse.

Shaking off the unease, she treaded down the stairs. Beginning a project of this magnitude was always the hardest part. She'd never relished any aspect of cleaning and the amount of junk that needed to be tossed on this job stifled her motivation. When she reached the bottom step a strange noise resonated from the entryway. Listening intently, she followed the melodious tune emanating from her knapsack.

"What on earth is that?" she whispered, opening the bag.

The Batman theme clamored from within its depths along with a light that flashed with each tonal outburst. Realizing it was the cell phone Danni had given her, she hit the green button and answered, "Hello?"

"What took you so long? I was beginning to think you were never going to answer."

"Seriously, the Batman theme?"

"Pretty cool, huh? That's how you know it's me calling."

"Danni, you gave me the phone. You're the only one who would be calling."

"I wanted to check in and see how things are going. You sound flustered. Everything OK?"

"Just a bit overwhelmed. This place is huge." Sarah huffed.

"You wanted this and now you've got it. No sense whining about it."

"Yeah, I know. I was getting ready to start working."

"Good, and keep this with you. That's the whole point of having a phone without a cord, so you don't have to run through the house to answer it."

"Got it. Good-bye, Danni."

Clicking the red button, Sarah shoved the phone into her pocket, grabbed the knapsack, and traipsed down the hall glancing in the main floor rooms as she went.

The front parlors hosted an array of fine antique furnishings, Adams-style mantels, gilt-framed oil paintings, and faded-silk curtains tattered by years of sunlight.

The formal dining room and eat-in kitchen were situated at the back of the first floor, all as spacious as the front parlors and equally in need of a good cleaning. Everything was cloaked in layers of dust with the pungent odor of musty papers and mildew.

It would appear Edie was a less than stellar housekeeper as well as a hoarder. Stacks of old newspapers, outdated coupons, and other assorted boxes of junk hovered in corners and under tables. With only three weeks to complete the inventory and clear the house, the cleanup and trash removal would hinder Sarah's progress significantly. But the outcome would be well worth the sweat and backbreaking efforts.

Plunking her bag on the kitchen table, Sarah pulled out the box of tea bags and studied the room. The outdated space was a mishmash of styles including painted cabinetry, a vintage gas stove and fridge, white Formica countertops with gold sparkles, and worn heart pine floors from years of feet plodding across them.

Sarah searched the cabinets for a mug, rinsed it out, and filled the teakettle with water. She rotated the sticky stove knob until a wave of gas scented the air, the pilot light glowing a soft blue. When the kettle screeched, she fixed her tea and headed to the front parlor with the knapsack slung over her shoulder. Setting the cup on the coffee table, she retrieved the clipboard, pen, and tape recorder. Sheets of rain cascaded down the paned windows punctuated by an occasional clap of thunder as she began recording.

"KITCHEN HAS LITTLE TO CONSIDER. Most of it can be boxed up and sent to the local thrift store. Contact Lisa at *Antiques and Coffee Beans* about the pub table and chairs. Front parlor appears to have a collection of Dresden figurines, Meissen porcelain, and Louis the Fourteenth furnishings."

She clicked off the recorder, took a sip of tea, and slipped a Miles Davis CD into the player. As the sultry trumpet sounds filled the space, Sarah fell into work mode as she rummaged through the curio cabinet. There was something intoxicating about the velvety notes of jazz that lulled Sarah into a state of reverie, clearing her mind so she could focus on her work.

She'd start by recording a basic listing of the items before tagging each one. Later she'd transfer her notes from the recorder to her ledger. Color-coding had been her means of organization since high school when she discovered the four-in-one ballpoint pens with different colored ink. Green meant the item would be sold in her shop, red was for the auction, blue was for consignment, and black was for donations. Despite her old-fashioned way of doing things, she was able to catalog estates in a detailed and efficient manner. While her methods may have seemed antiquated to others, it worked well for her.

Hours later, the rain subsided, giving way to a setting sun that emblazoned the far wall in snippets of orange and gold. When Sarah's eyes began to blur, she glanced at her watch; shocked to see it was seven-thirty in the evening. Lamplight cast shadows while odd noises emanated from walls and floors as if the house were struggling to breath. Staying here had seemed like a good idea in the light of day but now that night was taking hold, Sarah's composure was faltering. Her imagination had already wreaked havoc with her earlier in the day and now her fortitude was wavering like a flag in a hurricane. Now seemed like a good time to eat something and find all the light switches before she was lost in the dark.

Sarah traipsed across the hall and turned on the electrified oil lamp near the staircase. Its shimmering light cast shadowy figures against the mahogany balustrade as she made her way to the kitchen flipping on light switches along the way. Once in the kitchen, she fixed a cup of tea, grabbed the peanut butter and saltines, and sat at the table to make notations in her ledger.

With her notes complete, Sarah closed her ledger, cleaned the crumbs from the table, and set the tea mug in the sink when a cold chill slithered along her spine like an ice cube dropping down her shirt. When she looked up her lungs constricted at the sight of a glowing visage, its sunken eyes peering through the window.

A blood-curdling scream rushed from her lips as she jumped back, nearly falling over the table. A familiar howl of laughter pierced the air, revealing the ghostly specter as nothing more than Danni shining a flashlight beneath her chin.

"Dang it, Danni!" Sarah hollered, heading for the back door.

Danni was doubled-over on the back stoop laughing. "Oh, Sarah," she gasped, "You should have seen the expression on your face!"

"It wasn't funny. I almost fell!"

"But you didn't," she said, regaining her composure. "So you're a little rattled about ghosts in the old place, eh?"

"I'm not rattled about anything except seeing that scary mug of yours glaring at me! Honestly, it's a good thing I didn't have a gun, I might've killed you!"

Danni scooted past with a pizza box and a six-pack of beer. "Be serious. You'd have dropped the gun before you fired a shot," she replied, shaking her head. "I brought supper. You'll waste away on those power bars you're always ingesting, or was it peanut butter and crackers for dinner?"

Sarah rolled her eyes. Sometimes it was annoying how well Danni knew her habits.

Danni looked around with a grimace. "Not much of a kitchen for such a big house. I expected something grand with stainless steel appliances and tons of gourmet gadgets."

"Apparently, you've forgotten who lived here. It seems the place hasn't changed in decades," Sarah said, searching the lower cabinets.

"What're you looking for?" Danni asked.

"Something to drink. I can't stop shaking thanks to your juvenile stunt. I know Edie must have kept something around here."

"I brought a six pack."

Sarah wrinkled her nose, "I'm not in the mood."

"Forgive my impertinence, your highness, I thought it might

be nice to relive the old college days, maybe have a séance when we're done."

"Very funny. I need something stronger than beer to settle me now."

Sarah located an unopened decanter of peach wine, a carafe of vodka, and two bottles of Kentucky bourbon, all tucked beneath the sink.

"This will do," she muttered grabbing the bourbon.

Pulling a tumbler from the cabinet, Sarah sat at the table and poured a hefty shot. She took a sip and leaned back in the chair, savoring the slow burn.

"Honestly, I don't see how you drink that stuff straight. It's like lighter fluid," Danni said with a scowl.

"You have to relish the moment and drink it slowly."

"You're not right, you know that, don't you?"

Sarah leaned forward and cocked her head. "By the way, why are you here at this hour?"

"I brought pizza and beer, remember?"

"Isn't it a bit late for supper?"

"Are you kidding? It's never too late for pizza and beer."

Sarah shook her head with a grin. "It's good to know some things never change."

"Oh, I nearly forgot, William dropped this off today and wanted you to sign it." Danni dug around in her satchel and handed Sarah a file.

"I knew there was an ulterior motive. What is it?"

"Something about turning the house over by the thirtieth. He's in a hurry to get this place listed." Danni popped open a beer and took a swig.

"I thought I already signed the contract?"

"That was for the attorney. This is for the realty company."

"Whatever," Sarah replied, tossing the file on the table.

"You OK?" Danni queried, shoving a piece of pizza in her mouth.

"There's just so much to do." Sarah rubbed her eyes with the heels of her hands. "I managed to get most of the porcelain in the front parlor catalogued, but this place is huge. I'll have to work day and night to finish on time."

"Hire someone to help you."

"That would cut into my profits. Antiques aren't bringing the prices they used to and I'm going to need a new roof on the store before long, not to mention I'm paying Manny to run the shop while I'm here." She shrugged. "I'll get it all done somehow."

"Then you're gonna need some energy. Have a slice." Danni slid the open pizza box across the table to Sarah whose stomach rumbled at the smell of pepperoni. Reaching in, she grabbed a piece. The two ate and chatted until the box was empty.

"It's getting late, so I better skedaddle." Danni said, reaching for her keys. "You gonna sign that contract?"

"Do I have to?"

"Unless you want me to send William over to get it."

"Give me a pen." Sarah took the silver pen from Danni, signed, and handed everything back to her.

"Wanna take a walk? We can go down to Palmer's and watch the drunks sing karaoke." Danni shoved the paper into her bag, awaiting Sarah's answer.

"I need to do some paperwork before I go to bed." Sarah hugged Danni. "Sorry, I'm so grumpy. I really appreciate you getting me this job."

Danni returned the embrace, her demeanor softening. "I know you've got a lot on your mind. Get some rest." As she headed for the back door, Danni turned with a sheepish grin, "And watch out for those creepy ghosts!"

Sarah tossed a towel in Danni's direction as the door closed. She locked the deadbolt, switched off the overhead light, and started down the hall, turning off lights along the way. She left the old oil lamp on in case she needed to wander downstairs during the night.

She trudged upstairs, grabbed her nightshirt from the overnight bag on the bed before going to the bathroom to wash up. Staring at her image in the vanity mirror, Sarah noted the slight hint of crow's feet parading from the corners of her eyes, underscored by dark shadows.

"Dad always said I should work smart, not hard. Should've listened to him."

Sarah washed her face in the sink and reached for the towel, a shudder slithering down her spine as the temperature dropped. Straightening up, she noticed the shower curtain around the claw foot tub flutter as if it were breathing. She stared at the rippling fabric flowing in and out, its movement matching her own breath. Her inclination to run from the house and never return was thwarted by her need to act like an adult and ignore the crazy idea that something was behind the curtain. Determined to overcome her trepidation, Sarah moved closer to the tub, the air growing colder with each step. The scent of decaying dirt filled her nostrils as she grabbed the curtain and flung it aside, simultaneously jumping back. With a long exhale, Sarah stared at the empty tub. The room temperature rose and the sickening smell dissipated.

Frightened by the episode, Sarah removed the shower curtain from the rings, wadded up the length of plastic, and tossed it in the corner.

"That should fix it."

Determined to overcome the fear niggling at her nerves, she switched off the light and ambled to the bedroom window. Hoisting it open, she took in the salty evening breezes that soothed her troubled mind. She plugged in the phone, threw back the coverlet, and replaced the sheets with the fresh ones she'd found in the linen closet earlier in the day.

Climbing into bed, she jotted a few notes in her journal,

trying to occupy her thoughts and settle the disquiet simmering in the depths of her gut; then again it may have been the pepperoni. A clap of thunder rattled the walls making Sarah jump followed by a flash of light and another roaring boom.

Sarah loved thunderstorms. Something about rain pelting against windows and tap dancing on a tin roof gave a cozy feel to a place. She recalled her grandmother fussing at her when she was little to keep away from windows during storms for fear limbs would crash through the glass. Sarah never heeded the warnings, mesmerized by nature's showmanship.

Raindrops peppered the windowsill, picking up speed as winds swirled through the room inducing Sarah to close the window before water drenched the floorboards. A loud thud shook the walls temporarily paralyzing her with a rush of adrenaline. Another clap of thunder, along with a flash of light, coaxed the lamp on the bedside table to flicker once, twice, and then all went dark.

Great, no electricity and no flashlight. What was I thinking?

With no electricity and exhaustion tugging at her eyes, Sarah climbed into bed hoping to get some shuteye. As she settled between the cottony sheets, the bourbon kicked in sending her into a restful slumber as rain drummed a soothing cadence overhead.

PAUSED at the edge of a darkened ledge, Sarah's stomach turned as the dank smell of fresh dirt and death filled her nostrils. A distant voice gurgled, *"He's guilty."* She tried desperately to move, but her feet were fused to the floor. Luminous skin covered the bony fingers that tangled around her wrist like a vine. She opened her mouth to call for help but the words escaped in a silent shriek...

Sarah bolted upright, the scream on her lips materializing as she gasped for air. She glanced toward the alarm clock, its glowing digits blinking twelve o'clock. The power was back on. In an effort to tame her quivering body, she switched on the lamp, thankful for the light that washed away the disquiet. Now more than ever, she regretted letting Danni talk her into staying here.

Throughout childhood, Sarah had been plagued by life-like dreams where the cadaverous entities were so realistic she could feel their emotions and sense of touch. These individuals weren't familiar to her but more akin to spectral figures from the past as if she'd fallen through a portal into another era. Their icy fingers would clutch at her body while their eyeless faces scanned hers seemingly seeking assistance to a troubled past.

Reverting to her childhood defenses, Sarah shifted beneath the covers, pulled the sheet over her head, and willed away the frightful images until sleep rescued her from her turmoil.

DAYLIGHT PEERED through the wavy glass windowpanes rousing Sarah from her sleep. Stiff from the fetal position she'd maintained throughout the night, she stretched in an effort to loosen her cramped muscles.

Sarah padded to the bathroom, yawning along the way. Her body froze when she gazed at the shower curtain encircling the old iron tub while the scent of fresh dirt stung her nose. How had the curtain gotten back on the shower rod? She swallowed the scream hovering at her lips as the curtain began to sway in sync with her own breathing. Panic inched up her neck flushing her cheeks and stifling her breath, the stench of decay overwhelming her senses. She willed her feet to move but they wouldn't respond. The room began to fade in and out making her lightheaded.

Don't faint. It's only your imagination.

Whatever was on the other side of the curtain, she had to face it. It was probably nothing more than a draft or her mind playing tricks on her. She wasn't going to let all of this ghostly nonsense ruin her chances for financial security. Although she'd been dealing with the terrifying images her entire life, she'd never been harmed so there was no real reason to fret; at least that's what she kept telling herself.

Emboldened, she ripped the curtain from the rod. A sigh of relief blew across her lips when she saw the tub was empty. Scrunching the curtain into a ball, she shoved it into the wastebasket.

"I don't know what you want and I don't care! Leave me alone!" she hollered.

As she stomped from the bathroom, an icy current grazed her cheek in a soft kiss, the words, *not yet*, ringing in her ear.

Sarah hurried to the kitchen and started the teakettle, her limbs still shaking from the bizarre occurrence in the bathroom. She was always braver in the daylight. Gazing out the window, she noticed a sizable branch planted in a puddle near the overgrown rose gardens and stepped outside to investigate. Ivy trellised up the tabby exterior of the house as sunrays reflected from rippled windowpanes. The storm had littered the English garden with downed limbs and a few broken flowerpots, making the place seem bleak and forlorn.

That explains the crash I heard last night. I hope the roof isn't damaged. Thank goodness I'm not responsible for anything outside of the house.

A high-pitched squeal from the kitchen alerted her that the water had reached a boil.

Sarah scurried inside, removed the screaming kettle, and tipped it over the cup when a knock on the front door echoed through the house. Hurrying down the hall, her heart sank when she opened the door. Dressed in a dark-blue suit with a floral bow tie, William Devereaux stood before her, his haughty demeanor an instant annoyance.

"Good morning, William," she muttered with as much enthusiasm as she could muster.

"G'morning. Mind if I come in and take a look around? Danni said she okayed it with you." Without waiting for a response, he stepped inside.

"Go ahead. But make it quick, I've got a lot to do," she snapped.

"Sarah, why are you so defensive? You act like you don't want me around. A little bit of *down time* would do you a world of good," he purred, his deep blue eyes sparkling at the idea.

"William, if you recall, you're the one who gave me a short deadline for this project. I don't have time for social calls."

"No need to be bitter. I didn't decide on the date, my agency did. They want this place on the market as soon as possible," he said with a sheepish grin, his perfectly bleached teeth gleaming unnaturally.

"What's the rush? It's a mansion, so it'll take some time to sell."

"We've got a lot to do before listing it. The sooner we make the necessary repairs and get her on the market, the faster we can make a sale. You know my motto..."

"I know, 'an empty house is a lonely house.' Do what you have to do and get out. I'll be in the library," Sarah replied, a sneer curling her upper lip.

She turned on her heels, hurrying to the second floor to avoid any further contact with one of the most annoying people she'd ever known.

Stepping into the library, Sarah inhaled the stale scent of old books. The sheer number of items in the space was overwhelming. Hundreds of volumes overflowed from crowded shelves in addition to stacks piled in corners and along walls. The room was a mess, particularly the secretary, its desktop concealed beneath an avalanche of papers.

"This is a nightmare," she groaned as she started sifting through the piles. In her rush to avoid William she'd come upstairs without her tools. She snuck downstairs, retrieved her recorder, CD player, and hurried back upstairs.

Clicking on the recorder, she spoke, "The library appears to have a variety of genres including NYT best sellers, self-help books, and leather-bound classics. Check with Raven Booksellers on consigning the rare copies."

She clicked off the recorder and glanced around the disordered space. "May as well get started," she sighed when a voice tickled her ear.

"Why so glum?"

"Darn it, William!" Sarah hollered, startled by his stealth approach.

"You're awfully jumpy. I hope you aren't nervous being here by yourself." He leaned over and rested his hand above her head, sandwiching her between his body and the bookshelves. "I could stay if you need some company. These big old houses can be scary at night." A gleam flickered in his eye at the prospect of another conquest.

"I don't need your help. I'm perfectly capable of staying here *without* company," she said, scooting out from under him, hoping he'd take the hint.

"Suit yourself. If you change your mind, here's my card. Call me and I'll be over in a flash."

"I'd rather take my chances with the ghouls and goblins." Sarah snatched the card from his hand and shoved it in her pocket.

"Ouch. That hurt, Sarah," he mocked, grabbing his chest. "By the way, the attic is a mess. Have you been up there yet?" he said with a mischievous grin, apparently enjoying the fact he could get under her skin so easily.

"I only started yesterday afternoon. Don't worry; the house will be empty, attic and all, by the thirtieth. But the longer you hold me up, the less likely I am to meet the deadline."

When William realized he wasn't getting anywhere, he gave a slight bow and left.

Sarah glanced around the room with a sigh. The piles of outdated magazines, old mailings, and what appeared to be a year's worth of receipts were disconcerting. If she could get paid for the clutter she'd be able to retire tomorrow. "May as well get the trash bags from the truck. If the attic is anything like the rest of the house, it's bound to be a calamity."

5

———————

After cataloguing several boxes of books, many rare signed editions, Sarah stacked them neatly in the far corner of the library. Years of accumulated junk mail topped the Chippendale secretary, along with rusted paperclips and dried up pens, all of which found its way into a large garbage bag. She sat for a moment contemplating whether to take a break or tackle another project. Her motivation was dwindling after so much time in one room and changing tasks usually revitalized her.

Louis Armstrong crooned in the background as William's words replayed in her mind, *By the way, the attic is a mess.* She'd yet to make her way up there and now seemed as good a time as any, despite the unwavering sense that something was waiting on the other side of the attic door. She'd been spooked the day before but needed to get a grip. There wasn't time to be insecure. The best thing she could do was to confront her trepidation and investigate the cluttered disarray residing on the top floor. In her years as an antiques dealer, there were generally two discoveries in attics—the most valuable of treasures or the most notable of junk, usually the latter, making them a huge investment of time with little payoff. Nonetheless, she had to clear it out.

With tools in hand, she climbed the narrow staircase, treading carefully on each board. Fingers of fear squeezed the air from her lungs as she grasped the knob and nudged the swollen door with her shoulder. Amidst the creaking concerto of door hinges, the attic exhaled its stale, musty breath. Visions of teenage horror movies flashed through her mind making her pause. Holding her breath, she stepped into the dreary space, her lungs expanding when she realized she'd overdramatized the idea of some unknown entity hovering on the other side.

Dormers cast fragments of light across the floor, shadowing old furnishings, trunks, and boxes. The only light fixture in the space was a bulb dangling from a cord in the center of the vaulted ceiling. With a hard tug on the chain, the bulb flashed to life, revealing an array of clutter. An old settee and parlor chairs were stacked in one corner alongside a marble-topped bureau with a clouded mirror. A stockpile of boxes, old quilts, and a few framed portraits inhabited the other side of the room. Furnishings costumed in sheets, like worn-out Halloween ghosts, huddled against the remaining walls.

"As I suspected, mostly junk," she mumbled.

Warped floorboards creaked beneath each step as Sarah scanned the space for signs of anything valuable. The parlor pieces would need reupholstering, in addition to repairs where the wood frames had split. Most of the quilts were patchwork style probably used for covering furniture. Leaning over to examine a stack of boxes, Sarah yelped when her foot jammed against the corner of something.

Closer examination revealed a camel top chest buried under a hodgepodge of quilts. Kneeling to get a better look, Sarah startled when a giant flying cockroach, otherwise known as a Palmetto bug, scurried past sending her to her feet with a shudder. Southerners had a habit of giving genteel names to the most disgusting vermin on earth. Regardless of the name, Sarah despised the vile creatures.

Grabbing a small chair, she sat before the trunk studying the letters "EAM" below the rusted keyhole. When she lifted the lid, the strong scent of cedar assaulted her nose, triggering a sneeze. Faded newspapers, a few leather-bound scrapbooks, a blue velvet photo album, and bits of lace inhabited the space.

Sarah rummaged through decades of mementos her fingertips beginning to tingle as she gently sorted through yellowed newspaper clippings as frail as butterfly wings. Within minutes of perusing some of the memorabilia Sarah discovered the contents belonged to Edie's great-grandmother, Eleanor 'Nora' Alexandra Monroe. Sentimental well wishes regarding Nora's birth, along with announcements in local society papers littered the pages. Apparently, a long anticipated event for the Monroe family, the start to Nora's life seemed charmed and celebrated, much like the romantic fantasies Sarah held about the era no doubt created by reading too much Jane Austen growing up.

Even though she needed to focus on the job at hand, Sarah couldn't tear herself away from the trunk's contents. Something about memorabilia from the past had always intrigued her. It was probably one of the reasons she'd chosen to sell and appraise antiques in spite of her tumultuous night terrors.

Perusing one of the scrapbooks, Sarah was enthralled by the contents. An entire page listed baby gifts and their contributors, followed by a photo of Nora swaddled in a blanket. Other entries included pictures of her first pony, first birthday celebration, and first Christmas. Another scrapbook held school samples and early attempts at needlework as Nora learned the delicate handwork required of young ladies during the era.

A royal blue velvet album caught Sarah's attention. She reached for it when the Batman theme howled from her pocket, making her heart skip. A shaky "Hello" crossed her lips.

"Glad to see you're using this thing!" Danni said gleefully, "You sound out of breath. Did I catch you at a bad time?"

"You startled me, that's all."

"Where are you?"

"In the attic."

"I thought you were working downstairs today?"

Sarah searched for an excuse to pacify her best friend. Undoubtedly, Danni would scold her for scavenging through old documents instead of working.

"I decided to clear out some of the junk in the attic so I can concentrate on the important stuff in the rest of the house. William was all too happy to report that the attic was a mess."

"William came by?"

"Yeah. He gave his sickeningly sweet line of garbage and then left when he realized I wasn't interested."

Danni giggled. "Maybe you oughta get him to stay there with you. You've been pretty jumpy lately."

"Only because you scared me last night! I assure you I'm fine and William is the last person I'd ask for help," Sarah scoffed. "By the way, why are you calling?"

"Thought I'd bring over Chinese later and wanted to let you know ahead of time so you didn't have a coronary when I showed up."

"Very funny. Come over about six?"

"See you then."

Sarah slipped the phone back into her pocket and cradled the photo album in her lap, brushing her hand across the soft blue velvet. The word *Album* was scrolled in silver on the cover and an ornate clasp held it closed. On the first page was a photo of a young woman holding a baby dressed in a lacey christening gown. In fine script below the oval opening was written, Eleanor "Nora" Alexandra Monroe, and the date of her birth, May 26th, 1879.

Pictures of a little girl clad in frilly frocks with dark silky ringlets littered subsequent pages. Obviously a happy child, the images showed Nora accompanied by dolls, stuffed toys, and in one picture wearing a riding habit as she straddled a dapple gray rocking horse. Each image revealed her life in still shots from childhood, to adolescence, into a fine young debutant. Something in Nora's expression, the familiarity in the shape of her eyes and the curve of her smile resonated deep within Sarah, as if they'd always known each other.

Immersed in her explorations, Sarah was jarred back to reality when the doorbell rang. She returned the album to the confines of the trunk, brushed the attic dust from her shorts, and hurried downstairs.

Opening the front door, Sarah gazed upon a lovely white-headed woman wearing a floral cotton dress, black Mary Janes, and a wide-brimmed hat. She held a small basket covered with a blue and white checkered tea towel in her hands. When she spoke, a Lowcountry drawl accented each word, her 'I's' sounding like 'Ah' with an extra syllable added to words like 'chair' so that they came out as 'chayer.'

"I'm terribly sorry to bother you, but I thought perhaps you were the new mistress of the house?"

"No, ma'am, I'm here to clean out the contents for auction."

A hint of disappointment shadowed the woman's crystal blue eyes. "Oh, I see. I brought you some apple cinnamon muffins. You may as well enjoy them, even if you won't be livin' here." Her warm smile and friendly demeanor veiled loneliness.

Sarah's heart sank. With all the work to be done, she started to turn the lady away but remembered her mother's words regarding manners when a guest paid a call.

"Now, Sarah," she would say in her genteel manner, "a good southern lady is never rude, no matter how busy she may be. Chores can wait. Hospitality always takes precedence."

Sarah conjured a grin, "Thank you, I'm sure they're delicious. Would you like to join me for a cup of tea?"

The woman's eyes brightened and a smile spread across her face, accentuating the wrinkled roadmap of her life.

"I don't want to disturb you," she said as she stepped inside, looking about.

"It's no bother at all...Miss?"

"Dottie MacDougall. I've been curious about the old place since Edie passed. With no descendants, everyone's been talkin' 'bout who'd be taking it over. I suppose the house will be auctioned as well?"

"Actually, only the contents. The house will go on the market once it's emptied."

"No doubt it'll be some time before it's listed."

"I don't know. I'll be relinquishing that aspect to the real estate agent at the end of the month."

Dottie's eyebrows arched. "Only three weeks for all of this? Have they a buyer in mind?"

"Not that I'm aware of." Sarah took comfort that someone else appreciated the monumental task before her and the ridiculously short amount of time in which to accomplish it.

They walked to the kitchen where Sarah started the kettle and plopped tea bags into two mugs. Dottie sat delicately in a kitchen chair, placing the basket upon the table.

"Are you from 'round here?"

"Yes, ma'am. I'm Sarah Holden. I own the antiques store on Bridge Street."

Dottie's smile broadened. "Is Gerald Holden your father?"

"He's my uncle. I worked at his funeral parlor the summer before my junior year of high school." Sarah shuddered at the memory. She'd barely slept for three months because of the nightmares.

"Gerald served with my late husband on City Council for many years. Of course, you were probably too young to remember that. My dear Alfred had to relinquish his council seat after my arrest for protesting the removal of a giant cedar tree in town. One of those blasted developers wanted to take it down to construct some sort of hideous buildin'."

Dottie's eyes glazed as she reminisced. "Poor dear, didn't speak a word when he bailed me out of jail. Next day he resigned from the Council and never made mention of it again. He was a gentleman that way."

Sarah placed two cups of tea on the table and sat down, intrigued by the woman's stories. Over the next half hour, Dottie regaled her with stories of protests against unnecessary development and even a few tales about Sarah's Uncle Gerald. Apparently, he had a penchant for pranks, a side of him Sarah never knew. He always seemed so serious at work; then again, his job as a funeral director demanded it.

Once the teacups ran dry, the two women bid adieu, Sarah escorting Miss Dottie out with a promise to visit once the auction was complete. She wanted to know more about this woman's colorful past not to mention her Uncle Gerald's antics. Instead of returning to the attic, Sarah decided to go back to the library and work.

SOMETIME LATER, the doorbell echoed in tune with the chiming of the grandfather clock, alerting Sarah of the six o'clock hour. Scurrying to the door, she opened it to find Danni waiting with dinner and a bottle of wine.

"Ready to take a break?" Danni chirped as she walked past, the aroma of fried rice mingling with the stale air of the house.

Sarah's stomach grumbled, reminding her she'd skipped lunch. She rummaged through the cabinets in search of wine glasses and a corkscrew.

Danni served up the cartons with chopsticks while Sarah

popped the cork of the wine bottle and filled two Waterford goblets. Her mouth salivated as she joined Danni at the table.

"I'm famished!" Sarah declared, scooping Moo Goo Gai Pan into her mouth.

"Not taking lunch breaks again?" Danni queried, biting into a shrimp slathered in lobster sauce.

"Between inventorying the library and checking out the attic, I've gone nonstop all day. And then I was delayed when Miss Dottie came to visit. Sweet lady but I really didn't have the time to spare. I haven't even gone for a run since I started this project."

Danni rolled her eyes at Sarah's constant need for fitness. Danni's idea of exercise was walking from the car into the liquor store.

"What'd she want?"

"Just curious about the house. I guess she was one of the few people who claimed Edie as a friend."

Danni's eyebrows arched. "That says a lot."

"Don't be so negative. I kinda feel sorry for Edie. It's not like she was a bad person. Her protests actually did a lot for the preservation of this town. If I recall, you've been arrested for the same thing."

"Yeah but the charges were dropped and I didn't run around drunk and dressed like a hippie."

"Everyone has a story. I wonder what made Edie so odd."

"You mean crazy," Danni huffed. "Tell me more about your visitor."

"Miss Dottie shared all sorts of stories about my Uncle Gerald and some of the protests she attended back in the day. I think you'd like her."

Danni shrugged and took another sip of wine. "Anything interesting in the attic?"

Sarah's shoulders slumped as a sigh escaped her lips. "There's so much up there, it'll take a few days to get through it all, maybe as long as a week. I did find a hope chest belonging to Edie's great-grandmother, Nora. It's a virtual time capsule with newspaper clippings, diaries, and photo albums chronicling her life," Sarah said, perking up.

"Sarah, you're supposed to be getting everything ready for auction, not rummaging through old junk. This happens every time; you find some remnant of the owner's past and obsess over it. It's not like there are any descendants who'd want it. Toss the stuff."

"Heavens no! You know I love a good story," she said sheepishly. "Believe it or not, old photo albums and antique pictures are highly collectible."

"Do what you want, just make sure I don't have to deal with William because you didn't get the place cleared in time for his precious open house."

"Don't worry, I'll handle William. I already took one for the team when he came by."

Danni snickered at the comment. Over dinner they talked about mundane things like the upcoming Earth Day celebrations, the ongoing dispute over parking downtown, and where Sarah's parents were traveling next.

"Are your parents still in Italy?"

"Yup. They'll be home next month before heading out on their next adventure. I can hardly keep up with them."

Once they'd polished off most of the Chinese food, Danni yawned. "I better head out. I've got to be at the office first thing in the morning."

Sarah chewed the inside of her lip. She desperately wanted to ask Danni to stay but wasn't sure it was the right time. After all, she didn't have a reasonable explanation for her trepidation and Danni's no-nonsense way of thinking wouldn't respond well to the idea that there were ghosts making strange noises and re-hanging shower curtains.

"Thanks for bringing supper."

"Any time. See you tomorrow," Danni said, scooting out the door.

Sarah watched the headlights on Danni's Mercedes flicker down the drive before she cleaned the kitchen and headed upstairs to the library. Hopefully, keeping busy would drive her to the brink of exhaustion so she could sleep through the night without interruption.

As she emptied one of the shelves, Sarah was enveloped by the strong scent of Chanel No.5. Apprehension slithered down her neck as the memory of Edie's grisly image with its empty eye sockets pulled the breath from her lungs. She closed her eyes, telling herself the odor was probably resurrected from moving things around. It wasn't the first time she'd been inundated by odors trapped in old books and fabrics.

Satisfied with her justification, she exhaled and continued removing a complete set of Dickens' works when her hand brushed against something. Sarah reached into the dark recesses of the shelf and pulled out a brown leather bound tome simply titled, *Dreamist,* in raised gilt letters. Surprisingly, there was no mention of an author or editor, only the title. Opening the worn cover, she was shocked to find only *Dreamist* and London, England on the title page, nothing else. She turned a few more pages when an old photo of a young girl in a lace-trimmed dress fell to the floor accompanied by the sound of pattering overhead. Her gaze shifted to the ceiling, the hair on her arms bristling. She reached for the cell phone to call Danni but thought better of it, instead convincing herself it was probably a raccoon skittering about in the attic.

Sarah was adept at explaining away the unexplainable; it's how she'd kept her sanity throughout her life. She descended the ladder and picked up the photo. Studying the image, she was certain it was the same little girl she'd seen in the scrapbooks, tempting her to go to the attic and look through the hope chest.

No, she thought, slipping the photo into the back pocket of her khaki shorts and tossing the book onto the donation pile. *You have to finish this room if you're going to make the deadline. Confronting angry masked rodents isn't part of the job description.*

Despite the draw to investigate the attic, she worked for another hour until her vision began to blur. A yawn filled her lungs as she went downstairs to check the doors and turn off all the lights except the old oil lamp. Its soft radiance illuminated each step as she ascended the stairs.

She started toward her room when something tugged at her hand as if leading her to the staircase at the end of the hall. Common sense dictated she should be afraid, yet she felt strangely calm. *I suppose a little late-night reading wouldn't do any harm and the raccoon is probably long gone.*

Sarah hurried to the attic, taking a deep breath to steady her nerves, as she opened the door. A hint of burgeoning moonlight swept across the floor as Sarah pulled the chain on the bulb. Fixating on the hope chest, she padded across the space, sat down, and scoured through the contents. Retrieving a few of the scrapbooks, she switched off the light and hustled down the staircase. Her arms shook and her insides wobbled like jelly as she traipsed to her room. *I really need to start doing this in the daylight,* she thought, rotating her shoulders in an effort to release the tension holding them captive.

Sarah set the albums on the night table along with the photo she'd found earlier before changing for bed. Hesitating at the bathroom door she considered washing up in the one down the hall. *I can do this,* she told herself. With as much courage as she could muster, she stepped into the bathroom and flipped the switch washing the space in light. Thankfully, there were no signs of anything otherworldly in the bathroom. The plastic curtain was still balled up in the trashcan and the tub was free of ghostly entities. After brushing her teeth, she crawled into bed and opened one of the scrapbooks. Faded newspaper clippings, delicate as sandcastles in a windstorm, filled the pages forcing Sarah to handle them carefully to prevent them from disintegrating.

One image in particular caught Sarah's attention. A little girl in a lacey dress stood at the base of the stairs, the same little girl from the photo she'd found in the library. She reached for the loose picture, her fingers tingling as she held it next to the one affixed in the album. It was definitely Nora Monroe. Sarah slid the loose photo between the pages and continued perusing the album.

Blue ribbons, now faded purple, along with horse show listings cluttered several pages. A few pieces of poetry scribbled on yellowed parchment were tucked beneath the front cover. Apparently, Nora was an avid poet from an early age.

One poem, written when Nora was ten, caught Sarah's attention.

Wind in My Hair

Hoofbeats pound the earth in rhythm with the beating of my heart,
Just a girl and her horse, drifting, galloping through the wilderness as one,
Searching for the freedom to be who we were meant to be.

Sarah blinked away exhaustion as she placed the album on the night table, switched off the lamp, and fell into a peaceful slumber. As she slept, her heartbeat quickened when a skeletal hand emerged from the darkness, touching her forehead. At that moment, visions of a little girl astride a horse, the same child from the photo she'd found in the book, filled her dreams. Giggles emanated from the child as she rode wholeheartedly, the horse's mane flipping against her face while they galloped full speed toward the horizon.

When Sarah awoke the next morning, her muscles ached and her back was stiff as if she'd actually been riding all night long. It seemed all the moving of furniture and books was taking its toll on her body. Yet something else was plaguing her, something she couldn't identify. She grabbed her clothes and scooted down the hall to take a shower, too nervous to try the tub. As Sarah stepped into the bathroom, an icy sensation nipped at the back of her neck as an unseen skeletal hand reached for her hair. Thinking it was a bug; she swatted at her hair before grabbing a towel and starting the shower.

6

———————

Sarah braided her wet hair and slipped on a t-shirt, shorts, and running shoes. Her stomach rumbled and the idea of a bagel with some of Lisa's special cream cheese tempted her to make a trip to town.

She parked in front of her favorite haunt, *Antiques and Coffee Beans*, and jaunted inside. Miss Jess was already in her usual spot sipping her tea and polishing silver for Lisa while Kayla, the accountant for the shop, was going through the register receipts. Lisa was on the floor scrubbing the carpet.

"Hey Sarah," she said, "Wasn't expecting to see you this morning. How are things at the mansion?"

"Busy!" she replied. "Already had a spill this morning?"

"Not exactly. When I opened up there was an empty bottle of orange soda in the middle of the floor. Apparently, someone shook it up and it exploded all over the carpet and the ceiling," Lisa said with a smirk.

Sarah looked up and saw orange splotches on the ceiling. "Someone broke in and vandalized the place?" she said, looking around.

"No break in, everything was locked up tight," she replied, standing up.

"If no one broke in how do you explain the soda incident?" Sarah asked, her skin beginning to prickle.

"I can't," Lisa said, walking behind the counter to wash her hands. "Your usual this morning?"

"Actually, I was thinking about a bagel with olive cream cheese spread and a cup of tea."

"Join me over here," Miss Jess called out as she moved the silver to her side of the table, clearing a space for Sarah. "You know this place is haunted even if Lisa doesn't believe it."

"Sure seems that way," Sarah agreed, glancing around the room.

At that moment a woman entered, impeccably dressed in a flowing chartreuse blouse, turquoise silk scarf, and wide-legged linen slacks. Flaming red hair crowned her smiling face.

"Good morning, Lisa. I decided to stop in before I head to Fineland's Department Store. It's Senior Day and we're introducing a new fragrance at the Lauderdale counter."

"Ione, would you like a cup of coffee?"

"Yes, please."

Lisa filled a mug and handed it to Ione as she made her way to sit with Miss Jess and Sarah.

"How are you Ione?" Sarah asked scooting her chair over.

"Very well, thank you. And yourself?" She sipped her coffee leaving bright red lipstick on the edge.

"A bit worn out."

Lisa placed the bagel with a side of olive cream cheese and a cup of steaming tea in front of Sarah.

"Thanks Lisa," she said spreading cream cheese on the bagel. Sarah looked at Ione and smiled. "Have you been in any movies lately?"

"Not since last summer," she grinned, her eyes wrinkling with joy.

"How many does that make for you and Richard?"

Ione pursed her lips and looked at the ceiling. "Fourteen."

"That's a lot of filming," Sarah said, taking a bite of her bagel.

"Richard and I have been movie extra's for nearly twenty years now. *The Big Chill* was our first," she said proudly, taking another sip of coffee.

"That's pretty cool."

"What brings you down here?" Ione asked. "I thought you'd be buried in inventory at the Monroe place."

"Needed a break. Even though the house is huge I was beginning to feel like the walls were closing in," Sarah sighed. "I don't think Edie threw anything away which has created more work than I'd bargained for."

"I'm not surprised given Edie's proclivity for unusual behavior," Miss Jess said, raising her eyebrows.

Lisa walked over and joined them. "*Unusual behavior* is a nice way to put it," Lisa added with a chuckle.

"Did you guys know Edie?" Sarah asked, placing the bagel on the plate and focusing her attention on the three ladies sitting with her. Perhaps they had information that could explain some of the things happening at the mansion.

"Can't say that I knew her all that well. She came in here every so often for a cup of coffee but most of what I know about her I've heard from others or read in the paper," Lisa replied.

Miss Jess chuckled. "I think her most notorious escapades were during the nudist colony years."

"Nudist colony?" Sarah exclaimed.

"You've never heard about that?" Ione asked.

"No. I didn't realize Edie ever lived anywhere but here."

"The nudist colony *was* here," Miss Jess added.

"I think I still have the article about it," Lisa said, walking to her desk in the back room. She returned moments later with a yellowed newspaper article dated May 15th, 1971 and handed it to Sarah.

Nudist Colony Shuts Down, Property to be Sold

AFTER A BRIEF RUN of three months, the residents of the nudist colony on Crane Island have called it quits. Harriet Peabody purchased Crane Island late last year with the intention of turning it into a community for those "who wished to break free from the restraints of societal fashion." One of the most notable residents of the colony is Edie Monroe. It came as no surprise that the endeavor was doomed to failure when the weather shifted bringing with it swarms of sand fleas and mosquitoes.

Mr. Devereaux, of Devereaux Real Estate, said he's been fishing off the shore of Crane Island for the past few months. He claims it's the only spot where the fish are biting making it the perfect location to build a cabin. For more information about the land contact Rodney Devereaux, broker in charge.

SARAH ROLLED HER EYES. She wasn't the least bit surprised that a Devereaux would be hanging around a beach filled with naked people under the pretense of fishing.

"So, Edie was part of this nudist movement?" Sarah asked.

"According to the article and the town gossip. I remember her parents were furious with her for bringing more disgrace to the family. Her father's drinking increased exponentially after the article came out," Miss Jess added.

"Why do you have the article here?" Sarah queried.

"Harriet Peabody bought this place after she sold the island. Granted she didn't stay long and ended up moving to Arizona where she started another nudist commune. I guess wearing clothes was too much for her." Lisa chuckled.

Sarah finished her tea and the rest of her bagel and stood up to leave. "I really need to get back to work ladies. Thanks for the company and the interesting conversation," she said with a smile.

"Anytime," Lisa replied.

Sarah hopped in her truck and drove back to Monroe Manse mulling over the idea that there had been a nudist colony in town and that Edie had partaken of it. She parked the truck and hurried inside as birdsong floated on marsh breezes.

She trudged to the library for another day of inventory. Sliding the ladder over to the far wall, she started clearing the upper shelves. A thick layer of grime encased this section; making it obvious the books had not been handled in years. Blowing dust from a faded spine, Sarah held one of the volumes toward the light to get a better look at the title. In faint gilded lettering, it read, *Pride and Prejudice I*. Volume two and three sat beside it on the shelf.

She cradled the book in her hand as if it were a piece of fine bone china, carefully opening the cover. Her breath caught when she read the publication date of 1813. Closing the book, she held it to her chest, taking a moment to process the treasure —a first edition of Jane Austen's masterpiece. *Pride and Prejudice* had been one of her favorites since childhood, and now she held this rare jewel in the palm of her hand. The last set she'd seen at auction brought eighteen thousand dollars.

If only I had the funds, I would treat myself, she thought. *How ironic that I'll have to sell them to make the money to buy them.*

Carefully descending the ladder, she placed the three volumes on the desk and climbed back up to discover first editions of *Sense and Sensibility* as well as *Emma*. These were also worth thousands and would sell quickly.

Additional literary treasures included a leather-bound set

of Thackeray's classics and early printings by the Brontë's as well as Edgar Allen Poe. She'd consign these with Dan and Laura at Raven Booksellers. They had a loyal following of serious book collectors who would pay top dollar.

The scent of Chanel No. 5 wafted through the room as a vision of Edie's lifeless body flickered in Sarah's mind. Shrugging it off, she pushed the image from her mind and returned to the job at hand. The last thing she needed was to stretch her already overwrought imagination any further by trying to figure out where Edie's dead body was found or how long it was there before being discovered. Convinced that moving books around had resurrected the scent, Sarah continued her inventory.

Morning hours faded into afternoon with most of the library purged and organized. In one corner a stack of rare and valuable books were catalogued and boxed while numerous containers of best sellers and paperbacks would be donated to the library's annual fall book sale. Two garbage bags, which Sarah hauled to the curb for trash pick-up the next morning, overflowed with old mailings.

Pleased with her progress, she decided to take a break when the Batman theme blared from her pocket.

"Hey, Danni, what's up?"

"Sorry to bother you, but I just got word from William that he wants to photograph the house next week for his company website. Any way you can make that happen?"

"I suppose he can photograph the rooms that are cleared and inventoried," she sighed.

"I'll let him know he can come over next week," Danni replied.

"Make sure he doesn't show up before then. I don't need his interference."

"You want supper again tonight? I was thinking Mexican food from Avocados."

"Sounds good."

"See you at six."

Sarah clicked off the phone and started for the kitchen to fix a peanut butter sandwich for lunch. As she walked down the hall, she thought about the scrapbook she'd skimmed the night before and scrambled to her room to retrieve it. *Might as well look through it over lunch*, she thought.

AT SIX O'CLOCK SHARP, Danni arrived with enchiladas and Coronas, prompting Sarah to take a break for dinner. Danni plunked a couple of limes on the counter and began opening drawers in search of a knife.

"Got anything to cut with around here?"

"Try the knife stand on the counter," Sarah replied, pulling plates from the upper cabinet.

Danni sliced a lime into wedges and squeezed the juice into each beer. She handed a bottle to Sarah, grabbed one of the plates, and sat down. "What's that?" Danni asked, taking a swig of beer.

"It's one of Nora Monroe's scrapbooks I found in the attic."

"Sarah, you're doing it again."

"Doing what?" she said, taking a bite of enchilada.

"Getting distracted by inane stuff. You've only got three weeks to clear this place out. Stop goofing off."

"But it's interesting," she said slouching in the chair.

"No doubt," Danni said with a smirk. "The Monroe's have plenty of interesting stories."

"What do you mean?"

"Anytime a wealthy family does something outrageous, people talk, and in this case for more than a century."

"Why would anybody care about something that happened

a hundred years ago?" Sarah asked, reaching for the hot sauce. "Wasn't Edie scandalous enough?"

"For having been born and raised here, I'm shocked at how much you *don't* know about this town."

"I was only interested in the old houses and antiques. Besides, I never paid any mind to the gossip, you know Mother didn't let me."

"Where's the fun in that?"

"Come on, Danni, that's what I have you for, to fill me in on all the dirt around here," she said with a sheepish grin. "So, tell me about this scandal."

Danni began the story with as much drama as she could muster.

"Nora Monroe was the only surviving child of Arthur and Evelynn Monroe. They had two daughters, but the younger one, Ethel, died of influenza at the age of four.

"Nora was well educated and had all the things wealth could offer. Of course, the family was determined she'd marry well. Frederick Hamilton of Charleston was a few years older than her but considered a good match, so the arrangements were made." Danni paused to take a drink.

"That doesn't sound very scandalous," Sarah said.

"Be patient. It's a complicated story, I'm setting the stage."

Sarah rested her chin in her hand wondering if Danni was carrying on for the sake of hearing her own voice. Her profession as an attorney was definitely well chosen.

"Once the wedding date was announced, the preparations went wildly out of control, amassing an exorbitant price tag. Within a year, Nora was pregnant and gave birth to a little girl. That would be Edie's grandmother, Bitsy. And then one day, Frederick got up to discover Nora was gone. A thorough search of the place revealed she'd taken off with a few of her best dresses and some jewelry. The only thing she left behind was a note."

"What was in the note?" Sarah asked her interest revitalized.

"Something about needing to get away. Most people believed she ran off, too ashamed to admit she didn't like being a mother. Frederick refused to accept it. He never even finished the mansion he was building in Charleston for them. When Mr. and Mrs. Monroe passed on, they left the estate to their granddaughter, Bitsy, under Frederick's care. He lived here and continued to maintain Nora's rose gardens until his dying day."

"Wow, that's some story. Did anyone ever hear from Nora again?"

"Nope. Most people surmised she went to Europe to escape the gossip and probably met someone over there. It's like one of those mysteries you see on TV, where the person is living a double life."

"I still don't understand how you know all of this."

"Have you forgotten my mother's need to be part of high society? She pushed her way into as many garden clubs and charitable organizations as she could. These old stories floated around for years, especially anything to do with the Monroes. With all of Edie's drunken escapades and crazy antics, the family exploits continued well into this century."

Nodding in agreement, Sarah put the dishes in the sink, her mind processing the new information.

"Of course, Edie's ramblings about ghosts certainly didn't help her reputation," Danni added.

Sarah froze at the mention of ghosts when a loud *thump* echoed from above.

"What was that?" Danni whispered, her eyes widening.

"Probably another branch from the big oak out back. It dropped a limb the other night and the storm probably loosened a few more."

Danni nodded, her face paling as she stared at the ceiling.

"Now who's freaking out over ghosts?" Sarah chuckled.

"I'm not afraid, it caught me off-guard, that's all," Danni said defensively, trying to relax.

"I don't mean to break up this little party, but I still have a lot of work to do before bed," Sarah yawned.

"Sure you don't want me to stay here with you?"

Sarah's heart pounded at the thought of having Danni stay but quickly dismissed the idea. "You don't have an overnight bag."

"I could go home and get one," Danni replied reluctantly.

Sarah shrugged. "Bring one tomorrow and we'll have a slumber party like the good old days."

"I get it. Now that you've heard all the rumors about the Monroes, you want me to go," Danni said playfully, obviously relieved her friend wasn't taking her up on the offer to stay. She gave Sarah a quick hug before grabbing her keys. "I'll see myself out. Get to work, and stop all this gossiping!"

"Goodnight, Danni."

Sarah washed the dishes, relieved she'd found a way to get Danni to spend the night without revealing the reason she wanted the company. One more night alone and then she'd have someone here. The idea of having another *living* person in the house gave her the courage to face anything that might happen. Sarah secured the downstairs doors, grabbed the scrapbooks, and returned to the library.

Turning on the overhead light, she discovered what had caused the thump they'd heard earlier. The donation book pile had tumbled over, with the *Dreamist* book sprawled open. Sarah restacked the books and resumed her inventory.

After filling two more boxes, Sarah rotated her shoulders in an effort to loosen the stiffness in her back. She sat at the recently cleared Chippendale desk and made a few notations in her ledger. Switching off the light, she carried the scrapbooks to her room. A little late-night perusal of the contents would help her relax.

Dust and dirt adhered to Sarah's sweaty body like powdered sugar to a donut. A long soak in an old tub would go a long way to alleviating her stress. However, after the bizarre occurrence with the shower curtain she didn't dare soak in the tub. She'd have to settle for a shower.

Refreshed from her shower, Sarah snuggled into bed as the grandfather clock chimed midnight. She fluffed the pillows, grabbed a scrapbook and paged through until sleepiness tugged at her eyelids like window shades being drawn. Wearily, she scooted below the covers, pulling the sheet over her head with the lamp illuminating the room. Her mind began to submit to slumber when a bony finger reached out and touched her forehead. Suddenly, Sarah found herself in another time and place, helpless to escape.

7

———

Muffled voices roused Nora from her sleep. Sitting up, she cocked her head and surmised the sound was coming from the end of the hall. Curious, she slipped on her wrapper and tiptoed down the hall where a sliver of light streamed from the library. Her parents spoke in hushed, heated tones as she pressed her ear against the edge of the doorway. In all her years, she only remembered one argument between them and it had been mild.

"How are we to survive, my dear? We cannot lose this house, not to mention ruining Nora's chances for a good marriage. You must convince Mr. Devereaux to extend the loan," Mrs. Monroe pleaded.

"He's still indignant about our refusal of his offer for Nora to wed his son. I might be desperate but not so much that I would sacrifice my only daughter to *that* family. They're a dishonest lot."

"Yet you went to him for financial assistance," she said, disdain tinting her words. "You should have known better than to invest in any of his questionable schemes."

"What choice did I have? We needed money immediately

and Devereaux was the only one with the means to help. It's imperative we speak to the Hamiltons without delay. We've always considered Frederick a good match for Nora and their wealth would more than solve our issues."

Tears welled in Nora's eyes as she listened to the dilemma in which her parents found themselves and the precarious nature of her own marital future. How could she appease her parent's wishes to wed Mr. Hamilton when her heart belonged to another? Nora was well acquainted with the Hamiltons having attended their annual Christmas party, which was the most anticipated event of the season. Frederick was handsome and a much sought-after catch. He had always been attentive and kind to her but that wasn't enough to make a marriage, at least not in her mind. She blamed all those Jane Austen novels she'd read for putting such romantic ideas in her head. Granted, with a little time and effort on her part perhaps Mr. Hamilton could become her Mr. Darcy.

"I shall write to Mrs. Hamilton tomorrow morning and invite her to tea. And please, from here on out let me handle this situation. You've already made a mess of things," Mrs. Monroe scolded.

Nora scurried down the hall to her room, closed the door, and crumpled to the Persian rug in a sobbing heap. Any dreams of a future with Charles were decimated even though she'd always known it was unlikely. She crawled beneath the cottony sheets and stared at the hand-crocheted canopy above, despair weighting her chest as she deliberated how to break the news to her beloved. Somehow, she'd find a way to accept Frederick Hamilton and move past a love that never had a chance in a society dominated world such as hers.

As if someone pressed the fast forward button on a VCR, the scene shifted ahead several weeks. Nora rode a sleek chestnut horse alongside a lanky, distinguished gentleman. The conversation was pleasant as they plodded along the marsh's edge serenaded by seagulls squawking in bountiful blue skies. A soft breeze ruffled tree leaves and swept across tall grasses burgeoning from the sticky pluff mud.

It was all so realistic; Sarah could actually smell the pungent aroma of the marsh in the depths of her mind. She felt as if she was trapped inside of Nora's head, seeing, hearing, and feeling everything she did.

"Mr. Hamilton, how long will you be in town?" Nora asked, a shy smile lifting her lips.

"A few more days at least. May I call on you later?"

"I would like that very much."

"Shall we gallop back?" he proposed with a grin

Nora nodded as they spurred the horses into a bold pace, the salty air swatting their faces as they ducked and dodged all manner of low lying limbs. Unfortunately, Mr. Hamilton was not as familiar with the trails and dodged when he should have ducked, dislodging him from the saddle and planting him on the ground.

Nora dismounted and scurried to his side.

"Are you all right, Mr. Hamilton?"

"I'm fine, but I fear my hat may not be." Reaching beneath him, he rescued the crumpled remnants of his chapeau. He brushed it off and attempted to restore its form before placing the misshapen bowler back on his head.

Nora covered her mouth in an effort to muffle her amusement.

"No need to stifle your beguilement, Miss Monroe. Certainly, my disheveled appearance is laughable," he said, casting a sheepish grin in her direction. His dark eyes sparkled, letting her know he was amused at his happenstance and not the least bit unsettled.

She returned a smile as they remounted their horses and plodded to the barn at a leisurely pace.

A groom took the horses as Mr. Hamilton and Nora walked

side by side to the house. When they reached the portico, he removed his creased hat and bowed.

"Miss Monroe, I shall take my leave now. Thank you for a delightful afternoon."

"I enjoyed our ride and look forward to your visit later this evening."

With a quick curtsey, Nora slipped inside, her heart sinking with each step.

8

―――――――

Sarah sucked in air as the door in her dream slammed shut. Looking around, she tried to get her bearings. She was at Monroe Manse. Of all the dreams she'd had throughout her life none had ever been so lifelike or personal. Terror rippled through Sarah's core sending beads of perspiration down her back as she shivered from the experience. The clock showed three a.m., too early to call Danni. Even if she did call, what would she say? Danni would want to know about the dreams and why Sarah hadn't shared them with her before now. Not too many people accepted spectral visions and Danni's no-nonsense attitude, along with her military upbringing, wasn't likely to bend to the idea of haunted dreams.

Groggy, Sarah sat up in bed and reached for the scrapbook. She paged through several clippings before stumbling across a sepia photo with the image of a young lady upon a regal steed. The caption below it read, "Nora and Camden, afternoon ride."

Well, that explains why this particular horse is in my dreams. Rattled, she closed the album and plopped back against the pillows. After all these years, the dreams were intensifying in nature. And it frightened her. For a moment, she considered driving back to her cottage but scolded herself for being so ridiculous. She was an adult now and needed to deal with it.

Obviously her subconscious had amalgamated the dinner discussion about the Monroes with the image from the scrapbook. With a few deep breaths, Sarah felt the tension drain from her shoulders and spine. Parched from the experience, she decided to go downstairs for a drink.

She swung her feet over the edge of the bed when something tickled her foot. Frozen with fear, she glanced down to see a skeletal hand latch onto her ankle, and in one swift move yank her down to the floor. Screaming, she clawed at the Persian rug as the hand pulled her under the bed when a scratchy voice whispered, "We need your help."

Suddenly, everything went quiet and the grip on her leg released. Sarah gasped in deep breaths as she scurried from under the bed. With as much speed as her quavering legs could muster, Sarah ran downstairs and out the front door. Breathless, she looked back at the house, its tabby walls looming over her like a giant preparing to devour its prey. In all her years, she'd never had a ghost get physical with her.

Sarah glanced around in the darkness when she realized she didn't have the cell phone or her keys. Tears christened her lashes at the overwhelming loneliness that enveloped her. She had no way to call Danni and her parents were in Italy. Even if she could call, she wouldn't. No one would believe what just happened. Hopelessness tightened her chest as she hurried to her truck, climbed inside, locked the doors, and rested her head against the seat. Sarah took a few deep breaths like she'd been taught in therapy when she was a kid.

As her heart rate slowed, her mind drifted back to the slumber party in fifth grade. The image of Nancy's contorted face when Sarah shared her nightmare was etched in her memory. How was she supposed to know that the woman in her dream was Nancy's deceased grandmother? A shiver jolted her body. The dreams were getting worse and at this moment she couldn't deal with a reality she'd locked away for so long.

As Scarlett O'Hara would say, she'd think about that tomorrow. Since it was only a couple of hours before dawn, Sarah decided to sleep in the truck. First thing in the morning she'd venture back inside. If Danni couldn't stay with her tomorrow night she'd go back to her cottage. It would cost her time but preserve her sanity and possibly her life.

9

———

A low rumbling emanated from a garbage truck, rousing Sarah from her troubled slumber. Dazed, she sat up and rubbed her eyes. Even in the light of day, the house seemed forlorn with its weed-ridden gardens and misshapen bushes shuddering in the breeze. Outside the gate, a small dog marked the edge of the drive before tottering behind its owner who had stopped to admire the old house. At that moment, she wished she could be as carefree and unaware of the spectral occupants residing within the mansion's walls. Despite the tumultuous night, Sarah knew she needed to go back inside.

Mustering all of her courage, Sarah left the safety of her truck and trudged to the front portico. The door creaked as she opened it and stepped inside. Early morning light speckled the floors as dust particles danced on sunrays streaming through the transom windows. Not sensing anything otherworldly, Sarah exhaled. Maybe she'd overreacted last night. No doubt, her mind was muddled after the dream and could've been playing tricks on her. Chances were she'd tripped when she got out of bed and only imagined the bony fingers and the echo of someone calling for help. Pacified by her rationalization she went to the kitchen for tea and a power bar.

While the teakettle heated, Sarah jaunted up the stairs to fetch the cell phone. She hovered at the bedroom door garnering her courage to go in. Much to her relief, the room was in order except for the scrapbook that lay sprawled on the floor. She scooped it up, placed it on the nightstand, grabbed the phone, and dialed Danni's office number.

"Law office of Danielle Cook. Anita speaking."

"Hey Anita, it's Sarah. Is Danni in?"

"Sorry, she's at the courthouse until this afternoon. Would you like to leave a message?"

"Have her call me when she gets back. Thanks Anita."

Sarah clicked off the phone and dialed her father's cell number. Maybe talking with him would make her feel better and resurrect some of the excitement she'd had for this job. The phone rang several times before a computerized voice answered. "This voice mailbox is full. Please try again later."

"Great," Sarah mumbled. "I wonder how long before they realize they need to empty their voice mail. At this rate, I'll be done with the estate by the time I reach them."

Sarah sighed. There was no sense wasting any more time. She'd learned over the years that staying busy was the best way to battle her fears. Working herself to exhaustion helped her sleep. She changed, pulled her hair into a ponytail, grabbed her tools, and went downstairs to fix a cup of tea. After tea and a granola bar Sarah started working.

Now that the front parlor and library were complete, Sarah decided to work on the dining room. Of all the rooms, it was the least cluttered and close enough to the back of the house that she could escape quickly if need be. A long mahogany table and twelve chairs anchored the room beneath a shimmering crystal chandelier. In the center of the table, a sterling epergne in several shades of tarnish with cut crystal bowls stood between matching candlestick holders. The china cabinet was well stocked with twenty-four complete place settings of green Cockatrice by Minton. Sadly, entire sets of china didn't sell well, so she'd have to sell it off in pieces. Dinner at the Monroe mansion must have been an extravagant affair back in the day.

I'm surprised Edie kept all this stuff, no doubt she never made use of it, Sarah thought, clicking on the tape recorder. After listing the important pieces in the room, she turned the recorder off and began tagging items.

When the hall clock chimed twelve, Sarah decided to forgo lunch and keep working. She was making headway and didn't want to break her rhythm by stopping to eat. Thrilled by the extraordinary value of the items she'd categorized already, Sarah was driven by her desire to see what else she would unearth.

Once the contents of the china cabinet were recorded and packed, Sarah started emptying the buffet. She recorded several miscellaneous serving pieces including stray napkin rings and a cut crystal sugar shaker, none of which would bring much money. Opening the bottom drawer, she heard a *snap* echo through the room.

"Doggonit!" she grumbled.

Sarah saw dollar signs fly away as she considered the cost to repair whatever she'd just broken. She pulled the drawer out to inspect it for damage when her hand brushed across something underneath. Flipping the drawer over, she noticed an extra slat of wood. With careful wriggling, the slat gave way, revealing a small compartment holding a tintype photo and a gold ring with a horseshoe-shaped garnet and seed pearls. Sarah was shocked to find a hidden compartment in a buffet; usually secretaries and desks housed secret chambers.

Studying the photo, Sarah wondered about the identity of the handsome young man as a chill bumped across her skin.

Although the image was slightly faded, his soulful eyes, warm smile, and modest attire of a sack coat and plaid shirt showed clearly. Shadows imprinted on the edges of the picture suggested it had once been housed in a case of some sort. The mystery of the man's identity fueled Sarah's desire to investigate further; however, she reminded herself that she needed to stay on task if she was going to get everything complete by the deadline. Anyway, there was no way to identify him even if she wanted to pursue it.

The ring was obviously meant for a petite hand and was missing one of the tiny pearls. Sarah's heart palpitated and her fingertips tingled as she stuffed the ring in her pocket. Now was as good a time as any to take a break.

She strolled several blocks to Avant-Garde Jewelers on Bridge Street. Stepping through the door, she was welcomed by the official greeter to patrons of the jewelry store, a brindle boxer named Woodrow. She reached down to pat the dog's head, grinning at his protruding under bite and crooked teeth.

"Good afternoon, Sarah," Keith's voice rang out.

"Hey, Keith, how's business?"

"Can't complain. What brings you here? I figured you'd be swamped with the Monroe estate."

"I needed a break." Digging in her pocket, she pulled out the ring and handed it to him. "I found this and was wondering if it's a cheap piece of costume jewelry or something of value."

He walked behind the counter and placed the ring under the lighted magnifier.

"The garnet is well carved and the seed pearls are a bit discolored, but overall, it looks real. I'll check the gold content." Keith walked to the back room while Sarah glanced at china place settings labeled with the names of soon-to-be local brides. *Nothing in this place has changed*, she thought. It was still an old-fashioned, family-run jewelry store selling everything one would need for life's special occasions from high school graduation to marriage, births, and anniversaries.

A few minutes later, Keith returned. "It's about nine-karat gold, probably English."

"That's good news. How much to replace the missing seed pearl?"

"Not much. I can have it ready in a few days."

"That'd be great. Thanks, Keith."

"No problem."

Sarah started back to the mansion, the sun massaging her shoulders as she sauntered along the dappled streets of town. Jasmine scrambled over picket fences, its fragrant bouquet scenting the air, bringing forth fond memories from childhood when she'd go to Langdon's Pharmacy for an ice cream soda and a handful of butterscotch candies.

When she reached the mansion, Sarah wandered about the yard. Captivated by the rose garden, in spite of its overgrown condition, she noticed a single rose blooming on one of the larger bushes. She leaned over, taking in the sweet perfume before returning to the monumental undertaking waiting inside.

THE BATMAN THEME clamored from within Sarah's pocket startling her from her working stupor.

"Hey Danni."

"Anita said you called."

"Just checking to make sure you were still spending the night."

"Planned on it. I'll pick up supper on the way."

"Sounds good. See you later."

Sarah exhaled as she hung up the phone grateful that Danni would be here. Hopefully, she wouldn't have any nightmares with someone else in the house. Relieved, she traipsed to the dining room and resumed her inventory.

At six o'clock Danni arrived with a bottle of Chianti, Woodford Reserve, and ravioli from Delgotti's Pasta House. She was still sporting her business suit and heels with her hair pulled into a tight bun unlike her usual attire of blue jeans and a plaid shirt. Kicking off her heels, she pulled a bottle from a brown paper bag.

"Thought you might like some good bourbon," she said, placing the bottle on the counter.

"What's the occasion? You usually aren't so generous with the top shelf stuff."

"Landed another big account today. It's going to take a lot of my time, but I'll still bring supper."

"You don't have to do that, I'm perfectly capable of feeding myself."

"Peanut butter sandwiches and granola bars. You're my best friend and I feel badly you're stuck with such a short deadline. It's my way of helping out."

"Thanks, Danni. I really appreciate it."

Sarah pulled a couple of mismatched plates from the upper cabinet as well as forks from the drawer and set them on the oak pub table before pouring a shot of bourbon and joining Danni.

"How was court today?"

"Great. I love it when Judge Muller is on the bench. It's pure entertainment, like watching a sitcom. He should consider comedy when he retires. Makes arguing a case less stressful. He made a joke about the high-tech manner of doing business at the courthouse by drawing juror numbers from a Tupperware bowl after shaking it to mix up the slips of paper. You won't find this stuff in the big cities." Danni chuckled, uncorking the Chianti. "How about you? Uncover any priceless artifacts?" Danni asked.

"Discovered a secret compartment under one of the drawers in the buffet this morning with a ring and a photo of a man. Kinda strange since hidden cubbies are usually found in desks and trunks. I suppose with the house being used during the Civil War, it's conceivable they had all sorts of places to hide valuables."

"Who's the guy in the picture?"

"Not sure. My middle school teacher taught us that the house was used as a hospital during the war but the guy in the photo is white."

"Guess it's a mystery," Danni said. "Nothing about this place surprises me anymore. The history behind this house has more plot twists than a soap opera."

"I still don't understand how you know so much about it," Sarah said, taking a bite of ravioli.

"I told you, I heard stuff during Mom's garden gossip gatherings. The Monroes were at the core of the rumor mill. With their wealth and reputation, any bit of scandal caught attention, like a kite in a hurricane." Danni poured a splash of Chianti and swirled it in the glass apparently consumed by memories of adolescence.

"Poor Mom was always trying to make me into a debutante. I think she was disappointed when I decided on law school instead of becoming Susie homemaker. Thank goodness Dad understood me or I'd probably be married with two point five kids, a full social calendar, and the proverbial picket fence around a clapboard house."

"And a bottle of booze hidden in every cupboard." Sarah snickered.

"Better believe it!" Danni said before downing the swallow of wine and promptly pouring another.

"Too bad your marriage to Scott didn't work out."

"I think we were in love with the idea of the conventional American family. Let's face it, I'm a far cry from traditional."

"I'll drink to that," Sarah chuckled, holding up her glass.

"I'm surprised you never heard more of the rumors about the Monroes, especially since you grew up here."

"Like I said, Mom didn't like gossip and I wasn't exactly invited to every social gathering. I'm kind of an outcast, remember?"

"That's probably why I hang out with you. Since you're a loner I don't have to worry about you sharing my dirty little secrets."

"I don't think you have any secrets. Your escapades are public knowledge." Sarah snorted.

"True. Then again, real friends don't keep secrets, thus why you know everything about me."

A pang swirled through Sarah's stomach. She desperately wanted to tell Danni everything but still wasn't sure the time was right.

When they finished eating Sarah cleared the table while Danni got her bag from the car.

"Where am I sleeping?" Danni asked, holding her duffle bag.

"Upstairs, down the hall on the right."

Sarah finished cleaning up when Danni ambled into the room wearing a faded USC t-shirt and knit shorts, her shoulder length hair contained behind a headband.

"Is there a TV in this place?"

"Nope. If you want entertainment you'll have to settle for books."

"No thanks. Had my share of reading during law school," Danni shrugged.

"I brought my CD player. We could listen to the oldies."

"Like 80s music?"

"More like the 30s," Sarah replied, scrunching her shoulders.

"I thought this was supposed to be a slumber party? You

know, scary movies, spiked Coca-Cola, fun?" Danni said with hands on her hips. "I even brought microwave popcorn."

"You'll have to go somewhere else to pop it. There's no microwave in this place."

"Ugh, this slumber party is a bust."

"Consider it more of a sleepover. You could always help me out."

"Beats being bored," Danni shrugged. "What do you want me to do?"

"Grab the garbage bags from the library and help me pack the kitchen stuff up."

"Fine, but I'm drinking while we do this," Danni huffed as she wandered down the hall.

Danni and Sarah filled garbage bags with gadgets, silverware, old copper-bottomed pots, and mismatched dishes. Not surprisingly, they discovered drawers filled with junk ranging from an assortment of advertising bottle openers, expired coupons, a collection of wire bread ties, and folded sheets of once-used tinfoil.

Two hours, and several garbage bags later, most of the kitchen contents were in two stacks by the back door, one for garbage pick-up and the other for the Blue Moon thrift store. Sarah kept just enough dishware and glasses to use until she finished the job and completed clearing the kitchen.

"I've had about all the fun I can have for one evening. I'm going to bed," Danni announced with a yawn.

"G'night. Thanks for the help."

"Consider it a favor. I don't even do this at my own house," Danni replied with a sly grin. "See you in the morning."

Sarah poured a shot of bourbon, locked all the doors, and headed for bed. Flipping on the old oil lamp, she scaled the stairs, making a mental note to do more research into the Monroe history. If she could identify the man in the photo and the owner of the ring it could increase the value. Buyers loved to know the provenance behind the items they purchased.

Halfway up the staircase, Sarah's hair began to bristle as if someone was watching her. Inhaling, she slowly turned around scanning the entry hall below when she zeroed in on a misty form outside the dining room. She blinked a few times and it vanished making her believe it was nothing more than bleary eyes from a long day's work. Sarah shook off the uneasy feeling and scurried up the stairs to her room relieved that nothing had materialized. The last thing she needed was to burden Danni with her fears her first night in the house.

After changing into her nightclothes, Sarah settled into bed, propped the ledger against her knees, and hit the play button on the recorder. Clicking the different colored tabs at the end of the pen, she transferred the inventory information into the columns on each page, the colored ink corresponding with its designated category.

"Whoever invented these multicolored ball point pens was a genius," she quipped before switching off the recorder, closing the ledger, and setting them on the night table.

Yawning, she reached for one of the scrapbooks. A quick perusal revealed more of Nora's blissful life along with various awards for her gardening talents. When Sarah's eyes began to blur, she placed the album on the pile, switched off the lamp, and answered the call of dreamland, thankful for an uneventful evening and another living soul across the hall.

10

———

The scent of jasmine tickled Nora's nose as she walked along the terrace wall, cradling a bundle of freshly cut pink roses. Stepping into the kitchen, she began arranging the blooms in a tall Limoges vase with delicately painted violets roaming over the surface when Miss Biggs, head housemaid, walked in.

"Miss Monroe, Mr. Hamilton is here to see you."

"Oh dear, I wasn't expecting him so soon," Nora said, glancing at her dress and hands "Please tell him I'll be there momentarily. I need to make myself presentable."

Nora clambered up the back stairs to her bedchambers, rinsed her hands in the washbasin, and pulled a pale blue dress from the wardrobe. As she changed, the note she'd retrieved from the hollowed-out oak during her morning walk fell from her pocket to the floor. For months, she and Charles had discreetly left correspondence to one another in the old tree trunk to prevent anyone from discovering their ongoing tryst. Nora was determined to keep this secret, especially when so much was at stake.

She leaned over, retrieved the envelope, and stared at it,

tears christening her eyelashes. She hadn't the emotional fortitude to deal with this right now. She slipped the note into the drawer of her vanity and rushed downstairs, the strain of her family's expectations to wed a man of prominence weighting her shoulders. Pausing in the entry hall, she smoothed her dress, straightened her posture, and took in a deep breath before stepping into the front parlor.

The room was awash in the late afternoon sun as Frederick Hamilton stood at the window gazing out over the front lawn. His tall frame, dark hair, and handsome profile made Nora take pause.

This is a good man, she told herself. *You can learn to love him.*

"Mr. Hamilton, it's ever so good to see you," she said with a slight curtsey.

Frederick turned, a broad smile sweeping across his face as he bowed. He stepped closer, reached for her hair, and removed a crinkled rose leaf. "Miss Monroe, I see you've been tending your roses this afternoon."

"You're quite observant, Mr. Hamilton," she replied, a blush warming her cheeks.

Nora glided across the room, her silk skirts rustling like autumn leaves, and perched upon the velvet settee while Frederick began to pace. His finely tailored suit and neatly styled hair was the opposite of her beloved Charles whose sandy hair fell in curls at his shoulders, his loose fitting clothes always dappled with dirt.

"Miss Monroe, I need to discuss something of great importance with you."

With his hands clasped behind his back, Frederick stopped in front of the mantel and hesitated before speaking.

"It's no secret our families have hoped we would form an attachment. My goodness, they practically wrote our wedding vows!" he said with a chuckle. "I want you to know, despite the conspicuous arrangement for us to wed, I'm enamored with you. Regardless of my parent's wishes, I respectfully ask for your hand, without hesitation or inducement."

Unable to meet his gaze, Nora studied her hands, her chest tightening as she searched for the courage to close the door to her heart and accept the fate standing before her.

"If you're not inclined to marry at this time, I don't wish to broach the subject with your father. I think too highly of you to overlook your feelings on the matter," Frederick added as he began to fidget.

Her heartbeat quickened to a rabbit's pace as she considered his declaration. This was it. Her time had come. She had no choice but to say yes. Her family's financial future depended upon it.

"Mr. Hamilton, I too, have grown fond of you these past few months and gladly accept your offer. You may speak with my father."

Elated, Frederick let out a sigh of relief as he rushed to Nora's side. His eyes locked onto hers as he scooped up her hand, kissing it gently.

"You've made me the happiest of men, Miss Monroe! I shall speak with your father directly. Thank you for the great honor of accepting my proposal."

He rushed from the room as Nora leaned against the tufted back of the settee staring out the window where a Carolina Wren chirped out a melody from the branch of a crepe myrtle. Its melodious warbling plucked at her soul. Although her heart was heavy, she was relieved the engagement was official. Frederick was absolutely correct about the transparent attempt by both families to bind them together. Now that the decision was settled, there was no turning back, regardless of what happened or how she felt.

After an evening of toasts and felicitations, Nora was drained and headed to her room to prepare for bed. She shimmied into a cotton gown and sat before her vanity mirror, her deadpan stare reflecting the condition of her soul as she ran a silver-handled brush through her coffee brown tresses. Sadly, she didn't feel elation over a commitment that should bring indubitable joy. At that moment, her mind darted back to the note she'd stashed away earlier. Reaching into the vanity drawer, she retrieved the envelope, broke the seal, and took a deep breath.

My dearest Nora,

Please forgive my brash behavior at our last meeting. I beg you to reconsider my offer. In time your parents will find it in their hearts to forgive you. We can rendezvous at the destination we discussed. Do not leave me dangling with uncertainty. Meet me at the river oak tomorrow with your answer.

Lovingly yours,

Charles

Tears puddled in her eyes as she shoved the note back into the envelope. Gliding across the room, she peeled back a corner of the rug and lifted the floor panel. She reached inside and removed a collection of letters bound with a silk ribbon, adding the new one. A tear tumbled across her flushed cheek as she held the bundle to her chest. How could she go on like this? First thing in the morning, she'd leave Charles a note in the hollowed-out oak. She had to correct the situation and make things right, no matter how much pain it inflicted.

With the swiftness of a rabbit, the dream shifted to the next day. Dressed in a dark-blue riding habit, Nora mounted Camden, adjusted her skirt, and took the reins from the groom.

"Thank you, Charles. I shan't be long. I'm only riding as far as the *river oak*," her eyebrows arched as she studied his steely blue eyes.

With a nod, he stepped back and watched her lope languidly across the pasture toward the wooded trails.

Once in the woods, Nora slowed Camden to a walk as she watched seagulls dip and soar on morning breezes. Camden's hooves thumped rhythmically along the sandy path, relaxing her into a hypnotic reverie. As she rounded the corner, spectacular water views, framed by towering live oak trees unfolded before her. One oak in particular stood out, its branches sprawling in all directions from a trunk wider than the steed on which she perched.

She slid out of the saddle and led Camden to the river oak where she draped the reins over a low hanging branch. He grazed peacefully as Nora wandered to the water's edge. Moments later, the sound of footsteps caught her attention. She turned to see Charles striding toward her.

He was still as handsome as the first time they'd met when he'd helped her from the ground after Camden had thrown her. Her father had spared no expense on such a fine horse but he was a high-spirited animal and Charles had a way with him. Between Charles's time instructing Nora and training Camden, a friendship formed and quickly blossomed into something much stronger.

"Got here as soon as I could. George was acting strange about my departure, so I had to wait until he was engaged elsewhere."

"You don't think he suspects…"

"Not at all but it's good to be cautious."

Stepping closer, he reached for her hand only to have her withdraw it slowly.

"What's the matter?" he asked, furrowing his brow.

"Charles, please know I would never intentionally hurt you. I couldn't bring myself to deliver such news in a letter."

"Nora, what…"

"Let me finish before you speak." She paused before continuing, "It's no secret my parents have long intended I marry Mr. Hamilton. Last evening, he made an offer of marriage."

"I wondered when you'd tell me."

"You knew?" she queried, her voice cracking.

"News such as this travels quickly amongst the servants, and I am only a servant."

"You're more than that to me," she reached for his hand but this time he held back.

"Apparently not," he replied, his gaze holding hers.

Silence as thick as fog after a thunderstorm hovered in the air. Finally, Nora spoke.

"I don't know what else to say. My father has agreed to the proposal, as have I. Our wedding is scheduled for May of next year."

"So soon?" he declared.

"There's no reason to delay."

"Why not? Won't you please reconsider?" he pleaded.

"Charles, we've been over this many times. I thought I made myself clear about my situation."

"I never believed you'd actually go through with it. Why the sudden proposal? I assumed it would be months before anything was made official," he said, running his hands through his sandy curls.

"I don't know what precipitated his offer," Nora replied, looking at the ground to hide her deception. She couldn't let him know the reason was a financial one. "I haven't a say in the matter, especially since all has been settled."

"Of course you have a say in this. It's your life, Nora! Are you willing to spend it with a man you don't love?" Desperation punctuated his words.

"I don't dislike him. He's a fine man and quite fond of me. Our engagement has long been anticipated. I've always been forthright about it."

"But you love me. Isn't that enough to prevent you from marrying another man?"

"Charles, be realistic. We both knew I would marry someone else. As much as I care for you, my parents would never approve the match. Please, try to understand my position."

Charles rubbed his forehead, his expression forlorn.

"Nora, I'm begging you. Tell him you've had a change of heart. Ask for a longer engagement, anything, but don't go through with this, not yet. Give me time to find a viable solution."

She looked away to avoid witnessing the pain she'd inflicted.

"This isn't personal. It's about the family name," she swallowed hard, *and the family fortune, or lack thereof.*

"So now I'm not good enough for you? It didn't seem to bother you these past few months!" His face flushed as he tried to contain his agony.

Droplets dangled from Nora's eyelids, blurring her vision in a sea of sorrow. She had to end the relationship. If Charles knew she was marrying for money he'd find a way to convince her to run away with him, which at this point wouldn't take much to achieve.

"Charles, these aren't my wishes. I'm merely making the best of an impossible situation. I must follow my family's expectations. As much as I love you, we both knew this could never amount to anything more than"— she shrugged her shoulders— "whatever this is."

"I won't accept this. I can't let you go," he replied, a grimace wilting his handsome features. "I need to get back to work before anyone questions where I've been."

Without looking at her, Charles turned and started towards the barn. Nora watched him fade into the tree line, her eyes relinquishing the tears. Despair tightened her chest, as she feared what he might do next.

Remounting Camden, she headed for the barn, praying Charles would be elsewhere so she could slip back to the house and forgo any further discomfort.

Fortunately, he was nowhere in sight when she approached the stables. George was nearby, helped her from the saddle, and led Camden down the aisle to the tack room. Tugging at each finger of her leather gloves, she looked up to find Charles standing before her his hair tousled by the breeze and his eyes rimmed in pink.

"Where's Camden?"

"George is tending to him," she whispered.

"I'm Camden's groom." His voice shook as he fought to maintain his composure. "Or am I not good enough to care for your horse now?"

"You know full well that's not the case. George was here when we rode up and you were not."

"And asking for me is beneath you? After all, I'm *only* a stable hand with no pedigree or family connections," he grumbled as he brushed past her into the stables.

Nora squeezed her eyes shut to prevent the tears from falling as she started for the manse, her pace hastening in an effort to escape the anguish sweeping through her body. With each step, she persuaded herself that Charles was behaving like a spoiled child. As she approached the hollowed-out oak, a sob gushed from her lips. She leaned against its fractured trunk releasing the pent-up sorrow, tears dripping from her cheeks to the bodice of her riding habit. How could she go on like this? Trying to please her family and save them from financial ruin was stressful enough but being in love with a man to whom she could never officially commit was crushing her spirit. Wiping her cheeks, Nora inhaled and strode back to the house determined to find a way to heal her wavering heart.

11

———————

Sarah sat straight up in bed, her chest aching and her face stained with tears. She glanced at the clock with its bold green numbers glowing six o'clock. Experience told her sleep was out of reach, prompting her to get up and prepare for the day ahead. In all the years she'd dealt with the dreams, keeping busy was the best way to thwart the rising anxiety that plagued her. Besides, Danni would be up soon and she wanted to steady her frazzled nerves before her friend noticed anything unusual. Danni's observant manner made her an excellent attorney but could be harrowing as a friend. She'd likely pick up on Sarah's angst and question her about it and right now she hadn't the mental stamina to deal with Danni's interrogation tactics.

Sarah started the kettle and plopped in a chair. She rubbed her eyes trying to dismiss the images of Nora when Danni shuffled into the kitchen, her hair disheveled and eyelids drooping.

"Mornin'," Danni mumbled.

"Good morning. Did you sleep well?"

"Not officially awake until I've had coffee."

"Afraid there's no coffee but I do have some Earl Gray tea."

Danni sneered. "Not an option."

"Sorry, that's all I've got."

"You're killin' me," Danni said, trudging from the room back upstairs.

Half an hour later, Danni returned dressed in a suit with her hair neatly pinned at the nape of her neck.

"I'm going to Perk's for some java. How about Greek from Stephano's for supper?"

"How can you think about dinner this early?" Sarah asked, sipping her tea.

"What can I say, I have a two-track mind; food and booze."

"Greek will be fine," Sarah replied, her chin propped on her hand while she swirled the tea in her cup with the other.

"You alright?"

"Just contemplating everything I have to do today."

"All the hard work will be worth it," she said patting Sarah's shoulder. "See you around six."

Danni scooted out the door leaving Sarah to ponder the previous night's dream and its connection to the house. The images replayed in her mind sending a shiver down her spine. Why was Edie's great-grandmother haunting her dreams? Of course, with all of the scrapbooks she'd been looking through it was probably her subconscious creating its own version of Nora's life. But why had Edie appeared a few days before in a dream during the day? None of it made sense. Granted, dreams rarely made sense so why expect them to be plausible now?

Sarah huffed. She was beginning to see a parallel between her life and Edie's. They were the last of their family lines, unwed, and childless. A pang reverberated in Sarah's chest at the idea that someday all of her hard work in her grandfather's store would be meaningless. She'd be nothing more than a name on an old deed. Self-pity plucked at her heart. She was thirty-three with no prospects for marriage or children. She wasn't opposed to marriage but the likelihood of finding a man who would tolerate and accept her haunted nightmares didn't seem probable. Even as a child Sarah couldn't keep friends once the nightmares interfered.

The grandfather clock chimed seven o'clock prompting Sarah to adjourn her pity party when a thud overhead made her jump. Gulping down her fear, she hurried down the hall, grabbed a walking cane from the umbrella stand, and darted up the stairs two at a time.

She paused at the second-floor landing, trying to determine where the noise was coming from. At that moment, a crash emanated from her bedchambers followed by scuffling. If this was a ghost it was the noisiest one she'd ever heard. She crept to the doorway, her insides quaking. The room was disheveled with the night table lamp on its side, the brush, mirror, and comb of a dresser set scattered across the floor, and strange clicking noises coming from the area near the chest of drawers.

Curtains billowed in the breezes like laundry flapping in a windstorm. Her heart pumped as she raised the cane over her head and stepped into the room. Without warning, a bedraggled squirrel leapt from the shadows. Spooked, Sarah screamed and swung the cane, missing the squirrel, instead sending a porcelain figurine crashing to the floor. The fluffy tailed rodent darted across the room from floor to bed and out the open window.

"Stupid furry rat!" she declared, trying to steady her pulse. Glancing at the dismembered ornament, she mumbled, "Well, at least it wasn't Dresden." She knelt to pick up the broken pieces and the dresser set when she noticed a negligible protrusion beneath the rug. She lifted the fringed corner and spotted a slightly warped floorboard. Visions of Nora with her letters resurfaced. Sarah reached over and fiddled with the board, but it didn't budge.

"Honestly, you didn't think it was actually a secret compartment? It was only a dream," she murmured, standing up.

Sarah leaned the cane against the wall, pulled a change of clothes from her bag, walked down the hall to the bathroom, and prepared for the day. Reentering the bedroom, she stumbled on the bulge in the rug as the overwhelming scent of decay stung her sinuses. Unable to move, Sarah stared at the protrusion in the rug.

Be brave, she thought, closing her eyes and taking several deep breaths. Despite the fear rising in her chest like flood waters, she knelt down, peeled back the rug, and glared at the warped board. This time she pushed the end of the board with her heel, nearly falling forward when it popped open.

It can't be, she thought.

Sarah grabbed the flashlight from the night table, shining it into the cavernous space where a shadowy form caught her eye. She reached in and pulled out a stack of letters bound with a threadbare silk ribbon.

Holding the letters to her chest as if they were fine porcelain, Sarah sat on the bed, unfurled the ribbon, and began reading. Page after page of impassioned declarations spilled from the scripted documents in waves of adoration. As the dates progressed, the esteemed professions transformed from affection to desperate pleas for reconsideration of her impending nuptials. The letters correlated with the visions from Sarah's dream, proving Nora had a lover! Danni would flip when she heard this.

She placed the sentimental messages on the night table, accidentally knocking one of the albums off. She leaned over to pick it up and noticed a photo had dislodged from one of the crumbling pages.

A warm sensation ran up her arm as she grasped the cabinet card image of Nora in her riding habit with Charles holding Camden. To anyone else, the loving expression on her face may have been attributed to her horse, but Sarah suspected it was Charles who held her affectionate gaze.

"It must be true," Sarah whispered. "She did run off with him." A shock jolted through her fingertips causing her to drop the photo.

Sarah rubbed the sting from her hand before stuffing the photo back inside the scrapbook and setting it on the pile. While intrigued by the connections unfolding before her, Sarah knew she had to get to work. Temptation prompted her to call Danni and share her discoveries but she decided against it. Her best friend would chastise her for goofing off. She'd wait until Danni came for dinner and show her everything then. Once she saw the evidence surrounding Nora's disappearance, she'd not be so critical of Sarah's interest in the scrap albums.

Sarah scooted to the kitchen for a bottle of water before clambering up the stairs to start inventorying the bedrooms. As she reached the second floor landing the strong scent of dirt and decay overpowered her. Pulling her shirt collar over her nose, she was shocked when the tape recorder fell from her pocket and started playing. She reached down to grab it when a cold blast of air rushed down her back and a raspy voice on the recording hissed, "*He's guilty.*"

Repulsed, Sarah jumped back, catching herself before she tumbled down the stairs. All of a sudden, the recorder clicked off as the putrid odor evaporated. While Sarah could logically explain the recorder turning on when it fell, the voice was beyond explanation, especially since it *wasn't* hers.

Sarah drew a slow breath filling her chest in an effort to calm her strained nerves when a loud crash from the library shattered her ruminations.

"Darned squirrel must be back!"

Without thinking, Sarah bolted down the hall to the library door where she noticed the stack of donation books sprawled across the floor with the Dreamist book lying open. She glanced around to see if there were any squirrels before entering but the room appeared to be unoccupied. Cautiously, she walked over to the scattered volumes, a whiff of Chanel No. 5 lingering in the air. Her body froze. Unless the fuzzy-tailed rodent had raided Edie's perfume stash, this mess was caused by something spectral.

Too frightened to stay inside, Sarah ran down the stairs, out the back door, and plopped down on a scrolled iron settee near the roses. Spring's floral perfume mixed with the salty marsh breezes, which was a welcome relief from the odors in the house. Sarah inhaled several times, using the breathing techniques she'd learned in therapy when she was younger. Tears pricked her eyes as she tried to resolve what was happening to her. There was no one to talk to about this, not even Danni.

She was beginning to suspect the house really was haunted and that Edie was saner than everyone believed. Burying her face in her hands, Sarah sobbed. She ran through several scenarios of how people would react if she shared her experiences. Based on the reactions of her so-called friends in fifth grade she didn't think it would bode well. Ghosts and hauntings definitely hadn't improved Edie's reputation.

Despite the nauseating fear churning in her stomach, Sarah wanted to understand what was happening and why. It seemed as if everything she'd experienced throughout her life was coming to fruition and she desperately needed to make sense of it. Danni would be a great asset for figuring this out although Sarah didn't relish the idea of telling her. With Sarah's parents in Europe, Danni was the only one who could help even if she was reluctant to believe in ghosts.

Looking up at the wavy glass panes, Sarah reminded herself that she couldn't let fear deter her from achieving her financial goals. So far she'd not been injured by the spirit, only scared half to death. After considering all the facts, the prospect of reentering the house seemed less daunting. With a few more deep breaths, Sarah willed herself back inside to resume her work on the second floor.

Hours later, several large bags were stuffed with outdated comforters, worn sheets, and faded towels awaiting delivery to the Blue Moon thrift shop. Another garbage bag overflowed with a horde of brightly colored lipstick tubes, several empty bottles of Chanel No. 5 perfume, old toothbrushes, withered bars of soap, and various hand creams. Some of the stuff looked to be from the 70s, not surprising considering the junk cluttering the other rooms in the house.

Thankfully, the furnishings more than made up for the menagerie of worthless items. One room sported a five-piece Rococo bedroom suite while the room Sarah occupied was a patchwork of styles replete with an Empire canopy bed and a grouping of Renaissance Revival pieces including a dresser, chest of drawers, and wardrobe. Even better, the rugs were hand-woven and in pristine condition, the colors as vibrant as the day they were made. After an afternoon free of voices and odors, Sarah was satisfied with her progress.

Just before six, Sarah hurried downstairs, hauling the bags of linens, her ledger, and the recorder with her. She plunked the bags by the front door and headed to the kitchen to make some notations in her ledger before Danni arrived.

A short time later, the sound of tires crunching over oyster shells signaled Danni's arrival. Sarah put her work aside and started setting the table when Danni came through the back door with a large paper bag. The aroma of lamb kabobs and tzatziki sauce wafted through the air making Sarah's stomach rumble.

"Want a drink?" Sarah offered.

"You have to ask?" Danni snorted.

Sarah poured the wine and joined her friend at the table.

"Find anything interesting today?" Danni asked, tossing her high heels to the corner and opening a Styrofoam container.

"Not really. Spent most of the day packing up old bed linens and trash."

Sarah was tempted to share what had happened with the voice on the tape recorder and the strange odors but lost her nerve. *Maybe after Danni has a few drinks*, she told herself.

The two discussed the day's events while eating every morsel of the kabobs as well as baklava for dessert.

"I don't suppose you got any coffee today?" Danni asked with a yawn.

"Nope. Why would you want coffee at this hour?"

"Got some paperwork to finish."

"I'll check the cabinets again."

While rummaging through the corner cupboard, Sarah discovered a plastic bag sealed with an old bread tie. Grabbing it, she studied the shriveled mass of leaves within.

Danni's eyes widened, a goofy smile forming like that of a teen whose best friend just passed gas in science class.

"Oh my gosh! Edie smoked pot!" Danni exclaimed.

"Don't be ridiculous. I'm sure it's dried herbs from the garden or something like that." Sarah opened the bag and sniffed, pausing to identify the odd scent.

"Herbs my foot! The woman was loony as a tune and this is probably why! Edie was a pothead!" Danni declared, reaching for the bag.

Sarah turned, blocking her from grasping it. Sniffing again, she identified the aroma.

"It's rose petals. Here, take a snort."

Danni inhaled deeply. "You're right, definitely roses. Why would Edie keep potpourri in the kitchen cabinet? She really was nuts."

Sarah shrugged her shoulders when she noticed a small card on the shelf where the bag had been. In longhand, it read, *Rose hip tea from the gardens of Monroe Manse.*

"Apparently, Edie made her own tea. I'll have to try some tonight." Sarah handed the card to Danni.

Danni read the note and handed it back to Sarah. "Nothing

about that woman surprises me anymore. Are you really gonna drink that stuff before bed? You'll never get to sleep."

"There's no caffeine in this, only rose petals. They call it tea because you steep it like tea leaves."

"If it ends up being some sort of poison, make sure the cell phone is on the night table so you can dial 9-1-1 while gasping out your last breath," Danni huffed.

"Very funny. Besides, I don't need 9-1-1 since you'll be across the hall."

"Not a good idea. I sleep like the dead."

"Good point. How about another drink?"

"I need to stay awake, not pass out."

"Then try some of this tea and we can gasp out our last breaths together," Sarah chuckled.

"I'll pass," Danni replied, holding up a hand.

Sarah started the kettle and scooped some of Edie's rose hip tea into a strainer she'd found in the silverware drawer. Once the water rolled to a boil, Sarah poured it over the dried petals, scenting the room in fresh roses.

"If it tastes as good as it smells, this will be a real treat," she said.

Danni shook her head and sat down at the table. "If it's OK with you, I'm going to work down here for a bit."

"No problem. Make sure you lock up and turn off all the lights. Oh, and leave the lamp on in the front entry."

"Will do."

Sarah lingered in the doorway as Danni shuffled through her satchel pulling out files.

I need to tell her, she thought.

Danni looked up. "Everything OK?"

"Yeah, I was just thinking…"

"What?"

Sarah chewed her lower lip. "Nothing that can't wait. See you in the morning."

"G'night."

Sarah meandered down the hall, switching on the old oil lamp as she passed. Starting up the stairs, she stopped when the lamp began flickering on and off like a firefly in a summer night sky. Her stomach tensed as she walked over to the lamp, a chill slithering across her skin. She fiddled with the bulb until it stayed lit.

Sarah made her way upstairs, changed for bed, and slipped between the soft sheets. Breezes floated through the windows carrying the cadenced chirping of cicadas in harmony with the crooning of crickets. She sipped Edie's special blend of tea, the delicate liquid instantaneously bathing her in a wave of serenity. Knowing she wasn't alone in the house seemed to help too.

Sarah reached for the recorder and ledger when she realized she'd left it downstairs on the kitchen table. Weariness enveloped her. Instead of going back downstairs she decided to peruse one of the scrapbooks instead. Skimming through newspaper clippings and old photos, Sarah sighed when she read the announcement for Nora's engagement to Frederick Hamilton. She felt badly that Nora wasn't able to follow her heart and marry the man she truly loved.

Leaning her head against the headboard, Sarah tried to figure out how she'd come to experience Nora's feelings so vividly. It wasn't as if she'd known her personally. Of course, the imagination could weave elaborate tales from something as simple as old photographs and memorabilia.

She paged through the scrapbook reading subsequent entries including congratulatory notes to Nora on another successful state fair with her prize roses when a slip of paper fell to her lap. Gently unfurling it, she read,

T O MY BLUSHING ROSE,

. . .

CONGRATULATIONS on your accolades at the state fair. My heart warms knowing my future bride will not only fill our house with beautiful blooms but also with the tenderness and delight of a precious soul.

YOURS TRULY,
  Frederick

A DRIED ROSE bud fettered in a yellow ribbon shared the page from where the letter had fallen. Further reading disclosed an excerpt from the society section of the local paper announcing the upcoming nuptials between Nora and Frederick along with details of her wedding ensemble. Photos from their honeymoon in Europe and a few pictures of Nora with her horse, Camden, completed the volume.

Sarah admired Nora's determination to put her family's needs before her own desires. Still, it seemed unlikely she would run away after going to such lengths to fulfill her family's expectations.

What made you change your mind and leave with Charles? Sarah pondered, closing her eyes as her head rested against the pillow.

Sheer exhaustion overshadowed Sarah's sense of curiosity. She plopped the scrapbook on the floor, switched off the light, and settled in for the night. As she drifted off an ear-piercing scream echoed from below jolting Sarah from bed. She raced from the room and down the stairs nearly colliding with Danni who was as pale as a ghost, her eyes wide with fright.

"What's the matter?" Sarah asked, her heart drumming in her chest.

"Tell me what's going on here," Danni demanded.

"What do you mean?"

Danni held up the recorder, her hand shaking. "I accidentally knocked this off the table. When it hit the floor it started playing. There's a voice on there and it's *not* yours."

Sarah sighed. The wait was over. She had no choice but to tell Danni everything.

"Let's go to the kitchen. I'll pour you a shot of bourbon and explain everything."

"You know I don't drink that stuff."

"Trust me, you will after you hear what I have to say."

They traipsed to the kitchen where Sarah poured them each a hefty shot of brown liquor before sitting at the table. Sarah took in a deep breath and rubbed her temples trying to figure out how to broach the subject of haunted dreams with her friend.

"What the heck is going on?" Danni asked her gaze fixed on Sarah.

"I believe the house may be haunted."

"Haunted?" Danni asked bringing the glass to her lips and grimacing as she swallowed.

"Since I arrived, I've heard voices and smelled things."

Danni rubbed her forehead, mulling over what she was hearing. "You really believe this place is haunted?"

"Pretty sure," Sarah sighed, suddenly regretting her decision to share her secret.

"Sarah, there are no ghosts. Stop thinking about all the nutty stuff Edie used to rave about. You're just tired and imagining things."

"But I'm not. For example, today I found a bunch of love letters under one of the floorboards in the master bedroom."

"I'm not surprised Edie had secret hiding places, although I am shocked she had a lover." Danni snickered.

"The letters aren't Edie's. They belonged to her great-grandmother, Nora."

Danni shifted in her seat. "You found letters belonging to Nora Hamilton in the floorboards of your room?"

"Yes."

"What made you look there?"

"I saw it in a dream."

"OK, now you sound crazy."

"I know it sounds insane, but that's what happened."

Danni leaned forward, her forearms resting on the table. "You had a dream and then discovered a stash of letters from Frederick to Nora?"

"Actually, the letters were from Charles."

"Who the heck is Charles?"

"The groom."

"Nora was married twice?"

"Not a marital groom, a stable groom."

"What are you saying?"

"Nora was in love with another man," Sarah declared.

Danni's mouth dropped open. "Do you know what this means?"

"Yeah, she had a guy on the side."

Danni blew out a breath. "And you got this information from a dream which makes you believe the house is haunted?"

Sarah shook her head as she turned her glass on the table. "I know I should have told you everything years ago..."

"*Years* ago?" Danni downed the bourbon in one gulp and plunked the glass in front of Sarah who immediately refilled it. "I'm confused. What exactly are we talking about?"

"This may take a while," Sarah said.

"I've got all night."

12

———————

Sarah breathed a sigh of relief that her friend was willing to listen to her accounts of ghosts and mysterious voices. She started with the crazy dreams and strange occurrences that had plagued her since youth.

"Do you remember Nancy Smith?" Sarah asked.

"Wasn't she that snotty girl who thought she was better than everyone else?"

"That's the one. When we were in fifth grade she invited me to her slumber party. I was so excited because she was popular and, well, I wasn't. At first I was nervous about it but Mother reassured me that I'd have a good time if I gave it a chance. So I went. Things were going great. All the girls were being nice to me and we had pizza, cake, and a pillow fight. When we finally settled into our sleeping bags, Nancy started telling ghost stories."

Sarah paused to take a sip of her bourbon.

"Everything was fine until we went to sleep and I had one of my dreams. I dreamt about a short, plump woman with gray hair who was trying to tell me something. It wasn't scary until she reached out and touched my hand. Her fingers were like ice. All of a sudden her eyes were hollow and her face was a shadowy skull. I woke up screaming which of course woke everyone else. The other girls gathered around while I told them about the dream. That's when Nancy's face scrunched up and she wailed for her parents."

Sarah ran her hand through her hair before continuing. The memory of that night was as vivid as if it had happened a few hours ago.

"Turns out I'd described her grandmother right down to the floral dress and antique brooch she wore on her collar. Apparently, Nancy's grandmother had passed the summer before and they were quite close. Nancy said I was a mental case who was jealous of her popularity and trying to ruin her party. Of course, the other girls rallied around her. Nancy's mother called my parents in the middle of the night and demanded they come and get me. From that moment on I was a social outcast."

Danni swirled the brown liquor in her glass before responding. "Why didn't you tell me about this before now?"

"I didn't want to risk losing your friendship. I'd been a loner since the party and let's face it, you're not exactly the ghost believing type."

Danni huffed. "Yeah, I probably would've told you to seek therapy."

"Been there, done that. Didn't work."

"You went through therapy because of this?" Danni asked her eyebrows arched.

"Yup. My parents thought I was seeking attention and worried about my mental health so they sent me to a shrink."

"And?"

"His office was in an old house *with* ghosts. When I realized no one believed me, I told him I didn't really believe in ghosts and started talking about boys and clothes, and that was the end of it."

Danni snorted. "Boys? You've always been too focused on your studies or your work."

"That's how I keep my sanity. I've been dealing with this since I was little. It's a lonely road when your classmates think you're some sort of freak and your parents believe you're crazy."

Reaching across the table, Danni took Sarah's hand. "I don't believe in all this hocus pocus stuff but I do believe you."

Tears crested in Sarah's eyes. After all these years of living with a terrifying secret, someone finally believed her. Over the next hour, Sarah filled Danni in on all the strange things that had happened since she arrived at the house from the voices to the odors to the shower curtain incident.

Danni's eyes widened as she blew out a breath. "I can't believe you stayed here after the hand under the bed thing. That would've sent me running."

"I have a job to do and couldn't run away. Most of the ghost stuff usually happens at night but ever since I got this job more things have been happening during the day. It's like one of those full-blown hauntings you see on TV. I really want to finish this job. If all goes as planned I'll be able to pay off my house and have that mortgage burning party I've dreamt about." Sarah sighed and slumped back in the chair. "But first I have to get through this haunted nonsense without losing my nerve."

"Any idea who's leaving you messages on the recorder and messing with the shower curtain?"

Sarah swallowed the lump lodged in her throat. If she'd known Danni would take it so well she'd have told her years ago.

"Maybe Edie? Then again, I keep dreaming about her great-grandmother, Nora," Sarah shrugged.

Danni yawned. "It's late and my mind is frazzled. How about we tackle this in the morning?"

"Thanks Danni. I really appreciate it."

"What are friends for if not to solve mysteries and do battle with the undead?"

"Wish you'd been able to help me the summer I worked for my uncle at the funeral parlor."

"Ugh, I don't even want to think about that," Danni said with a shiver.

"Tell me about it. I hardly slept that summer."

Sarah and Danni rinsed their glasses and tromped up the stairs, tipsy from the late night libations. At the second floor landing they bid goodnight and went to their rooms. Sarah crawled into bed relieved she'd finally shared her long-held secret with Danni. For the first time in her life, she wasn't alone and it felt good. She clicked off the lamp and snuggled beneath the sheets as salty breezes wafted through the room caressing Sarah's cheek and lulling her to sleep.

13

———————

Nora galloped along the trail into Sarah's dream. Deep in the woods, she pulled Camden up in a remote location, dismounted, and draped the reins over a low-hanging tree branch. Camden lowered his head, nibbling the lush greenery while Nora walked toward the inlet. Captivated by her surroundings, she watched the tidal grasses swaying to and fro as marsh breezes caressed her cheek. The sound of footsteps shifted her attention as Charles made his way toward her.

"You're late," she said, playfully.

Sauntering up beside her, he reached for her hand. The two stood quietly, captivated by the serenity they found in each other's company.

"I'm glad you've forgiven me," he said, breaking the silence.

"You know I can't stay angry with you."

"Are you still going through with this crazy notion of yours?"

"It's not crazy, Charles. I haven't a choice in the matter." Hopelessness accented her tone as she removed her hand from his. Nora desperately wanted to tell him everything about her situation, but she hadn't the courage. The thought of her parent's financial ruin, as well as the disrepute that would result from her running off with a stable hand, silenced her.

"But you do have a choice. This is the 1890s! You don't have to comply with a prearranged marriage. This sort of pledge is from the Stone Age, not modern times."

"Please understand, I'm not entering into this marriage under duress but of my own will."

"Are you saying you love him and not me?"

"Why must we argue? I have a duty to my parents to abide by this agreement. My feelings for you are irrelevant."

"I'm irrelevant?" he asked, wrinkling his forehead.

"Please don't twist my words. I only meant my feelings are not enough to fulfill my family's wishes, nor provide for my future." Nora turned away, watching a flock of pelicans swoop and glide across the water's edge. In that moment, she wished she could be as carefree.

"So, you're going to marry a man you don't love?"

"Frederick is a wonderful man, and I'm quite fond of him. In time, I'll grow to love him, as I know he loves me." She turned back to Charles. "Eventually, you'll marry and forget I ever existed."

His stare cut to the depth of her being. "Nothing could ever wipe you from my consciousness. You've infiltrated my soul and I cannot survive without you. It pains me to know you can dismiss me so casually."

"I'm not dismissing you, Charles, only trying to make you understand the situation is out of our control," she replied, closing her eyes in an effort to corral the tears that were forming.

"Nothing is beyond our control. We could run away like we discussed. I have a bit of money saved, enough for train tickets. Hundreds of people are making their way West. We'd not have much financially, but we'd have each other. Please tell me you'll consider it."

Nora's heart thumped, prodding her to say yes but her mind silenced it. "I thought we could remain friends, but now I see it's impossible." Her eyes glistened. "I mustn't ruin the family honor; my father would never recover. I'm their only surviving child and they dote on my every breath. They've always provided for me and I cannot abandon them."

For a moment, the two stood in silence, neither willing to acknowledge the finality of their situation.

"Very well. If you must throw away love for money and family pride, there's nothing I can do to stop you," his voice cracked as he turned and marched away.

Unable to move, Nora watched him retreat down the path, tears cascading over her cheeks. If only she could make him accept her decision.

The dream shifted to Nora's bedchambers where she sat at her vanity staring at her image in the looking glass. "Mrs. Frederick Hamilton," she whispered, her stomach tightening as the words drifted from her lips.

Despite her meager attempts to convince herself otherwise, Nora's heart was anchored in the berth of her affection for Charles. She opened the vanity drawer, reached toward the back, and removed a small leather case imprinted with a flower basket design. Gingerly, she unhooked the side, nestling the open case in her hands, a warmth spreading through her body. Charles's rugged features and kind countenance had been perfectly captured in the tintype portrait.

Prudence dictated she hide the treasured image somewhere more discreet. Slipping the photo from its encasement, she decided to stash it with the ring in the secret compartment of the buffet drawer. Thankfully no one ever looked in any of the secret hiding places from the war. She gazed upon his likeness once more, her chest constricting, as she slid the tintype from its encasement into her wrapper pocket. Once the house staff retired for the night, she'd sneak downstairs to the dining room. Her heart felt as if it was tethered to an anvil, barely able to beat beneath the weight of her despair. She couldn't bare the agony much longer, leaving her with only one choice to salvage her sanity.

14

———

Sarah awoke from her peculiar slumber gasping for air. Another night of telling dreams haunted her to the point of wired energy. Now more than ever she was beginning to sense there was a message imbedded in the dreams, although she couldn't figure out what it was. Even stranger was the inexplicable connection she felt for Nora. Something in Nora's gentle spirit comforted her like an old quilt.

Sarah changed into a pair of khaki shorts and a tank top and headed to the kitchen for tea. She wanted to speak with Danni before she headed to the office.

"Good morning," Sarah said as she started the kettle. "You're not dressed for work. Late court time?"

"Called in. I've made pretty good progress on the new case and figured Anita could handle it for a few days. This way I can research some of the haunted stuff."

Sarah closed her eyes, took in a deep breath and blew it out, releasing years of pent up tension and loneliness. For the first time in her life she had an ally and she delighted in it. Moments later the kettle squealed and Sarah fixed her tea then sat across the table from Danni who was tapping away on her laptop.

"What're you doing?"

"Surfing through the archives at the records office for anything about the Monroe family."

Sarah sipped her tea when she noticed a large coffee cup with the "Perks" emblem on the side.

"You've already been out for coffee?" Sarah asked, shocked that Danni had been productive at such an early hour. Early for Danni was noon.

"Yup," she replied without looking up. With a heavy sigh, Danni stopped typing, closed the laptop, and leaned back in her chair. "This was a bust. There's nothing in this data base that we don't already know."

"Thanks for trying," Sarah replied.

"How about you? Any strange dreams?"

"Dreamt about Nora and Charles again," Sarah said, exhaling.

"Anything significant?"

"Not really. They met, they argued, Nora went back to her room and pined for him. Perhaps if we knew more about her life we could figure this out. Are you sure you told me everything?"

"The only thing I've ever heard was that Nora Hamilton ran off because she didn't like being a mother. Of course, Miss Ida might know something."

"The bee woman?"

"If you want to know anything about anybody in this town, she's the one."

"Mother never let me around her for that reason. Besides, I thought you were the town gossip," Sarah said playfully.

"No, I'm the one about whom the town gossips," Danni quipped, taking a sip of her coffee. "Miss Ida will be selling honey at the farmer's market this afternoon. How 'bout we pay her a visit?"

"We can take my truck and drop off the linens at the thrift store on the way."

"In that rust bucket? No thanks."

"Funny, you didn't mind my old heap in high school," Sarah smirked.

"Desperation makes you do strange things. I'd have ridden on a potbelly pig if it got me out of the house."

Sarah snickered.

"What's so funny?" Danni asked, squinting her eyes.

"Memories of you climbing over that ten-foot fence behind base housing to meet me in the truck when your dad took away your car for getting arrested."

"Hey, the arrest was dropped from my record and well worth the trouble. That protest helped the shrimp industry by stopping illegal dumping of waste in the river."

"If I recall correctly your father didn't see it as worthwhile, especially when the Senator got involved."

"Dad never saw anything that violated protocol as worthwhile," Danni replied with a snort.

"He may have been strict but he was a softy underneath that tough exterior," Sarah said with a grin.

"Maybe to you but to me he was worse than a drill instructor!"

"I hate to break up this stroll through memory lane but I need to get some work done if we're going to see Miss Ida later."

"Got it. I'm going to swing by my house and check on a few things. I'll be back before noon."

"Thanks Danni."

"No problem," she said, grabbing her car keys and coffee and scooting out the back door.

Sarah sipped her tea when a crash from the second floor reverberated through the house. She froze, listening intently. Maybe the squirrel had come back for a second round. Jumping from her seat, Sarah ran out the back door hoping to catch Danni but there was no sign of her. For a moment, she considered calling her friend but decided against it. She'd have to handle this on her own.

Sarah's head tilted back as she took in a deep breath. She walked inside, treaded down the hall, and clambered up the stairs, her muscles tensing as the strong scent of freshly dug earth saturated the air. When she reached the second-floor landing, she glanced over her shoulder, a feeling of déjà vu rankling her brain. All of a sudden, she made the connection with the familiar sensation. The dream of the misty figure with the skeletal hand was in this house, on this very landing!

Her lungs constricted as the temperature began to drop. Closing her eyes, she was overpowered by an arctic embrace that slinked along her shoulders and down her arms.

Take a deep breath, count to five, release, and repeat, she thought trying to steady her racing pulse. Suddenly the library door slammed shut breaking Sarah's concentration.

Aggravation mixed with terror as she meandered down the hall and stood outside the library. Perhaps if she confronted the ghost it would leave her alone. With a trembling hand, she gripped the doorknob, turned, and pushed the door open, its worn hinges screeching.

Sarah peered inside. Everything seemed to be in order except for the pile of donation books that had tumbled over with the *Dreamist* book lying open. Closing the book, she re-stacked it with the rest. Sarah glanced around, trying to determine what kept knocking the books to the floor and decided it was probably the house shaking each time a door closed. After all, Danni had just left when she heard the thump. It was the most logical explanation she could come up with. Relieved to have found a reasonable and non-haunted explanation, Sarah turned to leave when the *Dreamist* book flew across the room and landed at her feet, the slight scent of perfume wafting through the air. Paralyzed, Sarah stared at the small tome.

"What do you want from me?" she muttered.

Silence.

She reached down and grasped the book, running her hand across the cover. "Is this something you want me to keep?"

Nothing.

"Great, now you go silent," she muttered as she put the book back on the stack. "If you want me to know something you'll have to be more specific. And stop throwing books at me, I don't appreciate it!"

Pleased with her fortitude, Sarah drew in a deep breath, stood a bit straighter, and headed down the hall. She paused at the landing, scanning the space. Why had she dreamt about this house a week ago when she'd never been in it before? Then she remembered her middle school history lesson about Monroe Manse being a civil war hospital for the black soldiers. The teacher must've shown photos of the place and Sarah's subconscious had resurrected the image in her dreams. Maybe she was making more of this haunting thing than she should. In her heart, she knew these were only rationalizations to quell her fears but after a lifetime of finding ways to deal with her strange reality, it was working.

She padded down the stairs to the kitchen to grab her work tools and a fresh cup of tea before tackling the gentlemen's parlor. The water in the kettle was still hot as she filled her cup and plunked a fresh tea bag in it. Steam wafted from the cup curling into fingers that brushed against her chin, the strong scent of perfume stinging her nose. An icy sensation rattled her core as she turned. A scream caught in her throat as she dropped the cup sending hot tea splashing at her ankles. Petrified, Sarah stared at the *Dreamist* book now sitting on the kitchen table.

Her legs wobbled like Jello while her heart pounded against

her ribcage. The book cover flew open, an invisible finger leafing through each page until it stopped on the first chapter. At that moment, the scent of Chanel evaporated and the temperature returned to normal leaving Sarah dazed and unsure what to do next.

Her fortitude was waning. She wanted to run from the house and never return. Of all the entities she'd experienced this one was the most persistent and it was beginning to wear her down. At this point, all she wanted was to finish the inventory, auction off the items, and collect her profits. How had something so simple become so maddening?

"What is so important about this book?" Sarah asked, scanning the room.

Swallowing hard, she waited for an answer but silence ensued. The ticking of the grandfather clock in the hall grew louder and louder mimicking her heartbeat.

You can do this, she thought taking a step forward when her foot slid in the puddle of tea. Before she fell backward, unseen arms steadied her. She whipped around but nothing was there.

Sarah grabbed a towel from the counter and wiped up the mess. Tossing the towel in the sink, she sat down at the table and skimmed through the book. After several failed attempts to absorb what she was reading, she buried her face in her hands. She was beginning to feel as if her mind was slipping away like a ship without a heading.

"I don't have time for this," she muttered rubbing her eyes. Closing the book, Sarah gathered her recorder, ledger, and pen and trudged to the gentlemen's parlor to start inventorying the contents. If she could just keep busy, she'd be fine until Danni got back.

15

A few hours later, Sarah had tagged and listed most of the furnishings in the room, including an incredible 19th century Italian walnut desk in pristine condition. This would bring upwards of twenty grand and possibly more if the right bidders were present. Sitting in the tufted leather chair, Sarah ran her hand across the deep green leather top. She opened all the drawers and searched for hidden compartments, surprised when she didn't find any. Of course, a family of this stature probably kept important documents in a safe.

The back door slammed startling Sarah from her ruminations. She hurried to the kitchen where Danni was unpacking the contents of a large paper bag.

"I grabbed shrimp salad and fries for lunch from Nan's Café on my way over."

"Everything OK at the house?" Sarah asked, her stomach rumbling at the delectable aroma drifting from the bag.

"Yup. Then I swung by the office but as usual, Anita had everything under control. I swear she could run the place without me and no one would know the difference."

"Someone would notice, they may not say anything but they'd notice."

Danni shrugged as she handed a container of food to Sarah and sat at the table.

"How about you, find anything of interest?" she said taking a bite of shrimp salad.

"Since you asked," Sarah replied, sliding the book across the table. "The ghost has been rather active this morning."

"What do you mean?" Danni asked, her words muddled by a mouth full of food.

"Aside from having this book thrown at me in the library? Let's see, when I came downstairs it was sitting on the table. Before I could get to it, the blasted thing flipped open to the first chapter, *by* itself!"

Danni swallowed hard. "Are you saying something threw the book at you and then carried it downstairs to the kitchen?"

"Yup."

Danni's fork fell to the table with a clatter. "This is beginning to creep me out."

"Tell me about it."

"Why didn't you call me?"

"Because I didn't want to creep you out," Sarah chuckled.

With a huff, Danni leaned back in the chair. "What do you think all this means?"

"I suppose the ghost wants me to read the book. She went to a lot of trouble to get my attention with it."

Danni paged through the leather-bound volume before pushing it away.

"We can read through this later. We need to eat and head over to the farmer's market and speak with Miss Ida."

After finishing lunch, they climbed into Danni's Mercedes and drove to the park across from the Naval Hospital where a walking path snaked around an array of tented stands for the afternoon farmer's market. Merchants peddling everything from homemade bread, fresh produce, flowers, cookies, and all-natural dog biscuits filled the area.

At the end of the first row, a small tent trimmed with black and gold striped ribbons hailed the honey sign they'd been hunting for. An older woman with grayish hair pinned beneath a wide-brimmed straw hat was selling a mason jar of honey to a young couple. With a broad smile, she winked at Danni,

"There's my girl! I'll be right with ya."

She finished her sales pitch, bagged the jar of honey, and handed it to the couple.

"What can I do for my favorite little Rebel?" she asked, embracing Danni.

"I came to pick that brain of yours for some slanderous gossip."

Ida grinned, apparently delighted to share some dirt on her fellow residents. "Who you wantin' to gab about?"

"The Monroes."

"Ooo, a fine choice indeed." She glanced at Sarah and asked, "Who's your friend?"

"This is Sarah Holden."

Sarah held out her hand. "It's nice to meet you."

Ida returned the handshake and cocked her head, "You ain't Joe's kid, are ya?"

"No, that was one of my uncles. I'm Howard's daughter."

"Ah, the quiet one. Wise man, kept to himself, never much gossip on him, or your mama. But his brothers, Gerald and Joe, they were always into something. I remember the time your Uncle Joe took one of the coffins from Gerald's funeral parlor and entered it in the bed races during the River Festival. I can still see him wheeling the cart and coffin down Bridge Street with a sign that read, "Rest in first place." We were all laughing until he hit a pothole and capsized the thing. When the body rolled to the curb you could've heard a pin drop. I don't think your uncle Gerald spoke to him for six months after that.

Some of the kids who witnessed it are probably still in therapy!"

Ida chuckled at the memory, shaking her head. "Joe would've been commodore the following year if he hadn't been banned from the Festival for life. Shoulda checked that coffin before he took it."

Sarah grinned at Ida's blatant portrayal of her uncles. She remembered the story from family gatherings. It took Gerald a while before he forgave his brother. Fortunately, the relatives of the deceased agreed not to sue in exchange for a free funeral.

Miss Ida motioned for them to sit in the folding chairs behind the honey display.

"So, what do ya wanna know about Edie, aside from her being bonkers?" Ida grimaced. "I suppose I shouldn't make light of mental illness. Schizophrenia is a serious thing."

"Edie was schizophrenic?" Sarah asked. It was the first time she'd ever heard anyone put a name to Edie's irrational behavior.

"What else could it be? She complained of hearing voices and seeing visions. She'd putter around her gardens talking to the air. Then again, it could've been the alcohol." Ida shook her head. "She'd been such a proper young lady growing up until she turned eighteen. Then she disappeared for a year and came back, well, crazy."

"What made her change?" Sarah queried.

"No one knows. She went from being a debutant to a babbling fool. Of course, a lot of people thought she might be growing more than roses in the back yard, if you get my meaning. It was the early 70s, after all," Ida winked.

"Actually, we were more interested in her great-grandmother, Nora," Danni said, changing the topic.

"The one that ran off after havin' Edie's grandmother? Not much to say about her. Supposedly, she couldn't handle the responsibility of motherhood and left. Terrible scandal. That kinda thing was unheard of back then."

Sarah piped in, "Were there any other reasons given for her disappearance, besides wanting to escape?"

"Not that I ever heard. Something wrong with that one. Who runs away from a fortune and a good family? The Monroes were expected to carry on family traditions and all that aristocratic nonsense. Of course, that all ended with Edie." Ida huffed. "You know, it was strange how Edie fought all that society stuff but carried on the rose cultivation. She was obsessed with it."

"Why do you think she loved the roses so much?" Sarah asked.

"Probably because of her lineage. Supposedly, her great-grandfather continued tending the rose gardens after his wife ran off. Did it until his dying day. Taught his daughter Bitsy to carry on and she taught Edie's mama to do the same. The Monroe's roses are known throughout the state." Ida said.

"Can't imagine what poor Mr. Hamilton went through. That was a time when men didn't take on the responsibilities of raising a kid, especially families as notable as the Hamiltons. He was a businessman for goodness sake. Poor thing never gave up hope of Nora's return. He could've remarried a dozen times but never did. How's that for devotion? Couldn't throw a rock in a football stadium and hit a man with dedication like that today." Ida said, reaching for a bottle of water. "You two want something?"

"No, thank you," they responded in unison.

"Did you ever hear anything about ghosts in the place?" Danni asked.

"Just the usual stuff. No respectable southerner would have an old house without a ghost or two. With Edie being crazy, it's hard to tell if it was her mind or the house that was haunted.

A young woman approached the tent, studying the jars of honey.

"Pardon me, but I got to help a customer," Ida whispered with a wink.

Ida offered the woman a sample and began her spiel about the benefits of local honey.

Disappointed, Sarah and Danni looked at each other. It was obvious they weren't going to garner anything useful.

"I guess we can go. Doesn't sound like we're going to get any new information," Danni whispered.

Sarah nodded, and the two bid good-bye to Ida.

"Come back soon, Rebel!" she hollered after Danni.

As they walked down the pathway, Sarah asked, "Why does she call you Rebel?"

"Years ago, I helped her with a sit-in against the spraying of pesticides for mosquitoes. The chemicals being used were killing the bees, which in turn hurt her honey production. Granted, she'd have protested even if she weren't in business. She's a tree hugger who makes fabulous peach moonshine."

"Isn't that illegal?" Sarah gasped.

"Only if she gets caught," Danni giggled.

"By the way, how is it I never heard about this sit-in?"

"I think it was the summer you went to Canada with your parents."

"Was that the time you managed to sneak away before the cops showed up because you didn't want to lose your car for a year?"

"Yup. I may be resolute about protecting the rights of nature, but I'm no fool. Dad said I wouldn't have wheels until after graduation if I got arrested again. With you out of town, I couldn't afford to sacrifice my ride."

Sarah shook her head and grinned, silently rejoicing in the uncommon occurrences of small town life.

16

Sarah and Danni belted out the lyrics of Michael Jackson's *Thriller* as they cruised down Renault Road. Danni pulled between the iron gates of the mansion and parked the car.

"Sorry we didn't get anything useful from Miss Ida," Danni offered.

"It was worth a try," Sarah shrugged.

Once inside Danni plunked down at the table while Sarah put the kettle on. "Want a cup of tea?"

"Is it that rose concoction?"

"Yes."

"Then no."

Sarah scooped some of the shriveled petals into the strainer. Danni sighed and reached for the *Dreamist* book, skimming through the first chapter. "This is written in riddles. It's like those mind teasers, you have to play with the words and phrases to figure out the meaning."

"Probably why I couldn't make any sense of it. I've never been good at that kind of thing. Don't have the patience."

"I'll read through it later. Maybe I can figure it out." Danni closed the cover. "I need to get some work done. OK if I use the dining room? It has more space to spread out."

"Sure. I've already inventoried that room."

Danni grabbed her computer and files and padded from the kitchen. Sarah poured water over the rose hip tea, closing her eyes as she inhaled the fragrant aroma.

"Sarah," Danni called out.

Sarah grabbed the cup and traipsed to the dining room. "What is it?"

"Who's this guy?" Danni asked, holding up the tintype photo Sarah had found in the secret compartment of the buffet drawer.

"I completely forgot about that. I think it's a picture of Charles. I found it hidden with a garnet and pearl ring. Last night I actually dreamed about Nora hiding that photo."

"He's handsome. Is this the guy she was seeing on the side?" Danni asked, staring at the image.

"That's the one. In the dream, Nora was distraught about having to marry Frederick Hamilton when she really wanted to be with Charles. It was really sad."

"This is getting really weird. Are you saying you can read her mind?"

"I know it sounds strange but in the dreams, I can feel everything Nora does, like I'm trapped inside her head."

Danni rubbed her forehead. "I appreciate that you've been living with this for a while but it's still pretty bizarre for me."

Sarah patted Danni's hand. "I get it. Why don't you get some work done while I finish the inventory in the gentlemen's parlor?"

"Sounds like a plan."

Sarah went back to the front room to continue the inventory as evening shifted to nightfall. When her stomach rumbled, she wandered down the hall and popped her head in the dining room.

"You hungry?"

"Always."

"Taco pizza from Gillard's?"

"Got it." Danni dialed the number and ordered dinner for delivery. Half an hour later Danni and Sarah sat at the kitchen table eating pizza and swigging beer.

"Were you able to get much accomplished?" Sarah asked.

"I finished up the stuff for work and started looking through that *Dreamist* book. Whoever wrote it had a way with words. The riddles are complex but I think I'm making headway with it. I always loved brain teasers."

"As much as I love to read I've never been very good with poetry or any kind of riddles. What I'd really like to know is why the ghost wants me to read that book. I mean if she wants me to know something why not just show me instead of moving an old book around?" Sarah shrugged.

"Who knows? It's not like there's a ghost manual that explains this stuff." Danni's eyes widened and she sat up straight. "Maybe that's what this book is, a manual of some sort. Think about it. You're having these haunted dreams and the ghost keeps pushing this book aptly titled *Dreamist.*"

"Makes sense but why me?"

"Cause you're the one that's here," Danni replied, leaning forward.

Sarah contemplated the idea but was too tired to pursue the notion. "I can't keep my eyes open. I'm going to bed," she said, rising from the chair in a stretch."

"Go ahead. I'm going to work on this a little while longer."

"Thanks for all your help Danni. It means a lot to me." Sarah patted Danni's shoulder.

"I'm glad to help but you're going to owe me for this," Danni replied with a sly smile.

"Not a problem. Next time you're overrun by spectral visitors I'll be there to help," Sarah giggled.

She scooted out of the room before Danni could retort. Walking down the hall, she switched on the old oil lamp, grabbed her recorder and ledger from the gentlemen's parlor, and made her way upstairs. She set the recorder and ledger on the night table and stepped into the bathroom. With Danni downstairs, she wasn't afraid of the room like she had been after the shower curtain incident. Thankfully, there were no signs of any spectral visitants. Weariness enveloped her as she changed into her nightshirt and crawled into bed. Instead of transferring inventory into her ledger she rested her head on the pillow and closed her eyes. Moments later, her mind drifted and the dreams began.

17

The sun's orange glow broke free from night's captivity as breezes filtered through the open window, rousing Nora. Wedding plans were inundating much of her day, leaving little time for tending roses or trail rides. Still, she was determined to escape the deluge of preparations, at least for a small respite. Now more than ever, she longed for a leisurely ride with Camden.

She ambled to the vanity and scrutinized her reflection. How had her existence become so chaotic? This should be the happiest time of her life, and yet she felt nothing but turmoil and regret.

Nora's imagination ventured to a different scenario, where her betrothed was Charles. Her heart danced at the thought, raising the corners of her rose petal lips. But the blissful moment swiftly turned to woe when she realized her love for Charles was deeper than she'd thought.

In a few weeks, she would be Mrs. Frederick Hamilton. Any woman would celebrate such a match, yet she was consumed in self-pity. Who would suspect that Nora Monroe, daughter of a distinguished family with all the material advantages a person could hope for, was miserable because she was compelled to marry for suitability and financial security? In essence, she was being traded like a prize horse; the owners interested only in pedigree and financial gain.

After readying herself for a ride, Nora strolled to the barn, lamenting the hopeless paradox of her life. *Stop wallowing*, she thought. *Frederick is a wonderful man whom you'll grow to love.*

When she approached the barn door, she saw Charles grooming a bay gelding.

"Good morning, Charles. I hope this day finds you well."

Without looking her direction, he continued brushing the horse. "It does indeed. Thank you."

Nora watched him run the brush in long strokes across the horse's coat.

"Is there something you want, Miss Monroe?" he said, turning to face her, his expression set in an emotionless glare.

"I need to know we can still be..." Her voice trailed off when she realized the insensitivity of her suggestion.

"I'm at your service Miss Monroe. If you need something, I'll dutifully oblige." His steely eyes cut through her soul like a knife through butter.

"Please do not address me so formally. We're too dear to one another for such apathy." Instinctively, she reached for his hand but stopped herself.

"Perhaps at one time. But it's clear we crossed a line we shouldn't have."

His disdain was crushing. Her legs wobbled and her breath came in short bursts. She wanted to cry out in anguish and tell him everything, but family honor rendered her mute. Finding her voice, she whispered,

"Did you receive my note?"

"I did."

"Will you meet me at the river oak so we can talk?"

"I have work to do."

The brusque nature of his words stabbed at her heart, the reality of her situation crashing down upon her in an avalanche of regret. She'd wanted for nothing her entire life and now the one thing she desired most was to love Charles openly and freely, and yet she couldn't. If only she could escape the emotional prison between family loyalty and true love.

Nora walked to Camden's stall and caressed his velvety muzzle as he nuzzled her hand in search of carrots. Even her beloved steed couldn't chase Charles's indifference from her mind. If only she could marry for love instead of family names and finances. The turmoil swirling within knotted her stomach and squeezed her lungs. How could she go on like this? Without warning, everything blurred and reeled, sending her to the floor in a crumpled heap.

Charles raced to her side, lifting her shoulders as consciousness cleared through her mind's fog.

"Nora, are you all right?"

"I'm fine," she said, pushing herself up to a sitting position. "I lost my breath for a moment."

He helped her to her feet, steadying her arm in his.

"Let me get someone to escort you back to the house. You need to rest."

"I'm quite well, I assure you." Her gloved hand rested on his. "I just need some fresh air. If you'll prepare Camden for a ride, I'd be most grateful."

A tender smile erased the contempt from his handsome face.

"Are you sure you're able?"

"I'm certain."

Nora waited as Charles groomed and tacked Camden. He slid the stall door open and led the sleek cinnamon gelding to the front of the barn where she waited. With a gentle hoist, he helped Nora to the saddle. She adjusted her skirts and reached for his hand, a slight smile brightening her eyes.

"Let's not be angry with one another. I cannot bear it."

"Enjoy your ride, Miss Monroe." He tipped his worn hat, overlooking her outstretched hand. Without uttering another word, he returned to the horse he'd been grooming earlier who pawed impatiently at the ground.

Nora headed for the trails, trying to escape the anguish of Charles's apathy. Her shoulders were in knots and her mind raced with all the things she wished she'd said to him. She nudged her heels against Camden's sides sending him into a canter. The soothing beat of his hooves as his elongated stride rocked along the sandy path began to ease the tension from Nora's body. Quiet moments like these were a balm to the woes of everyday life. She halted Camden, taking time to admire the mesmerizing beauty of the marsh; the sun glimmering across its choppy tides. All of a sudden, the pounding of hoof beats shattered the serenity of the moment.

"Charles, what are you doing here?"

"Bear needed the exercise, and I wanted to make sure you were all right."

"I assure you I'm well."

"All the same, I insist on accompanying you for the remainder of your ride."

They rode side-by-side in silence, their inherent communication eliminating the need for words. Nothing could ever sever their connection, not even marriage to another.

In her entire life, no one had made her feel more at ease than Charles. He viewed her as a living, thinking individual with ideas that mattered, not some fragile, thoughtless creature. He listened to her opinions with interest and challenged her to think beyond the narrow scope of her existence. Privilege had its benefits but true freedom to do and love as she pleased was something outside of her purview. Her time with Charles allowed her to be her true self without pretense. Even with all that was happening, he remained a true gentleman, not by monetary means, but by his very nature.

Half an hour later when the trail curved toward the barn, Charles spoke, "I'd better start back. If we arrive together, there'll be no explanation to pacify the curiosity of others." Charles smiled, spurring Bear into a canter.

Nora's chest tightened as he disappeared into a forest of live oaks.

How can I possibly stop seeing him? she thought. Camden clopped along at a carefree pace, allowing Nora to escape her burdens a while longer. In the woods, she was unfettered by family pressures and the constraints of life. Only here could she truly be free.

THE DREAM SHIFTED to a warm spring afternoon where an ivory silk gown, adorned with layers of frothy lace and orange blossoms, hugged Nora's delicate figure, her hair crowned with a headband of tiny pink roses. Frederick stood by her side beaming with delight at the loveliness of his new bride. Dressed in a finely tailored dove gray suit with white brocade waistcoat, he was the perfect image of a debonair gentleman.

Wedding guests held crystal flutes filled with sparkling French wine, raising their glasses as Mr. Monroe made the first toast. The bride and groom stood before the mantelpiece in wedded bliss.

"To my darling daughter and son-in-law. May you be blessed with longevity, joy, and a house full of boys!"

Laughter erupted amidst the clinking of crystal.

After downing the contents of his glass, Frederick whispered in Nora's ear, "What is he referring to, my dear?"

She leaned in and spoke softly, "My father adores me but always hoped for a son to carry on the family name. This is his way of wishing you better luck at preserving the family line. But not to worry, if we have a house filled with little girls, he'll dote on them just as he has on me."

The four-piece ensemble began playing a waltz, inviting all in attendance to dance. Frederick swept Nora into his arms, leading her across the ballroom floor in their first steps as husband and wife. They swayed and twirled within the walls of Monroe Manse amidst a rainbow of taffeta gowns pirouetting in a whirlpool of color.

Unbeknownst to the wedding guests, Charles hovered in the bushes outside the mansion listening to the music and laughter emanating from the ballroom, his heart breaking with every note and giggle. He couldn't let this go on. Somehow, he'd find a way to make Nora his.

18

———————

Sarah stirred and rolled over, instantly resuming her sleep. The dream had shifted several days to Nora standing beside her husband aboard a steamer for Europe. As the ship navigated from the dock, well-wishers fluttered hankies in an enthusiastic bon voyage. Nora's chest seized momentarily when she caught a glimpse of Charles standing on the pier, watching the ship sail away with his heart. Dismissing the image from her mind, she focused on the six-month excursion ahead. She hoped the extended absence from home would suppress the lingering feelings she held for her former love.

The dream fast-forwarded to a scene months later. Nora and Frederick had returned, settling into married life with exuberance. His attentive and compassionate nature during their grand tour of Europe had drawn them closer, easing her conscience regarding her decision to marry him.

Thrilled to be back, Nora embraced the allure of ancient oaks, rippled Spanish moss, and sultry marshes. They would be staying at Monroe Manse until their new house in Charleston was completed.

As she sashayed past the ballroom something caught her eye. She stepped inside and stared at the newly hung portrait over the mantel. She'd sat for hours in her wedding gown while the artist captured her likeness. Her image exuded a subtle happiness in the slight turn of her lips and the sparkle in her eye. To a stranger, the woman in the painting appeared gracefully shy and pleased with her circumstances. Yet Nora could see the hint of despair and emptiness staring back at her. Nothing could heal the hole in her heart, not an expensive ceremony or a gown created by a notable Paris designer. But she was determined to make the most of her situation and love her husband to the fullest.

Throughout their European travels, Nora had missed her family home. It had always held a special place in her heart. Most of all, she longed to take a ride on Camden. She changed into her emerald green riding habit and strolled to the stables feeling secure in her relationship with Frederick, certain her feelings for Charles were well contained. After all, it had been months since she'd seen him and she'd mentally rehearsed her response in the event he attempted to revive their relationship. There was no turning back now and she was determined to stand firm in her devotion to her husband.

Nora approached the barn smiling warmly at George who issued an earnest welcome.

"Miss Monroe...forgive me...I mean, Mrs. Hamilton, it's good to have you back. I hope your time away was pleasant."

"Indeed it was, George, thank you. Would you ready Camden, please?"

"Yes ma'am."

George headed into the barn while Nora sat upon the wooden bench, watching the clouds drift in the sky like sheep stalking across a pasture of blue. The clopping of Camden's hooves caught her attention as George led her beloved horse through the barn door. Caressing Camden's nose, she planted a kiss upon his velvety muzzle.

"I missed you, Camden."

George helped Nora into the saddle and handed her the reins.

"Thank you, George. I shan't be long."

She nudged Camden forward with her heels and felt the enthusiasm in his stride, letting her know he too had missed their outings.

Nora's body relaxed, absorbing the rhythmic rocking of Camden's stride as they cantered along the sandy path to the river oak. She pulled him up to watch a heron land in a mound of pluff mud where the stagnant water licked the stems of marsh grasses. Remnants of autumn tinted the sun's rays a deep golden hue as winter's gloom waited in the shadows. A chilly current of air fluttered the veil of Nora's riding hat, sending an uneasy sensation hastening down her spine.

Turning instinctively, she noticed Charles standing at a distance watching her. For a few moments, the former paramours gazed at each other. When Charles started to walk away, Nora called out to him.

"Where are you going?"

"Back to the barn. I heard you'd returned and wanted to see for myself."

"How have you been?" Her chest tightened as Charles walked towards her, the leaves crunching beneath his boots and the curls of his sandy brown hair bouncing with each step. He stopped in front of Camden, reaching out to stroke his muzzle. Despite the months in Europe and her efforts to focus her affections on her husband, she was still affected by Charles's rugged good looks and deep blue eyes. No matter how hard she tried, she couldn't sever the deep-rooted ties of her heart.

"Things have been quiet since you left. The only time I see your parents is when they request the barouche. I'm sure you've heard that your father acquired two new horses," he said, staring at the ground and tufting the dirt with the toe of his boot.

"I've not had an opportunity to speak with him. Today is my first full day at the mansion since our return from Europe."

Nora fidgeted with the reins, perspiration building beneath her riding gloves as her efforts to suppress her feelings dissolved.

"I've thought of you often since your departure."

Nora gazed into his steely eyes. The sentiments for him came flooding back in a surge of profound affection weakening the dam she'd constructed around her heart.

"I don't believe we should be discussing this. Things are different now. There's no returning to past infatuations."

Charles started to respond when the sound of hoof beats caught their attention.

"Someone is coming. You must leave," she said, her words rushing from her lips in a panic.

Without arguing, he vanished into the trees as Frederick galloped up beside her.

"I heard you went for a ride and decided to join you."

"I'm ever so glad you did," she replied, trying to steady her quavering voice.

"Are you feeling all right? You look a bit flushed."

"It's the chilly air." She turned her head for a moment, closing her eyes in an effort to suppress the tears. "Perhaps we should head back. I believe some tea would take the nip from my cheeks."

"Shall we see who's faster?" he said with a sheepish grin, spurring his horse into action.

Nora took the challenge, urging Camden into a full gallop.

Racing side-by-side, ebbing and flowing from first to second place; they dodged tree limbs and dashed across open spaces. Nora rode wholeheartedly in an effort to outrun the painful feelings she held for Charles, all the while dashing to victory against her husband. When she reached the barn first, Nora declared with a laugh, "My Camden is still the finest horse in the county!"

"Well ridden, my love." Frederick dismounted and handed his horse off to George before reaching up to help Nora from the saddle. He pulled her close, his dark brown eyes simmering in adoration, making her blush as another stable hand took Camden away. Frederick offered his arm which Nora accepted as they strolled back to the house.

Once inside the house, Nora and Frederick joined Mrs. Monroe in the front parlor for tea, reminiscing about their European travels. When the teapot ran dry, they excused themselves until dinner.

"Come with me," Frederick whispered, clutching Nora's hand.

They climbed the stairs and slipped into the grand ballroom where Frederick pulled her close.

"What are you doing?"

"Dancing a waltz with my beautiful bride."

"But there's no music."

"There's always a melody in my heart when you're nearby."

She followed his lead as they sashayed across the room, shame weighting each of her steps. Despite the wonderful and loving husband holding her, Nora's mind waltzed back to the one man she'd always hold dearest in her heart.

And then the dream altered to another scene.

Nora waited beneath the river oak while Camden grazed nearby. The soft thumping of hoof beats announced Charles's arrival. He dismounted and walked over to her.

"I'm surprised you showed up."

"Charles, we must stop meeting. If we were discovered..." Nora glanced around nervously.

"No one knows about us, unless you've mentioned it."

"Of course not!"

He took her hands in his and spoke gently. "So long as we're careful, nothing can stop us from seeing each other. We're not doing anything wrong."

"I'm married! Rendezvousing with a single man would tarnish the family reputation! Especially when I'm in lo..." Her voice trailed off as she looked down.

His hand, rugged and tanned, gently lifted her chin. He flashed a smile that made Nora's stomach flutter. "Finish what you were about to say. You're in love with me. If this is all I can have of you, then so be it. I'd rather see you here than not at all."

"We have to stop this. If we were caught..."

"And what if we were? I'm Camden's groom. We could say I came out to check on a loose shoe."

"And how did you find out about the loose shoe? Everyone knows you'd never let him out of the barn unless he was safe to ride."

He stared off for a moment, pondering her question. "I'll come up with something. Don't worry."

"But I do worry. Not just for me but for you too. If we were discovered, Frederick would run you out of town. With his connections, you'd be unable to find work anywhere in the state."

"Nora, I cannot give you up. I won't give you up."

"But I have to give you up. Please honor my wishes and stop sending for me. Every time we meet, my resolve weakens. Frederick deserves all my love, not the remnants of my affections." She pulled her hand from his and mounted Camden.

"This isn't over, Nora," he called out.

"Yes, it is," she replied, spurring Camden into a canter and disappearing in a cloud of dust.

"I won't give up," he whispered. "Not when I know your heart belongs to me and not him."

19

____

Sarah sat up in bed, rubbing the sleep from her eyes. The dreams were becoming more vivid and while they weren't overly frightening, they were disconcerting. She tried to remember the details but the only thing that stood out was Charles's indignation over losing Nora to Frederick and Nora's unwavering love of Charles.

She swung her legs over the edge of the bed, her feet dangling above the sun-dappled floor. She was making decent progress with the inventory, better than she would have thought in spite of the haunted activity. Her chest tightened when she considered all the things that remained to be done. The attic alone would take days to catalogue, not to mention clear out.

Grabbing a change of clothes, Sarah padded down the hall to take a shower. She rotated the knobs and stepped into the tiled enclosure letting the hot water massage her tight muscles. She lathered her hair and imagined the mortgage to her house disintegrating in the fire pit in her garden. That's why she was doing all of this, to be debt free. At that moment, a wave of regret crashed over her. The most momentous occasion she hoped to achieve in life was financial freedom. No love affairs or children, just paying off her house. Even the image of her mortgage burning was solitary. Outside of Danni, Sarah was alone in the world. She had her parents but they were abroad and rarely in town.

Without warning the water ran ice cold, forcing a yelp from Sarah's lips as she turned the water off. Breath billowed from her lips in a misty cloud as if she were standing in the artic. Terror squeezed her heart in a vice-like grip as she gently slid the shower curtain open expecting to witness some sort of gruesome, eyeless figure. Her shoulders slumped when she gazed at the empty room. Shivering from the cold, Sarah stepped from the shower and wrapped herself in a plush towel. One great thing about Edie was that she spared no expense on the quality of linens regardless of the outdated 1970s orange and gold design. Sarah walked to the vanity, wiped steam from the mirror, and gazed at her reflection.

A faint mist hovered in the air, clouding the mirror and exposing the words 'he's guilty' as the stench of dirt and decay stung Sara's nostrils. Staring in horror, she screamed when a skeletal figure appeared behind her, its hand reaching for her neck. She whirled around to find the room empty and the foul stench dissipating. Terrified, she ran down the hall to her room and collapsed onto the bed clutching the towel to her chest when Danni appeared.

"What's wrong?" she asked breathlessly.

"Creature in the bathroom," Sarah gasped, trying to steady her shaking limbs.

Danni's skin paled as she glanced down the hall. "What sort of creature?"

"The one from my dreams! A skeletal entity that reeks of rotting flesh!"

"Delightful," Danni responded. "Eau de death. Maybe you can market it to funeral directors."

"Not funny. I've had my fill of funeral parlor employment, thank you."

"Seems like your uncle's funeral parlor wasn't half as bad as this place."

Danni had a point. The summer Sarah had worked for her uncle wasn't nearly as unsettling.

"Sorry to scare you. Let me get dressed and I'll meet you downstairs," Sarah said, her breath beginning to slow.

"Sure you don't want me to wait?"

Sarah pursed her lips. "Would you?"

Danni plopped onto the bed. "Get changed. I'll stay right here."

"Thanks Danni, you're the best."

Too frightened to return to the bathroom, Sarah snatched a t-shirt and khaki shorts from her overnight bag and slipped them on. She braided her dark brown hair, laced up her sneakers, and sighed. Somehow Danni's presence gave her a sense of peace and courage.

"Let's go downstairs, I need some tea."

Danni shuffled down the stairs ahead of Sarah who glanced over her shoulder to make sure the skeletal figure wasn't following them, relief washing over her when nothing appeared.

"Smells like coffee," Sarah announced as she stepped into the kitchen, her eyes resting on the coffee maker next to the kitchen sink. "When did you get that?"

"Brought it with me. I couldn't handle any of that rose petal stuff you've been pedaling. I needed a jolt of caffeine with java beans, not tea leaves and potpourri."

Sarah shook her head as she filled the kettle and turned the stove knob.

"What are your plans today?" Sarah asked, prepping her teacup.

"Thought I might visit the Historical Foundation and see if

I can find anything pertaining to the Monroes and this house. If we learn more about the history maybe we can figure out why Nora is haunting this place. Although, after what you told me about this Charles fellow, I'm beginning to believe she really did run away with him."

"No one knew about the affair and they didn't have the means back then to locate a missing person like we do today. Maybe that's what all of this is about. Nora wants people to know the truth. She didn't run away from motherhood, she ran off for love."

"Still pretty scandalous, even by today's standards. Why reveal one dishonorable act to replace another?"

"Don't' know."

"And you're certain Nora is the ghost?"

"As certain as I can be. It's not like I can prove anything but she is the one I keep dreaming about."

"If you're OK being here alone, I'll head out," Danni offered. "Unless you want to come with me."

"I'm fine. The ghost keeps scaring me but she hasn't hurt me yet. Maybe I'll find some answers while I clear things out."

"You sure?"

"Yeah. I need to stay busy, it's how I deal with all of this," Sarah replied, with a sigh as she rubbed the tension knotting the back of her neck. "I need to get back to work. I have more to do than I have hours to do it."

"I've got my cell phone with me. Call if you need anything."

"Will do."

Danni grabbed her coffee and keys and scurried out the back door, seemingly relieved to escape the oppressive nature of the house.

Sarah sat down with her tea and paged through the *Dreamist* book. Page after page revealed riddles and prose about visions and shadowy dreamscapes but none of it made any sense. She remembered a quote from one of her favorite childhood stories when Alice said *Nothing would be what it is because everything would be what it isn't. And contrariwise, what it is, it wouldn't be, and what it wouldn't be, it would.* Slamming the book shut, Sarah huffed. She didn't have time for childhood nonsense; she needed adult intervention for whatever was trying to communicate with her. She took another sip of tea when the faint tinkling of Bach's Piano Concerto No. 1 floated through the room.

"What on earth?" she muttered, trying to ascertain where the music was emanating from. Maybe there was a radio on somewhere in the house, or so she hoped. Sarah ambled down the hall past the dining room and the scrutinizing stares from the framed portraits of Monroe ancestors. When she reached the front entry, she realized the music was coming from upstairs. Pausing at the base of the staircase, she gazed up to the second-floor landing pondering whether to investigate on her own or call Danni.

She told herself it was probably a clock radio Danni had set and forgotten to turn off. Satisfied with her rationalization, Sarah climbed the stairs, the air getting thicker with each step. The hair on her arms prickled as she reached the top and realized the piano music wasn't coming from Danni's room as she'd suspected; it was coming from the ballroom. Sarah hesitated. She didn't remember seeing a radio or a piano in that room but then again she hadn't spent much time in there either.

"You've got this," she whispered, goading herself forward. With each footfall, the air grew colder until she stood at the door of the ballroom. Music resonated from the far corner from something shrouded beneath a dustcover.

How did I miss that?

Trudging across the room, Sarah stopped at the blanketed form, the prickling of her skin spreading across her scalp and down her back. She reached out and yanked the cover off, revealing a piano. At that moment, the room warmed and the music ceased.

Her breath caught as she gazed at a Becker Brothers piano, the sheer opulence of the instrument temporarily dissolving her fear. She'd learned how to play the piano the summer before sixth grade when her parents sent her to stay at her grandmother's home in Edgefield. Sarah had inherited the instrument but her small cottage didn't have space for a grand piano so she stored it at her shop. Sometimes when business was slow or she was stressed, she'd tickle the ivories. Playing always gave her a sense of peace and brought about fond memories.

Despite her apprehension, she couldn't shake the pull toward the instrument. It was like some sort of magnetic force. She reassured herself that the entity had frightened but not harmed her so a few moments of playing wouldn't be harmful. In all her years, Sarah had never played an instrument as valuable as this one. Awe over the rarity of it momentarily chased the trepidation from her mind.

She perched on the needlepoint-covered bench, rested her right hand on the keys, and began to tap out a melody. The piano was slightly out of tune but the sound was still as rich as velvet. In good condition a Becker Brothers could bring upwards of twenty-five grand. She lifted her left hand but before her fingers made contact, the keys started playing on their own. Sarah jumped up sending the bench tumbling to the floor. Everything went silent except for the fright ringing in her ears.

She backed from the room, her stare fixed on the piano. Once she reached the hall she turned to run but stopped.

"For goodness sake," she scolded. "Grow up; you have a job to do." Using the technique, she'd learned in therapy as a child, Sarah inhaled deeply, held it for a count of five, and released.

She repeated this several times until her muscles released the tension and her breathing returned to normal.

Despite the calming techniques, Sarah didn't feel like staying in the house. She needed a break and decided to take some of the valuable books to Raven Booksellers on Craven Street. At least she'd accomplish something while avoiding the ghostly presence.

Sarah scooted into the library, grabbed the box with the Jane Austen volumes and Poe's works, and plodded down the steps, beads of sweat gathering on her forehead. She placed the container on the kitchen table, plopped her wallet and keys in with the books, and carried the box to her truck. Opening the truck door, she pushed the box across the seat and slid behind the steering wheel. The engine coughed and sputtered as she turned the key and pulled out of the drive onto the road.

She drove to town, stopping to let one of the tours pass, its horse-drawn carriage filled with people gawking at the antebellum mansions while the tour guide divulged historic facts. When the carriage turned down North Street, Sarah drove two more blocks and parked in front of the old brick building where Raven Booksellers was located.

The engine of her truck cackled as she shut it off, grabbed the box, and headed inside. Raven Booksellers was an Edgar Allen Poe themed bookstore specializing in rare and valuable editions and was a popular destination for book lovers across the state.

"Hey Laura," Sarah called as she stepped inside.

"Good morning, Sarah. How are things going at the mansion?"

"Busy. I brought some books that may interest you. Is Dan here? I think he'll want to see these too," she said, setting the box on the desk.

"He's meeting with a guy who wants to sell his vinyl collection," Laura replied, peeking inside the cardboard container.

She removed one of the books and flipped to the copyright page, her eyes widening when she saw the date.

"A first edition of *Pride and Prejudice*? Do you have all of the volumes?"

"Yup. I've also got *Sense and Sensibility* and *Emma*."

Sarah helped Laura pull books from the box when she noticed two distinguished gentlemen sitting in the far corner in what appeared to be a heated discussion. One seemed rather flustered, his cheeks red and his mouth clamped in a hard line.

"Sarah, what are you staring at?"

Looking at Laura, she grinned. "The two men over there. The one guy seems..." Sarah gulped. When she glanced back there was no one there.

"Don't be alarmed. Lots of people see them," Laura chuckled.

"What do you mean?" Sarah asked, a flush coloring her cheeks.

"It's an old building and we often get reports from customers who see ghosts. People actually like the idea that the place is haunted. Good for business, especially one that has a Poe theme."

"Makes sense, I suppose. Do you know who they are?"

"If you believe in that kind of thing, we surmise it could be the lawyers who used to work here back in the 1800s when the building was a law office."

Now that she thought about it, Sarah was pretty sure the men were dressed in period attire. She shuddered at the thought.

"Are you alright? I assure you they're harmless."

Regaining her composure, Sarah forced a smile. "I was just startled."

"OK if we consign these? I might have a buyer for the Austen books although I'll have to hide the Poe volumes from Dan. He'll want to keep those for himself."

"Not a problem. Send me an invoice and a check once they sell."

Sarah hurried out the door relieved to stand in the warm sunshine. She'd been in that bookstore a dozen times and had never seen anything otherworldly. Why now?

20

———————

Sarah slid onto the vinyl seat of her truck trying to figure out what had changed to increase the visions. It seemed as if her ability to see ghosts was intensifying in frequency not to mention the scents and voices accompanying the images. Absorbed in her thoughts, she didn't notice the figure coming toward her or the hand reaching for the door of her truck.

"William, you stupid jerk! What are you doing?" she yelled, her blood racing as she tried to catch her breath.

"Aren't we jumpy," he said with a Cheshire cat grin as he positioned himself inside of the door so she couldn't close it. "Thought you'd be at the mansion, not out shopping."

"I'm not shopping, I'm working. If you'd kindly remove yourself, I'll get back to work," she grumbled.

William leaned in causing Sarah to tip back. "Stop with all of the fake animosity. Just give in to what your heart and body desire," he purred, his gaze traveling up and down her body. "Haven't you wasted enough time avoiding me and every other man in town? If you're not careful people will start to assume things about you."

"Let me ask you something. How long were you married to your first wife?"

"Ten years," he said straightening up, his eyes shifting to meet Sarah's. "She was a shrew. Nobody blamed me for leaving her."

"Maybe she was a shrew because you couldn't keep your pants zipped."

"That's cold."

"Cold is having an affair with your secretary and half the bar floozies in town. How many times have you been engaged?"

"What's your point?"

"You're a philandering pig. You were the same way in high school and you haven't changed."

"Can I help it if women are obsessed with me? It's not my fault I have a long list of *formers*. Most women can't handle all this," he replied with a sly grin.

"Any woman obsessed with you needs therapy. Either way, you're not worth the time and definitely not the trouble. Speaking of time, I need to get back to work."

Sarah shoved William who tottered backwards as she slammed the door. He leaned forward resting his arms on the open window of the driver's side.

"I'll be out next week to photograph the mansion. Maybe we could take some naughty shots while I'm there," he said, the right side of his mouth curling.

"Only after I gouge out my eyes and have a lobotomy."

"Finally, I made it into the lineup. Sounds like a challenge and you know I love a good challenge," he winked before jaunting across the street.

Sarah plunked her head against the steering wheel. The man was sickening. The idea that he thought she'd acquiesce to what he considered charm was laughable. Sarah cranked the truck and started down the street, her mind still reeling from the encounter with William. She'd known him her entire life and never understood how any woman could stand him. At this point she'd rather face the ghosts than William's advances.

Lost in her thoughts, Sarah drove toward the mansion, defeat weighting her shoulders. While she had the support of her best friend with the spectral visitants, the stress of clearing the house and warding off William's obnoxious proposals were beginning to hamper her enthusiasm for the end result. She didn't relish going back to the house without Danni. Even though the ghost hadn't harmed her, the scare factor was a definite deterrent.

Oyster shells crackled and popped beneath the tires of Sarah's truck as she pulled down the drive. She cut off the engine and stared at the tabby walls of the mansion. Mentally, she went through the list of things that remained to be done making her heart palpitate. There was so much left to do and yet her curiosity over Nora's disappearance, the dreams, and the ghostly occurrences were perplexing. Regardless, she had to get back to work if she was ever going to be free from the ghost and her financial constraints. Sarah opened the truck door and slid from the seat when the Batman theme roared from her pocket.

"Hey Danni."

"What're you doing?"

"Just got back from Raven's. Any luck with your search?"

"Nothing we didn't already know about the place. I spoke with Dr. Bristow at the Historic Foundation and she's going to look for some resources."

"You didn't tell her about the ghosts, did you?"

"Of course not. I told her we needed information about the estate for the auction brochure."

"Brilliant," Sarah said.

"By the way, who's going to handle the auction?"

"Alyssa if I can catch her."

"I need to stop by the office. Anita called earlier and needs my signature on a few things then I'll be over. How about the Tavern for supper?"

"Sounds great. I could use a break from this place," Sarah sighed, her shoulders slumping.

"Something else happen?"

"Yeah. I'll fill you in when you get here."

"You sure? I can get Anita to bring the papers by on her way home."

"No need. Like I said, the ghost hasn't harmed me, she just scares me," Sarah replied, trying to convince herself she was braver than she felt.

"Alright, but if you change your mind call me."

"Thanks, Danni."

Sarah slipped the phone in her pocket as she plodded to the back door, the broken stepping-stones wobbling beneath her feet and weeds brushing against her legs. Stepping into the kitchen, she tossed her wallet on the counter and grabbed a power bar. She peeled off the wrapper and plunked into a chair, eating her meager meal. Her appetite was practically non-existent and she had too much to do to stop for lunch, especially if she and Danni were going out later.

Sarah trudged down the hallway and up the stairs reassuring herself that the ghost was frightening but harmless. If she could just stay focused on the job at hand the end result would more than justify the unnerving aspects of it. The more she got done the sooner she'd be free of the nightly visions and spectral shenanigans and the sooner she could achieve her financial goals.

Sarah blew out a long breath. Her entire existence hinged upon being debt free. The main goals in her life consisted of keeping her business afloat and burning the mortgage to her house once it was paid off. For a moment, Sarah envied Nora's predicament. While it was a distressing situation, at least Nora had the love of two men with no worries about her finances. The only thing Sarah had was her parents, best friend, and a career but nothing that created the depth of feeling she experienced when she was dreaming about Nora's life.

As Sarah reached the top of the stairs, a cross breeze fluttered down the hall from the open windows in the rooms. She inhaled the scent of low tide and jasmine, the very aroma that had soothed her throughout life. There was nothing more fragrant or comforting than springtime in the Lowcountry.

She walked into the bedroom and sat on the bed, deciding to transfer the inventory she'd failed to complete when she fell asleep the night before. With pen in hand, she opened the ledger and pushed the play button on the recorder. She started writing when the recording on the tape altered, playing slower and slower until her voice was nothing more than a moan. And then the device clicked off.

"Great, the batteries must be dead," she mumbled, popping the plastic cover off the battery compartment and removing the batteries.

Sarah searched her overnight bag for replacements when she remembered they were in her backpack downstairs. Scurrying down the steps, she rummaged through the backpack, grabbed fresh batteries, and jaunted back upstairs. She grabbed the recorder and started to slide the first battery in when the device slipped from her hand and hit the floor. When Sarah leaned over to pick it up, it started to play, a crackling voice screeching out, *he's guilty*, before clicking off.

Sarah jumped back, terrified by the fact the blasted thing was playing without batteries! Unable to move, she stared at the machine too petrified to retrieve it. She took in a breath, held it for a count of five, and blew it out when a slow moan began to filter from the tiny speaker. Without thinking, she slammed her foot down smashing the device into plastic shards.

"Why are you doing this? I need to work!" Sarah yelled, fraught with terror as her limbs quaked. Instead of continuing with the inventory she ran downstairs to wait for Danni's return. She'd had enough at this point and wasn't sure how much more she could endure.

21

———————

Sarah stomped down the hall, ready to quit. *Let someone else handle this mess*, she thought as she stormed past the dining room. Out of the corner of her eye she glimpsed movement and instinctively stepped inside. A strong breeze tickled her cheek, rousing the loose wisps of hair framing her face. A sense of peace embraced Sarah as she realized the movement she'd noticed was probably just spring's breath billowing through the open window. She was being ridiculous. There was no need to run away from a career defining opportunity regardless of the circumstances. Sarah closed her eyes and filled her lungs, holding for a count of five, and releasing. As the tension drained from her limbs, she decided to tackle the first-floor closets when the doorbell rang, interrupting her thoughts. Sarah hurried down the hall and opened the door to an elegant woman dressed in white cotton pants and an indigo silk blouse, her blond hair swirled neatly into a French twist.

"Hello, I'm looking for Ms. Cook. Is she here?" Her words flowed in a melodious English accent.

"I'm sorry but she's out. I'm Sarah Holden. Can I help you?"

Smiling, she held out her hand. "I'm Dr. Bristow. I spoke with Ms. Cook the other day regarding the history of the house. I found an interesting book which might provide the information she's searching for."

"Would you like to come in for a cup of tea?"

"No, thank you. I'm giving a lecture at the museum and thought I'd drop the book off on my way."

"I'll let Danni know." Sarah took the hefty volume. "Have a nice day."

"And you."

Sarah shut the front door and walked to the kitchen. She sat at the table skimming the pages of the book hoping to glean more information about Nora and the house. Unfortunately, its contents rehashed stories from the Civil War and its time as a hospital for the black soldiers, but nothing of significance about Nora.

"Looks like this is a bust," she said, sliding the book across the table. "Time to get back at it," she mumbled hoisting herself from the chair and plodding down the hall.

THE AFTERNOON PASSED with the downstairs closets purged of crocheted afghans, placemats, and a pile of Battenberg lace tablecloths along with a menagerie of cut crystal vases, bowls, and candlestick holders. The clock rang out six in cadence with the sound of Danni's Mercedes' tires crunching down the drive. Relieved that her best friend was here, Sarah finished the notations in her ledger and went to the kitchen as Danni popped her head in the back door.

"You ready to go? I'm starving," Danni said.

"More than ready," Sarah replied, grabbing her wallet and scooting out the door.

Danni chatted about the day as they strolled beneath a

canopy of moss-laden oak trees, past picket fences and church-yards, until they reached Bridge Street. Salty breezes from the waterfront wafted past as they climbed the steep staircase to the Tavern. Danni and Sarah entered the darkened eighteenth century structure where they were greeted by the smell of burgers frying and raucous laughter emanating from the bar. Several of the pub's regulars perched on bar stools slinging back beers, reminiscing over the day's events.

Waving to the crowd at the bar, Danni and Sarah slipped into the dining room and sat at a wobbly pub table covered in stiff white paper. The Old Tavern had been in Henry's family for three generations and was steeped in legendary tales including those surrounding famous buccaneers and a well-known parson. The colonial décor was reminiscent of the New England style complete with Williamsburg blue wainscoting and built-in corner cupboards.

Henry was known for his burgers and fries but not his reno-vation skills. The place was clean, albeit in desperate need of restoration. Admittedly, it was the food and fun-loving atmosphere that attracted patrons, not the crumbling 200-year-old structure.

Vicky, the Old Tavern waitress for more than a decade, navi-gated through tables issuing a warm greeting.

"Hey, guys. How's it going?"

"Fine," Danni replied.

"It's been a while since you've been in."

"Too long. How's your son?" Danni asked.

"Doing well in the Marine Corps. He picked up Sargent and leaves for California next month."

"Congrats!"

Pulling a pad and pen from her apron pocket, Vicky asked, "The usual for you ladies?"

"That'd be great. Thanks!" Danni replied.

Vicky headed for the kitchen, gathering up dirty dishes

along the way. Always smiling, she was beloved by regulars, having the memory of an elephant for the menu preferences of those who frequented the place. On her way back, she placed two frosted mugs and a pitcher of beer on the table before taking the order of a couple on the other side of the room. Danni filled each mug and offered a toast.

"To your fortune."

"If I can tolerate the ghostly antics," Sarah said, clinking her mug against Danni's and taking a long drawl.

"What happened today?"

Sarah fidgeted with the corner of the paper placemat while she filled Danni in on the piano music, the gentlemen specters at the bookshop, the tape recorder playing without batteries, and her run-in with William. Danni grimaced.

"Yikes, I don't know which is the scariest; the ghosts or being propositioned by William."

"I'll drink to that," Sarah said, draining her mug and plunking it on the table for Danni to refill.

Vicky returned, setting down two plates.

"Cheeseburger with onions, extra pickles, and fries"—then turning to Sarah—"cheeseburger all the way, fries, and a side of ranch dressing."

"Thanks, Vicky," the two chirped in unison as she scurried back to the bar. Danni and Sarah erupted in laughter. They'd been finishing each other's sentences and responding simultaneously for years. It reminded Sarah how truly connected they were and how thankful she was to have Danni on her side.

"Dr. Bristow dropped off a book earlier about the house," Sarah said, taking a bite of her burger.

"Anything good?

"Same stuff they taught us in school about the architectural features and being used as a hospital during the war. Nothing that can help us figure out the ghost thing."

"So, what are you going to do?" Danni asked with a mouth full of fries.

"I don't know. My motivation is wavering making it harder to stay focused. I lost a lot of time running from ghosts today, not to mention my productivity was greatly reduced when I obliterated my tape recorder."

Danni slumped back in her chair. "Maybe this is too much for you."

"I could get it all done without the distractions but every time I try to ignore or justify the occurrences the ghost gets active. I *really* want to finish this job."

Danni pursed her lips and stared at her beer mug. "I'll call Anita tomorrow and tell her to clear my calendar for the next two weeks. I can help with the inventory."

"I can't ask you to do that," Sarah said, resting her chin in her hand.

"You're not asking, I'm offering. Besides, with both of us rummaging through all that junk we have a better chance of finding pertinent evidence of Nora's disappearance."

Sarah chewed her lower lip as she considered her friend's offer. It would help to have an extra set of hands not to mention reduce the fright factor of being alone in the house.

"You're sure this won't mess up any of your cases."

"Positive. As of tomorrow, I'll officially be a ghost hunter apprentice."

Sarah chuckled as they clinked their mugs and finished the beer. After paying the bill and bidding the regulars goodnight, Sarah and Danni stepped into the stale night air. As they meandered down the darkened streets shadowed by streetlights and the serenade of cicadas, Danni prattled on about her theories regarding the ghost and the circumstances surrounding Nora's disappearance. Sarah hadn't seen Danni this enthusiastic since high school when they attended a sit-in protesting the clear-cutting of trees on Balding Island. Her lips curled as she recalled the satisfaction beaming from Danni's face as she, along with Sarah's Aunt Millie, were hauled to the police station for refusing to disperse from the gathering. While Aunt Millie was out within an hour with only a court date to hamper her future, Danni had the added imprisonment of being grounded for six weeks. Nevertheless, their efforts resulted in the developer being fined an exorbitant amount thus thwarting future destruction to the natural landscape.

When they reached the house, Sarah unlocked the back door and flipped on the kitchen light as Danni followed.

"Want a drink?" Sarah asked, reaching for the bourbon.

"Why do you always ask when you already know the answer?"

"I like to keep life interesting," she replied, her eyebrows raised as she held up the bourbon bottle.

"I'll have a beer, not that lighter fluid," Danni responded opening the fridge and grabbing a can.

"You didn't seem to mind it the other night."

"I needed it after your haunted revelation," Danni said with a huff.

Sarah sat at the table and swirled the amber liquid in the glass.

"What's the matter?" Danni asked.

"I'm trying to get a grasp on everything. It's all so overwhelming with the inventory and the ghost. I feel like I'm swimming in pluff mud."

"But I'm going to help you out so there's no reason to be stressed."

Taking a sip, Sarah sighed. "There's plenty of time for us to search for answers to Nora's disappearance *after* I finish with the estate. I really need to stay focused."

Danni's shoulders slumped. "I realize you have a lot to do but once you leave this place we won't have access to the ghosts or your dreams. Didn't you say the dreams don't occur outside the house?"

"Generally, that's the way it's been in the past. I usually only dream about the ghosts when I've visited a place or I'm staying there."

"Then we need to keep working on this while you're here."

Sarah nodded her head. "Alright. We can keep investigating but you'll have to do most of the research while I clear things out. If I find anything that relates to Nora's disappearance I'll add it to the stuff we already have."

"Sounds like a plan." Danni yawned. "I'm going to turn in early and read through the *Dreamist* book. Maybe I can find some answers to help us make sense of your dreams."

"I've got to make some more notes in my ledger, especially now that I don't have a recorder."

Danni went upstairs while Sarah rinsed her glass and locked the back door. She plodded down the hall past the portraits, a shiver rippling across her flesh as if the ancestral eyes were scrutinizing her every step. Turning, Sarah studied the stalwart gazes of the Monroe family with their stern expressions and judgmental stares.

Her lack of sleep and frazzled nerves were beginning to wreak havoc on her mind. Sarah's eyes were dry and her eyelids drooped. She shook her head in an effort to restore her wakefulness but fingers of fatigue wrapped around her body like a warm blanket on a winter's night. She trudged up the stairs, changed for bed, and slid between the sheets. Too tired to work, she rested her head upon the pillow and closed her eyes. Unbeknownst to her, a skeletal finger swept a loose hair from her from her forehead as her mind drifted to a time long past.

22

———————

"Reynolds, I need to discuss something of a delicate nature and would appreciate your discretion in the matter," Frederick said to his footman. "You will be handsomely compensated.

"I'm at your service, sir."

"My concern for Mrs. Hamilton has grown since our return from Europe. As of late, she has seemed - distant. I'll be away on business for a few weeks and ask that you keep close watch over her, in case she should need anything. Make note of any anomalies in her mood and report to me when I return."

"I'm honored to have your trust, sir," the footman replied with a bow before leaving the room.

The scene shifted to an overcast morning at the entrance of Monroe Manse with Nora bidding adieu to Frederick as he prepared to leave on a business excursion.

"Safe travels, my dear." Nora said as Frederick planted a kiss on her cheek.

"I'll be thinking of you," he whispered with a tip of his hat before climbing into the carriage. The driver slapped the reins against the horses' haunches, lurching the carriage forward. Nora watched as it tottered down the drive and out of sight.

Stepping inside, Nora called for Miss Biggs.

"I'm going for a ride should anyone ask for me."

"Yes ma'am," Miss Biggs replied with a nod, her white apron clinging to the black dress that stretched around her ample figure.

After changing into her riding attire, Nora traversed the well-worn path to the stables, embraced by the early morning grandeur. The air was fresh as birds serenaded the day in a melodious ballad and flowers breathed their sweet fragrance amongst towering oaks. Nora followed the dirt path to the stables where she found George sweeping the aisle.

"Good morning George."

"Good morning, Mrs. Hamilton."

"Would you ready Camden for me?"

"I can send for Charles if you'd rather," George offered.

"No, thank you. I'm on a tight schedule and haven't time for him to be located."

With a nod, George trudged down the aisle leaving Nora waiting. Shortly thereafter, the clip clopping of Camden's hooves echoed through the barn. George assisted Nora into the saddle.

"Camden is feelin' his oats this mornin', so you need to stay sharp," he said taking a step back.

"Thank you, George, I shall be attentive to his antics."

George gave a slight bow and returned to his morning duties. With a prod of Nora's heel, Camden plodded along the trail, exceedingly skittish, spooking at every moving leaf and scattering squirrel. Fortunately, Nora was an exceptional horse-woman, able to anticipate his high-tempered mannerisms, and recover his demeanor when he began to shy.

The trail rounded, unveiling the expanse near the river oak.

A rhythmic thumping caught Nora's attention as Charles rode up next to her.

"I wasn't expecting to see you." Her voice faltered.

Camden pawed the sandy ground with his hoof. With a quick nudge of her heel, he stopped, tossing his head in protest.

"He seems a bit antsy this morning," Charles said.

"He's probably reacting to my anxiety."

"What's bothering you?"

"You know exactly what's bothering me. The thought of acrimony between us is unbearable."

"I feel no animosity toward you, Nora. It's the situation that infuriates me. The idea that two people can care so much for each other, yet be divided by something as trite as money is maddening. Do you think I can tolerate the notion of you being married to another man? I can hardly function under such circumstances."

"There's nothing that can be done about it now," she replied her gaze drifting toward the marsh.

"I understand Mr. Hamilton has gone away on business for a few weeks."

"He has."

"Then we have a few weeks to ourselves."

"Charles there's something I need to say to you," she said, fidgeting with the reins.

"Go on."

Nora inhaled. "I am with child."

Charles swallowed hard and peered toward the horizon before speaking.

"It's not too late for us. I have a bit of money saved. We could leave for Europe, or Mexico." Optimism tinted his words.

"I'm going to have a baby! I can't possibly run away now!"

"Bring the child with you. Or better yet, we leave immediately. You can have the baby wherever we settle. I can raise it as my own."

"Are you mad? Do you think I would keep this child from its home, from its family? Have you any idea the consequences of such actions?" Exasperated, Nora shook her head at the absurdity of his suggestion.

"We can be together, if you'd only trust me."

"Charles, we're getting nowhere with this discussion and I think it best that I leave before I say something I'll regret."

"Very well, but this discussion isn't over!" he declared, turning his mount and galloping away.

Sarah rolled over glancing at the glowing green numbers on the alarm clock that read three a.m.

"Ugh, too early to get up," she grunted, squeezing her eyes shut and willing herself back to sleep. Fortunately, weariness tugged at her eyelids like shades being drawn sending her back to dreamland where Nora sat upon a scrolled wicker rocker in the nursery, humming a lullaby to the small cooing bundle in her arms. Miss Biggs entered and smiled at the scene.

"Pardon the interruption Mrs. Hamilton, but I have an urgent letter for you from the stables."

"I hope all is well with Camden. He was lame last week after throwing a shoe."

Nora rose, placing her daughter in the bassinet. She recognized the penmanship, her chest tightening as she took the letter and walked to her room. The correspondence was brief, merely asking that she come to check on Camden at her earliest convenience. But she knew the real reason for the request. Even though she was troubled by the prospect of meeting him, it was better than not seeing him at all. She'd just started riding again following her lengthy confinement.

Early next morning, donning her finest blue riding habit, Nora headed for the stables. She had sent word to have Camden tacked and ready to ride, and per her request, found him waiting on the cross-ties as George tightened the girth.

"Good morning George."

"G'morning Mrs. Hamilton," he responded, leading Camden from the barn and helping Nora mount.

With a nudge of her heal, Nora sent Camden forward in a lively gait toward the edge of the trail where they rocked into a canter. When she approached the river oak, she slowed him to a walk, dismounted, and waited for Charles. Moments later he rode up, tipping his hat, and in one fluid motion, alighted to the ground. The two horses grazed as he sidled up beside her.

"I wasn't sure you'd come."

"I almost didn't."

He took her hand, his smile melting her resolve. "I had to try once more. Please reconsider my offer?" His eyes pleaded for acceptance.

She looked away, unable to meet his gaze for fear she would succumb to his request.

"Nora, look at me," he said.

Her pulse raced as she scanned his chiseled features and deep blue eyes. The beautiful soul standing before her, one so much like her own, compelled her to consider running away. She loved that he treated her as an equal rather than a porcelain doll to be fawned over. He accepted the depth of her intellect as well as her desire to be more independent, something Frederick could never understand. Her husband loved her but his view of a woman's role was more traditional.

"Charles, I..." Nora couldn't form the words for fear the pressure building in her chest would stifle the beating of her heart.

"Say what you must. I promise this will be the last time I ask."

23

———————

The bleeping of the alarm clock chased Sarah from dreamscape to reality. Hitting the button, she sat up in bed, rubbed her eyes, and ruminated on the sorrow emanating from Nora as well as the agony of Charles's despair. Oddly, his emotions hadn't come through as strongly until now.

"Frederick definitely wasn't her true love," she murmured, "which explains why she ran away and left her family behind." Before Sarah could delve deeper into the previous night's vision, she caught sight of something out of the corner of her eye moving behind the curtain. Her skin prickled as her back tensed. She shifted her feet from beneath the covers and lowered them toward the floor, her nerve endings pounding. Sarah leaned forward, peering down to make sure the creature under the bed didn't grab her ankles again. Despite her trepidation, Sarah was determined to confront whatever hid behind the curtain, whether living or not.

Her toes touched the woolen rug as she slowly lowered her heels to the ground and started across the room. With each footfall, the air grew colder until she stood inches from the wavering drapery. Sarah pulled her nightshirt over her nose as the scent of decay stung her nostrils at the same time the words *"he's not what you think"* tickled her ear. Simultaneously, the curtain caught the breeze, flapping like laundry in a cyclone, sending Sarah scurrying across the room. She stared at the window as the drapery wafted back into place and the stench dissipated.

Sarah closed her eyes and took a few deep breaths, thinking about the most recent visions. Reynolds was new to the dreamscapes making her contemplate the significance of his role in the mystery. More disturbing, why was the ghost revealing all of these things? Why not just show what she wanted to convey? Of course, now wasn't the time to deliberate on such things. Sarah was beginning to fall behind on the job and needed to get back to work before her timeline in the house expired.

"Sarah?" Danni's voice rang out from the hallway.

Whirling around, Sarah held her chest, unable to steady her breathing as she stared at her friend.

"Doggonnit Danni, you scared me half to death!"

"What's wrong?" Danni asked, standing next to Sarah.

"There was something behind the curtain."

Danni's posture straightened. "Like what?"

"The ghost. I heard her whisper 'he's not what you think' in my ear."

Danni scanned the room, her eyes wide. "What do you think it means?"

"I'm not sure but it was the same voice that keeps saying 'he's guilty'."

"Are you positive that's what you heard? This blasted house makes a lot of noise with all its creaks and groans."

Sarah rubbed her forehead. It seemed as if Danni was beginning to doubt the ghost thing. "I'm not sure about anything anymore. I'll change and meet you downstairs."

"Need me to stay with you?"

"I'm fine," she sighed. Although Danni was supportive, Sarah accepted that she was still alone in her spectral awareness and probably would be for the rest of her life.

After changing into a tank top and shorts, Sarah scurried down the stairs relieved to see Danni sipping coffee and perusing the *Dreamist* book. She fixed a cup of tea and joined her friend at the kitchen table.

"Anything interesting?" Sarah asked, taking a sip of tea.

"Actually, yes. I've been able to decipher a few pages. From what I can tell it's some sort of instruction manual for people who dream about ghosts."

"Like me?" Sarah's eyes widened and she sat straighter.

"Exactly! Apparently, these people can communicate with the dead through their dreams. Think about how cool it would be if you're one of these dreamists!"

"Easy for you to say, you're not the one being haunted," Sarah huffed, propping her elbow on the table and resting her chin in her hand. The whole thing was absurd, like she was some sort of side-show freak in a back alley. After years of mental isolation and living with the frightening images, Sarah was finally getting answers that could help her cope with her abilities, or whatever they were. At least she had someone to support her. Sarah blew out a breath, and sat up. She might as well learn all she could. "Tell me more."

Danni smiled. "According to what I've read so far, there are people who can interact with ghosts through their dreams. Apparently, these 'dreamists' as they're called, are like conduits for the dead. Ghosts communicate their needs while the dreamist is sleeping."

"What else?"

"That's all I've been able to figure out so far, aside from the fact that there's a genetic component to it."

"That can't be unless it skips a generation. My parents definitely don't believe in the ghost thing," Sarah said, scrunching her eyebrows. "So, you really think I'm one of these dreamist people?"

"Considering you keep dreaming about a woman from the 19th century who used to live in this house and reportedly disappeared, I would say yes. Maybe that's what these ghosts have been trying to tell you. You're not crazy, you have some sort of strange gift that allows you to communicate with the dead."

"If that doesn't make me crazy I don't know what does," Sarah said, slumping back in the chair.

"It would explain all of the weird things you've experienced throughout your life. Most of the haunted visions you've shared with me have taken place while you were asleep, right?"

"Yeah, but sometimes I see things during the day."

"I can't explain that, at least not yet. Based on the first chapter of the book, ghosts seek out dreamists to help them find peace to some unsettled situation that causes them to linger after they've passed."

"So, you're saying Nora is trying to tell me something?"

"Do you have a better explanation for what's happening to you?" Danni asked.

Excitement bumped across Sarah's skin at the idea that there could be an explanation for her lifelong turmoil with spectral visitants. "Not really. This is the closest I've ever come to a reason for the dreams."

"I'll keep working on it. Speaking of dreams, did you have any good ones?"

"Don't know that they were good but they were interesting."

"Do tell," Danni said, planting her elbows on the table as she leaned forward.

"I dreamt about Nora having a baby. Charles was still trying to convince her to run away with him even though she was married with a kid."

"Talk about persistence," Danni said, taking a swig of coffee.

"The saddest part was that Frederick was beginning to sense something was wrong with Nora. He even asked his footman to keep watch over her when he wasn't around in case she needed something."

"Didn't she have a lady's maid for stuff like that?"

"This seemed more about her mental state. I think Frederick was worried about her emotionally, like postpartum or something."

"Talk about dedication. She was a fool to run off and leave him behind." Danni said, rolling her eyes.

They both jumped when Danni's cell phone blared. With a trembling hand, Danni glanced at the number before answering it, "Hey Anita. Yeah...OK...not sure. Have you checked the file cabinet in my office? Tell him to stay calm, I'm on my way."

Hanging up the phone, Danni sighed.

"I gotta go. Mr. Sandlin is at the office giving Anita a fit. You know if she can't fix it, it must be a problem. Will you be OK until I get back?"

"Sure. I've got plenty to keep me busy in the attic."

"Be back as soon as I can," Danni said, grabbing her keys and scurrying out the door.

Gulping down the last swallow of tea, Sarah stood, took in a deep breath, and started for the stairs. She didn't relish the idea of working in the attic without Danni close by, but with the deadline a little over two weeks away she needed to get going on the rest of the house. If she could just stay busy, she'd be all right. Hopefully she'd find more answers to the century old mystery while she dug through the stuff in the attic.

SARAH'S CHEST tightened as she glanced around the attic space, amazed at how much stuff was stored there. Setting her ledger and pen on a mahogany plant stand, she tugged off an old sheet that was covering a Renaissance Revival dresser and two marble-topped tables. The dresser was pristine, despite its age, and still retained working locks with the original key. A search through the dresser drawers revealed a few lace petticoats, two pairs of silk stockings, and an old celluloid glove box. Sarah opened the box and removed three pairs of gloves, two of ivory kid leather and one pair of delicately crocheted lace. As she handled the lace gloves, a strange sensation tingled up her arm. A fleeting vision of a woman hovering over a large mound of freshly dug earth, her visage contorted and her skin gray, flashed through Sarah's mind.

Startled by the image, Sarah tossed the gloves to the ground. This vision was more disturbing than the rest and was accompanied by a feeling of loss and betrayal. Sarah cupped her face in her hands and sobbed. The woman's loneliness saturated Sarah's soul, making her feel discouraged. Her parents were half a world away, Danni was working, and an impending deadline loomed before her. While she wasn't technically by herself, her career and financial goals suddenly seemed hollow and meaningless. Whoever this spirit was, her emotions were beginning to tangle with Sarah's. The Batman theme wailed, breaking Sarah out of her self-pitying stupor.

Steadying her voice, Sarah answered, "Hey Danni, were you able to pacify your client?"

"For now, but he's one of those persnickety types who wants everything immediately. I've got to swing by the county office and while I'm there I'll poke through some of the records. How are things going there?"

"Overwhelming, but nothing I can't handle," Sarah replied, wiping a tear from her cheek. She decided not to mention anything about her sudden onslaught of melancholy in the hope it would subside.

"I'll call you later," Danni said.

"Sounds good."

Sarah hung up, slipped the phone back in her pocket and retrieved the gloves from the floor. She replaced them in the box, which she promptly shoved back into the drawer as a shiver shook her shoulders.

In the far corner of a darkened alcove, Sarah foraged through several more boxes of junk, making notations in her ledger with each item. Without the recorder, she had to write everything down as she went, which significantly slowed her efforts. When the clock downstairs chimed three, she decided to take a break and trudged to the kitchen. After ingesting a couple of power bars, Sarah grabbed a bottle of water and dashed back to the attic hoping to find more hidden treasures in addition to any clues related to the mystery of Nora's disappearance.

Afternoon transitioned to evening with sunlight dappling the attic walls in shifting contours, creating the illusion of spectral activity. Having found a steady rhythm, Sarah kept working, shrugging off the phantasmal feel of the room. She dug through nooks and crevices, unearthing strange objects, including a withered leather shoe with black buttons. She recalled nineteenth century superstitions where a shoe was placed inside a wall to ward off evil spirits, but this was her first experience with it and she hoped it was an indication that the spirit haunting her was benevolent.

Sarah swiped the sweat from her brow when her cell phone rang, her eyebrows arching when she saw the time was seven o'clock. *Can't believe it's that late*, she thought answering the phone.

"Hey Danni. How's it going?"

"This is taking longer than I thought and may morph into an all-nighter."

"Sounds pretty intense."

"It is but I can still bring you some supper. However, I'm not sure if I can spend the night," Danni said, her voice wavering. "Maybe you should go back to your place tonight."

"Don't worry about it, I can handle being by myself for one night. Honestly, I don't have much of an appetite, not to mention I'm in a zone and making good progress, so if you don't mind..."

"Got it. You're in a zone. If you get too scared call me and I'll come over."

"Thanks, but I'll be fine. Take care of your client. I'll see you tomorrow."

Sarah hung up, her gut churning at the idea of being alone in the house. All of a sudden, every shadow and creak seemed ominous.

Keep working, she thought.

Staying busy would distract her from the macabre and help with her progress. Pacified, she returned to the task at hand. A few more hours passed with three distinct stockpiles earmarked for the thrift shop, auction, and trash.

"I think that's enough work for one day," Sarah whispered, stretching the stiffness from her back. She grabbed the ledger and tugged the light chain before sauntering downstairs in search of something to eat. Fortunately, there was leftover Chinese food in the fridge, which she ate cold while reviewing her logs.

A slight sense of relief took hold. She was making more progress than she'd thought.

Sarah scribbled a notation to contact Alyssa about the auction hall, that is, if she could catch her. Alyssa Gordon was the epitome of southern grace, often clad in tattered jeans, cowboy boots, and pearls. Whether at the auction house or the farm, she had the gift of hobnobbing with the wealthiest of clientele or wrangling a passel of goats from one end of the barn to the other. Without doubt, Alyssa could do it all with a smile on her face and grace in her step. The moment Sarah accepted the Monroe estate; she knew Alyssa would be the perfect choice to handle the auction end of things.

Sitting up, Sarah gazed around the room. Between the sweltering working conditions, the haunted dreams, and the ghostly whispers, Sarah felt as if she'd been at the mansion for years instead of a few days. At least she still had two weeks left but at this pace she'd be cutting it close. A yawn drifted from her lips prompting her to turn in. It was almost midnight and she was tired enough to sleep through anything, even a visit from the dead.

She secured the back door, turned off the kitchen light and meandered down the hall where she flipped on the old oil lamp. It flickered several times sending a sense of unease trickling down Sarah's back. Hesitantly, she reached out and fiddled with the bulb until the light steadied.

Thank goodness it was only a loose bulb, she thought, blowing out a breath. Contented that the flashing lamplight was not the result of supernatural intervention, she trudged up the stairs and changed for bed. Sarah desperately wanted to wash away the day's grime but the idea of stepping into the shower with no one else in the house deterred her. She crawled between the sheets and glanced at the time. Midnight. Plunking her head against the pillow, she was relieved when weariness weighted her eyelids as sleep escorted her to another time.

24

———————

Standing beneath the sinewy branches of the river oak, Charles handed a small box to Nora. She opened the lid and gasped.

"Charles, it's stunning!"

"I know I promised to leave you alone, but I wanted to give you something to remember me by."

"Charles, this is too much. I cannot accept it," she replied, staring at the glittering facets of each carved garnet in the horseshoe shaped brooch.

"You had no qualms keeping the ring I gifted you last Christmas."

"And I never wear it for fear someone may question its origin."

"Then where is it?"

"In a secret place. I keep it with your portrait."

"I'm glad you think of me. I only wish I had an image of you."

Shaking her head, she handed the brooch back to him. "I can't keep this."

"No one has to know where you got it. Wear it and think of

me. If anyone asks, say you purchased it on one of your shopping excursions. Surely no one would question a minor acquisition such as this."

Nora gazed at the garnet-studded horseshoe, the rawness of her emotions leaking in tearful streaks across her flushed cheeks. "I shall wear this every time I ride. Even though we cannot meet privately, when you see me wearing it, know you're with me in spirit."

"That would give me great joy. However, I may not be here to witness it," he said, looking away.

"What do you mean?" she gasped, her eyes darting from the brooch to his face.

"I can't stay here, Nora. Every time I see you, a small part of me dies. It's best if I leave."

All of a sudden, the stays of her corset felt tighter. Regardless of the circumstances, she couldn't bear the thought of never seeing him again. "Where will you go?" her voice cracked as she breathed out the words.

"I'll find work elsewhere. Anywhere but here. There are too many memories, too many shattered dreams," he whispered. "How do you think I feel every time I think of you being married to another man? I tell you I can hardly stand the thought." His jaw clenched as he glanced at the water.

"I know it's selfish, but I don't want you to go," she said, grasping his hand.

"You could always join me." He gave her fingers a squeeze, hoping this time she would acquiesce.

Slowly she withdrew her hand, averting her gaze from his pleading expression as she garnered all her courage.

"If you must go, then so be it. I'll always love you no matter where you are. But I have a duty and an obligation to my husband and my daughter. You may not agree, but I know you understand. If I did anything untoward, I wouldn't be the person you profess to love."

A grin lifted his sculpted cheeks. "You're a wise woman, Nora Hamilton. I'll love you until the end of time."

Gently lifting her hand to his lips, he planted a kiss, bowed, and walked away.

Sorrow washed her porcelain features in tears as she fondled the brooch in her hand. Even though she knew nothing could ever come of their relationship, she'd taken comfort in knowing he was close by. For her, seeing him was enough. Now she realized she was being cruel to him. She plunged the keepsake into her pocket, mounted Camden, and prodded him forward.

A short time later Nora arrived at the barn, leaving Camden in George's care, before wandering back to the manse. She ascended the back stairs to her bedchambers where a travel chest rested at the foot of the bed. Nora lifted the lid, removed the brooch from her pocket, and placed it lovingly within the secret compartment used to store valuables when traveling.

At the sound of footsteps, she closed the lid and stood, straightening her skirts as Frederick entered the room.

"My love, I was told you've already been for a ride. I'd hoped to join you," he said, brushing her cheek with a kiss.

She met his gaze, conjuring as much affection as she could, Charles's image still lingering at the forefront of her mind.

"My apologies, but I needed some time to think," she responded, her chest constricting as she spoke.

"Is everything alright?"

In an effort to ward off further inquiries, she forced a smile. "Of course. I've been so involved with Bitsy and making selections for our new house that I needed a few moments of quiet for myself. I feel quite refreshed."

"I've been worried about you lately with all of the preparations for our home in Charleston and believe I may have a solution to ease your burdens."

Nora tilted her head.

"I've spoken with your parents. They've agreed to have us stay a few months longer whilst you adjust to all motherhood has bestowed upon you. Your restlessness has not gone unnoticed, my dear. The house in Charleston has taken this long, it can wait a few more months before we make the finishing touches and move in. And I think your parents enjoy having little Bitsy here. I must travel to Georgia for a few weeks on business and we'll resume the interior work on our new home when I return."

"Oh, Frederick, thank you ever so much! This is a wonderful surprise!"

She embraced him, a wave of relief flooding her body. He held her briefly before gazing down upon her delicate features, his expression revealing the love swelling within the sea of his chest.

"If I'd known it would bring you this much joy, I'd have made the arrangements to delay our move sooner."

"Frederick, you know how much this place means to me. While I'm excited about the house in Charleston, I haven't the affection for it as I do my family home."

"Until I return, indulge in all that brings you joy and let Mrs. Stokes care for Bitsy. There's a reason we have a nanny," he said, arching his eyebrows.

With another long embrace, Nora felt the tension abating. To be free of the stress of relocating was a true blessing, although it wasn't the real reason for her relief.

"Bitsy and Mrs. Stokes are in the rose garden. Why don't you change and join them for tea?" Frederick suggested.

"That sounds wonderful."

He kissed her cheek and left the room.

He's such a wonderful husband, she thought. *If only I could feel about him as I do about...* She let the idea drift from her mind trying to squelch her longing for Charles. Nora wanted to love Frederick as she did Charles but there was something missing, a connection that only Charles could provide. Theirs was an unexpected amalgamation of the soul. If only she'd never discovered her parent's financial difficulties then things may have been different.

Regardless, Nora knew she had to bolster her courage and end things with Charles. She'd made so many attempts to end the relationship only to waver when she saw the devotion emanating from his sultry blue eyes or the angle of his jawline when he smiled.

No sense dwelling on past decisions or failures, she thought, shaking her head and taking in a deep breath. She'd done the right thing marrying Frederick and saving her parents from the humiliation of financial ruin, even if she'd sacrificed her heart in the process. Her stomach churned as she stared out her window in the direction of the hollowed-out oak where she and Charles usually left their correspondence to each other. Nora pondered her predicament unsure which was more distressing, the guilt of her indiscretion or her inability to be with the man she truly loved.

Nora felt badly for her husband. Instead of her love for Frederick growing, it seemed to be fading into indifference. He was a good man and deserved better than a wife who could never give him her whole heart.

I must end things with Charles, she decided, her heart wilting beneath the weight of her sorrow. If she didn't sever the relationship now she feared she never would. Even though Charles had mentioned leaving, she hoped in her heart he'd reconsider if they could return their relationship to one of propriety. After all, he was the best groom in town and had a way with Camden who could be high-spirited and difficult to handle at times. Nora sat at the writing desk, removed a crisp sheet of parchment from the lower drawer, dipped the silver pen into the ink well, and scripted a quick note.

Once she sealed it, she hurried down the stairs, hoping to

slip away before anyone took notice or questioned her intentions.

"Good day, Mrs. Hamilton," Mr. Reynolds said with a slight bow.

Nora spun around, grabbing her chest with one hand while shifting the letter into the folds of her skirt with the other.

"Mr. Reynolds, you gave me a fright!"

"My apologies, Madame. Are you going out?"

She fumbled for a quick excuse that would avert further inquiry, "I thought I might take a stroll before the midday meal."

"You seem flushed, Mrs. Hamilton. Should I send for Mr. Hamilton?

"No!" she exclaimed. "I don't wish to trouble him. He has business to tend to."

"May I be of further assistance?"

"Not at this time, Mr. Reynolds, thank you."

The footman bowed again before treading down the hall. Nora retreated to her room, too nervous to journey out. Frustrated, she knew she'd have to find another opportunity to leave the note in the old hollowed-out oak.

THE FOLLOWING MORNING, Nora rambled through the garden. Roses perfumed the air as she gently pruned branches, documenting the growth in her leather journal. She hoped the time away from Charles would lessen her feelings for him. To make matters worse, she'd not been able to get the note to him.

The creaking of hinges interrupted her ruminations as Mr. Reynolds emerged from the kitchen and stood on the back porch. She'd noticed his presence more often lately, and it warmed her heart to know he was so attentive.

"Mr. Reynolds, is anything the matter?" she queried.

"All is well, Madame. I only stepped out for some fresh air." Observing the basket of cut roses at her feet, he offered, "Would you like me to take the flowers in for Miss Biggs to arrange?"

"No, thank you."

With a slight bow, he returned inside.

Nora continued her work for nearly an hour when Frederick sauntered up beside her.

"My dearest, how long have you been working in the garden?"

"Most of the morning. What brings you out here?"

"I wanted to spend time with my beautiful wife since I leave on the early train tomorrow. How shall I survive three weeks away from you and Bitsy?"

"Business will occupy your time, leaving no opportunity to think of us."

"Impossible! You consume my every thought." His lips pressed against her hand making her stomach knot.

Miss Biggs stepped out the back door and announced, "Lunch is served."

"Shall we go inside?" He lifted the basket of freshly cut stems in one hand and offered his arm to Nora, who graciously accepted.

After washing up, Nora joined the family at the dining table for lunch.

"Frederick, we're thankful you've allowed our Nora and little Bitsy to stay here. It gives us great joy having our family together under one roof," Mr. Monroe said, placing the napkin in his lap.

"It gives me peace knowing they're here, sir, especially with this new account in Atlanta that is taking so much of my time."

The conversation transitioned from Frederick's upcoming business travels to the rose gardens to the sweltering summer temperatures.

"Nora, you've not been to the stables for some time. Is

everything alright?" Mr. Monroe asked, taking another bite of chicken.

"This heat has been unbearable, not to mention having to prepare for the rose show next month."

The ease with which the justification flowed from her lips, surprised her. She yearned to ride but dared not for fear of encountering Charles.

After lunch, Nora withdrew to her room passing Reynolds as she made her way up the stairs. She sat before the looking glass and gazed at her reflection, noticing the dullness in her eyes and the pallor of her skin. Her heart was withering in the desert of her despair. Despite the outward signs of her internal strife, Nora was determined to stay the course of loving her husband.

Early the next day, as the sun painted the sky in shades of glowing orange and lavender, Frederick stepped into the carriage en route to the train depot. Nora waved farewell from the portico, holding Bitsy in her arms. Once the carriage vanished, Nora went inside to commence her daily duties. Following a morning of recording the growth of her roses in her journal and pruning them, she joined her mother for tea at the mahogany tea table in the ladies' parlor.

"Nora, my dear, I'm concerned about your health. You seem forlorn and peaked. Please tell me what's distressing you," she said, lifting the cup to her lips.

"I'm not sure I can explain it in a manner you'd understand." Nora sighed, pondering her response. "My life is not as I imagined it would be."

"What more could you possibly desire?" Mrs. Monroe placed the cup in its saucer, giving her full attention to her daughter.

Nora's palms moistened as she wrung her hands contemplating a viable explanation to appease her mother's queries.

"Please don't misunderstand me. I love my daughter, my family, my home, yet...something is lacking."

"What about your husband?"

"What about him?"

"You listed all the things you love about your life, but his name was not mentioned," she said, raising her eyebrows.

"He's part of my family, so I need not distinguish him from the rest." Satisfied with her explanation regarding the faux pas, Nora sipped her tea. But Mrs. Monroe was not easily dissuaded.

"Bitsy is also family, but you named her specifically."

"You're placing too much emphasis on this. I love my husband. Are you happy now? I expressed my love for him *specifically*."

"I'm not entirely convinced by your explanation." The firmness in her mother's tone alluded to her suspicion that something was awry.

"I assure you I'm quite well, just a bit tired."

Mrs. Monroe's lighthearted demeanor promptly returned. "Motherhood takes its toll on a woman. Is Mrs. Stokes not doing enough? Perhaps we should employ additional help to assist her."

Nora grasped her mother's hand, forcing a smile. "That's not necessary. It's been difficult trying to balance the demands of motherhood along with my other responsibilities, but I'm adjusting."

"I too had difficulty adjusting to the obligations of motherhood. I'm glad it's nothing more than that. If you need more support let me know and I'll gladly arrange for additional help. As women, we must take care of one another. Men haven't a clue of the strains associated with our daily responsibilities."

Relieved to have pacified her mother's inquiries, Nora excused herself and retreated to her bedchambers. Once there, she reclined on the settee near the window and closed her eyes, willing the tension to release its hold on her body. Her nerves were raw as she fought the urge to go for a ride. She tried to concentrate on her roses but Charles's image flooded her mind in waves of adoration, his blue eyes glimmering and his smile tugging at the strings of her heart.

Her fortitude failed. Rising, she changed into her black riding habit, grabbed her riding hat, retrieved the brooch from her trunk and affixed it to the collar of her shirt before heading down the rear stairs. Unbeknownst to her, Reynolds stood in the shadows at the base of the stairs watching as she crept out the kitchen door.

25

The door in Sarah's dream slammed shut as she sat up and turned on the lamp on the bedside table. Of all the dreams she'd had so far this was the most intense. Not wanting to forget any of the details, she reached for her ledger and jotted a few notes of what she'd witnessed in the dream. Her hand shook as she wrote, the urge to call Danni increasing with each word. She glanced at the clock, which read four-thirty a.m. She couldn't call this early.

Sarah considered everything she'd seen in the vision and one thing struck her as familiar. The trunk. It was the same one in the attic where she'd found the scrapbooks. She leapt from bed, grabbed the flashlight from the night table, and hurried to the end of the hall. She stood before the attic door, her hand resting on the glass knob contemplating whether she wanted to search the trunk alone. Closing her eyes, Sarah puffed up her chest, turned the knob, and stormed into the darkened space before she overthought her actions.

She tugged the light chain and padded across the wooden floors to Nora's trunk. Sarah kneeled before it, opened the lid, and shone the light inside where she noticed a small blue leather diary resting against the back corner. Lifting the small book, she cradled it in her hand, gently turning the yellowed pages as she tried to make out the feathery script. After skimming several entries, she selected one and began reading.

SEPTEMBER *28, 1899*

MY ADORABLE DAUGHTER, Bitsy, delights my every waking moment. Her rosy cheeks and melodious cooing cause my heart to sing. Motherhood is a true blessing. I can hardly stand to leave her in the bassinet for fear I may miss some precious sound or endearing expression. She will no doubt be a fine horsewoman and enjoy the out of doors, as do I. I look forward to instructing her in the ways of needlework and cultivating roses as my mother did for me. The sparkle in Bitsy's eyes alludes to a bright child who will relish all the world has to offer. I thank God every day for such a blessing.

"DOESN'T SOUND like a woman who didn't like motherhood," she muttered, pulling several more items from the trunk.

Running her hand across the bottom of the chest, she gasped when her fingers brushed against an uneven surface bumping below the papered interior. With renewed gusto, Sarah peeled away the paper and pointed the flashlight at a secret compartment. She wriggled the small slat of wood until it came loose revealing a small leather box. Her mouth went dry as she removed the box and opened the lid, her hand trembling. Inside was a horseshoe shaped brooch with faceted garnet beads along with a tintype photo of Nora wearing the brooch.

"What are you trying to tell me Nora?" Sarah whispered, fingering the blood red stones. As soon as the words left her mouth, the scent of decaying dirt filled the room. Sarah jumped up, her knees quivering. This was not the situation she'd hoped to find herself in, *alone*.

She scanned the room looking for the source of the odor but everything was quiet and in its place when an icy finger traced her shoulder. Sarah grabbed the box, photo, and diary, and ran for the attic door turning to see what had touched her. Nothing. Breathless, she hollered, "I can't help you if you keep scaring me away. Either leave me alone or tell me what you want but I'm getting tired of these games!"

Proud of her gutsiness, Sarah marched down the attic steps slamming the door behind her for good measure. Once in her room she placed the diary and photo on the night table and opened the leather box to study the horseshoe brooch. It amazed her how something considered ordinary a hundred years ago was now worth a small fortune. The piece was valuable and would bring a decent price at auction. When she picked up the ring from Keith she'd have an appraisal done on the brooch. Oddly, she hadn't found any other jewelry items during her inventory. Knowing Edie, she probably pawned most of it. As far as Sarah could recall, she didn't remember Edie ever working. No doubt, the Monroe family must have had an abundance of valuable pieces that were now long gone to support Edie's drinking habits.

Pleased with her discovery and its direct connection to her dream, Sarah placed the small box on top of the diary as her eyes blurred. She turned out the light, rested her head against the pillow and promptly fell asleep.

26

———————

Nora marched along the well-worn path past the hollowed-out oak, her fortitude strong in case she should encounter Charles. She was tired of hiding from him and not being able to ride.

As she approached the barn, she saw George grooming a dapple gray, while other workers swept walkways and tidied aisles.

"Good afternoon, Mrs. Hamilton. It's good to see you. Camden has missed your visits."

"Could you ready him for me?"

"Of course, ma'am."

With a slight bow, George disappeared into the barn leading the gray to his stall and retrieving Camden. Shortly thereafter, George led the glistening chestnut gelding to the front of the barn. After helping Nora into the saddle, he handed her the reins and stepped back.

"Thank you, George." Nora clucked to Camden and trotted off.

Charles was exercising a dark bay thoroughbred in the

small ring behind the barn when Nora rode past. Moments later, he exited the ring, and followed the trail to the river oak where he rode up beside her.

"I've missed you."

"Charles, I hoped to avoid such a meeting. Please go back to the barn. There's no need to conjure up past feelings. I need some time to clear my head."

"What's troubling you?"

"You know exactly what's troubling me. Please, won't you abide by my wishes and leave me be?"

His eyes rested on the sparkling brooch pinned at her collar, a slight grin wrinkling his cheeks. "Is that what you want or is this a passive way of avoiding me?"

"I'm trying to do what is right by my family. Each time we meet, the same discussion ensues with identical results. If only you would honor my requests..." her voice trailed off. "Can't you see that I'm torn? I must abide by my commitments. Your presence distracts me from giving my whole heart to my husband. He deserves better than the remnants of my affections."

"I won't give up. It's not too late for us. We can go away and leave all this behind," he declared, obviously emboldened by the idea that she'd kept the brooch, thus giving him hope.

Nora's pulse quickened, her words rushing from her lips. "I won't leave my child, nor disgrace the family." Gathering the reins, she started Camden forward when Charles moved his horse to block them.

"Get out of my way and let me pass," she demanded.

"Not until you tell me the truth. Have you any affection for me? If you don't, I'll leave and never speak with you again. Otherwise..."

"This conversation is over. Please move aside." When Charles refused, she reined Camden around and spurred him to a gallop.

"You'll regret this!" he yelled. Charles watched her dash down the path. "You'll never forgive yourself for not following your heart, Nora," he mumbled in her wake.

From that point on, Nora remanded herself to the house and filled her time with tending roses, reading, and needlework. The days passed with the swiftness of an ebbing tide and much to her surprise, Frederick's return was a welcome respite to her loneliness.

On his first evening back, Frederick sat in his study at Monroe Manse finishing paperwork from his recent business trip when Reynolds rapped on the door.

"Sir, I have some information of particular interest."

"What is it?"

"While you were away, I followed Mrs. Hamilton when she went for a ride." Reynolds paused, knowing the information would displease Mr. Hamilton "I'm afraid to say there was an incident."

"Go on," Frederick replied.

"She was joined by one of the grooms."

"That's not unusual. Was there a problem with Camden?"

"It didn't appear so. They had words, and then she galloped off, seemingly distressed. He yelled out a threat as she rode away."

"But he did her no harm?" Frederick straightened in his chair, indignation furrowing his brow.

"Not that I could see. I've seen him working with her horse, but this is the first time I've witnessed such animosity."

Frederick sat back in his chair mulling over the information.

"Reynolds, do you believe this man is harassing Mrs. Hamilton?"

"I cannot say; however, their meeting did appear to be strained."

"Thank you, Reynolds. I appreciate your attention to the matter."

"It's my honor to be of service."

Reynolds returned to his duties, leaving Frederick seething with rage.

Frederick had noticed the alteration in his wife's moods over the past few months; she was distant, fatigued, and rarely went for a ride. He'd attributed the changes to motherhood but now reconsidered that theory. Reynolds's words echoed in Frederick's mind fueling the notion that the groom was pursuing his wife with unwanted advances. *Well, that will come to an end*, Frederick thought as he opened the top desk drawer and fingered the revolver within it.

Days passed to a different scenario where Nora sat at her writing desk, scripting a few sentences to Charles. During her last visit to Charleston, she'd taken the liberty of having her image made wearing the garnet brooch. She hoped giving Charles something to remember her by would help make a clean break and sever their romantic ties permanently.

Nora reread her words, content that the message was clear. This was the end of their relationship. She slipped the letter into an envelope along with the tintype and sealed it with a deep red wax mark. The thumping of her heart rang in her ears as she rose from the chair and hurried down the stairs in hopes she could get to the hollowed-out oak without interference. At the base of the stairs, Nora rounded the newel post when Frederick stepped from the gentlemen's parlor where his office was temporarily housed whilst they stayed at the manse.

"My dearest, where are you off to in such a rush?"

"Frederick, you frightened me," she gasped, startled by his sudden appearance and nearly dropping the note.

"How so?"

"I was deep in thought and didn't notice you."

"My apologies. I didn't mean to alarm you. Where are you going?"

Nora swallowed hard. "I was on my way to the gardens."

"May I join you?"

Fearful Frederick would discover the envelope in her hand, she shifted her right foot back one step and slid the note into the pocket of her dress.

"I'd like that very much," she said, forcing a smile.

Frederick offered his arm and escorted her to the rose garden. They strolled amongst the red, pink, and yellow blooms, relishing the budding paradise as they ambled along. However, Nora was antsy to get back to her prior endeavor and made excuses about forgetting her journal. Fredrick noticed his wife's subtle anxiety and escorted her inside before returning to his work in the gentleman's parlor.

Once he was out of sight, Nora hurried out the back door to the hollowed-out oak. Looking around to ensure she hadn't been followed, she pulled the envelope from her pocket and started to place it inside the tree. A twinge gripped her stomach. What if Charles refused to accept her request? He might take the photo to mean she wasn't serious in her commitment to cease their relationship.

As she stood in the shadow of the old tree, she pondered what had prompted her to attempt something so irresponsible. The best thing she could do was to avoid any interaction with Charles outside of his grooming responsibilities. Satisfied with her decision, she tucked the note back in her pocket and rushed to the house. Once in her room, she stashed the photo with the brooch and crumpled the note into the fireplace. Striking a match, she held the flame to the paper and watched it disintegrate into ash.

Nora's concentration shifted when she heard the cooing of her daughter from across the hall. Sauntering to the nursery, she lifted the cherished bundle from the crib and settled in the rocker. She cradled Bitsy in her arms, humming a lullaby as elongated shadows danced across walls, the afternoon sun beginning its waltz with the evening tide.

Engulfed in adoration, Nora gazed at her daughter's rosy cheeks. Under no circumstances could she abandon the most important person in her life, reinforcing her decision to permanently end her relationship with Charles. With a sigh, the tension in her back and shoulders subsided. Focusing on her daughter gave her a slight sense of peace. Mrs. Stokes appeared in the doorway and smiled.

"Mrs. Hamilton, may I take Bitsy for her feeding?"

"Of course." She handed the babbling bundle to Mrs. Stokes who stepped from the room, speaking softly to her charge.

Nora's emotions felt like a train wreck, her heart derailed by the pending finality of her relationship with Charles. She ambled down the hall to her chambers and changed for dinner. Donning a soft green brocade gown with lace overlay, she sat before the vanity mirror fixing her hair into a loose coiffure.

From within the velvet jewelry case, she took out the set of earrings and matching brooch Frederick had given her as a wedding gift. Seed pearls wreathed in garnets adorned the lustrous gold swirls. She fastened the ornament at the base of her lace collar, slipped on the earrings, and peered into the looking glass once more. It never ceased to amaze her how something as simple as jewelry could make a wardrobe selection seem more elegant. If only her feelings matched her appearance.

She clasped the cut crystal bottle near the mirror, removed the stopper, and rubbed the fragrant rose oil along the crest of her wrist. Inhaling deeply, she took in the calming fragrance, hoping to soothe her raw nerves. The last thing she wanted was a barrage of questions about her emotional state. Contented with her appearance, Nora made her way downstairs, her skirts sweeping the floor in a rhythmic rustling. She entered the dining room where her parents and Frederick were seated around the table in lively conversation.

"I was getting ready to send for you, my darling," Frederick said, pulling the chair out for her.

"I apologize for my tardiness, but I was with Bitsy and lost all sense of time."

"We understand," her mother replied.

Dinner was served amid discussions of upcoming business trips for Frederick, in addition to stories of Mr. Monroe's encounters with an astute, yet arrogant, banker.

"The young fool thought he could pull the wool over my eyes, but I'd have none of it. I told him to rectify the mistake or I'd take my accounts elsewhere." Mr. Monroe punctuated the story with a swig of scotch before continuing his diatribe. "Then the rascal strode off to speak with the manager..."

While her father prattled on, Nora's mind wandered to her last rendezvous with Charles and the complexities of her current situation.

"Nora. Nora?" her mother repeated emphatically. "Is everything alright? You seem distant this evening."

"Forgive me. I was thinking about the garden club gathering next week and how to arrange my roses."

The answer seemed plausible and was readily accepted by all at the table. Following dinner, Mr. Monroe and Frederick retired to the gentlemen's parlor for brandy and cigars while Nora and her mother moved to the front parlor.

The two enjoyed tea, discussing everything from gardening to needlepoint to Bitsy. Nora tried to concentrate but couldn't stop thinking about Charles. Finally, she feigned exhaustion and excused herself for the evening.

Once in her room, Nora changed for bed, retrieved her diary from the locked drawer of her writing desk, and rested on the wing chair by the window. Weariness consumed her. She scripted a few lines about the day's events before replacing it in the drawer. Unbeknownst to her, Charles hovered in the shadows just beyond the garden wall staring at the flickering light emanating from her room.

27

———————

Sarah startled awake, her nightshirt soaked and the sheets clinging to her legs. Glancing at the clock, she rubbed her eyes, and muttered, "Only six-thirty?" Unable to settle, she decided to make an early morning of it. With a stretch, Sarah looked at the small leather box sitting on the night table and reached for it when the Batman theme rang out.

"G'morning," Danni declared, her voice chipper for such an early hour, especially for her. "Did I wake you?"

"Just got up."

"I found something interesting when I was at the county offices yesterday and thought I'd bring breakfast over from Palmetto Bagels."

"That sounds good. See you soon."

Sarah hung up, opened the small box, and gazed at the jeweled horseshoe. Danni was going to flip when she told her about the brooch and the dream. Stiff from days of moving furniture and cleaning out closets, Sarah slid from bed, went into the bathroom to change clothes, and dab on some concealer. As she pulled her hair into a ponytail the tinkling of piano keys floated through the room. She stared at her reflection in the bathroom mirror, her body tensing as the glass began to fog and the scent of fresh dirt filled the space.

"No!" she yelled, scooting from the room as the odor dissipated and the music stopped. She stood at the top of the staircase, her chest heaving. The sound of tires crunching over oyster shells sent her running down the stairs to the kitchen. Thank goodness, Danni was here. Sarah threw the back door open as Danni sauntered up with a brown paper bag and a manila folder.

"Are you OK? You're pale as a gho…" Danni blushed. "Sorry, wrong choice of words." Danni walked past planting the bag of bagels and a cup of coffee on the table. "What's going on?"

"Sit down and I'll fill you in."

Danni doled out bagels and cream cheese while Sarah fixed a cup of tea. With steaming cup in hand, Sarah sat down and proceeded to tell her friend about the dreams and her middle-of-the-night excursion to the attic where she discovered the brooch. Danni's eyes grew larger with each story.

"This is unbelievable," Danni said, shaking her head.

"Tell me about it," Sarah mumbled.

"No, I mean your dream and what I found in the newspaper archives." Danni slid the folder across the table.

Sarah opened the folder and started perusing the articles. A chill slinked down her back as she read through the article about Nora's disappearance dated August 5, 1900.

SEARCH CONTINUES *for Mrs. Frederick Hamilton*

MRS. FREDERICK HAMILTON, *also known as Nora, disappeared Monday of last week. This is uncharacteristic for Mrs. Hamilton and thus Mr. Hamilton is offering a reward for any information leading to his wife's location. Their infant daughter, Bitsy, is doing well although missing her mother's care. All correspondence regarding Mrs. Hamilton should be addressed to the offices of Devereaux and Greene.*

"DEVEREAUX? AS IN WILLIAM'S FAMILY?" Sarah asked.

"Probably. Supposedly his ancestors have been here for generations, at least that's what he boasts about."

"And Frederick offered a reward for information leading to Nora's location? The poor guy sounded desperate to find her," Sarah said, shaking her head.

"This Charles guy must've been something special for her to walk away from a man like Frederick, not to mention her daughter. I mean, what kind of woman abandons her only child?"

"From what I gathered from my dreams, she tried to love Frederick but couldn't let go of Charles." Sarah popped a chunk of bagel into her mouth. "The evidence really does suggest she ran off to be with him. Except..."

"What?" Danni asked.

"In my recent dreams, Charles seemed irritated with Nora for *not* running away with him. Then last night I dreamt about Charles giving Nora this brooch and with a little searching, voila I found it. It's all so confusing."

"What else did you dream about?"

"Random things. I saw Nora tending to her roses, spending time with her daughter Bitsy, writing a letter to Charles ending the relationship..." Sarah gasped. "There was a scene where Reynolds told Frederick he'd witnessed Charles threatening Nora."

"Charles threatened her?"

"He was frustrated because she wouldn't run away with him and yelled that she would regret it."

"Sounds like a threat to me," Danni said, stuffing the last bite of bagel in her mouth.

"I suppose it might seem that way if you hadn't seen the entire conversation." Sarah sucked in a breath. "What if Charles did do something terrible to Nora?"

Danni's body stiffened. "Like what? Kidnap her?"

"Or worse, what if he killed her?"

"I thought he loved her?" Danni asked.

"He did but it wouldn't be the first love affair to morph into obsession and end in murder."

"Are you suggesting he killed her because he couldn't have her?"

"It's not that farfetched and it would explain the voice that keeps telling me "he's guilty," Sarah argued.

"So, you're suggesting Nora Hamilton didn't run away but was murdered by her psycho-possessed lover?"

"I don't know. Maybe. There's something more going on but I can't figure it out," Sarah replied, staring at the brooch. "With a bit more digging we might be able to find the answers."

"Any ideas where to search?"

"Everywhere."

"That narrows it down," Danni said with a huff.

Before Sarah could respond, Danni's phone rang, her brow furrowing when she looked at the number. Sitting straighter, she answered.

"Danni Cook...yes sir...it will take some time...but the contract says...that could land you in litigation...no I'm not threatening you...I'm aware...I'll tell her." Danni hung up and rubbed her forehead.

"What's wrong?"

"That was Jerrod Devereaux."

"William's uncle?"

Danni nodded. "He just took over the legal end of the estate."

"What?" Sarah hollered, her eyes widening.

"Apparently, Davidson and Davidson have been indicted on tax fraud and their cases transferred to other offices."

"How did Devereaux end up with this one?"

"I'm sure it's not a coincidence," Danni replied with a smirk.

"That little weasel! I'll strangle William when I see him again."

"You'll want to do more than that."

"Why?" Sarah's tone sobered.

"They've moved the deadline up one week."

"They can't do that!"

"Sadly, they can, especially when other auction houses still want this estate."

"But I've already done some of the work," Sarah declared.

"Which will make it easier for the next company."

"So I'm fired?" Sarah said, slumping back in her chair.

"Not if you agree to the new deadline, otherwise you're out."

"Isn't there something in the contract?"

Danni's face flushed. "It had a clause."

"A clause?" Sarah's voice went up an octave as her forehead wrinkled. "You didn't mention a *clause* when I signed."

"I didn't think there'd be reason to invoke it. Knowing your obsessive methods, I knew you'd complete the job on time. And I've known Frank Davidson for years. He's a solid attorney. His son and partner however…"

"Let me guess, his son drew up the contract."

"And also handled the taxes for the firm." Danni said, holding up her hands.

Sarah closed her eyes and exhaled. "The end result is I have to agree to the new deadline or forfeit everything."

"I'm so sorry Sarah. I never thought they'd lose this account to another attorney who would alter the time frame."

"Then I don't have a choice, especially now that we we're getting closer to discovering what the ghost is trying to tell us. I won't lose this job, especially because of a Devereaux!"

28

———————

Sarah thrummed her fingers against the kitchen table, her nerves on edge. Now more than ever she was determined to finish this job and solve the mystery surrounding Nora's disappearance.

"You're scaring me," Danni said. "You have that look that says you're contemplating something serious."

"I'm going back to the attic to look through the trunk," Sarah announced, standing up. "I need you to find anything you can on this house and the Monroes. Between the two of us, and whatever this entity is trying to convey, I think we can solve this thing."

"Are you sure you want to be here by yourself?"

"Absolutely. I'm tired of living in fear. It's time I face this dream stuff and learn how to cope with it," Sarah said with a glint in her eye.

"What about the new deadline?"

"I'll still be working but I can search for clues at the same time."

Danni didn't argue. Instead, she grabbed her keys and headed for the door.

"Where are you going?" Sarah asked.

"You said to get more information about the Monroes and the house. I'm going to the city offices," she replied, shrugging her shoulders.

"At this hour? It's too early."

Danni grinned. "Not when you have friends with access."

"You still have a key?" Sarah queried, raising her eyebrows. "Does Scott know?"

"He knows I like to work without interruption and that I'll put everything back in its place before I leave."

"He's the best ex a girl could ask for," Sarah said with a giggle. "Think you'll find anything new?"

"Won't know until I look. The recent information from your dreams gives me other avenues, which may lead to something I overlooked when I was there last time. I'll check the newspaper archives again too."

"Good luck," Sarah said as Danni hurried out the door.

Sarah's need to confront her fears and figure out who, or what, was behind the voices and dreams chipped away at the wall of trepidation she'd built over the course of her life. Positive that Nora's disappearance was the reason behind the haunting, Sarah was confident she and Danni were on the right track to discovering the untold story. More importantly, she wanted to prove that she could finish clearing the estate regardless of the impossible deadline placed upon her.

Sarah went to the dining room and placed the horseshoe brooch on the table with Charles's picture. He was definitely a good-looking guy, but then again, so was Frederick. Yet there was a charisma about Charles that Frederick didn't possess. Of course, that may have been influenced by the intimacy of Nora's thoughts in the dreamscapes.

A shiver rattled Sarah's body as she pondered her new reality as a dreamist and the fact she'd actually experienced Nora's thoughts and feelings. After years of confusion, she was beginning to accept the idea that her ghostly experiences were some sort of gift, not insanity.

Equipped with a bottle of water and her work tools, Sarah dashed up to the attic, excited to delve deeper into the trunk and Nora's past. Shadows skirted across the floor as clouds meandered through the sky lending an eerie feel to the space. A rumble shook the floors announcing an impending storm, dampening Sarah's motivation. Despite the angst niggling at her nerves, Sarah persisted with her search. She needed answers and was not going to be deterred by thunder and over-cast skies. Looking around the shadowy space, she contem-plated where to begin. Although she longed to search for clues about Nora, responsibility tightened around her chest like a lasso. Before she indulged in sleuthing, she needed to get some real work done, otherwise, she'd lose this job.

A clap of thunder shattered the stillness, sending Sarah's heart racing and her limbs quivering. The room darkened as rain began pinging against the windowpanes. Sarah yanked the chain on the light bulb washing the room in a soft glow. The lure of Nora's past was magnetic, preventing Sarah from focusing on anything else. Despite her need to work, she knelt by the trunk and lifted the lid.

Sifting through bits of lace, loose photos, and a few yellowed cards, Sarah sucked in a breath when she noticed a lone newspaper article crumpled against the side of the chest. She removed it carefully, smoothing out the wrinkles without damaging the print. A distinguished looking gentleman stood next to a little girl in a calf length frock. The caption below read, *Mr. Frederick Hamilton and daughter Bitsy at Monroe Manse garden party.*

Bitsy's smile revealed a couple of missing teeth as she gazed lovingly at her father whose sagging expression and hollow stare seemed to reveal the despair of being abandoned by his wife.

"Poor Frederick," Sarah mumbled.

A bolt of lightning, along with a roaring boom, shattered the darkened space, unraveling Sarah's fortitude like twine. With a few deep breaths, she was able to slow her racing pulse and settle her frazzled nerves. She sorted through a stack of cabinet card photos, the type primarily seen at the turn of the twentieth century, picturing Bitsy and her father. It appeared they held a special bond by the loving expression captured in the photos even though Frederick's countenance seemed eclipsed by the disappointments of his marital circumstances. She could almost feel the turmoil of his existence. Up to this point, Nora's perspective had been the primary one. Now, Sarah wondered if there was a way to expand that ability to include Frederick. Regardless, anyone could look at the photo and sense Frederick's internal battle that showed in his sullen expression and shadowed eyes.

Sarah put the newspaper clipping and photos back in the trunk and looked around the cluttered room. Her attention swung like a pendulum between searching for clues and completing the inventory. Admonishing herself for being irresponsible, she walked across the space and started sorting through a tower of sagging boxes.

The cadenced pattering of rain against the roof increased to a pounding drumbeat soothing Sarah into a steady work rhythm. It seemed the louder the rain, the calmer her nerves. Each container was labeled in magic marker with contents ranging from tax returns and bank statements to canning jars and paperback books. "More junk," she whispered. However, one box at the bottom of the stack caught her attention. Squinting, she was able to make out the faint handwriting, *l-e-d-g-e-r-s*.

This looks interesting, she thought.

Sarah removed the boxes piled on top and pulled the crumpled container to the middle of the floor beneath the bulb where the light was better. Several leather-bound ledgers hibernated within the flimsy mildew ridden enclosure. Gingerly, she removed the volumes from within and grabbed a nearby chair. She sat down, paging through the first ledger, admiring the elegant handwriting that scrolled across the lined pages.

Entries such as kitchenware, grains, and furnishings filled each account. The next book contained the salaries of the house staff from the cook to the lady's maid. Sarah enjoyed the bird's eye view into the economic history of bygone days, astounded by the pittance paid to servants of the time, when one name in particular grabbed her attention. Oddly, this servant's salary was notably higher than the others, but she surmised it was probably due to the footman's *extra* duties. It would seem watching over the boss's wife was a profitable endeavor.

After searching through the remaining journals, and finding nothing of significance, Sarah glanced around at all the unopened containers. The sheer number of them was mind-boggling. It was as if the boxes had multiplied overnight.

"I guess Edie wasn't the only hoarder in the family. Looks like these people never threw anything away," she chuckled. "The television network should do a special antique version of hoarders gone wild."

Foraging through boxes, she searched for any evidence of Nora's encounters and relationships with family and friends, making inventory notations in her ledger as she went. After sorting through several boxes of junk, Sarah was thrilled when she removed a sheet unearthing an old Hoosier cabinet, complete with a flour sifter and potato bin, several salt-glazed crocks, and a butter churn. Granted, these country style items weren't as popular as they'd been in the 1980s but there was still a small market. It would just take some time to sell unless Alyssa snatched them up. She was always searching for old farmhouse pieces for her cabin.

Hours later, Sarah's shoulders ached from lifting, not to

mention, her stomach was beginning to protest. She stacked boxes of worthless junk by the door to be hauled to the dump. Brushing the dust from her khaki shorts, she headed to the kitchen for a peanut butter sandwich.

Sarah gazed out the kitchen window as she stood at the sink eating. The rain had cleared, leaving a sea of gray clouds in its wake. In the garden, splinters of color peeked through tight-fisted rosebuds as they began to release their imprisoned petals. Sarah caught a glimpse of something moving amid the roses, making her limbs tingle and her pulse quicken.

She marched out the back door and called out, "Who's there?

A rustling emanated from the depths of the nearest rose-bush, making the hair at the nape of her neck bristle. Sarah grabbed an old rake that was leaning against the house and stalked toward the bush, her heart hammering within her chest. She raised the rake over her shoulder and shouted,

"Come out or I'm sending you to the hospital!"

A furry gray blur leapt from the bush. Alarmed, Sarah swung the rake with the force of a lumberjack, swiping the rosebush and scattering leaves everywhere as a large raccoon scurried past in a frightful scamper.

"Pesky vermin!" she yelled, lowering the rake to her side. With shaking hands, she filled her lungs with air, held it for a count of five, and released. Her racing pulse began to steady as she propped the rake against the wall and stepped back into the kitchen to finish lunch before returning to the attic.

29

The afternoon passed with more furnishings tagged and a second stack of junk destined for the dump. Satisfied with all she'd accomplished, Sarah started toward the other side of the attic when the house shuddered from a door slamming below, Danni's frantic voice echoing through the halls.

"Sarah?"

Hurrying down to the second-floor landing, she leaned over the railing and shouted, "Up here!"

Out of breath, Danni ran to the base of the stairs. "Where've you been? I've been calling since three o'clock!"

Sarah patted her empty front pocket recognizing the source of Danni's alarm.

"I'm sorry. I must have left the cell phone downstairs."

"Thank goodness you're OK! You scared me!" Danni declared, her hand resting on her heaving chest.

"I'm really sorry." Sarah checked her watch. "I could use a break. Want a drink?"

With hands on her hips, Danni huffed, "Of course."

They went to the kitchen where Sarah poured two glasses

of wine and joined Danni at the table. Danni took a long sip and slumped back in the chair.

"How'd your search go?" Sarah asked.

Danni tossed a manila folder on the table. "Interesting. It took a lot of digging and a bit of help from Scott but I found something strange in the old deeds section."

"Scott was there? How's he doing?"

"Same. His youngest son just made the all-star team for little league."

"That's great! You gonna go to any of the games?"

"Too busy right now."

Sarah shook her head. "You're an enigma. I've never known anyone who gets along so well with their ex-husband *and* his new wife."

"Scott and I were never meant to be more than friends. And I like his wife, Gina, she's good for him."

"You seemed like a good match at the time."

"Like I said, he's a good friend and I love him but I'm not cut out to be married. I'm too set in my ways and I like my freedom. After graduation from law school I thought getting married was the next logical step in my life. But it didn't take long to realize that Scott was the settling-down-family-man kinda guy and that wasn't for me. Seriously, can you see me with kids?"

"Maybe hovering over a cauldron like the old woman in Hansel and Gretel," Sarah said with a chuckle as she opened the folder and started paging through the contents. "These are property deeds for all of the Monroe's holdings as well as Frederick's." Sarah skimmed each copy, fascinated by the old script and the manner in which land ownership was recorded more than a century before. "Wow, looks like the Monroes owned a good portion of land at one time."

"And then it tapered off." Danni reached over and pointed at the page Sarah was looking at. "Seems that Mr. Monroe started selling off large tracts of land just before Nora's wedding."

"My first dream showed Nora eavesdropping on her parents when they were discussing their financial difficulties. It's why she was rushed into marrying Frederick. And if the dream of her wedding day holds any merit it looked like a pretty expensive event. Her gown alone had to have cost a fortune."

"I remember seeing something in one of the articles I found in the archives that her dress was made by someone named Worth out of Paris."

"Charles Frederick Worth?" Sarah declared.

"That's the name. Is he someone special?"

"He's the father of haute couture! My gosh, Nora's wedding gown must have cost thousands."

"No wonder her father had to sell off land to pay for it," Danni said, taking another sip of wine. "Never understood why women spend so much for a dress they're only going to wear once. It's a total waste of money."

"Thus, why you and Scott were married at city hall." Sarah chuckled. "I remember your mother had a fit."

"Poor Mom. She was so disappointed that she didn't get to have a fancy wedding event for her only child; just a phone call saying I was married and then five years later another call announcing the divorce."

"I didn't think she'd ever forgive you."

"But she did," Danni sighed. "Of course, she still tortures me with reminders that she doesn't have any grandchildren." Danni took a long gulp of wine. "Anyway, there's an interesting deed for a 23-acre plot on Balding Island that was given to a guy named Reggie or Reinhold, something like that."

"Reynolds?"

"That's it. How'd you know?" Danni asked.

"He was the footman. I actually dreamed about him last night."

"Any idea why a footman was given a 23-acre tract of land?"

"In the dream, Frederick was worried about Nora and asked his footman Reynolds to watch over her while he was away on business. I found an old ledger in the attic this afternoon showing substantial payments to him."

"Humph, sounds like a pretty big payoff for keeping an eye on the boss's wife."

"A good footman was a highly regarded employee at that time. I suppose Frederick felt Reynolds deserved a substantial retirement for his years of service. Makes you wonder why Nora would leave such a great guy, and her daughter. Seems to me she could have tried harder to make her marriage work."

"What kind of guy has someone spy on his wife? Sounds a bit controlling if you ask me," Danni said with a shrug.

"He wasn't spying per se, it was more like making sure she was safe. Frederick was concerned about Nora's moods and was away a lot for business. I think it gave him peace knowing someone was watching over her."

"Still seems a bit extreme."

"Did you find anything else interesting?"

The broad smile and sly look on Danni's face answered her question. She'd found something big.

"Check this out," Danni said, pushing another stack of photocopies across the table. "I went back through the newspaper microfiche and as I suspected, was able to find more information when I searched under Charles's name."

Sarah skimmed the first article. "This is a report of Charles's disappearance following the accidental death of Nora's parents?" she gasped. "You're kidding me?"

"Looks like there was good reason for Charles's departure. I know we originally suspected he ran away with Nora but now that we know he left a few weeks after her disappearance, it kinda squashes that theory. Now it seems his departure was for something much more sinister. He may have been responsible for her parent's death."

"Why would he kill her parents?

"Who knows? Why does anyone kill? Love, money, revenge, jealousy, it's all there."

Sarah kept reading. "It says the carriage wheel fell off. Seems like an accident not murder."

"Until you read the rest of it. Turns out the wheel wasn't properly secured and guess who was responsible for maintaining it?"

"Charles?"

"Yup. And guess when he vanished?"

"Around the same time as the accident?"

"Sarah, you should've been a detective," she said sarcastically. "After the incident, he was never seen or heard from again. Sounds like a pretty strong coincidence, if you ask me."

"Or a whole lot of circumstantial evidence."

"Now you sound like a lawyer," Danni teased.

Sarah shook her head in disbelief. "A wheel falls off a carriage resulting in the death of the people riding in it. The person responsible for the maintenance of the vehicle leaves without a trace, the same man who was trying to convince their daughter to run off with him. I still don't see motive." Sarah snapped her fingers. "Wait a minute, the voice on the recorder said '*He's guilty*'. Do you think this is what she's been trying to tell me?"

"Maybe. He wouldn't be the first man to seek revenge after being turned down by a woman. You said she married to save her parents from financial ruin. I wonder if she ever told Charles? It would explain his need for revenge."

"It seems more likely he ran away to be with Nora or to escape his heartbreak. He did mention looking for work elsewhere. I can't imagine he'd kill anybody, especially the parents of a woman he professed to love."

"Just read the article," Danni said.

The Daily Gazette
August 25, 1900

Suspicions Raised in Stable Hand's Disappearance

CHARLES DONAHUE, a groom for the Monroe Stables, is suspected of negligence regarding the upkeep of his employer's carriage. His dereliction of duties resulted in the rear wheel falling off as the vehicle rounded Bellamy Curve. The Monroes perished when the carriage careened into the river.

Further investigation by police found Mr. Donahue's residence empty of clothing and personal effects. Interviews conducted with his colleagues revealed they had no knowledge of his current location.

Additionally, Mr. Frederick Hamilton reported a burglary after discovering his missing wife's jewels had been taken along with a small amount of cash. Mr. Donahue's disappearance, and possible involvement with the crimes, has police ardently searching for him. Mr. Hamilton is offering a reward of $1,000 for any information leading to Mr. Donahue's whereabouts, and the return of the stolen jewels.

Mrs. Hamilton's whereabouts are still unknown since her disappearance on July 29th.

"THIS IS UNBELIEVABLE," Sarah muttered, shaking her head. "Why would the police question him without solid evidence to suspect him? And I still don't believe Charles would go to such extremes to prevent them from searching for their daughter. If he wanted to eliminate people searching for her he'd have to kill Frederick too. After all, he'd put ads in the paper looking for leads to find Nora."

"I think Charles was trying to save his own hide. Typical guy," Danni said with a snort.

"Now that I think of it, Charles seemed agitated with Nora in my last few dreams. And the voice on the recorder kept alluding to someone's guilt. Maybe that's what Nora has been trying to reveal, the identity of the man who killed her parents!" Sarah's hand covered her mouth. "Oh, my gosh, what if he murdered Nora too?"

Danni leaned forward, her brows furrowing. "Go on."

"We know Nora disappeared without a trace and that no one knew about the affair with Charles until my dreams. What if Frederick was supposed to be in the carriage and at the last minute changed his plans? Maybe Charles thought Frederick would be with his in-laws and die in the accident. You have to admit it was a pretty brazen move for Charles to sneak into the house and steal stuff, especially if Frederick was home."

"Makes sense and would explain why no one ever found Nora." Danni blew out a breath. "You hungry?"

"Starving."

"I didn't stop for lunch today and I can't think clearly when my stomach is playing soccer with the inside of my ribs. I'll pick up something from Boundaries. We'll work on this after we eat."

"How can you stop to eat when we're on the verge of discovering the reason for Nora's disappearance and possible murder?"

"Because I'm hungry and that takes precedence. You want fried oysters and blue cheese lima bean slaw?"

"Of course."

"When I get back I'll tell you about the things I learned

from the *Dreamist* book," Danni said as she slipped out the door.

"You can't leave now!" Sarah hollered, rising from her seat as the door shut.

She plopped down in the chair, her nerves prickling with anxiety. It was just like Danni to leave her hanging. Sarah's stomach rolled with anticipation and a hint of hunger, prompting her to take the new articles to the dining room. She placed them on the table along with the other items and started rearranging them like a puzzle, trying to connect everything they'd discovered through her dreams, the contents of the trunk, and the century old rumors. The pieces were beginning to fall into place but there were still too many gaps to solve the mystery. Sarah picked up the diary, sat down, and started paging through it when an entry dated a few days before Nora's disappearance caught her attention.

July 25th, 1900

I do not know how much longer I can live this lie. The misery is creating such tension between Frederick and me. I fear he senses something is awry and it breaks my heart to hurt him, but a lifetime of despair is more than anyone can tolerate. I'm plagued by my thoughts that drift from leaving to staying. I must find a way to escape this agony before I lose my nerve.

"I can't believe this," Sarah mumbled.

Oddly, only a few more entries were made, ceasing on the day of Nora's disappearance, July twenty-ninth. Sarah's thoughts were interrupted when the back door opened and closed announcing Danni's return. In the kitchen, she found Danni unpacking a large paper bag, the scent of food making her stomach rumble.

"Got us an order of crackle fries. With all this investigating I figured we'd earned it."

Sarah grabbed one of the waffle cut fries sprinkled with fresh black pepper and Parmesan and popped it in her mouth. She closed her eyes, smiling as she savored the different flavors.

"I'm going to have to run five miles to work off this dinner but it'll be worth it," she said, reaching for another fry and grabbing two beers from the fridge. Hunger prompted her to hold off showing Danni the diary entry until they finished eating. She didn't want to get grease on it.

Dipping one of the fried oysters in spicy cocktail sauce, Sarah looked across the table at her friend. "OK, what did you learn from the book?"

"I knew you'd stew while I was gone," Danni said with a sly grin. "According to what I read last night, dreamists have other skills than just communicating with the dead through their dreams."

"Other skills? Not sure I'm going to like this."

"Have you ever gotten a vision from touching an item?"

Goose bumps raced across Sarah's skin, her voice a mere whisper. "Yes."

"Great. When we finish eating I want to try an experiment."

"You want to use me as a test subject?"

"Pretty much. Can't try this with anybody else, you're the only dreamist I know. Come on, you said you wanted to improve your skills and now it's time to do your part."

Sarah shrugged, "Alright."

When they finished the last fry, and cleared the table, Sarah and Danni traipsed to the dining room.

"First, we need an antique item, preferably not something that belonged to Nora."

"Does it matter what it is?"

"Nope, as long as it's old, but don't touch it."

"Why?"

"Stop with the questions and follow my instructions," Danni commanded.

"Fine. How about one of the silver napkin rings?" Sarah pointed to the small assortment on the buffet.

"Perfect." Danni grabbed one and held it up. "I'm going to hand this to you and I want you to tell me the first thing that pops into your head.

"Huh?"

"Just do it," Danni moaned. "Remember, tell me the first thing that enters your mind."

Sarah held out her hand and closed her eyes as Danni placed the napkin ring into her outstretched palm.

With a shiver, Sarah blurted out, "a linen table cloth." Opening her eyes, she cocked her head. "What was the point of that?"

"According to the book, a dreamist can decipher something about a previous owner by touching an object. The first image that enters the mind is generally accurate but if you dwell too long your own thoughts can taint the original message."

"All I saw was a linen tablecloth. That doesn't tell me anything about the owner of this."

"It takes practice so we'll have to keep at it. Chances are your preconceived notions about the napkin ring being affiliated with table settings interfered. The book says it takes time and training to perfect. The most important thing is to make a mental snapshot of the first image that presents itself. Let's try again."

"How does this relate to the dreams?"

"It's all interconnected. You have to hone one ability before moving on to the next. Each chapter is a foundation for the following chapter."

Sarah's eyebrows scrunched as she pursed her lips. "This sounds a bit farfetched."

Danni sighed. "You see ghosts in your dreams and you

think this is farfetched? You can always read the book yourself and try to figure it out. I'm merely the messenger."

"No, I trust you. Let's try again."

For the next thirty minutes they traversed the house, Sarah picking up an item and saying the first thing that entered her mind.

"How do we know what I'm seeing is accurate and not my own imagination," she asked.

"Supposedly, as you learn to identify the initial image the snapshots in your head will relate to the dreams and eventually give you access to the thoughts of more than one entity."

Sarah nodded. "This is a bit overwhelming. I feel like I'm catapulting from a plane without a parachute."

"It'll get easier as your skills improve, at least that's what the book says."

Sarah's heart swelled. The idea of being a dreamist wasn't as daunting with someone else helping her through it. If she could grasp the skills necessary to deal with the visions maybe she could finally have something of a normal life. Up to this point, she thought financial security and a successful career was what she wanted but now she realized being free from fear had always been at the core of her existence.

"Maybe with a bit more practice we'll be able to figure out why Nora left a wonderful man like Frederick for a guy like Charles," Sarah said with a smirk. "Apparently, even 19th century women were attracted to bad boys."

30

Sarah and Danni startled when a loud *thwack* echoed from upstairs.

"What was that?" Danni whispered, staring at the ceiling.

"Sounded like a door slamming. The windows on the second floor are open and a breeze probably blew a door shut. I'll go check."

"You sure about that?" Danni asked, her face pale.

"Won't know until we look."

Sarah started down the hall with Danni lagging behind.

"Come on slow poke," Sarah taunted.

"I'll let you go ahead in case there are zombies waiting to suck out our brains."

"Don't be ridiculous, zombies don't exist."

"Apparently, you've never been to night court," Danni replied, grasping the stair railing as she ascended the stairs a few steps behind her best friend.

When they reached the second-floor landing, Sarah shuddered. She looked down one side of the hall and then the other. All of the doors were open.

"I don't see any closed doors," Danni muttered, glancing around.

"Maybe something blew over. You check the bedrooms while I search the library and the ballroom."

"No way! I'm sticking with you."

Sarah shook her head. "Library first."

They walked down the hall and peered into the library. Stacks of books were piled in the far corner along with four boxes of paperbacks, as well as a garbage bag filled with outdated coupons and sweepstakes ads. Nothing was out of place. From there they crossed the hall into the ballroom. Sarah shivered at the memory of the piano playing. A soft knocking interrupted the quietude.

"What was that?" Danni whispered.

"Not sure but it sounds like it's coming from behind the far wall."

"Well it's freaking me out," she hissed.

"Stay here, I'm going to check it out."

Danni grabbed Sarah's arm. "Are you nuts?"

"No, just haunted. Stop being such a baby, it might be a rat or something trapped in the wall," Sarah replied with a smirk. "And why are you whispering? We're the only ones here."

"So you say."

Sarah started toward the knocking sound when a door slammed again. "It's coming from the end of the hall!" Sarah declared, running past Danni.

Evidently, not wanting to stay alone, Danni followed. Sarah stood at the bottom of the small staircase staring at the attic door.

"This is where the noise came from but I know the door was already closed."

"Sure you didn't leave it open earlier?"

"Positive," Sarah replied.

"Maybe it was something else."

"You heard it too. Are you saying it wasn't a slamming door?"

Danni's shrugged her shoulders.

"We need to find out what made that noise," Sarah declared.

A wave of courage surged through Sarah's veins. She marched up the steps, grasped the doorknob, her chest tightening as she flung the door open. A breath blew across her lips when she peered inside and found everything in its place. Sarah tugged the light chain and scanned the space with Danni close behind.

"This place is seriously creepy," Danni said, looking around the room like a soldier on a secret mission searching for the enemy.

"Don't be so melodramatic."

Shattering glass jolted them from their conversation.

"What was that?" Danni asked, her voice trembling.

Sarah shrugged, her knees quivering as she stepped toward the section of the room where the sound originated.

The bulb dangling from the ceiling sprinkled slivers of light across the floor where a large oval frame lay face down in a puddle of glass shards at the base of the opposite wall. Walking over, Sarah lifted the frame. The portrait of a gentleman with a neatly trimmed beard, dark hair slicked away from his face, and a forlorn expression clouding his brown eyes stared back at her.

"Handsome fellow," Danni said, studying the image.

"Looks a lot like Frederick." Sarah replied, checking the back of the frame and the wall to determine how it had fallen. "The hook is secure and the wire is intact."

"Let me guess, it didn't like where it was hanging and threw itself onto the floor," Danni smirked.

"Well, there's no *logical* explanation for it to fall."

"You think the ghost did this?"

"Do you have a better reason?"

"At this point I can't explain anything except that you have some sort of bizarre connection with the dead," Danni said, running her hands through her hair.

Sarah hugged Danni. "Thanks for believing in me."

"What are best friends for if not to slide down the rabbit hole of insanity with them?"

"I'll clean this up tomorrow. It's not like anyone will be walking around up here, at least not anyone who could be injured by broken glass."

"Ha, good one," Danni said, hurrying for the door.

"Before we leave, I want to look in the trunk once more."

"Haven't you gone through that already?" Danni whined, her shoulders slumping.

"I've been trying to clear this place out and the trunk is bigger than you think. There are still some things I haven't pulled out yet."

Sarah knelt before the chest, opened the lid, and dug around. Wrapped in tissue was a petite volume with *journal* imprinted in gilt. Danni peered over Sarah's shoulder as she opened the front cover and paged through.

"What is that?" Danni asked, squinting. "It looks like a diary for a gnome."

"It appears to be Nora's rose journal."

"How many diaries did that woman have?"

"This isn't her personal diary, it's a journal to record garden work. Nora received numerous accolades for her rose cultivation. These are her personal notes about the growth and care of her prized roses." Sarah skimmed through a few notations and exhaled. "People would pay a small fortune to get information like this. The Monroe roses are considered heirlooms and still highly sought after."

"I forgot you're into all that gardening stuff. I don't suppose there's anything in that journal that would explain Nora's disappearance?"

Sarah flipped to the last entry. "The last date in this journal is July 29th the same day she vanished."

"If she was going to run away, why would she make notations about her roses on the day she planned on leaving?"

"To make it look like she was going about her daily business so no one would question her behavior? Think about it. She had to be a nervous wreck and was probably trying to appear as normal as possible."

"I still think Charles was up to no good."

"I know the evidence looks that way but in my dreams he seems completely enamored with her. I don't think he would have hurt her," Sarah said, pursing her lips.

"But he killed her parents."

"There's no proof of that, only speculation."

"There's no evidence because he robbed the house and ran away before the police could question him! Why do you keep defending him?" Danni asked, planting her hands on her hips.

"I don't know, something tells me he's innocent."

"Well until we find evidence otherwise, he looks pretty guilty to me."

Sarah yawned. "Maybe I'll dream about something that will confirm or deny his guilt."

"Let's hope so," Danni replied, rubbing her eyes. "I'm going to read more of the *Dreamist* book before I go to sleep. Maybe if we can strengthen your abilities we can finally get this mystery solved.

"Let's hope so," Sarah replied. "I'm exhausted. Think I'll turn in too."

Sarah followed Danni, turning off the attic light and closing the door behind her. When they reached the hall, Sarah stopped Danni.

"I really appreciate all your help with this."

"It's pretty fascinating stuff, even if it is a bit scary at times," Danni replied.

"Glad you think so," Sarah said, scrunching her lips.

"You can't tell me you're not enjoying some of it."

"I'm relieved to learn I'm not crazy and that I have some sort of gift. Maybe I'll enjoy it more once I get a better understanding of it."

They bid goodnight and headed to their respective rooms. Sarah placed the rose journal on the night table, slipped on her nightshirt, climbed into bed, and promptly drifted off to sleep.

31

Nora sat on the nursery floor playing with Bitsy when Frederick entered.

"My dearest, shall we go out on the trails after lunch?"

Nervous about seeing Charles, Nora scrambled for an excuse to avoid the barn.

"I have work to do in the garden. The state competition is next month and I fear I'm not well prepared."

"Darling, is everything alright? You've not been yourself lately."

"I apologize for causing any worry. The upcoming rose competition has weighed heavily on my mind."

His eyes glimmered as he knelt beside her, reaching over to tickle Bitsy's chubby feet as they kicked the air.

"I wish you'd reconsider and take a break. It would do you good."

"I'd love to, but I really must log the roses' growth in my journal," Nora said, her heart weighted by deceit.

"Perhaps another day," he said, kissing her cheek before leaving the room.

Guilt squeezed Nora's chest. How could she be so selfish? A couple of hours wouldn't have hindered her work; then again, gardening wasn't the true reason for avoiding the stables.

Bitsy cooed, distracting Nora from her thoughts. She jangled a rattle above her daughter's head watching the baby's eyes twinkle with glee. When a yawn curled Bitsy's rosy lips, Nora lifted the precious bundle and gently placed her in the bassinet before kissing her daughter's forehead and crossing the hall to her room.

She sat at her desk enjoying the breeze that shuttered through the lace curtains. Opening the small journal, she paged through it, scripting notations about recent buds and weather conditions. The quietude was shattered when Bitsy's cries summoned Nora back across the hall.

"My darling girl, what's the matter?" Nora murmured to the chubby cheeked cherub as she scooped her from the bassinet. Beguiled, Nora gazed upon her daughter's toothless smile as her tiny fisted hands batted the air. Nothing could ever hold her heart like her dear daughter did. Unbeknownst to her, Frederick stood in the doorway, taking in the splendor of the heartwarming scene, seemingly content in the knowledge that all was well with his precious family.

Without warning the dream altered.

Frederick walked along the cobblestone streets beneath afternoon's golden rays, to the offices of Devereaux and Greene. An impressive building of tabby and brick, it exuded the judicial character its proprietors wished to display. The jingling of a brass bell welcomed Frederick as he opened the heavy oak door where a young man in his twenties sat at a slant top desk.

"Good day, Mr. Hamilton. How may I be of service?"

"I'd like to speak with Mr. Devereaux."

"I'll tell him you're waiting, sir."

The clerk disappeared through the glass-paneled door behind his desk. Moments later, a rotund gentleman wearing a dark frock coat, striped ascot, and hounds tooth trousers emerged, a smile elevating his chubby cheeks. With a hearty greeting, he extended his hand.

"Frederick, my good man, always a pleasure to see you. Terribly sorry to hear about your wife. Still no word on her whereabouts?"

Returning the handshake, Frederick replied, "Noting yet. Please forgive the intrusion, but I have some pressing business to discuss."

"Of course. Follow me."

The two men stepped into the office and closed the door. Once beyond earshot of the clerk, Mr. Devereaux chided, "Are you mad? How dare you come to my office?"

"For goodness sake, Dixon, calm down. Trust me, meeting publicly will arouse less suspicion than if we were caught skulking around. No one will suspect a thing."

"Very well," he grumbled. "What do you want?"

"I've thought extensively about what we discussed the other day and wish to go forward with our plan. But I need assurance that you will employ someone who is discreet and will not share this *endeavor* with another living soul. Have you such a person?"

"Indeed I do, but he will come at a handsome price. Are you sure you want to do this? It isn't too late to change your mind."

"I've never been more certain of anything. No one makes a fool of me and gets away with it. He must pay for what he's done," Frederick growled, the muscles in his cheeks tightening.

The dreamscape altered to another place and time with Frederick summoning Reynolds to his office.

"Mr. Hamilton, you called for me?"

"Yes, Reynolds. I need you to deliver this note to the police chief."

"Has something happened, sir?"

"Actually, Reynolds, we've been robbed. My wife's jewels are missing as well as a small amount of cash from my desk drawer. I need Captain McClure's assistance immediately."

"Of course, sir," Reynolds replied with a bow as he left the room.

Frederick rubbed his temples. The stress of his wife's disappearance followed by the death of his in-laws and now having to report a robbery weighed heavily on his psyche.

Days later, headlines circulated news of the robbery leading to rumors and theories behind the crimes and the short period of time in which they had transpired. Many began to suspect that Frederick was cursed.

Sarah shifted, rubbed her eyes, and glanced at the clock. *Ugh*, she thought, *only two in the morning.*

"Go back to sleep," she muttered, rolling over and promptly resuming her slumber.

Frederick sat at his desk, holding a leather-embossed case with a portrait of Nora in her wedding gown. A forlorn expression exposed the pain over his wife's inexplicable departure. With the unexpected deaths of Mr. and Mrs. Monroe, in addition to the police investigation, Frederick could barely function. If it hadn't been for his precious daughter he was certain he'd lose his mind beneath the strain of it all. Bitsy was his only saving grace. But was she enough to prevent him from seeking the revenge he so fervently desired? If only he could erase all of the pain and distress of the past few weeks. His ruminations were interrupted when Reynolds walked into the room.

"Mr. Hamilton, the work is complete. Would you care to inspect it?"

With a nod, Frederick placed the photo in the top drawer of his desk and followed the footman to the second floor. Frederick stepped into the elongated room where he'd danced a waltz with his true love on their wedding day. This was the room where Nora played piano while he read and the room where all the family celebrations took place. It was also the room with the most memories and that caused the most heartache. He scanned the freshly plastered wall that now concealed the hearth.

"Does it meet your approval, sir?"

"This is quite nice," he said, running his hand across the smooth surface. "Please extend my gratitude to the workmen for their diligence."

"Of course, sir. They'll return tomorrow to paper over the plasterwork."

"Thank you, Reynolds, for your discretion in this matter. Your loyalty is appreciated and will be amply rewarded, I assure you."

32

Sarah jolted awake stunned by the recent images in her dreams. There was something familiar about the building where Frederick met with Dixon. All of a sudden, a chill ran down her spine. She knew the building. It was noticeably different now since all of the interior rooms had been reconfigured. However, there was no doubt it was the same building that currently housed Raven Booksellers. A shiver rattled her body when she realized the two men she'd seen in the corner when she'd dropped off the box of books a few days before were Frederick Hamilton and Dixon Devereaux.

It seemed like her visions were becoming more intense and oddly involved the perspectives of more than just Nora. Sarah made a few notations on a pad of paper by the bed so she could remember as much as possible when she discussed it with Danni.

One thing was abundantly clear; Frederick's sorrow in the dream was palpable. His wife had disappeared, his in-laws were dead, and his home had been robbed. To complicate matters, he was left to raise his daughter alone. Despite the turmoil swirling around him, it seemed his dedication to finding his wife was steadfast. Yet, his need to wall away the fireplace in the ballroom remained a mystery. It was an extreme measure, but then again, he'd been through a landslide of bad luck.

Sarah rushed to the bathroom and prepared for the day, relieved when nothing otherworldly steamed the mirror or appeared in its reflection. Meandering down the hall she peeked into the ballroom, realizing what had bothered her about the space all along. There was no fireplace. She walked across the room and ran her hand over the faded wallpaper, snapping it back when her fingers brushed against an indentation. Her lungs constricted as she slowly raised her hand and slid it along the wall finding more grooves and imperfections.

"Why did you wall away the fireplace, Frederick?" Sarah whispered, pondering the reason for such a drastic and strange act. She stood there staring at the wall when an idea popped into her head.

Sarah bolted down the stairs into the kitchen to update Danni on the latest information. When she walked in the lights were off and there was no sign of her best friend. Her shoulders slumped when she saw a note taped to the fridge. She pulled it off and read Danni's sloppy script.

COULDN'T SLEEP SO GOT an early start. I'm going to stop by the office and then go to the library to search for any supplemental research related to the Dreamist book. See you later.

SARAH CONTEMPLATED CALLING Danni but decided to let her get some of her own work done before Anita arrived and clients started calling. She'd already monopolized much of her friend's time with this haunted mess and wanted to give her a break.

Grabbing a power bar, Sarah skipped her morning tea and went to the dining room to look through some of the paperwork hoping something might correlate with the new information from her dreams.

Paging through the ledger, Sarah was struck by something Danni had said. With practice Sarah would be able to gain perspective to more than one entity through her dreams. Frederick's feelings were definitely more prominent than before, but why?

Unable to contain her curiosity, Sarah dialed Danni's number.

"Hey, what's up?" Danni asked, sounding chipper letting Sarah know she was probably on her second cup of coffee.

"Wanted to talk to you about the *Dreamist* book, specifically having access to multiple perspectives."

"I read more about it last night. I need to do a few more things here and then I can stop by before I go to the library."

"Sounds great. By the way, could you pick up a few tools on your way and bring them over?"

"What sort of tools?"

"The kind to strip wallpaper. And maybe a sledgehammer."

"You need a sledgehammer to take down wallpaper?"

"I'll explain everything when you get here."

"This oughta be good. I'll be there as soon as I can," Danni said before hanging up.

Too antsy to work, Sarah decided to visit Miss Dottie. Maybe she could shed some light on the spirits residing in the mansion.

Sarah shoved the cell phone in her pocket, headed out the front door, and across the street, making her way down the alley behind the condos. There was no mistaking Dottie MacDougall's residence. Nestled amid a concrete jungle of parking spaces and garbage cans, was a virtual Eden. Miss Dottie had mentioned her parking lot garden during their conversation when she'd brought the apple muffins, and there it was in all its glory.

A bistro table took center stage surrounded by potted hydrangeas, hibiscus, and small fruit trees. Raised flower beds hosted a menagerie of foliage and carefully manicured boxwoods. Statuary of an angel and other woodland critters kept vigil amongst the plantings, while the trickling of a two-tiered fountain saturated the atmosphere in tranquility. Hedged by parked cars, the landscape was a conspicuous sight.

Sarah stepped through the white picket gate, up the back stairs, and knocked on the bright red screen door. Miss Dottie appeared, her snow-white hair neatly contained by a plastic headband.

"Hello, Miss Dottie. I hope you don't mind the intrusion, but I thought I'd come by for a visit."

"It's not an intrusion! I'm always happy to have visitors." Hospitality percolated in her smile. "Give me a moment, and I'll join you," she replied, her melodious Lowcountry accent tinting her words.

She disappeared into the kitchen while Sarah took a seat at the bistro table. Moments later, Miss Dottie emerged carrying a round tray with a carafe of orange juice and two glasses. Sitting across from Sarah, she poured juice into the cut crystal goblets, and handed one to her guest.

"Thank you." Sarah took a drink and nearly spit it out.

"Oh my, you do drink mimosas, don't you? If not, I can start some water for tea."

"It's very good, I just wasn't expecting alcohol this early," Sarah choked, wiping the juice from her chin.

"My dear child, this is the South. You know libations are always acceptable, regardless of the hour."

Sarah chuckled at her statement. Miss Dottie was a true southerner and fast becoming a favorite.

"Have you accomplished much at the mansion?"

"Actually, I have a lot to do but I needed a break and decided to take you up on your offer to visit," Sarah said.

"I'm delighted. Most young people aren't interested in spending time with an old woman."

"Do you have family close by?"

"Gracious no, it was only me and my husband, Alfred. He's been gone nearly thirty years now." A wave of nostalgia sailed across the sea of memories in her blue eyes. "What about you? Any gentlemen friends?"

"I'm too busy," Sarah replied, a blush coloring her cheeks.

"You're young and have plenty of time," she said, patting Sarah's hand.

Sarah hesitated, contemplating how to pose her questions without seeming too intrusive.

"Miss Dottie, how well did you know Edie Monroe?"

"She was a dear friend. We spent many afternoons here in the garden reminiscing about the good old days. Edie was an amiable soul."

"Did she ever mention anything about ghosts in the house?"

Miss Dottie raised an eyebrow. "Yes, she did. Poor thing had a terrible time sleeping. She'd hear all sorts of strange sounds in the middle of the night, not to mention the terrible nightmares. She'd swear she could hear spirits whispering inside her head."

"Did she say anything more specific?"

"Not really. I told her she had an overactive imagination and that old houses often made noises. People 'round here claim that ghosts exist, but I don't believe in such things. Edie was always reading about hauntings and such. Those kind of books put ideas in your head. I remember when she brought in a psychic hoping for some answers."

"Did she get any?"

"Heavens no. Only thing that woman did was burn some

incense, mutter a few phrases, and take Edie's money," Miss Dottie scoffed, shaking her head.

"Can you remember if she mentioned anything else about the spirits?"

"As I said, it's usually the sign of an overactive imagination. I told her to take a nip of bourbon before bed to help her sleep."

"So, most of the activity took place at night?"

"Every once in a while, she'd talk about shadows during the day or thumping in the attic, but most things happened after dark. She tried drinking some of her rose tea to relax before bed, but that seemed to make the nightmares worse." Miss Dottie took another sip of her drink before continuing. "I always got the feeling she'd been plagued by these nightmares throughout her life. Her only means of solace seemed to be cultivating her roses."

Miss Dottie placed her glass on the table and leaned forward, worry wrinkling her brow.

"Why're you asking about ghosts? Are you having problems over there?"

"I heard stories about the place being haunted and was curious," Sarah shrugged, still uncomfortable sharing her experiences, especially with someone she barely knew who didn't believe in ghosts.

"Like I said, it's probably your imagination playing tricks on you. Once the mind latches on to the idea of hauntings all of a sudden every noise and creak is a ghost." Miss Dottie chuckled.

"What about Edie's family, do you know anything about them?"

"Not really, Edie didn't like to speak about unpleasant things, particularly when it involved her family. They had a strained relationship."

"How so?"

"All I know is she hardly spoke with her parents when she returned to town after spending a year abroad. That was right after her high school graduation. Come to think of it, I don't recall her ever speaking about her childhood. Went so far as to change her name from Hanover to Monroe as a final insult to her father. Said the Monroe name represented the last time the family had any dignity. She never gave a reason for the rift with her parents and I didn't pry. Of course, her father's reputation for indulging heavily in the bottle didn't help matters."

Miss Dottie reached for the carafe as Sarah emptied her glass. "Would you like a refill?"

"I should get back to work. Thanks for the drink, and the conversation."

"You're welcome to stop by any time you feel like chattin'."

"I'd enjoy that."

Sarah started for the mansion as Miss Dottie stood to speak with a neighbor walking past with a small scruffy dog.

Sarah crossed the street, contemplating Edie's family history and the estrangement from her parents. It's no wonder she was always drunk. Oddly, Sarah hadn't thought about the fact that Edie's last name was Monroe. She'd assumed Edie used the name due to its prominence in the area. She never imagined it was due to a family squabble. It must have been one heck of a falling out for her to legally change her name.

For the next two hours Sarah cleaned, organized, and cataloged the attic all the while pondering what had caused Edie to disown her parents and alter her last name. Lost in her work, Sarah jumped when the phone bellowed from her pocket. She tapped the green button. "Hey Danni."

"On my way over."

"Did you get the tools?"

"Yup."

A short time later, Danni arrived with a tool bag in one hand and a sledgehammer in the other.

"So, tell me why you need a sledgehammer?" she asked,

plunking the tool bag on the table and leaning the sledge-hammer against a chair.

"You'll see." Sarah grabbed the bag of tools and the sledge-hammer and scrambled up the stairs with Danni trudging close behind.

When they reached the ballroom, Danni looked around. "How does a sledgehammer come into play for wallpaper removal?"

"I'm not taking down the wallpaper, I'm taking down the wall. Well, part of it." A mischievous grin spread across Sarah's face.

"You're going to demo a wall on the offset chance of?"

"I believe there's a fireplace behind it," Sarah said, reaching for the sledgehammer and scanning the wall for a starting point.

"Wait a minute. You want to tear down a wall because there *might* be a fireplace behind it?" Danni asked, her eyebrows arching.

Sarah looked at her friend and quipped, "Not just a fire-place, a fireplace with a secret."

"Have you lost your mind? You could get sued for tearing the place up! And all because you want to find out if there's a secret fireplace?" Danni's voice rose with each declaration.

"Danni, I know what I'm doing." Sarah ran her hand along the surface until she found the indentation below the peeling wallpaper and swung the sledgehammer over her shoulder. Danni grabbed her arm.

"I can't let you do this! What do you hope to gain from it?"

"The truth." Sarah wrenched her arm free and swung with all her might. The iron head slammed into the wall leaving a gaping hole. After a few more blows, she choked through the cloud of dust and began ripping off chunks of plaster as Danni watched.

Sarah picked up the sledgehammer and with one final

thwack, left a significant void. Danni joined Sarah yanking chunks of wood from the opening, widening the opening. As the dust dissipated, the top of an ornately plastered mantel appeared.

"How did you know this was here?" Danni murmured.

"I dreamt it."

"You just vandalized a house because of a dream? What if you'd been wrong?" Danni was nearly shouting.

"The dreams haven't been wrong yet."

Danni pursed her lips. "That's not the point."

Sarah raised the sledgehammer once again, when Danni stopped her. "Obviously, something significant happened in your dreams. Before you do any more damage I want you to tell me everything."

Sarah leaned the sledgehammer against the wall. "Fine. Let's go to the kitchen. I need a cup of tea."

"I'm going to need something stronger than tea." Danni grumbled, following Sarah downstairs.

"OK, tell me what's going on," Danni said, plunking into the chair as Sarah started the kettle.

"You said something the other day about dreamists being able to sense the feelings of more than one ghost. Tell me more about that."

"Not sure I can at this point. I'm still trying to decode the meaning. That blasted book reads like instructions for hooking up a TV, VCR, and gaming system. It's anything but clear," Danni said, rubbing her eyes with the palms of her hands. "So what did you dream about?"

"Last night I dreamt about Nora with the baby and then about Frederick. It was strange because it's the first time I've sensed his feelings although they're not as strong as what I get from Nora."

"From what I've read so far, there's a way to connect with a spirit by touching an item he or she handled in the past. Maybe when you went through the ledger it opened up your dreams to Frederick's perspective."

Sarah sighed as she poured hot water into a mug and sat at the table. "I realize this gives me more perspective but it's a bit overwhelming right now, especially with the new deadline and trying to piece together this mystery."

"Don't think of it as being more complicated, but as growth in your skills. We need to hone in on this and strengthen your abilities. You have to admit things haven't been as frightening lately."

Sarah shrugged. "You've got a point. All the same, I feel like I'm back in college trying to cram for a final exam."

"How did you get through college with all this haunted stuff? The dorms were like a million years old. There had to be some serious ghost activity hovering around," Danni said, grabbing a soda from the fridge. She sat back down, popped the top, and took a long swig.

"It was terrible! I can't tell you how many nights I lost sleep because of the nightmares or a shadow floating through the room. Thank goodness my parents paid extra for me to have a private room. There's no way I could have had a roommate." Sarah bobbed the tea bag in the cup waiting for the water to cool a bit.

"How did you pull that off? Your parents have always been so frugal."

"Convinced them that I needed complete quiet to study and that I was afraid I might end up with a roommate who partied. Dad wasn't about to risk losing tuition money because I couldn't maintain my grades." Sarah sipped her tea.

"That was pretty clever. I'm surprised you did so well without sleep," Danni chuckled.

"I went to the infirmary and asked for sleeping pills. Took them when the dreams got bad," Sarah said, staring at her cup.

"Sadly, the pills made me groggy during the day so I had to stop taking them."

"Wow, the dreams must have been rough for you to take drugs." Danni rubbed her forehead. "At least now we have a manual to guide you through this process."

Sarah nodded. "It's still mind-boggling. I feel like I'm catapulting from a plane without a parachute.

"That's because it's new. Once you perfect your skills things will get better."

Sarah inhaled deeply hoping her best friend was right and that a normal existence was somewhere in her future.

"So, tell me more about the dreams last night."

Sarah filled Danni in on Nora with Bitsy and then the meeting between Reynolds and Frederick after the fireplace in the ballroom had been walled up.

"It was the strangest thing," Sarah said, shaking her head. "I mean, why board up a fireplace?"

"Maybe there was something wrong with the chimney and he was trying to keep out a draft, or *critters*," Danni grimaced.

Sarah snickered. "Your irrational fear of wildlife astounds me. You'll fight for environmental protections but the idea of a squirrel sends you scurrying in the opposite direction."

"Ick. Squirrels are rats with bushy tails," Danni mumbled, her upper lip wrinkling.

"Aunt Millie had a squirrel named Dinky when I was growing up. He'd fallen out of his nest so she nursed him and then kept him as a pet. She had to disconnect her doorbell because the ringing sent him scurrying through the house knocking everything over as he flew to the back room."

Danni smirked. "A flying rat as a pet. Don't think so."

"He was cute," she said, taking a sip of tea. "Anyway, the next part of the dream was shocking. Frederick paid a visit to a man by the name of Dixon Devereaux."

"As in the same family from which our favorite little toadstool was spawned?"

"Probably, since I felt like I needed a shower after the dream. I think all the Devereaux' are related somehow. If this guy's physique is hereditary, William has a rather sprawling middle in his future," Sarah giggled with a sly smile.

"What sort of business did they have?"

"Not sure but Frederick made some sort of deal with him."

"And they didn't divulge the nature of their transaction?"

"No, but it seemed seedy. Hopefully, the reason will be revealed in my dreams tonight. Until then, we need to keep searching for clues."

"Shouldn't you be working on the inventory?"

Sarah shrugged. "Don't worry, I'll get it done somehow."

Danni checked her watch. "I'm going to the library. I'll see if I can figure out the connection between Dixon Devereaux and William's family and then I'll look for more information about the Monroes."

"I'm going to do some more work in the attic. I'm making progress with the inventory up there."

"I'll bring supper later. Holler if you need anything before then," Danni said hurrying out the back door.

Sipping her tea, Sarah paged through her ledger double-checking her figures. The potential sales were substantial making her stomach flutter. If she could finish the inventory, solve the mystery behind Nora's disappearance, and hone her dreamist skills perhaps she'd finally be able to relax for the first time in her life.

33

Sarah gazed out the kitchen window at a kaleidoscope of blooms as she washed her teacup. Colorful petals in shades of pink, red, and coral monopolized the rose bushes as squirrels scampered about to a symphony of birdsong.

Lost in the moment, Sarah didn't notice the front door opening and closing or William's presence behind her until he tapped her shoulder. Alarmed, Sarah dropped the cup in the sink, her fist poised in the air as she spun around.

"William, you sleazy jerk! What're you doing here?" she hollered, lowering her arm.

"Calm down," he said with his hands in the air. "I'm supposed to take pictures for the listing, remember?"

"Yeah, I remember. Hurry up and take your pictures, then get out. I don't have time for this." Sarah walked away shocked by her own rudeness.

"Sarah, are you OK? You don't seem like yourself." William's demeanor shifted to concern, something Sarah had never experienced in all the years she'd known him. For a moment she softened.

"I'm just a bit stressed. Go ahead and take your photos."

She dashed to the dining room hoping to clear the table before William noticed all the paperwork littering its surface. No doubt he'd question why she was investing so much time in an age-old mystery instead of doing inventory.

She grabbed a box from the closet and began placing the memorabilia and photocopies inside when an ear-shattering howl came from the second floor. Dropping the box, Sarah ran up the stairs, her heart pounding. When she reached the second-floor landing, she found William in the doorway of the ballroom staring at the battered mess with his mouth gaping open.

"What the heck have you done? You're supposed to clear the place out, not demo walls!" His voice raised an octave with each declaration.

Sarah fought the impulse to laugh. After all these years, she'd found something to drive William to the brink of insanity, and she was enjoying it.

"Is there a problem?" she asked in a lilting voice.

His face flushed as his words seeped through gritted teeth. "You idiot! This is going to cost a fortune to repair and I'm not paying for it! You had no right to do this!"

"I'm sorry, but I don't recall anything in the contract stating I couldn't take down a wall or two in search of inventory." Her taunting pushed him over the edge.

"Don't pull that crap with me!" he yelled.

Anger flooded his face turning it a dark shade of crimson as he lunged at her with both hands. Sarah braced for the impact, panic turning her muscles into cement. But before he could reach her, William flew backward, slammed against the wall, and landed with a thud. The strong scent of Chanel No. 5 permeated the air.

Rising slowly, William straightened his jacket.

"What just happened?" he exclaimed, the color draining from his face as his eyes darted around the room.

Sarah shrugged her shoulders and bit her lower lip, trying to hide her amusement at his bewilderment.

Her resolve seemed to rekindle William's anger. He stepped closer, fury simmering in his eyes as he growled, "This isn't over. My agency will be in touch!"

"I'm sorry, but I'll be too busy with the new deadline to take any calls so you'll have to speak with my attorney. I believe you already have Danni's number."

He stormed down the stairs with his fists clenched, the floor shaking as the front door slammed shut. Still puzzled by what she'd witnessed, Sarah knew it was Edie who'd intervened.

"Thanks, Edie," she mumbled. Sarah dialed Danni's number and left a voice mail warning her about William's probable tirade before returning to her work.

Hours later, snippets of light crept across the dusty attic floors as the sun shifted in the sky. A mountain of crumbling magazines, outdated clothing, record albums, and cases of Christmas ornaments were stacked at the doorway, destined for the Blue Moon thrift shop.

Sarah needed a break and decided to search Nora's trunk again. Digging through old newspaper clippings, many praising Nora's continued success at state rose competitions, Sarah found a neatly folded piece of yellowed parchment. She unfurled the paper to discover a silky dark curl bound with a pink ribbon. On the inside of the paper was written, "Lock of my darling Bitsy's hair."

The heartfelt words contradicted much of what Sarah had believed about Nora's inexplicable departure. It seemed unlikely she would have abandoned her daughter, even for her beloved Charles.

"Where did you end up, Nora?" Sarah whispered, tensing as if a voice from beyond would issue a response. When silence ensued, Sarah refolded the paper, convinced Nora wouldn't have left Bitsy. Then again, the term 'postpartum depression' was unheard of in those days. Maybe Nora reacted to a hormonal imbalance. One thing was certain, once she'd run away, she couldn't return with the disgrace surrounding her disappearance. Perhaps that's why she never came home.

Sarah pondered what Frederick might have told Bitsy about her mother's absence. If Danni and everybody else believed she ran off to avoid the drudgery of motherhood, surely, he did too.

Then again, if her dreams held any merit, he was devoted to his wife and determined to protect her. Sarah's gut churned. What if Danni was right and Charles had done something terrible to Nora? The idea was beginning to seem plausible. Nora disappeared shortly before Charles who was suspected of causing her parents' deaths and robbing the mansion. While Nora's feelings wavered between Frederick and Charles, her devotion to her daughter was steadfast. No matter what the evidence suggested, Sarah didn't want to believe Charles was a cold-blooded murderer.

Frustrated that she hadn't uncovered anything new, Sarah headed to her room to clean up before Danni arrived. As evening tide rolled in, Sarah sat at the kitchen table making entries in her ledger, pleased with her progress despite her demolition duties earlier in the day and her bizarre encounter with William. She smiled when the back door opened and Danni stepped inside.

"Hey! I brought wraps from the Speckled Goose. You hungry?

"Actually, I am."

Sarah closed the ledger and grabbed plates and silverware

while Danni poured the wine. Sarah salivated as she removed the paper from one of her favorite meals, a veggie wrap with humus and a side of bacon broccoli salad. Taking a bite, she closed her eyes savoring the sautéed veggies and homemade humus.

Danni took a long sip of wine. "Heard you had a visitor today."

"Did William call you?"

"Oh yeah. He was livid, rambling on about lawsuits and other nonsense. I let him carry on for a while before I hung up. Who'd have thought the little nitwit could be so temperamental?"

"That's not the half of it. I heard him holler while I was in the dining room. When I got upstairs, he was standing there like a lunatic staring at the hole in the wall. He was so angry he came at me. Then all of a sudden he flew backward. I'm not sure who was more stunned, him or me."

Danni was about to take a bite of her wrap but placed it on the plate instead. "What are you saying?"

"Edie shoved him before he got to me. I wouldn't have believed it if I hadn't seen it with my own eyes."

"You're saying Edie's ghost pushed William against the wall?"

"That's what I'm saying."

"What makes you think it was Edie?"

"Her perfume. Remember, I've smelled Chanel No. 5 ever since I saw Edie's ghost in the shop that day."

"Why would Edie defend you? It's not like you two were friends when she was alive."

"I know it sounds crazy, but maybe she likes me and wants me to finish the estate."

"At this point, nothing sounds crazy," Danni said, shaking her head.

"Nonetheless, I need to get this house cleared. I have less

than a week thanks to William's uncle and I'm not about to walk away from a fortune."

"Is it really going to bring that much?" Danni asked.

Sarah reached for her ledger and paged through it. "So far, I have an estimated $3.1 million in furnishings, $1.2 million in art and porcelains, and about ten thousand in silver. That's just the auction inventory. Then there's the stuff I'll put in my shop and consign to local dealers. The percentage I'll get from everything is substantial."

"Phew, that's a lot. No wonder so many auction companies wanted it. And when you're done with this, you can add ghost hunter to your résumé."

"No thanks. I'll stick to the antiques and estate business. This ghost stuff is too stressful."

"How close are you to finishing the inventory?"

"Closer than you'd think but I'll be working until the last minute to finish."

For a few minutes, they ate in silence when Sarah brought up Nora's disappearance. "I was going through the trunk earlier and found a lock of Bitsy's hair."

"And?"

"I'm starting to question the theory that Nora ran away with Charles. Everything suggests she was devoted to her daughter."

"So now you think Charles may have done something terrible to her?"

"Yeah," Sarah's shoulders slumped, disappointed that he may turn out to be a jerk.

"Makes sense that he'd be guilty considering everything you've dreamed about and all the articles we've found," Danni replied, taking a bite of her wrap.

"I'm still bummed about it. It's like reading a murder mystery and finding out your favorite character was the bad guy." Sarah took a sip of wine. "Did you find anything today?"

"Yup. Turns out Dixon Devereaux was William's great-great uncle. Apparently being despicable runs in the genes."

Sarah snickered. "Maybe we'll find out Charles was part of the Devereaux line."

At that moment, a loud crash emanated from the entryway.

"What was that?" Danni muttered, her eyes as wide as quarters.

Sarah shook her head. Inhaling deeply, she got up and treaded down the hall with Danni close behind as the air around them cooled. On the floor across from the stairs was the old oil lamp in a jumble of glass shards, sparkling in the luminescence of the chandelier.

"How did the lamp get to the other side of the hallway?" Danni asked, her voice shaking.

"I don't know." Transfixed on the shattered remnants, Sarah wondered out loud, "How did it get unplugged?"

"That's what you got from this? How'd it get unplugged? What about the fact the blasted thing smashed against a wall several feet away?" Danni's voice grew louder and louder as she flung her hands in the air. "Maybe the plug popped out of the socket when the lamp threw itself across the room!"

"Calm down, Danni."

"I'm beyond calm! This was interesting in the beginning but now it's getting dangerous." Danni rubbed the back of her neck. "Might as well clean this up. Where's the broom and dustpan? And don't tell me a witch flew off with it in the middle of the night!"

Sarah sensed the strange occurrences were beginning to drive Danni to the brink of her sanity.

"In the kitchen pantry. Relax, once you get used to this, you won't feel as demented."

"Maybe for you. You've had a lifetime to adjust but for us mere mortals it's unnerving when spirits throw things!" Danni stomped to the kitchen, obviously irritated by the madness unfolding around her.

Sarah approached the area searching for a logical explanation for the lamp's sudden ejection from the top of the chest. The lamp had flashed a lot over the past several nights. Perhaps there was a short, which rocketed it across the room. Electricity could do strange things.

Moving the chest a few inches from the wall, Sarah checked the light socket for burns. A litter of dust bunnies converged along the baseboards, in addition to a ballpoint pen, a couple of paper clips, and a rubber band.

Danni returned with the broom and began sweeping up the mess.

"Danni, there has to be a sensible explanation for this."

"You really think so?" Danni leaned against the top of the broom handle. "You've been dealing with this haunted stuff your entire life but I'm still new to it all. And now you have objects flinging themselves against walls and a book with directions on how to communicate with the dead. Does logic ring true in any of it?" Danni huffed as she resumed sweeping.

"I can't explain it either. All I can say is something in this house is trying to reveal its secrets. We just have to open our minds to it."

"How can you be so calm?"

"Because I've been grappling with this since childhood and for the first time in my life I'm not alone and I want to understand it!" Tears stung the back of Sarah's eyes. She was addled by everything that was happening. Part of her wanted answers while the other part wanted to finish up with the estate and leave.

Shaking her head, Danni stood there. "I get that this is difficult for you and I want to be supportive but sometimes it's a bit more than I can handle. Give me time to adjust so I can help you through it." She turned on her heel and carried the dustpan of broken glass to the kitchen.

Sarah exhaled. Now more than ever she needed to be patient with Danni. She knew her best friend was having a difficult time adjusting to the bizarre nature of haunted dreams and ghosts but at least she was still here and hadn't abandoned her like her so-called friends from middle school.

Sarah started to push the chest back against the wall when something underneath caught her attention. She reached down and retrieved a small envelope that was stuck in the crevice of the baseboard. Carefully, she plied it open and pulled out a note, her fingers numbing as a chill raced up her arm.

"What are you looking at?" Danni asked, walking up behind her.

"It appears to be a note from Nora."

"Maybe Nora knocked the lamp off when she was hiding it," Danni snorted.

"Oh my gosh, that's it!"

"Seriously? You think a ghost stashed a note and then threw a lamp across the room to get your attention?"

"Have you got a better explanation?"

Danni rolled her eyes. "What does it say?"

Sarah stepped under the chandelier to read it.

MY DEAREST CHARLES,

I can deny my love for you no longer. You are etched on my heart and soul. Meet me at the river oak tomorrow to discuss our future. Somehow, I'll find a way to bring Bitsy with me when we leave.

Lovingly yours,
Nora

THE TWO LOOKED at each other, stunned by the composition.

"She did run off with him," Danni whispered.

"Then why not lead us to the note to begin with instead of sending us on a scavenger hunt for the past week?"

"Who knows? But this confirms she ran away with him."

"Except we know they didn't leave together."

"Maybe that was the plan. They left at separate times so she could take Bitsy with her."

"But she didn't take Bitsy." Sarah thought for a moment. "Perhaps they decided to settle somewhere first. Didn't you say Nora left a note for Frederick claiming she was overwhelmed by motherhood?"

"That's what the rumor mill says. I wish we could get hold of *that* letter."

"Well, it hasn't turned up yet and we're running out of time."

"Speaking of which, it's pretty late and I'm beat. Sorry for my reaction earlier. I'll try to hold it together from here on out."

"No need to apologize, I understand completely," Sarah said with a smile. "I'm tired too."

"Maybe your dreams will tell us where the good-bye note to Frederick is hidden. I'll read some more in the *Dreamist* book before bed. Hopefully it'll give us some guidance."

"I'll add this note to the stuff in the dining room."

Sarah padded to the dining room and plopped the note in the box with the rest of the information and climbed the stairs with Danni. They bid goodnight as Sarah went to her room and prepared for bed. After changing into her nightclothes she sat on the edge of the bed, her mind racing with possibilities about the note when she remembered the diary. That was it!

She hurried down to the dining room, grabbed the small diary, and returned to her room. She scanned the yellowed pages once more. Maybe she'd overlooked something seemingly inconsequential that might make sense now.

As she paged through the diary, a chill raced through her

body when she reread the entry dated a few days before Nora disappeared.

J ULY 25, 1900

I do not know how much longer I can live this lie. The misery is creating such tension between Frederick and me. I fear he senses something is awry and it breaks my heart to hurt him, but a lifetime of despair is more than anyone can tolerate. I'm plagued by my thoughts that drift from leaving to staying. I must find a way to escape this agony before I lose my nerve.

"I CAN'T BELIEVE THIS," Sarah mumbled. "This goes along with the note."

Sarah was tempted to wake Danni but thought better of it. They both needed to get some sleep. She switched off the lamp and closed her eyes hoping her dreams would reveal more answers.

34

———

Frederick sat at his desk composing a note. His hair was disheveled and dark circles eclipsed his eyes. He sat up, his shoulders and back pinched by the strain of the past few weeks. He placed the pen in its holder and ran his fingers through his unkempt hair. His mind drifted back to the previous night when he'd rambled down the upstairs hall in the shadow of darkness carrying a small candle.

He could still smell the stagnant air as he crept into the ballroom, where he made his way to the hearth, set the candle on the floor, and pulled a silk pouch from his jacket pocket. Tears had puddled in his eyes as he worked a loose brick from inside the hearth and placed the pouch within the brick tomb. Sliding the brick back in place, he brushed the soot from his knees, scooped up the candle, and left the room as stealthily as he'd entered. As he made his way to his quarters, darkness blinded him; then again, it may have been the tears. How could he go on without her? Nora was everything he'd dreamed of, the perfect wife and mother, and now he was alone. Well, not completely alone, he still had Bitsy.

Shaking the memory from his head, Frederick sat up at his

desk. He resumed his writing, the ink from the fountain pen staining his hand as it raced across the parchment. He opened the top drawer of the desk, reached inside, and opened a back panel. Withdrawing cash from the compartment, he counted out a large sum before wrapping it in the letter and sealing it in an envelope. For a moment, he considered the ramifications of the endeavor but dismissed his skepticism. His soul simmered with rage as he marched from the room determined to exact revenge on the man who had stolen his happiness.

"Reynolds," he called, adjusting his top hat.

The footman appeared with a bow. "Yes, sir."

"I'm going to town should anyone ask for me."

With a nod, Reynolds opened the front door as Frederick darted past.

His heart pounded with the force of a steel drum as he traversed the shaded streets of town to Mr. Devereaux' place of business, the clanging bell on the door announcing his arrival.

The office clerk looked up from his work.

"Good day, Mr. Hamilton. Mr. Devereaux is expecting you. Go right in."

Frederick removed his hat, entered the office, and took a seat in the tufted leather chair across from Devereaux' desk.

"Frederick, you look dreadful."

"I'm not here to discuss my appearance," he grumbled. "Let's get to the business at hand and be done with it."

"Have you got everything I need?"

Frederick pulled the envelope from the pocket of his frock coat and handed it to Devereaux.

"You give your word I'll not be implicated in this?"

"I assure you from this point forward, you've nothing to be concerned about." A devious smile crossed his portly face as he opened the envelope and counted the bills. "It's been a pleasure doing business with you. Feel free to return anytime you need assistance with your *legal endeavors*."

With a nod, Frederick replaced the hat on his head and rushed home. A knot formed in the pit of his stomach, partly with worry but mostly with indignation toward the lowly groom who had destroyed his life. Vengeance saturated his soul.

He slipped through the front door of the mansion and placed his top hat on the hall tree. A squeal of delight echoed from upstairs drawing him back to reality. His chest swelled at the sound of his daughter's voice. He strode up the stairs, peeking into the nursery where Bitsy played with one of her dolls.

"Mr. Hamilton, what a pleasant surprise. We weren't expecting you," Mrs. Stokes said, rising to greet him.

"I just returned from town when I heard the voice of my little angel." He scooped the child into his arms planting a kiss on her cheek. "How is my precious one?"

With wide-eyed joy, Bitsy giggled and grabbed at his tie. He gazed lovingly upon the curly-headed child, her complexion colored in delight.

"Would you like some privacy, Mr. Hamilton?"

"I only wanted to see my Bitsy for a moment." He kissed her forehead and put her down, watching as she toddled back to her doll. Frederick proceeded downstairs to his office and closed the door, worry infiltrating his soul.

Without warning, the scene altered.

Charles rushed through his cottage shoving things inside a satchel. With rumors circulating about his involvement with the Monroe's demise he realized his only hope was to run away. He'd already stayed longer than he should have and chided himself for being so foolish. Once Nora was gone he should have left.

Opening the top drawer of his dresser, he stared at the stack of letters from Nora. Anguish squeezed his chest as he reached for the treasured correspondence. He couldn't leave them behind. It would only fuel the speculation of nosey socialites and gossiping servants. This was one secret he'd take to his grave. He owed Nora that much. Stuffing the letters in his satchel, he slung the strap over his shoulder and started for the door. He had to get out of town before the police caught up with him. They weren't likely to take the word of a groom, no matter how convincing. They'd convict him based on his rank in society not the evidence, even if there was none to be found.

Blood pulsed through his veins making his limbs throb and his lungs constrict as he gave one last glance around his quarters. Nothing was left but shattered dreams and misunderstandings. His only hope was to get far away as quickly as possible. Charles opened the back door and snuck into the darkness leaving his heart and all his hopes behind.

The dream altered to another scene weeks later where Frederick stood at the gravesites of Mr. and Mrs. Monroe.

The pastor completed the closing prayers whilst the family stood on either side of Frederick in a wall of sympathetic support. When the service concluded, the crowd dispersed, the murmur of whispered condolences filling the air. Frederick stared at the freshly dug graves wondering what had gone wrong.

The pastor approached, resting his hand upon Frederick's shoulder.

"Mr. Hamilton, I realize you've been through a great deal these past weeks. Please know I'm at your service should you need spiritual comfort."

"Thank you, Reverend Wilson."

Gray skies misted the earth, making the circumstances seem grimmer. As the drizzle intensified, Frederick opened his umbrella and marched across the churchyard toward town. By the time he reached the offices of Devereaux and Greene, he was chilled and damp. He closed the umbrella and stepped inside.

"I need to speak with Mr. Devereaux. It's of the utmost importance."

"I'm sorry, sir, but Mr. Devereaux is out of the office. Would you like to schedule an appointment for tomorrow?" the young clerk asked.

"No, thank you."

Frederick exited the building, a barrage of rain pelting the dirt road. Too distraught to return home, he went in search of Devereaux, forging ahead at a strong pace, not even opening his umbrella.

Droplets peppered his hat as the wind picked up, transforming the rainstorm into a deluge of misery as he approached the residence of Dixon Devereaux. Massive Georgian columns supported double verandas overlooking the river on Bridge Street. Knowing Dixon, he'd gone to the house to avoid any acknowledgement of the funeral.

Frederick walked to the back door and rang the bell. A woman with ruddy cheeks and bulbous eyes greeted him, her crisp white apron covering the black dress straining against her figure.

"Good afternoon, sir."

"Good afternoon. I'd like to speak with Mr. Devereaux."

"I'm terribly sorry, but he's unavailable."

Before Frederick could protest, a voice from within declared, "Show him in, Mrs. Ainsley."

A blush reddened her already crimson complexion as the woman stepped back, allowing Frederick to enter. Dixon lounged at a plantation desk in the gentlemen's parlor, smoking a cigar and clasping a cut crystal snifter of brandy.

"Had a feeling I'd be hearing from you." Turning to the housemaid, he spoke, "Mrs. Ainsley, would you give us some privacy?"

"Yes, sir," she said with a nod, leaving the men to talk.

"Frederick, please sit down. Would you like a brandy, my good fellow?"

"Yes, thank you," Frederick replied, his skin chilled by the dampness.

Dixon poured the drink and handed it to his client.

"I take it you've already been to my office."

Frederick let the slow burn of the brandy warm his body, before responding. "They said you were out so I decided to take a chance of catching you here."

"This must be more than a friendly call."

"I think you know why I'm calling. I need to know what went wrong and if there's any way it can be traced back to me?" Frederick growled.

"Come now, Frederick, I told you everything would be fine. No one will ever know what transpired. Unless of course, you've shared the information with someone else."

"Goodness no! I'll take this to the grave." His voice trailed off.

"Then no one will be the wiser. I must say you're looking frazzled. Are you getting enough sleep?"

"How can you be so casual about everything? Two people are dead!" Frederick declared.

Dixon leaned forward furrowing his brow. "Keep your wits about you or others will become suspicious. Thus far, all is working as planned."

"Working as planned? The carriage was to be damaged with the blame going to that philandering scoundrel of a groom! I wanted him sacked, I didn't want anyone killed!"

"Frederick, calm yourself. No one suspects any wrongdoing on your part. The town has sympathy for you, my good man. Your wife has run away and your in-laws have perished in a tragic accident due to an irresponsible stable hand who has conveniently disappeared. What more could you want?"

"You're unbelievable. Despicable is a better term!" Frederick said, rubbing his forehead.

"Please do not insult me, Frederick." Dixon swirled the liquor in the glass, his demeanor eerily calm. "Keep in mind the extent of my knowledge regarding your involvement in this little endeavor." Sipping his brandy, he continued. "You have your daughter, the family fortune, and the Monroe estate, not to mention you're rid of an irritant. I don't believe anyone will ever question the circumstances. No doubt, Mr. Charles Donahue will never show his face in our town again. So you see, you got your money's worth and a bit more." He reclined in the Windsor chair, his lips rounding into a devious grin as he puffed his cigar.

"It's true. I've not seen that wretched man since the newspapers connected him to the accident. If he has any sense at all, he's far from here."

"That's the spirit. Perhaps now that the news has made its way around the state, your lovely bride will return home," he snickered.

"What are you suggesting?" Frederick spat, his eyes forming slits.

"Come now, Frederick, no need to put on airs with me. We both know she ran off for *personal reasons*. Once she learns of her parent's demise, she'll return."

"If only it were true," Frederick whispered, his expression forlorn, as he thought about Nora.

"If you don't mind, I have work to do." Dixon stood, motioning toward the door.

"Thank you, Dixon, for your candor, and discretion." Bile filled Frederick's mouth as he forced the words from his lips. The last thing he needed was to make an enemy of Dixon.

Defeated, Frederick placed the hat upon his head, gave a nod, and exited the premises. On his way back to Monroe Manse, he mulled over all that had transpired. He felt as if someone had thrown acid on his emotions dissolving the ardent affection he'd once held for his wife. Of course, it wasn't Nora's fault. *If it hadn't been for that meddling groom all would be well*, he thought, clenching his fists.

From what he'd garnered from Reynolds a few days earlier, Charles was gone. When the police arrived at his cottage to question him, the rooms were in a state of disarray with no indication as to his whereabouts. Unfortunately, the carriage scandal added more momentum to the gossip regarding Nora's absence, making it difficult to shield Bitsy from objectionable attention. The more Frederick dwelled upon it, the more convinced he became that the Monroe tragedy, and his wife's absence, were entirely Charles's fault.

"I should've shot him when I had the chance," he whispered. If only he had, Nora would still be here and their beautiful family would be intact. Then again, he'd have gone to prison for murder thus disgracing the family name, something he would never risk. No, this was a much better outcome, even if he'd lost his in-laws in the process.

35

Sarah shifted in bed as the alarm clock blared its early morning wake-up call. She hit the button and sank back against the pillow. Even though she'd slept through the night, her energy was depleted and her muscles tight. Sitting up, she rubbed her eyes when images from the previous night's dreams flooded her consciousness. Suddenly energized, she hopped from bed, changed, and hurried downstairs, hoping Danni was awake. She'd flip when she heard about the dreams.

Sarah stepped into the kitchen where Danni was perusing one of the files and sipping coffee.

"Good morning. What are you reading?" Sarah asked, starting the kettle.

"I'm rereading the articles about Charles's disappearance and his involvement with the Monroes' demise. Something about it doesn't sit right with me."

Sarah grinned. "Probably because he didn't do it."

Danni removed her glasses and glared at her friend. "What do you mean he didn't do it? The investigation showed the wheel fell off due to his negligence. With his simultaneous disappearance, it's obvious he planned it. Not to mention, your ghost friend keeps saying he's guilty."

"Charles had no part in it," Sarah said flatly.

"You had another dream!" Danni leaned forward, her eyes sparkling with anticipation.

"Frederick was responsible."

The kettle screeched. Sarah poured a cup of tea and joined Danni at the table.

"OK, let's hear it," Danni said, raising her eyebrows.

"Remember Frederick was doing business with a man by the name of Dixon Devereaux?"

"I remember."

"Last night's dreams were strange but revealed a great deal." Sarah took a sip of tea before continuing. "Frederick made arrangements with Dixon to make it seem as if Charles had been careless in his duties. Apparently, the only thing that was supposed to happen was the inconvenience of a broken carriage wheel resulting in Charles's dismissal. But when the Monroes died as a result, it complicated matters."

"Are you telling me this was a murder for hire?"

"Like I said, no one was supposed to die. The main reason for the setup was to get Charles fired. Keep in mind, Frederick was under the impression Charles had threatened Nora."

"Huh?"

"If you recall, in one of my dreams, Reynolds told Frederick he'd heard Charles threaten Nora."

"Oh yeah, forgot about that," Danni said, wrinkling her nose.

"If Frederick believed Nora ran off out of fear, then maybe he thought getting rid of Charles would make her come back."

"So, the message from the ghost was telling you Frederick was the guilty one. Do you know what this means?"

"Yes, we have all this information about a century-old case with no viable evidence to support it."

"Aren't we pessimistic this morning?" Danni quipped. "Maybe with a little more sleuthing, we can piece the rest together. This could be the reason you're being haunted. Nora wanted the world to know the truth about her lover. He didn't murder her parents, he was framed."

Her suggestion made sense. If they could clear Charles's name, perhaps the haunting would stop.

Danni rubbed her forehead, obviously still unsettled by the newest revelation. "What about the letter Nora supposedly left Frederick saying she needed to get away?"

"Wish we could find that letter," Sarah said, slumping in her chair.

They'd yet to find the elusive letter and time was ticking away with the deadline for clearing the house fast approaching. Sarah and Danni sat in silence trying to figure out how the goodbye letter correlated with the dreams.

"Actually, the letter stating Nora ran away due to the stress of motherhood lends credence to this new theory," Sarah offered. "Think about it. She had a child with a man she admired but was in love with another. Perhaps she ran off because the strain of it all was too much."

"It's possible," Danni said, taking another sip of coffee.

"Wait a minute," Sarah declared, jumping up nearly toppling her chair. With the surprising revelations of the previous night's dreamscapes Sarah had completely forgotten about the diary entry she'd read before bed. She bolted up the stairs, grabbed the diary from the bedside table, and raced back to the kitchen.

"What's gotten into you?" Danni asked, furrowing her brow.

"I read an interesting passage in Nora's diary last night that alludes to her running away." She handed the blue leather diary to Danni. "Read the entry dated July 25th. She talks about her struggle between leaving and staying."

Danni's mouth dropped as she read it. "Didn't she disappear a few days later?"

"On July 29th. This confirms that a few days prior to her disappearance she was seriously contemplating leaving her husband and kid behind to run away with her lover."

"Definitely looks that way except we know differently." Danni shook her head. "Why would the ghost go to this much trouble to reveal something that could further tarnish her reputation? I mean, why not just let the world believe she ran away from her family? That in itself was bad enough but having an affair and leaving her child? That's incomprehensible."

"Maybe she wanted people to know she did it for love and not because she didn't care about her daughter."

"It's scandalous no matter how you view it. No wonder Edie was such a mess with a family history that included an alcoholic father and a malingering great-grandmother."

Danni's coffee cup flew across the table and smashed against the far wall. Too startled to move, she sat for a moment before speaking.

"What the heck just happened?" Danni's eyes widened as she glanced around.

Unfazed by the incident, Sarah smiled. "It would seem Nora doesn't like you referring to her in such a derogatory manner."

"I thought you said she wasn't dangerous."

"Generally, she's not," Sarah said with a sheepish grin. "Perhaps you should be more careful how you speak about her."

"Sorry, Nora, I didn't mean to insult you," Danni said. She got up slowly, grabbed the broom and dustpan, and cleaned up the mess. Opening the upper cabinet, Danni grabbed another mug, filled it, and sat down at the table, her eyes scanning the room for signs of movement.

Sarah's chair scraped the floor as she stood.

"Where are you going?" Danni asked, grabbing her arm.

"To the dining room to look through the papers. With this new knowledge, I might notice something I didn't before."

"No way you're leaving me here alone with a mug-tossing ghost!"

"What's the matter? Afraid of ghouls and goblins?" Sarah's mocking didn't deter Danni.

"Yes! I admit it! I've been trying to put on a brave front for you but this haunted stuff is creeping me out!" Danni's sleep ruffled hair intensified the crazed expression on her face giving her the appearance of a mad scientist.

"Calm down. The ghost didn't throw the mug *at* you; she tossed it *away* from you. No harm done," Sarah said, pursing her lips, enjoying the fact that her friend was getting a taste of what she'd endured throughout her life. Even her own fears were beginning to dissipate. "If you want, I'd be happy to string several cloves of garlic together for you to wear while you're here."

"Ha ha, very funny," Danni replied, rolling her eyes. She grabbed her coffee mug and paused. "Do you think it would actually work?"

"Bejeweling yourself with garlic won't help unless the ghost doesn't like Italian food. Let's keep working on this and maybe we can put an end to this haunted stuff so I can finally finish this job. Once we solve this mystery the only thing I'll have to ward off is William," Sarah said over her shoulder as she ambled to the dining room.

"The only way to keep him at bay is if you're a corpse and even then he'd still probably hit on you. You'd need a serious talisman to repel the likes of William."

Sarah shuddered at the thought. "My Uncle Joe used to take curses off of people when he was mayor. Aunt Millie said she found a drawer in his office filled with requests from residents for intervention after they'd had a curse put on them by that old man on the island. According to her, Uncle Joe was the only one in town with the ability to remove the spells."

"Do you hear yourself?" Danni asked, planting a hand on her hip. "No wonder communicating with ghosts doesn't seem strange when you have a family history that includes curse removal."

Sarah chuckled, "When you put it that way, haunted dreams don't seem so crazy."

36

Sarah set her teacup on the dining room table, emptied the box, and started perusing the paperwork.

"What else did you dream about?" Danni asked.

Sarah paused. "I dreamt about Charles packing his things to leave and Frederick at the Monroe's funeral. After the funeral Frederick went to Devereaux' house and confronted him about the mishap with the carriage."

"How'd he take the confrontation?"

"Dixon was snide about it. He actually laughed and suggested Frederick should be pleased because he got more than he paid for."

"Sleazy must run in the DNA with that family," Danni said, shaking her head.

"This was the first time I've dreamed from Charles's perspective. I don't recall touching anything he would have touched."

Danni pointed to the horseshoe brooch on the table. "The brooch."

"Oh my gosh! I nearly forgot about the bag!" Sarah declared.

"What bag?"

"In one of the dreams, Frederick went into the ballroom and stashed a small bag in the fireplace."

"What was in it?"

"Don't know," Sarah said, shrugging her shoulders.

"Well let's find out," Danni said with a grin.

"How?"

"We go upstairs and look."

"I didn't see which brick he removed, it was pretty dark."

"What about the book Dr. Bristow dropped off?" Danni asked.

"How's that going to help?"

"Obviously, the loose brick was already there, unless you saw Frederick chisel it out."

"No, he removed it with his hands."

"It may have been one of the hiding places when the house was occupied during the war. All we have to do is look through the book and find out if it mentions this particular hiding place."

"Danni, sometimes you're a genius."

"You're just noticing?" she chuckled as Sarah rolled her eyes.

Danni grabbed the book and paged to the chapter about secret portals. A smile radiated across her face as she tapped the page. "Here it is. The ballroom fireplace was one of the hiding spots. It's the fourth brick from the left, tenth brick from the bottom."

Sarah grabbed a flashlight as they dashed from the room and raced upstairs to the ballroom fireplace.

They plodded to the newly exposed hearth, Sarah shining the flashlight into the darkened space as she stooped to count the bricks. She tugged at the brick but time and humidity had sealed it in place. Sarah reached into her pocket for the pocketknife she always carried and pried at the edges of the charred brick, jiggling it from the crevice.

Reaching inside, Sarah gasped when her fingers brushed against a soft object. Danni's eyes widened as she looked on. Gently, Sarah brought the dusty pouch into the light, its blue silken fibers beginning to shred. With great care she tugged at the edges revealing several pieces of jewelry.

"Why did he put jewelry in the hearth?" Danni asked.

"Maybe after the robbery Frederick was afraid someone would come back to steal the rest of it."

"He was rich. Why not stash it in a vault or a safe deposit box?" Danni asked, her eyebrows arched.

"Who needs a bank vault when you have all these hiding places in your house?"

"Yeah, I suppose."

"Some of this stuff looks valuable." Gingerly, Sarah closed the bag, replaced the brick, and stood up. "We can get a better look at the contents under the kitchen light."

"I thought we had this thing figured out. Now it seems like we were mistaken about what happened to Nora *and* what the ghost has been trying to tell us." Danni scoffed. "It's all so confusing. If you've already solved the mystery about Charles' innocence, why is the ghost leading you to the jewelry?"

"Maybe Nora is rewarding me. The jewelry is probably valuable, and this is her way of saying thank you."

Danni snickered. "Only you could find the silver lining in a haunting."

Once they reached the kitchen, Sarah emptied the contents of the pouch onto the table. A strand of pearls, gold bracelet, diamond teardrop earrings, and a brooch with matching earrings glittered and glinted like pirate treasure beneath the luminescence of the overhead light. Sarah picked up an ornately scrolled gold brooch sporting a wreath of garnets and seed pearls.

Immediately, Sarah dropped the piece, a numbing sensation crawling up her arm as an image flashed in her head.

"What's wrong?" Danni asked.

"This brooch was a wedding gift to Nora from Frederick."

"How do you know that?"

"It was in one of my dreams. She wore it to dinner with a green dress," Sarah muttered, the image parading through her mind as if she'd actually been there instead of witnessing it in one of her dreams.

"If it was a gift from him, then it must be real gold and gemstones. I doubt Frederick would dabble in the fake stuff."

Sarah inhaled as she rubbed her hands together.

"You OK?" Danni queried.

"It made my hand tingle is all," she replied. "I wonder who I'll connect with in my dreams tonight since both Frederick and Nora handled this."

"Not sure. I'm still trying to make sense of that book," Danni said. "Last night I read about being able to make connections by touching areas of a house where the ghost spent a lot of time when he or she was alive."

"That could explain why I dreamt about Frederick hiding the jewelry. Still doesn't explain the relevance of it or why I dreamed about Frederick at the Monroes' funeral. We already knew they were dead so nothing new was revealed."

"Are you sure?"

"As sure as I can be when I'm getting information from dead people via my dreams," Sarah shrugged.

Danni looked around. "Now what?"

"I'll take these pieces to Keith when I pick up the ring I left there and get them appraised. All of this might add substantially to the bottom line," Sarah said, studying the stash.

"Do you think this is why Frederick walled away the fireplace?" Danni asked pointing at the jewelry.

"Seems a bit extreme. Unless…"

"What?"

"Maybe there's something else stashed in the fireplace."

"Looks like we have some more detecting to do this morning."

"I need to get some real work done first," Sarah said, carrying her cup to the sink.

"You take all the fun out of shirking off work to solve mysteries," Danni retorted. "I suppose I could do some more digging at the county records office. Maybe I'll find something I overlooked before we got this new information."

"I'll get some inventory catalogued and then we can discuss any new findings over lunch."

"How about I pick up chicken from Myra's," Danni offered.

"Sounds good. But get me the grilled chicken, nothing fried," Sarah said, rinsing her cup and setting it in the drying rack on the counter.

"You're not right, you know that?"

"Maybe so, but at least I won't drop dead from clogged arteries when I'm sixty."

"I'm not gonna die of a heart attack, my liver will give out long before that," Danni chuckled as she scooted upstairs to change.

Sarah stood at the sink looking through the wavy glass panes at the gardens beyond when an icy sensation trickled down her spine. With a shiver, she turned slowly expecting to see some sort of paranormal entity but the room was empty. She exhaled the pent-up fear. Despite her relief, something niggled at her subconscious letting her know she was far from solving the mystery of Nora's disappearance

37

Sarah started to walk past the dining room when a cool breath fluttered her hair, sending chills bumping across her skin. She stopped to gaze through the doorway, her heartbeat quickening as her eyes scanned the room for movement. Stepping into the room, Sarah looked around but didn't see anything out of place. At that moment, a strong breeze whirled through like a cyclone, scattering papers across the table onto the floor. The scent of Chanel No. 5 stung Sarah's nostrils, alerting her that Edie's ghost was close by.

"Edie, what are you trying to tell me?" Sarah's words came in a whisper as fear squeezed her lungs.

Silence.

She took a step backward and bumped against a body. Screaming, she spun around.

"Doggonit Danni! Make some noise when you enter a room!" Sarah's hands shook as she ran them through her hair.

"What the heck is wrong with you?"

"Edie was here," Sarah said, trying to steady her breathing.

"How do you know?" Danni queried, gazing at the papers strewn across the floor.

"Can't you smell the cologne?"

Danni sniffed the air. "Not really."

Sarah inhaled. The odor had dissipated.

"Why'd she make such a mess?" Danni asked.

"Who knows?" Sarah replied as she started picking up the papers. Danni helped until everything was crudely stacked on the table.

"You gonna be OK here by yourself?" Worry wrinkled Danni's brow.

"Yeah. Go to the county office, I'll be fine. I was just startled."

"Call if you need me to come back," Danni said, giving Sarah a quick hug before scurrying to the kitchen, obviously glad to be leaving the house.

The floor shook as the back door slammed shut. Sarah turned to leave the room when she stepped on a small piece of paper. Bending over, she lifted the crinkled sheet. Most of the ink was faded preventing her from reading the specifics; however, the name of the local architectural firm was clear.

Apparently, Edie had hired Benfield & Benfield to help with some structural issues. Sarah stared at the name and smiled. This was Caleb's firm. She'd known Caleb through her visits to *Antiques and Coffee Beans* over the years and had a good idea where he'd be at this hour. Perhaps he could explain the walled-up fireplace in the ballroom. Sarah grabbed the box of Limoges porcelains from the floor, snatched her wallet and keys from the kitchen table, and headed out the door.

Stuffing the box of Limoges into the Beast, Sarah hopped in the truck, drove to town, and parked in front of the antebellum mansion on Bridge Street. The rich aroma of coffee scented the air as she grabbed the box and made her way through the front door of *Antiques and Coffee Beans*.

Lisa stood behind the counter placing a freshly toasted bagel on a plate with a container of spicy cream cheese on the side. Miss Jess sat at one of the bistro tables, giving advice while pouring tea from a small brown teapot. Miss Jess was the renegade tea drinker in this establishment.

"Are you letting them live rent free in your head? Don't let their dishonesty ruin this opportunity. Tell them how much you're willing to pay and be done with it," she said, setting the teapot back on the table.

Sarah grinned. It was Miss Jess's signature comment when people were dwelling on negative things. It had soothed Sarah on several occasions when she'd been irritated by an uncompromising customer or an impossible antiques dealer.

Smiling, Lisa set the bagel and cream cheese in front of Miss Jess. "Here you go, a bagel, well done, with spicy cream cheese."

"Thank you, my dear. Now about the offer," Miss Jess said, spreading cream cheese on her breakfast when she looked up at Sarah and grinned. "Hello, Sarah."

"Morning, Miss Jess."

"Good morning, Sarah. How are things at the Monroe place?" Lisa asked, returning to the counter.

"Almost done. I only have a few more things to sort through." Sarah placed the box on the table. "I found this Limoges chocolate set and serving dishes and thought you might be interested. I've also got an English pub table with four Windsor chairs to consign."

A sparkle flickered in Lisa's eye. "Sounds great. Let's see the porcelain."

As they unwrapped each piece, a lanky gentleman walked in wearing a red T-shirt with the word "Local" printed in bright white letters.

"Hey, Lisa, you won't believe the deals I landed at that estate sale yesterday. Got the truck full of great stuff." He walked to the coffee bar, poured a cup of java, and joined Miss Jess at the table.

"Sounds good, Pete," Lisa said as she checked the porcelain markings with a loop.

Sarah shook her head. "Pete, you never cease to amaze me with the deals you find."

He sipped his coffee before addressing Sarah. "The secret is getting there early with cash in hand and not being afraid to make an offer that might insult the seller. You'd be surprised how many people are willing to accept low ball offers because they want to get rid of the stuff. Good business means taking risks. Speaking of business, how's it going at the big house?"

"The usual, exhausting and tedious, except this one is twice as big, and I have half as much time."

"How much time did you get?" he asked.

"Originally three weeks but it's been reduced to two."

"Are you kidding me? Who made that decision?"

"Jarrod Devereaux."

"Why the heck didn't you tell him to go jump in the river?" he said with a sneer.

"Don't give her a hard time Pete. I doubt she had a choice in the matter." Miss Jess turned to Sarah, "You'll get it done. I have faith in you."

"Thanks, Miss Jess."

Sarah grinned as the morning regulars began to meander into the space. The rhythm of the shop was like a symphony, each member engaged in their respective routines. Lisa was the conductor brewing coffee, doling out bagels, and attending to each person's request without missing a beat.

"Leez," a balding man in an Oxford shirt and khakis called from the doorway. "I need the jumper cables. Christine's battery gave out, and I've got to get some tools dropped off to Ben before I take Derrick to school."

Lisa reached below the counter and tossed the man a set of keys. "In the trunk of my car. I'm parked over by the church."

Sarah's eyebrows arched. "Christine?"

"My husband's truck seems to have a life of its own, so we call it Christine, like the car from the Stephen King movie."

"That's funny. I call mine the Beast."

The two women chuckled when a dark-haired woman with glasses strode through the door. "Good morning all," Renita called out as she poured her coffee and started searching behind the counter. "Got any creamer Lisa?"

"In the corner," Lisa said, pointing to a box of individual creamer cups.

Renita fixed her coffee and sat down with the others.

The coffee maker began to spit and sputter announcing a freshly brewed pot. Lisa made her way to the counter, filled a stainless steel carafe, and carried it to the vintage buffet where she placed it beside three other decanters, each with a different blend.

Returning to the box of porcelains, Lisa asked, "How much do you want for all of it?"

"Make me an offer. At this point, I need to clear out as much as possible from the house."

"How about $100 for the lot?"

"Sounds fair."

Lisa pulled cash from under the money tray of the register and handed it to Sarah.

"Good luck with the estate."

Sarah hesitated. She was about to ask about Caleb Benfield when he walked through the door. He was with his wife, Jill, a tall, slender woman cradling their dachshund, affectionately known as Daisy.

"What's in the box?" Caleb asked, a lilting English accent highlighting his words as he stood next to Lisa.

"Sarah brought some pieces from the Monroe place," she replied. As Caleb perused the serving dishes, Lisa asked, "You want a bagel?"

"Yes, please. Have you got any of the spicy cream cheese?" he asked.

"It's on the table."

Sarah walked over to Caleb and smiled. "Hey Caleb, I found a receipt for some work your firm did for Edie Monroe a few years back."

With a chuckle, he nodded. "Ah yes, I remember it *distinctly*."

"How so?"

"Bloody place was haunted!" he declared.

"You saw a ghost?" Sarah queried trying to feign surprise.

"Didn't see it, exactly. I was working in the attic when I heard footsteps and saw shadows on the far wall. Needless to say, I scuttled out of there rather quickly and didn't look back."

"You believe in ghosts?"

"Not particularly but being alone up there was, well, daunting," he replied, arching his eyebrows. "Have you experienced something?"

Sarah shrugged. "I'd heard rumors about the place being haunted and was curious. By the way, do you have any idea why the mantel in the ballroom was walled away?"

"Don't know the reason but it probably had something to do with crumbling brick or vermin. A lot of people enclosed fireplaces when they had problems with animals making their way inside through the chimney."

"Is that what your firm was working on? Structural damage?"

He sighed. "Edie complained about noises in the attic and was worried that maybe the house was shifting or settling, but we didn't find anything structural. Place is as solid as a fortress," he said, taking a plate with a freshly toasted bagel from Lisa and joining the others.

Disappointed she wasn't able to garner better information, Sarah got ready to leave when a woman with steely blue eyes, coiffed gray hair, and wearing a beaded necklace, walked in.

"Good morning, Lisa. I've got a few more pieces to add to the jewelry showcase," she said pulling several sparkling necklaces from her purse.

"Glad to hear it Sophia," Lisa replied, handing her a cup of coffee.

"Bring everything over here," Renita said. "I'd like to see what you made."

Sophia took a seat at the bistro table, which seemed to be shrinking with each new guest. The conversation ricocheted back and forth as all huddled around sipping tea and coffee, munching on bagels, and studying Sophia's latest creations.

Sarah smiled as she left them to their morning discourse and drove to the manse. The Beast sputtered to a halt in the drive as Sarah slid from the tattered bench seat. Once in the kitchen, she made a notation in her ledger and paper-clipped the cash to the page until she could get to the bank.

"Better get to work," she said, trying to motivate herself. It seemed the closer she got to the end of a job, the harder it was to stay focused, especially with the lingering mystery of Nora's disappearance and the pressure of the impending deadline. Grabbing her tools, Sarah jaunted up the stairs, stopping at the landing to glance down the hall.

Her nerve endings prickled as she made her way to the ballroom and peered inside. She ruminated on what Caleb had said about crumbling brick and critters but something about it didn't ring true. Most people boarded up the fireplace not the entire wall.

"What made you go to such extreme measures Frederick?" Sarah muttered as she set her tools on a parlor chair and stood before the cavernous hole she'd made in the wall. A soft breeze wafted through the room and whistled up the fireplace sending bits of charred debris floating to the grate.

Kneeling down, Sarah sifted through the ashes when something caught her eye. She reached in and grabbed a stack of cabinet card photos from the back corner and blew the dust from the one on top. A shudder rattled her body as she gazed at a newlywed couple standing in front of this fireplace. The next photo showed a glowing Nora holding a small bundle, obviously her daughter Bitsy. The last image was of Frederick and Nora with baby Bitsy in front of the hearth next to a tall pine tree decked out in Christmas finery.

They must have used this space like a family room, Sarah thought, shuffling through the pictures once more. But why wall away precious memories such as these?

Sarah continued the search, shining her flashlight into the darkened space when she noticed a shred of pale blue silk. She lifted the scrap and closed her eyes. Her fingers numbed as an image of Frederick hovering over a fire flashed through her head. Sadly, the scene dissipated quickly, leaving Sarah aggravated at her underdeveloped dreamist skills. She put the scrap aside and looked for more items but found nothing.

Sarah grabbed the scrap of silk and the photos and rose to her feet when a strange sensation encapsulated her body, as if invisible hands were pulling her away from the hearth. Her heartbeat hastened as the grip tightened around her upper arms, its icy grasp stinging her skin. In an effort to calm her nerves, Sarah took several deep breaths until she felt the grip loosen and her heart rate return to a steady pace.

Aggravation tapped at her nerves. She didn't have the luxury of digging for answers. With only a couple of days left in the house, she'd be hard pressed to finish the inventory, not to mention figure out what happened to Nora. Exacerbation pumped through her veins, flushing her cheeks and warming the tops of her ears.

"What are you trying to tell me? I don't understand!" Sarah screamed, stomping her foot.

All of a sudden, the breeze went still and the odor of dirt and decay filled the room. A flash of lightning and a rumbling boom followed as the room darkened and the pitter-patter of raindrops began to pepper the windowsills.

Thwack! The sledgehammer leaning against the wall near the fireplace slammed to the floor causing Sarah to jump.

"You want me to do more demo?" she whispered, her limbs quivering.

Nothing.

Sarah placed the photos on the piano and picked up the sledgehammer as the thrumming of rain intensified. With quivering hands, she swung the sledgehammer back and slammed it into the wall, sending plaster dust and wood chips flying. A few more hits and she'd managed to widen the chasm. Her mouth dropped open as she stood back and stared at a large framed portrait still affixed to the wall over the mantel. The soft brown eyes, mahogany tresses, and lacey gown left no doubt that this was Nora's wedding portrait. But why was it hidden up here and not with the other ancestral paintings lining the entryway?

Poor Frederick had to have been on the brink of insanity to go to this much trouble to cover up his pain. Lost in her thoughts, Sarah startled when the Batman theme clamored from her pocket.

"Hey Danni," Sarah said, her heart pounding.

"How's it going?"

"Interesting."

"Did you find something?" Danni's voice went up an octave in anticipation.

"Found several things that indicate Frederick was devastated by Nora's disappearance but nothing about where she went. How about you?"

"Getting ready to go through some old police records."

"They kept stuff like that?" Sarah asked.

"Apparently in a little town like this they did. Is it raining over there?"

"Buckets."

"If you're OK, I'll take my time here until the storm lets up. See you at lunchtime."

"See you then."

Sarah slid the phone back in her pocket, snatched up the fabric scrap and photos, and dashed downstairs to the dining room to add them to the rest of the evidence. Her nerves were still raw from the strange encounters in the ballroom, prompting her to fix a cup of tea. No matter the circumstances tea always calmed her.

While she waited for the water to heat, Sarah watched sheets of rain cascade over the rippled windowpanes until the kettle let out a high-pitched squeal. Pouring hot water into a mug, she noticed the cadenced beat of raindrops was slowing and the room was getting lighter. She glanced through the window and smiled, pleased to see the storm moving on.

"Better get some work done," she mumbled, grabbing her tea and starting down the hall. As she climbed the stairs, the hair on her arms stood on end as the tinkling of piano keys whispered from above.

38

———

Sarah made her way back to the ballroom and peered inside. The music had gone silent leaving an eerie feel hovering in the atmosphere. Her stomach churned and her chest tightened as she made her way to the piano. Closing her eyes, she touched the keys hoping an image might materialize. As her fingertips brushed the ivories, a vision of the attic flashed through her head.

"That was weird," she muttered, trying to figure out why her mind had drifted to the attic. Although the vision didn't make any sense, Sarah decided to follow the lead anyway. Determination dissolved the fear bubbling in her chest. With renewed fortitude, she walked down the hall and climbed the attic stairs.

The attic smelled mustier than usual, but considering the heavy rains it wasn't surprising. One thing was certain; the humidity following a Lowcountry rainstorm was almost as soggy as the rain itself.

Sarah set her teacup down and opened the window to circulate some fresh air through the stale space. Sunlight sparkled from puddles in the overgrown gardens below. She inhaled deeply, taking in the comforting scent of fresh rain and spring flora.

One corner of the attic had yet to be inventoried, but Sarah's worry over the deadline was beginning to wane. The more she thought about it the more she was determined that William's uncle Jarrod would have to give her an extension. It hadn't occurred to her until now that the house would be harder to sell with a bunch of junk cluttering up the rooms. She'd discuss it with Danni later and insist that an extension be granted.

Content with her rationalization, Sarah started digging through a stack of boxes. The first box held memorabilia from Edie's childhood. Faded photos, report cards, school samples, and a giant paper Easter egg colored in pink, green, and lavender marked her formative years.

Sarah moved on to the next container filled with mementos dating back to the 19th century, including a portable writing desk. Intrigued by the find, Sarah placed it upon her lap and opened the lid. Rich plum velvet lined the writing surface with a small compartment holding an inkwell, mother of pearl handled dip pen, and extra nibs. Shifting a small lever, she raised the velvet-covered board revealing a small space filled with blank papers and a letter. Sarah removed the letter from its one-hundred-year-old tomb, delicately unfolding the yellowed parchment, and began reading.

MRS. MONROE,

I AM APPEALING to your good nature and strong virtues and ask that you reconsider your decision. I find your rejection of our offer deeply offensive and beyond forgiveness. How dare you and your husband refuse an arrangement benefitting both families? Dixon is a remarkable young man, well suited to any young lady. Have you no honor?

Our families founded this town; therefore, it is sensible our children should marry someday. Please reconsider your decision, as it is unlikely Nora will have another opportunity for such a fine match.

SINCERELY,

 Mrs. Hampton Devereaux

SARAH'S STOMACH FLOPPED. THE DEVEREAUX' had tried to arrange a marriage between Nora and Dixon? Now she understood why the Monroes had pushed the marriage with Frederick as hard as they did. Obviously, marrying a Devereaux was as repugnant back then as it was today, although the Devereaux men never seemed to have a shortage of women chasing them. Granted, it was probably due to their money, which was more abundant than their moral code. Sarah sucked in a breath when another thought crossed her mind. What if Dixon told the man he hired to sabotage the carriage to make sure the Monroes died in order to enact revenge? It wasn't beyond their duplicitous nature. After all, their egos were wider than the Broad River.

She sat for a few moments considering the implications. It made more sense than Charles killing the Monroes. At that moment, Sarah remembered the dream where Frederick gave money to Devereaux. He'd removed the cash from a secret compartment of his desk, the same desk in the gentlemen's parlor below. She stuffed the letter in her back pocket and scampered downstairs to the front room. Sarah walked to the corner and perched on the high-backed leather chair. Although she'd emptied the desk and checked for hidden cubbies the week before, she decided to try again.

Sarah opened the top drawer like she'd seen in her dream, reached to the back, and gasped when her finger caught on something. She fiddled with a small indentation until she heard a *pop*. Squeezing her hand into the crevice, she gulped when her fingers brushed against something. As she struggled to clutch the mysterious item, the Batman theme blared from her pocket.

"Hello!" Agitation highlighted her voice.

"You alright? You sound upset."

"The phone startled me," she said, catching her breath. "Any luck with the police archives?"

"Not much. What about you?"

"You won't believe it."

"On my way!"

Danni hung up without waiting for a response. Sarah grinned at her best friend's enthusiasm. "She's going to flip when I tell her about all of this," she chuckled.

Sarah removed a crumpled paper from the hidden compartment and held it toward the window to get a better look at it. Sadly, the ink was faded to the point of being illegible.

Maybe a magnifying glass will help, she thought.

She ventured down the hall to the dining room where she found the magnifier with some of her other tools. The full extent of the fading was confirmed beneath the convex glass, eliminating any hope of deciphering the message.

"Hope it wasn't important, and even if it was it wouldn't matter because I can't read it anyway," she fumed. Sarah tossed it into one of the boxes destined for the dump and added the letter from Mrs. Devereaux to the paperwork on the table.

A short while later, Danni returned with lunch and a gallon of sweet tea. "Sorry it took so long but the drive-through at Myra's was wrapped around the building. What'd you find?" Danni blurted out as she set the food and the tea jug on the table.

"Calm down. Let me get some food in me, I'm starving."

"Fine," Danni grumbled.

Danni served the food while Sarah filled glasses with ice and poured the tea. They settled at the table as Sarah took a bite of chicken and started sharing all she'd discovered.

"Earlier I was in the ballroom when I found some family photos and a scrap of silk in the fireplace grate. Then a disgusting odor filled the room and something grabbed my arms."

Danni stopped eating and leaned forward. "Do you hear yourself? You're talking about ghosts grabbing you like it was a normal occurrence."

"I suppose I'm finally adjusting to all of it," Sarah shrugged.

"That's probably a good thing," Danni replied, popping another French fry in her mouth. "Go on."

"Then the ghost knocked the sledgehammer over so I took a few more hits at the wall."

"And?" Danni's eyes widened.

"Found Nora's wedding portrait."

"Seriously? Why would Frederick stash all of that stuff in the fireplace and then wall it away?"

"I'm beginning to wonder if he was losing his mind. It's pretty extreme behavior," Sarah said. "Anyway, I took the photos to the dining room and then fixed a cup of tea. That's when I heard the piano playing in the ballroom."

Danni's eyes widened as she blew out a breath. "This is getting seriously creepy."

"Tell me about it. When I got back upstairs the music had stopped. I decided to touch the keys to see if I could get a vision."

"Did you see anything?" Danni asked, perched on the edge of her chair.

"I saw the attic."

Danni's shoulders slumped. "Well that was anticlimactic."

"Not really. While I was in the attic, I stumbled across an

old portable writing desk belonging to Nora's mother. There was a letter from Dixon's mother inside. Evidently, the Devereaux' tried to arrange a marriage between Nora and Dixon, but the Monroes refused."

"You're kidding me?"

"Nope. Remember the business deal gone wrong between Frederick and Dixon?"

"Yeah."

"I wonder if Dixon knew about the Monroe's refusal for him to wed Nora and made sure they died in the carriage accident."

Danni sat back in her chair and sighed. "This is stranger than a reality show!"

"I thought the same thing," Sarah replied with a chuckle.

"Does any of it relate to what you've felt from Frederick in your dreams?"

Sarah thought for a moment. "I get a sense of despair and disillusionment from Frederick but not to the level of boarding up everything related to Nora."

"Sounds like you're starting to adjust to all of this."

"I guess so," Sarah said with a shrug. "What about you? Find anything significant?"

Danni pulled a folded paper from her pocket and handed it to Sarah. "Thought this was interesting."

Sarah scanned the photocopy, arching her eyebrows as she read. "This is a list of the jewelry that Charles supposedly stole from the house."

"Yup."

"These are the same items we found in the silk pouch hidden in the ballroom fireplace."

"Looks like Frederick faked the robbery too."

39

———

"Unbelievable!" Sarah declared. With wide eyes, she stared at her friend. "This must be what the ghost has been trying to tell me! Frederick was guilty of fraud."

"Could be," Danni said, taking another gulp of tea. "Still doesn't explain where Nora went or why Edie has been haunting you."

Sarah slumped back in the chair and pondered everything. "Nora was Edie's great-grandmother so it makes sense that she would want the family history clarified."

"Seems like a lot of trouble to show Frederick as an unsavory fellow while clearing the name of a man her great-grandmother had an illicit affair with. Frederick was family, Charles was merely a servant."

"The one thing that is consistent is the involvement of the Devereaux family throughout the scandal. I remember in one of my first dreams about Nora, she was eavesdropping on her parents. They were discussing their financial problems due to some poor investments with a Devereaux.

"Then Frederick did business with Dixon to sabotage his in-law's carriage in order to get Charles fired, except it resulted in their deaths. And now I've discovered the letter from Mrs. Devereaux chastising the Monroes for refusing their offer to arrange a marriage between their son Dixon and Nora. It seems the Devereaux family is a driving source of the Monroe's misfortune."

"Maybe the ghost was trying to tell you that Devereaux was the guilty party," Danni suggested.

"Who knows?" Sarah took another bite of chicken.

"Aside from the ghost hunting, were you able to get any work done?"

"A bit more in the attic but there's more here than I can get done in a day and a half."

"What are you going to do?" Danni asked.

"Finish what I can and demand an extension. William won't be able to make any repairs with all the antiques here and if they go with another agency it will take weeks longer. I assure you Christies and Sotheby's won't be fazed by some little small town twit and his ridiculous deadlines," Sarah said as she refilled her glass.

"Good for you!" Danni declared. "I think this dreamist stuff is making you bolder. I've never seen you this rebellious," she said, grinning.

"Speaking of which, have you read any more of the book?"

Danni's expression turned serious. "I have, but it's getting more complicated. There's a way you can control who you dream about but I've only figured part of it out."

"Tell me what you know so far. Maybe between the two of us we can unlock the meaning."

Danni dashed upstairs to retrieve the book and returned a few minutes later, puffing from the exertion.

"You need to get more exercise," Sarah said with a smirk.

"What makes you say that?" Danni queried, her lower lip protruding in a pout.

"You're winded from running up the stairs."

"I'll have you know I'm breathing heavy from excitement," Danni replied.

"Umhm," Sarah said, trying to suppress a smile.

Danni paged through the book. "According to what I read before bed, you can handle something that belonged to a person in order to dream about him or her specifically. Kinda like cuing the dream by connecting with a personal item before going to sleep."

"So, if I wanted to dream about Nora I should touch something that belonged to her before I go to sleep?"

"I think that's what it says. It also talks about being able to control who you dream about once you're asleep but I haven't figured that part out yet."

"It's a start. I'll try it before bed and see what happens. Meanwhile, I have a job to do." Sarah got up from her chair and started clearing away the remnants of lunch.

"I'm going to head to the office and check on a few things. Haven't heard from Anita and want to make sure everything is alright."

"Wouldn't she call if she needed anything?" Sarah asked as she rinsed the tea glasses.

"Yeah." Danni's shoulders slumped. "She does fine without me. It's scary how *well* she does without me. The woman is an enigma. The only reason I check in is to make myself feel necessary," Danni said with a grimace.

Sarah chuckled. "See you later."

"I'll pick up supper on my way back," Danni said, grabbing her keys.

"Something light, please."

Danni rolled her eyes and slipped out the back door. Sarah dried her hands, collected her tools, and started cataloguing the portraits and miscellaneous items in the entryway.

AFTER CATALOGUING everything in the downstairs entry as well as the upstairs hall, Sarah was relieved when she heard Danni's Mercedes crunching down the drive. It was well past six o'clock and much to her surprise, she was famished. Sarah brushed her hands against her khaki shorts and made her way to the kitchen as Danni came in carrying a large brown paper bag. The scent of barbeque wafted through the air making Sarah salivate.

With a sly grin, she looked at her friend. "You went to Bridge Street BBQ."

"Yup. Ran into your dad's old partner, Harlan. He said to tell you hello."

"Love that guy," Sarah replied, peeking in the bag and taking a long whiff. "Not surprised you saw him there. He and Dad used to frequent that place at least once a week."

"Can't believe he's still practicing law. I thought he'd retire after your dad did."

"Dad retired pretty early. Said he didn't want to be an old man confined to home because he and Mom were too frail to travel."

"Where are they in Italy?" Danni asked as she handed a carton of chopped barbeque and potato wedges to Sarah.

"Tuscany. They're supposed to tour Rome and Venice next."

Sarah poured two glasses of wine and sat across from Danni. She scooped a fork full of chopped beef into her mouth and closed her eyes savoring the hickory-smoked meat.

"This is sooo good," Sarah mumbled.

"I know you said to get something light but I drove past it on my way from the office and had to stop."

"No complaints here," she replied as she reached for a smoked potato wedge. "Everything OK at the office?"

"As always, Anita has everything running smoothly." Danni replied. "Did you get much accomplished?"

"I did but it won't be enough. I'm definitely going to miss the deadline. Do you want to call Jerrod or would you rather I break the news to him?"

"Why don't you call William? I'm sure you could persuade him," Danni chortled.

"I'd rather not," Sarah said with a shudder.

Danni cocked her head. "What is about him that you dislike so much? I know he's an irritating little mongrel but you seem to loathe him at a much deeper level."

"I don't despise him. Something about him makes my skin crawl, like I need to take a shower after I've been near him. Can't explain it really."

"I'll contact Jerrod tomorrow, if he doesn't call me first. I'll explain the situation and add a few threatening innuendos if he blusters on."

"Thanks Danni. I appreciate it. Since my timeline has been unofficially extended, I'm going to turn in early tonight. I'm beat."

"Sounds like a plan. I'll read some more of the *Dreamist* book. Maybe I'll figure out the rest of the riddle about controlling who you communicate with during a dreamscape."

After a few more glasses of wine, they bid goodnight and went to their rooms. Sarah washed up, changed into her nightshirt, and slid between the cottony sheets as warm breezes ruffled the curtains. *Only a few more nights and then it's back to your own bed*, she thought.

She'd grown fond of the old house over the past two weeks despite all the haunting and spooky occurrences. A twinge of sorrow tickled her stomach at the thought of relinquishing the place to William. Would the next owners appreciate the architecture and historical aspects of the place? And what about Nora? Obviously, her ghost was trying to communicate something. Sarah felt responsible for helping her and now more than ever longed to know Nora's fate.

In an effort to calm her racing thoughts, Sarah reached for one of the scrapbooks on the bedside table and leafed through the delicate pages. This one was different than the others in that it appeared to house photos after Nora's disappearance. Pictures of Bitsy in various stages of growth alongside her father littered the pages. A yellowed newspaper article quoted Frederick as saying he intended on instilling a love for gardening in his daughter to honor his beloved wife's talents. One line in particular tugged at Sarah's heart. "My sincerest hope is that Nora's memory will continue to grow in our daughter as she sustains the family reputation with award winning blooms."

"He truly loved her," Sarah muttered as her eyelids began to flutter.

With pleasant thoughts drifting through her mind, she set the album on the night table and switched off the lamp. A soft pitter-pattering tapped against the windowsill as spring rains spilled from night's embrace. Closing her eyes, Sarah's breathing slowed as she succumbed to another round of complicated dreams.

40

Frederick stepped into the back garden where Bitsy tottered near the rose hedge with Mrs. Stokes in close proximity.

"How is my beautiful cherub this morning?" he queried.

"Energetic, as always," Mrs. Stokes replied.

With an expression of nostalgia, Frederick looked upon the delicate features of the most prized person in his life. Burnished ringlets framed her porcelain face, her eyes sparkling. Everything about the child emulated her mother, even her love of the outdoors.

Bitsy scampered about when she glimpsed her father. With a gleeful squeal, she ran into his arms.

"Papa!"

"How is my angel this fine morning?" Scooping her up, he hugged her close, showering her rosy cheeks in kisses.

"I well," she giggled. Her attention span altered as she squirmed from his embrace and resumed running around in the early morning splendor.

"Mrs. Stokes, I'm going to town on business and won't be back until late."

"We may still be here when you return. In all my days, I don't recall caring for a child with such spirit."

Frederick smiled and disappeared into the house.

Then the dream shifted.

An older Bitsy grasped her father's hand as they strolled amongst the burgeoning flush of roses, the sun beating down upon the waxy emerald leaves and silken petals. Frederick plucked a flaming red blossom from the thorny branch, inhaling its fragrant perfume. Gently, he slipped the rose beneath the silk ribbon corralling Bitsy's shimmering ringlets.

Her deep brown eyes, the same as her mother's, gleamed as she gazed up at her father. "Papa, may I have another rose?"

"Of course, my cherub. What color would you like?"

"A pink one, if you please. It's my favorite."

Frederick reached across the hedge and plucked a bloom from the bush, catching his finger on one of the thorns. Blood bubbled at the site.

"Oh, Papa. You're hurt."

"It's only a pinprick," he said, sucking on his finger.

"Then why does it bleed so badly?"

"Sometimes the smallest things can cause the greatest damage."

He handed the flower to his daughter who motioned for him to lean over. He obeyed her command, as she snuggled the rose into the band of his hat.

"Thank you, my dear."

"Papa, why do you spend so much time with the roses?"

"Because I enjoy it."

"But we have gardeners. Why not let them do the work?"

"Aren't we full of inquiries today?"

Bitsy looked away before responding, "Some of my friends say you care for the roses because you think Mother will return someday."

His smile faded. For the past eight years, he'd done everything in his power to shield her from controversy, but he could protect her no longer.

"My dearest Bitsy, please don't concern yourself with idle gossip."

"Are they wrong?" she queried, cocking her head.

"Not exactly. Your mother spent a great deal of time and energy in the rose garden." He looked solemnly toward the house. "This is your family home, with a reputation for its gardens. I do this as a legacy for you. Someday, you'll care for these bushes, and your children after that."

"Does this mean Mother will never return?" she asked, her brow furrowing.

"I don't have an answer to that question, my dear. However, we can keep the roses growing and hope one day she'll come back and be proud of what we've done in her absence."

"Oh, Papa, I do hope she comes home. Will you teach me to care for the roses so I can make her proud?"

"Of course."

Bitsy hopped up and down. "May we begin today?"

He grasped his daughter's hand, leading her through the garden, identifying different rose varieties as she listened intently.

Sarah gasped as she bolted upright in bed. Looking around the darkened room, she rubbed the back of her neck trying to settle the hairs standing on end. Until now, she'd forgotten about her discussion with Danni about touching something in order to connect with the ghost in her dreams. The last thing she looked at was the scrapbook with images of Frederick and Bitsy. It had worked. Sarah's heartbeat increased as she slid from bed and padded down the stairs to the dining room. She flipped on the light, grabbed the threadbare silk pouch of jewelry, and hurried back to her room.

Slipping back into bed, Sarah pulled the garnet and pearl brooch from the bag and turned it over in her hand. She studied the faceted jewels as they sparkled in the glimmering gold setting. The image of Nora wearing the brooch to dinner with the matching earrings flashed through her mind. Satisfied that she'd made a connection to Nora, she placed the brooch back in the pouch, turned off the light, and went to sleep.

41

Nora paced the floor of her bedchambers wondering if Charles had received her note. The sooner she was able to escape, the better. Her nerves were raw as she struggled with the uncertainty of her decision. But there was no turning back now. Once Charles read the note, he'd meet her at midnight. She recalled the rendezvous they'd discussed a long time ago when they toyed with an elopement. They'd planned to run away to the Outer Banks of North Carolina where they would board a ship for Europe.

In all her life, Nora had never strayed from societal expectations or disobeyed her parents and the thought of stepping outside of her conventional existence was exhilarating. Simultaneously, the idea of causing so much pain, not to mention abandoning her daughter, hung like a noose about her neck. Nevertheless, the anguish of being separated from her true love was more than she could bear. In time, she'd seek forgiveness and hopefully gain access to her beloved Bitsy.

The grandfather clock chimed eleven, interrupting her ruminations. At this hour, the house was eerily still as the servants had already closed up for the evening and retired to their own quarters. With another hour to go before her departure, Nora's anxiety intensified, moistening her palms and hastening her heartbeat. Thankfully, Nora had asked to sleep in separate chambers after Bitsy was born in the event she needed to tend to the baby in the middle of the night. Frederick readily agreed, believing her ruse of not wanting to wake him. Remorse squeezed her chest with the ropes of her dishonesty. Frederick had been a supportive and loving husband and yet she couldn't commit her heart to him.

By morning she'd be gone, subjecting her family to heartache and social disgrace. For a brief moment, Nora reconsidered her plans but quickly suppressed her doubts. She couldn't go on like this. Perhaps if she scripted an explanation to each of them, it would ease the burden of her departure and give them some peace.

Sitting at her desk, she grasped the pen and began composing the first letter.

Frederick,

You are a wonderful man who deserves much more than I can give. I am not a fit mother as no woman who would do what I am embarking upon could refer to herself as motherly. By the time you read this I will be gone. Nonetheless, I love Bitsy with all my heart...

A rap at the door startled her. Before she could conceal the note, Frederick marched into the room. She could tell by his demeanor something was wrong. Nora rose from the desk, her insides trembling.

"Frederick, you surprised me. Is everything alright?"

"No, my dear, it is not."

He stepped toward her, gently grasping her shoulders. "I don't know how to broach such a delicate subject, so I'll be blunt. I know about the stable hand, Charles."

Nora's heart drummed at the mention of his name. How could Frederick know? Did he intercept her correspondence? Panic swirled through her mind like a typhoon, causing her knees to buckle. Frederick caught her and guided her to the tufted bench at the foot of the bed.

"I see by your reaction that what I've learned is true."

Her mouth was a desert. "What have you learned?"

"My dearest, do not be afraid. I know he's made threats, but you must be brave and tell me everything."

Frederick's words resonated in her ears. *I know he's made threats...* "What are you talking about?"

"Please don't hide the truth from me any longer. He cannot hurt you. Tell me what has happened and I'll have him dismissed immediately. He'll be exiled from the state if need be!" The gentleness in his voice gave way to indignation, his statements intensifying with each declaration.

"He's made no threats. Why are you saying such things?" Nora exhaled, relieved Frederick didn't know of her plans.

"Nora, I know you're impressed with his manner of caring for Camden, but that's no cause to shield him from the punishment he aptly deserves." Frederick paced across the room as Nora struggled for an explanation to appease him.

"I'm unsure how to respond, except..." Before she could finish, Frederick glanced down at the desk, his eyes settling on the note.

Her body went numb.

Frederick lifted the parchment, his hand beginning to tremble as he scanned the letter, his voice little more than a whisper. "What is this?"

"Frederick, if you'll let me explain," she said, jumping to her feet.

"Explain? Where are you going?"

"Nowhere, I was just writing my feelings down. I haven't been myself lately and thought if I captured my thoughts on paper I could address them more clearly," she replied, her voice faltering.

"Are you running away from *him*? Don't you trust your own husband to deal with that scoundrel? I'll have more than his job!" Frederick's voice escalated, his face reddening. He threw the note to the ground and marched for the door.

"No!" she pleaded, catching him by the arm. "I assure you he's done nothing wrong!"

Frederick wrenched his arm free from her grasp and growled, "Stop defending him! He's crossed a line and will pay for distressing my wife!"

"Please believe me, he's done me no harm!"

"He's a miscreant! Why do you continue to defend him?"

"Because I love him!"

The color drained from Frederick's face. Shaking his head, as if trying to toss her confession from his mind, he muttered, "You love him?"

"Oh, Frederick, I never meant to hurt you. This is entirely my fault."

"You're running away with him?"

Wringing her hands, she glanced at the crumpled note. "I don't know what I would have done. But things are different now. I'm not going anywhere," she reached for him but he backed away.

Frederick ran his hand over his face, trying to process his wife's revelation. Her words fueled his wounded pride like a spark to tinder setting his anger aflame. Madness brewed in his eyes and pulsed through his limbs as he grabbed her upper arms.

"You were going to leave me for a filthy, lowlife stable hand? I am a Hamilton!"

"Frederick, please, you're angry and rightfully so. We can discuss this once you've calmed."

"You think you can explain this away? What could you possibly say that could make me forget your indiscretions? You've made a fool of me!" He tightened his grip, his face only inches from hers, his hot breath stinging her eyes.

"Frederick, you're hurting me. Let go or I'll scream for help!" she pleaded, hoping to reason with the deranged creature before her.

"How dare you threaten me? Servants know their place and would never intervene between a husband and his wife, you little trollop," he hissed through gritted teeth.

His face reddened and the veins in his neck pulsed. In a rage, he shoved her, knocking her to the floor. Before she could cry out for help, his hands were wrapped around her neck. Gasping for air, she fought to escape, but his weight and strength were too much for her. Her hands began to numb as she pried at his ironclad grip around her throat. She tried to plead with him, but no sound escaped, his hold crushing her airway. Each agonizing second felt like an eternity. The room blurred and she felt herself growing dimmer. *No*, she told herself, *you can't give up...* And all went dark.

42

———

A scream escaped Sarah's lips as she jolted up in bed. For a moment, she didn't recognize where she was, but the fog dissipated from her mind when Danni ran into the room.

"Are you OK?" she asked breathlessly.

Sarah nodded. "Sorry I woke you."

Danni switched on the overhead light and glanced at Sarah's neck, "What happened?"

"I had another dream?"

"No, I mean your throat. It's red!"

Reaching for her neck, Sarah could feel the radiating heat. She scooted to the bathroom to get a closer look. Faint marks covered her throat as if she'd been strangled. She walked back in the room and plopped onto the edge of the bed. "This is getting way out of hand."

"You want to fill me in?" Danni asked, sitting across from her.

"Nora had finally decided to run away with Charles and they were going to meet at midnight. She was writing a note to Frederick apologizing for what she was about to do, hoping it would give him some peace after she left. Frederick showed up unexpectedly and confronted her about what he believed to be harassment on Charles's part based upon Reynolds's report. Nora panicked and blurted out her true feelings. Then Frederick went mad. He shoved her down, and," Sarah paused, trying to process what she'd seen. "He choked her."

"So that's why she ran off, she was trying to get away from Frederick's abuse! I'll bet your next dream reveals he blackmailed her into leaving without Bitsy while he played the sorrowful spouse to cover it up," Danni declared.

"She's dead."

"Of course, she's dead. She's haunting you."

"No, he killed her!"

"You can't be serious," Danni said, sitting straighter.

"Look at my neck and tell me I'm imagining this! She didn't run off, he murdered her!" Sarah rubbed her throat.

"Let's try to figure this out. Did you do something different before bed?"

"I looked through one of the scrapbooks. It was obviously post-Nora because it was filled with photos of Frederick and Bitsy. Then I dreamt about them. When I woke up I remembered what you said earlier about touching something belonging to the person in order to connect with their ghost in the dreams. I went downstairs, grabbed the pouch with the jewelry, and held the garnet and pearl brooch in my hand hoping to connect with Nora. Initially I was connected with her but somehow Frederick broke through."

Danni chewed her lower lip. "I might not have explained that clearly enough. Nora may have handled the brooch before her death but Frederick was the last one to touch it when he hid it in the hearth. Sounds like the connection got crossed since there was a strong attachment to the item for both of them."

"How do I keep that from happening again?" Sarah asked, rubbing her forehead.

"Don't know yet." Danni blew a long breath across her lips. "If Frederick killed Nora, where's the body?"

"I have no idea. I woke up when she died." Sarah's words were barely a whisper.

"This seems a bit farfetched. I can believe some of the other stuff, but murder? Surely, someone would have noticed him dragging a corpse from the house."

"Maybe Reynolds helped him. It would explain some of the bonuses he received." Sarah paused, mulling over the situation.

"Still doesn't explain why Nora's body was never discovered. They had a house full of servants, as well as her parents to question her whereabouts. Surely someone would've noticed something." Danni snapped her fingers. "Why don't you go back to sleep and see if you can dream where he buried her?"

"I'm not sure I ever want to sleep again."

"Want me to stay in here with you?"

Shaking her head, Sarah mumbled, "Go back to bed. I'll be all right."

"Are you sure?"

"Yeah, I'm sure. There's nothing you can do to stop the dreams and I don't think Nora would let anything serious happen to me."

"There can't be much left to reveal except where her body is buried." Danni stood up. "Sure you don't want me to stay?"

"I'm good, don't worry."

"Holler if you need me."

"I will. Thanks."

Danni paused in the doorway, switching off the overhead light, her playfulness resurfacing. "Sweet dreams!"

"Very funny!" Sarah tossed a pillow at Danni as she scurried from the room giggling. Danni always knew how to lighten the mood, even when haunted dreams and violent ghosts awaited.

Sarah rested her head against the pillow, willing herself to sleep. After listening to the rhythmic tick-tocking of the grandfather clock for over an hour, she finally dozed off.

43

———

Frederick shook Nora trying to revive her but to no avail. She was gone. Burying his head in his hands, he wailed, "Why did you do this, Nora? How could you make me do such a horrid thing?"

He slumped against the bed, gazing at her lifeless body. He had to do something before anyone stumbled upon the scene. Frederick struggled to his feet, covering Nora's body with a quilt before making his way downstairs where he summoned Reynolds to his office.

Moments later, the footman appeared, haphazardly dressed with puffy eyes.

"Come in and close the door behind you." Frederick leaned across his desk. "I need your assistance with something of a delicate nature. I assure you the compensation will be substantial. Are you with me?"

"I'm at your service, sir."

"Follow me."

With a nod, Reynolds accompanied Frederick upstairs to Nora's bedchambers. They stepped inside and closed the door.

Drained of emotion, Frederick motioned toward the corpse

beneath the quilt, "Reynolds, Mrs. Hamilton has had a terrible accident. Please don't ask about the circumstances, the less you know the better."

Reynolds nodded.

"We must remove her body without alerting anyone," Frederick stated.

"What shall we say when people question her absence?"

"Let me deal with that. As far as anyone is concerned, you know nothing of her disappearance. In the meantime, I need you to gather the necessary tools to bury her."

"Of course, sir."

"Meet me in the kitchen in fifteen minutes."

Reynolds checked his pocket watch, acknowledged his orders with a nod, and started for the door.

"Reynolds, I cannot express the depth of my appreciation. Your loyalty has been invaluable."

"Thank you, sir."

Fifteen minutes passed at the pace of a tortoise as Frederick gazed upon the quilt shrouding Nora's lifeless body. His muscles were in knots as he stood and hurried down the stairs, grabbed the oil lamp from the chest outside his office, and joined Reynolds in the kitchen.

"Were you able to procure the tools?" Frederick asked.

"Yes, sir."

He handed Reynolds the oil lamp. "I'll go and get the body. Meet me in the garden."

With a nod, Reynolds did as he was ordered.

The house had taken on an unnervingly tomblike feel, chilling Frederick to the core of his soul. Never in his life had he felt so devoid of emotion, as if all the love he had for Nora had been siphoned from his soul leaving nothing but an empty shell of a man. His stomach twisted as he ascended the back stairs and entered the bedchambers. He wrapped the quilt snuggly around the body, hoisted the bundle over his shoulder, and skulked into the darkness.

Having successfully maneuvered the narrow back staircase, Frederick slipped out the kitchen door. Moonbeams washed the garden in an unearthly glow, illuminating the rose bushes where Reynolds waited with shovels, a pick, and the flickering oil lamp.

Frederick rested the body on the ground and helped Reynolds dig a narrow plot between the rose hedge and tabby wall, checking frequently to make sure no one was aware of their clandestine activity. After an hour of sweat induced labor, Frederick carefully placed the corpse into the welcoming embrace of freshly dug earth. Nora's hand shifted from the edge of the quilt as if she were reaching for him. He grabbed the shovel and tossed dirt onto the body as quickly as possible trying to erase the nauseating scene before him. Once he and Reynolds had refilled the hole they covered the area in a blanket of pine needles, leaving nothing notable in view.

Frederick instructed Reynolds to return the tools, wash up, and say nothing about Mrs. Hamilton's absence.

"I'll take it to my grave, Sir."

Frederick slipped in the back door and settled into his study to prepare for the flood of questions that would inevitably follow. He poured a double shot of whisky and began formulating a scheme.

After plotting for hours, Frederick was pleased with his solution. He'd express his devastation after discovering a note from Nora stating she'd run away due to the stress of motherhood. If anyone inquired about the actual letter, he'd say he burned it in a state of despair. Devereaux would know how to get rid of the stable hand. Ruination of Charles's reputation would prevent anyone from believing him should he reveal the affair or question Nora's absence. Frederick's relationship with his in-laws was strong enough that they would accept his disclosure of the facts surrounding their daughter's departure. The plan was perfect.

The thought of raising Bitsy alone was frightening, but he'd maintain appearances for her sake. Shielding her from gossip and disrepute would be his primary objective. His head ached over what had transpired, but he convinced himself it was justified. After all, it was Nora's betrayal that had forced him to react so violently.

SARAH ROUSED FROM HER SLEEP. Her clothes were damp with sweat and her neck was still tender. Disturbed by the night's visions and the horror Nora had endured, Sarah tried to push the memories from her head when her last dream jolted her fully awake. She jumped from bed and ran across the hall where Danni snoozed, her face squished against the pillow with her hand draped over the edge of the bed.

"Danni, wake up," she said, shaking her friend's arm.

A moan slid from Danni's mouth as she swatted at Sarah.

"Come on, Danni, this is important," Sarah said, shaking Danni's arm again.

Danni rolled over, squinting as she grumbled, "What time is it?"

"Time for you to get up," Sarah answered, anxiety pumping through her chest.

"It's too early. I haven't had a full night's sleep," she replied, rolling back over.

"I know where Nora is buried!"

Danni sat up, rubbing her eyes with the heels of her hands. "Seriously?"

"Yes! I had another dream and I'm pretty sure I know where she is."

"Let me change," Danni muttered, her mind wakening as she ran her fingers through her hair.

"Meet you downstairs."

Sarah hurried back to her room, changed, and went to the kitchen to start the kettle. Moments later, Danni trudged in and started the coffee maker before plunking down at the table.

"Tell me what happened."

"Let me fix a cup of tea first. I need some caffeine before I launch into this story."

Sarah fixed a cup of coffee for Danni before pouring water in her cup. She set the cups on the table and sat down swirling the teabag as she spoke.

"After Frederick killed Nora he enlisted the help of his footman, Reynolds, to dispose of her body."

"What?" Danni asked, taking a swig of her coffee.

"They waited until everyone was asleep, wrapped Nora in a quilt, and buried her under one of the rose bushes."

"That's crazy!"

"Exactly, which is why, now that I'm awake, I question it. Surely someone would have discovered remains in the rose garden after all these years."

"Maybe not. Wasn't Frederick adamant about tending the roses himself?"

"That's what the rumor mill says."

"Now we know why. It wasn't to keep them blooming for Bitsy, he wanted to prevent anyone from finding Nora's body."

Sarah pondered the notion but countered it. "Frederick has been dead for decades. What stopped someone else from finding Nora?"

"The responsibility of caring for the roses was passed on to Bitsy and then to her daughter and then to Edie. It's one of the few family traditions Edie honored. The bushes are ancient and no one would risk digging them up. All Edie had to do was take care of them and no one would be the wiser."

Sarah sipped her tea. "I suppose there's only one way to find out."

"How's that?"

"We start digging."

Danni leaned forward, her eyes widening.

"You aren't suggesting we look for a body in the garden? Those rose bushes are heirlooms. It will push William over the edge if we destroy them."

"So, there's a fringe benefit," Sarah chuckled. "If Frederick was able to bury a body without killing the bushes, I'm sure we can excavate without doing much harm. We just have to be careful."

Sarah thought about Nora's death. She deserved a proper burial and if digging around some fancy rose bushes meant exposing the truth and giving her peace, it was worth it.

"We've come this far, we can't stop now. Let's do this," Sarah said, raising her eyebrows.

"Alright," Danni replied before gulping down the rest of her coffee.

They walked to the garden shed and emerged with shovels.

"Do you remember exactly where they buried her?"

"Between the far hedge and the garden wall," Sarah pointed.

Danni examined the tight space. "There's no way we can get back there without thorns tearing us to pieces. We need to prune it back. I saw some clippers in the shed."

Hurrying to the shed, Danni retrieved the garden shears while Sarah studied the area behind the rose bushes.

"We're about to find out if I inherited any of my mother's gardening skills," Danni declared, holding up the shears.

Danni snipped at the branches, careful not to catch her skin on the thorns, until a mound of spiked limbs grew and a narrow path formed. She stepped back and admired her handiwork.

"Not bad."

"Don't quit your day job," Sarah snorted. "Ready to excavate?"

"Let's make like Indiana Jones and dig."

With shovels in hand, they gouged and burrowed at the sandy soil for an hour. With a hole several feet deep, there was still no sign of a body.

"I don't think we're going to find anything," Sarah panted, sweat trickling down her neck.

"We've done this much, maybe we should dig a bit more."

"You go ahead. I'm going to grab a bottle of water. Want one?"

"Yeah, thanks."

Sarah walked inside, grabbed two bottles of water, and ran back outside to find Danni sinking the shovel down another layer. The two friends continued digging when something came into view. Sarah dropped to her knees and cleared away sand with her hands until she caught a scrap of fabric.

"Look!" Sarah held a calico remnant in her dirt caked hand.

"Please tell me that's not what I think it is."

"There's only one way to find out!"

The two started pawing at the soil with the fury of a dog after a bone. More scraps of fabric emerged and then Sarah's hand brushed against something hard. She recoiled, nearly tumbling into the barbed bush behind her.

"What is it?" Danni asked, her voice barely a whisper.

Sarah leaned over and scraped at the dirt until a skeletal hand poked through. Danni gasped, stumbling backwards into the garden wall. Sarah sat back. Sweat trickled down her forehead intermixing with her tears.

"Meet Nora Monroe Hamilton," she murmured, wiping the sweat from her brow, leaving a streak of dirt across her forehead.

"I can't believe it. She's been here all along," Danni said, craning her neck to peer in the hole from a safe distance.

Sarah closed her eyes, Nora's image filling her thoughts. All those years she'd been discarded like garbage while the world believed she'd abandoned her husband and only child. No wonder she wasn't able to rest peacefully, even amongst her beloved roses.

Danni looked at Sarah, "What do we do now?"

"We better call the police."

"How do we explain finding 100-year-old remains in the garden? I don't think they're apt to buy the haunted house story."

"The body has been here longer than we've been alive. It's not like we're going to be arrested for murder. Nora deserves a proper burial. I'll think of something logical to tell them."

Danni shook her head, "Tell the cops whatever you want. Who's going to break the news to William?"

"We'll let the police have that privilege."

Sarah brushed the dirt from her legs before jaunting inside. She called Captain Harris who arrived a short time later with a team of investigators. Sarah and Danni watched from the kitchen window as crime scene experts exhumed the skeletal remains. Shortly thereafter, the slamming of a car door, followed by flagrant yelling, interrupted the scene.

"What the heck are you doing? Who gave you permission to be on this property?"

Sarah looked at Danni with a sly grin. Their words rang out in unison, "William's here!" followed by raucous laughter.

They watched the episode unfold like a TV police drama as a red-faced William blustered at the detectives to cease and desist the destruction of the property. Captain Harris was all too happy to escort the raging lunatic back to his car with a warning to stand back and let them work. William clamored about legal suits before hopping into his Lexus and speeding off. Seconds later, Danni's cell phone rang. Glancing at the screen, she smiled. "Guess who?"

Sarah giggled, "Put it on speaker."

"Hello," Danni said in a lilting tone.

"What has your idiot friend done at the mansion?"

"Who is this?" Danni crooned.

"You know darn well who it is you stupid..."

"William, is that you? I didn't recognize the high-pitched voice."

Sarah stifled a laugh as Danni taunted William.

"What's happening at the mansion? I just left there and the police are in the backyard wreaking havoc on the landscape!"

"Sarah is fine, thanks for asking."

"She won't be when I get hold of her! It's bad enough she dismantled the wall upstairs, but now this? What's going on?"

"I don't know, William, but I'll let you know as soon as I hear something."

"Don't you dare hang..."

Danni pressed the red button, disconnecting his rampage.

"William says hello." And laughter echoed through the kitchen.

They watched the forensic team work for more than an hour when Captain Harris made his way up the back stairs into the kitchen.

"Well, it's definitely a human body. It appears to be female. CSI is taking it to the lab for identification."

"Any idea who it could be?" Sarah asked.

The captain shook his head. "With this family, it's hard to tell, but I know Edie's great-grandmother was never accounted for. Maybe this is why." He gave a nod and stepped out the door.

The two friends smiled knowingly at each other when Danni asked, "You hungry?"

44

———————

Two weeks later, Sarah's truck sputtered and coughed down the oyster shell drive as she pulled behind a sleek gray BMW. She'd not been back to Monroe Manse since she'd removed the last of the inventory the week before. Even though she was relieved to have everything done and to be back in her own cottage, she missed this place. There was something special about it that she couldn't quite understand. Perhaps it was the realization that her years of being haunted had a purpose, one that she was pursuing with the help of her best friend.

Thankfully, Jerrod Devereaux had granted an extension allowing Sarah to complete her work. He seemed less than pleased about the scandalous discovery but there was nothing that could be done about it now. As she parked the Beast, a pristinely dressed woman emerged from the BMW, her sandy blond hair drawn back in a bun.

"Good afternoon. You must be Sarah Holden," she said, offering her hand.

Sarah returned the handshake. "And you must be Cindy Vallion. It's nice to meet you."

"Thanks for coming over. I found a few things you left behind."

"Sorry about that. I thought I'd cleared everything out."

"There were three boxes in the attic that were well hidden. I'm not surprised you missed them."

As they stepped into the kitchen, an old familiar feeling swept over Sarah, like walking into a warm embrace. Traces of orange oil- and pine-scented cleaners lingered in the air and all the surfaces gleamed. Glancing out the kitchen window, Sarah gazed at the rose hedges robed in brightly shaded petals of red, yellow, and pink.

"It must have been shocking to discover Nora Hamilton's body after all these years. I wonder how she ended up in the gardens?" Cindy said as they traipsed through the house.

Sarah shrugged her shoulders. "I suppose we'll never know."

"I'm not happy they found a body in the backyard, but I am pleased to get this listing."

"I was surprised William gave it up. I've never known him to walk away from potential profits, especially when millions are involved."

"His agency didn't want to be affiliated with the *unfortunate situation*," she said raising her eyebrows. "I can't imagine any buyer would be deterred. The woman has been dead for more than a century and there's no proof she died in the house."

Sarah bit her lower lip. They reached the attic space where three boxes rested near the doorway.

"I called as soon as we found them. Don't have any idea what's inside, I left that for you."

Melodious notes emanated from Cindy's pocket. She glanced at the number and smiled. "I really need to answer this. I'll be right back." Her voice echoed down the stairs as she took the call. "Hey James, I'm at the Monroe mansion with Sarah Holden…"

Sarah knelt down and opened one of the boxes. Cookbooks, kitchen utensils, and several round silver plated trays occupied the space.

"More junk," she muttered and opened the next container.

Stacks of gardening magazines from the seventies spewed their musty breath as she dug through the cardboard container. She pushed it aside and reached for the next one.

Perhaps three is a charm, she thought, opening the last box. Disappointment brimmed as she peered inside to find vibrantly hued polyester slacks and blouses. She dug around hoping to discover something of value when her hand brushed against a hard surface. Her fingers prickled as she extracted the item from the depths of its paperboard tomb. She held a small burled walnut box monogrammed with the initials *EAM*. Before she could investigate, the strong scent of Chanel No. 5 stung Sara's nose.

"Anything of interest?" Cindy asked, standing in the doorway.

"Doesn't look like it, but I'll get a better look at the shop." Sarah replaced the treasure, refolding the box tabs and brushing the dust from her jeans as she stood.

"I've got a client meeting me here in half an hour. Let's hope it's a sale," Cindy smiled as she held up her manicured hands with fingers crossed.

"Good luck."

"Do you need help carrying these downstairs?"

"That'd be great, thanks."

Cindy lifted the box of kitchenware while Sarah grabbed the box of magazines. Both women were winded by the time they reached Sarah's truck where they plunked the cardboard containers in the back with a resounding thump.

Sarah sprinted back to the attic, hoisting the last box into her arms. Sorrow plucked at her emotions like fingers on violin strings as she looked around the emptied space.

"Well, Nora, I guess this is truly good-bye." Her eyes moistened as she ambled to the first-floor landing where Cindy waited.

The two women started for the front door when an icy finger traced the back of Sarah's neck. She glanced over her shoulder to see a shadowy skeletal form at the top of the stairs, the same one from her dreams. She sucked in a breath as the image transformed into a lovely young woman with coffee brown locks framing a luminous visage. A pale blue gown hugged her corseted figure as the scent of roses infiltrated the air. Sarah smiled as Nora gave her an approving nod before dissipating into nothingness.

Cindy opened the door for Sarah. "You know, they say this place is haunted. Have you ever heard anything so ridiculous?"

Sarah walked past her and whispered, "If you only knew."

45

Sarah drove to her shop and unloaded the three boxes from the bed of her truck. Once inside, she pulled the walnut box from the cardboard container and sat at her desk digging through the top drawer for the bag of skeleton keys she kept for these occasions. It took a few tries before she found one that would unlock the box. Anticipation jiggled her nerves as she gently lifted the lid only to discover a stack of papers tucked inside. Her adrenaline rush subsided as her hopes for something of value dissipated. Sarah removed the pile of tri-folded papers, the one on top catching her attention. It appeared to be a high-end linen stationary neatly folded with the words *To my daughter*, scripted on the outside.

I thought we'd found all of Nora's correspondence, Sarah thought. Unfolding the letter, she began to read.

My dearest daughter,

Chances are you will never see this letter since your identity has been hidden from me but it gives me peace to write it. There are so many things I wish I could tell you. Regardless, I never stopped loving you and think of you daily.

After my parents forced me to give you up, in order to spare their precious social standing, I disowned them, adopting my great-great-grandparent's name of Monroe. They seemed to be the last in our family line with any sense of dignity. I have resigned myself to doing all I can to break free from the constraints of societal expectations. They have destroyed my life. If I can make the world a better place, while bringing shame to my parents, then so be it.

As for your sperm donor, I'd admired him all through school but my father refused to let him court me. When he approached me at our class graduation party, I thought I was finally free to love him. Sadly, I soon discovered my father's opinion of him was correct, adding salt to the wound of my heart.

There's not much else I can say except I never wanted to give you up and I should have fought harder to keep you. I pray you were raised in a loving family and that life has been good to you. Most importantly, follow your dreams my dear child, no matter what.

Your affectionate mother,

Edie Anne Monroe

STUNNED, Sarah leaned back in the chair, trying to make sense of what she'd just read. Edie had a child? The strong scent of Chanel No. 5 filled the room as the air turned frigid. Sarah's shoulders slumped as she exhaled her frustration. There wasn't time to solve another mystery, especially since she no longer had access to the mansion. She still had to formally appraise the estate items, not to mention prepare for the auction. The idea of more haunted dreams made Sarah cringe.

The shop phone rang startling Sarah from her stupor. She glanced at the number and smiled.

"You're home," she answered. "I wasn't expecting you for another month."

"Got home last night. We'd really like to see you." Her father's soothing baritone voice boomed from the other end.

"Of course. I'm at the shop, come on by."

"Why don't you come to the house?"

"Dad, is everything OK?"

"We're fine but we really need to see you."

"I'll be right over."

Sarah's mind raced with a myriad of dismal scenarios. Was one of her parents sick? Did someone in the family die? Had her uncle Joe stolen another car from the retirement facility and taken off again? Grabbing her keys, she locked up the store, and sped to her parent's house on Dove Point.

Sarah cruised down the paved drive to the modest painted brick ranch overlooking the Intercostal Waterway. Salty breezes caressed her skin as she hurried to the front door of the house, her mind jumbled with disastrous thoughts. Their early return and the insistence on seeing her at her childhood home suggested something dreadful.

She reached for the knob when the door opened, her father's sculpted cheeks forming the grin that always melted away her fears. She took in his special scent of aftershave and lavender soap as his long arms pulled her close.

"How's my pumpkin?"

"Fine Daddy. Missed you guys and can't wait to hear about your latest trip."

She followed him to the living room where her mother was setting a tea tray on the center table. Sarah's mother didn't believe in doing anything half way. Always a silver teapot, always loose-leaf tea brewed to perfection, and always china cups. The room was well furnished with two substantial empire sofas facing each other, divided by an oblong seventeenth century table. An entire wall of windows provided a spectacular view of the river. Her mother gave her a quick hug and whispered,

"You're looking thin my dear. We need to work on that."

Sarah glanced down at her body and shook her head. "You always say that Mom and I just don't see it. If you'd seen all the take-out food I've eaten with Danni the past few weeks you'd freak out! Maybe if you'd stay put long enough to have me over for supper I might eat better."

"Humph," her mother grunted as she walked to the other side of the coffee table.

Sarah sat across from her parents feeling a bit more comfortable since their relaxed demeanor didn't suggest someone was in poor health or dying. They'd probably changed their travel plans, booked a yearlong cruise, and wanted to spend some time with her before they left. Nonetheless, she was anxious to hear what they had to say.

Her mother handed her a cup of tea and took a seat. Sara guzzled it down in a few gulps inducing a look of consternation from her mother. Sarah held out her hand when her mother lifted the teapot offering to refill her cup.

"Forgive me, but I'm a bit worried about whatever it is you have to tell me. Could we skip the niceties and get to the matter at hand?" Sarah asked.

Her father smiled, "That's my girl, straight to the point. You should've gone into law."

"I love what I do, Dad." Sarah scooted to the edge of the sofa, "What's going on?"

Her mother started to speak when Sarah's father rested his hand gently on his wife's arm. He gave her a knowing glance that said, *Let me handle this.*

Her mother acquiesced, taking a sip of her tea.

"Please let me say everything before you comment or ask any questions. This is the most difficult thing I've ever had to do," her father said.

Sarah nodded, a lump forming in her throat as tears stung

her eyes, her trepidation returning. *Which one of them is dying?* she thought.

Her mother's deep blue eyes gazed at her with great concern as her father began his summation, much like he did in the courtroom.

"We got a call from my old law partner, Harlan, while we were in Italy. He told us about the Monroe estate you've been working on. He heard about it while he was at the barbershop and contacted me immediately."

"Why would he care..." Sarah stopped mid-sentence as her father arched his eyebrows and straightened his shoulders letting her know it was time to listen, not speak.

"We're aware that a great deal of information was revealed during your time at Monroe Manse, including the discovery of Edie's great-grandmother, Nora Monroe Hamilton. We were concerned that other family secrets might have come to light."

Sarah chewed her bottom lip to prevent a flood of words from pouring out of her mouth. Her mind clamored with all the things she wanted to say like how she'd discovered Nora's body and that she was something called a dreamist who could see departed spirits in her dreams. She wanted to scream that she wasn't crazy and ask why her mother hadn't mentioned the genetic part of the dreamist abilities before now?

"Anyway, as you're aware, your mother and I had been married for some time when you came along."

"I know," Sarah said. "You told me that's why I never had any siblings."

"Please know that we love you more than anything," he said, grasping her mother's hand as they gazed into each other's eyes lovingly. "There's no easy way to say this." He inhaled deeply, watching for Sarah's reaction. "What I'm trying to say is that we weren't able to have children."

Sarah cocked her head and furrowed her brow. "You mean after you had me?"

"We were never able to conceive. You were adopted."

Adopted, I'm adopted. The words echoed through Sarah's mind with the resounding force of an avalanche. Her mouth was dryer than the Sahara Desert as she tried to form the words. "You're not my parents?" she muttered.

"Not biologically."

"I don't understand," Sarah said. "Why didn't you tell me before now?"

"We never thought we'd have reason to tell you," her mother replied.

"What possible reason would cause you to tell me now? I'm an adult for goodness sake! This is not the kind of thing you drop in a person's lap!" Her emotions took control as her mind relinquished any sense of logic. A sob broke loose as her mother moved to the sofa beside her. Sarah shifted away, too shocked to accept any comfort.

"We didn't make the decision lightly but we had good reason for not telling you before now. When we heard you were working on the Monroe estate and had discovered certain secrets, we knew we had to come home," her father replied, his voice steady in the face of his daughter's agitated state.

"What does the estate have to do with any of this?" Sarah demanded.

"Because Edie Monroe is your biological mother," her father said flatly.

"What?" She sucked in a breath. Her body numbed and her head began to ache as she tried to process everything her parents were telling her.

"Edie had an unfortunate encounter at a high school graduation party. She'd had a bit too much to drink and was taken advantage of by one of the young men in attendance. When her parents learned she was pregnant they contacted my law partner, Harlan, about making arrangements for the baby. Edie was sent to live with her aunt for a year with plans for her to return a few months after the baby was born. That way no one would ever know she'd been pregnant."

Sarah exhaled when she noticed the strong scent of Chanel No. 5 wafting through the room. Her resolve strengthened as her mind darted back to the contents of the letter she'd read at the shop.

"Go on," she whispered, trying to control her emotions.

"Your mother and I had resigned ourselves to a life without children when Harlan told me about Edie's predicament. Her father wanted it taken care of without anyone in town learning about it. It seemed like the perfect scenario. We would finally have a child and the Hanovers would be rid of anything that could tarnish Edie's chances at the aristocratic life they'd planned for her.

"You mean the Hanovers didn't know you adopted me?"

Her father shook his head. "It was all very private. The only ones who knew were Harlan, your mother, and me. It was easier to hide these things back then. But when Harlan told us about the details you'd unearthed at the mansion, we were worried Edie might have hidden a diary or something that would reveal your true lineage."

"Don't you think if I'd discovered something like that I would have called you?" Exasperation punctuated her words. "Granted, every time I called you were either boarding a plane or the voice mail was full."

"I'm sorry about all that. Regardless, we knew we had to speak with you before you discovered the truth on your own." Her father paused, giving Sarah time to process everything.

Sarah slumped back against the sofa, her mind racing as tears flowed across her face. All of a sudden, her entire life began to fall into place like a puzzle; her mother shielding her from gossip, her dreamist abilities, and Edie haunting her.

Sarah wiped the tears from her cheeks, her eyes swollen and red. No wonder her parents didn't understand her gift; they were completely unaware of it because they weren't biologically connected to her.

"Are you alright?" her mother asked, reaching for Sarah's hand, which she allowed.

"I think so. I just need some time to sort through it all and try to make sense of everything."

"We understand if you're angry with us..." her father started when Sarah interrupted.

"Dad, I'm not angry, only shocked. I think I understand what you guys were trying to do and I'm thankful for it. But I still don't get why you didn't tell me before now. Wouldn't it have been easier than worrying I might inadvertently discover my parentage from someone else?"

"As I said, the only people who knew were Harlan, your mother, and me. Until you started working on the Monroe estate we always believed our secret was safe. We did nothing illegal, albeit slightly questionable. Archibald Hanover was adamant that the baby was placed where Edie would never find it. His actions were reprehensible eventually leading him to drink heavily. But there's more at stake here. There's the matter of your inheritance."

"Inheritance?"

"Yes darling, you're the rightful heir to the Monroe estate," her mother said. "Everything will come to you."

Sarah sat up straighter. "What? That doesn't seem right. Who inherits a multi-million-dollar estate from someone they never knew?"

Her father smiled. "It's an exceptional situation but it's all yours, the contents and the house. Think of the possibilities..."

"Maybe I don't want the estate," Sarah interrupted, overwhelmed by it all. "I mean, can we even prove this?"

"Don't make any rash decisions, not until you've had time to absorb everything," her father replied. "I spoke with Danni last night and she verified we have the necessary documentation to transfer the estate to you."

"Danni knows about this?" Sarah yelled, heat radiating across her cheeks as her arms trembled. The idea that her dearest friend was part of the deception was too much. Danni should've called her immediately.

"We asked her to keep it quiet until we had a chance to speak with you first and she agreed. She did the right thing letting us tell you. Just because we didn't approve of her antics during high school doesn't mean we don't like her. She's always been a good friend to you and we appreciate that."

Sarah's shoulders slumped as the anger toward her best friend abated. They were right.

"What proof do you have of my lineage?"

"We have the original birth certificate with Edie's name on it."

Sarah's insides shriveled. Just when she thought the situation couldn't get any stranger another aspect rose to the surface. "Does it have the father's name too?"

"Yes," her father sighed heavily.

Sarah's tongue stuck to the roof of her mouth, impeding her speech. She cocked her head questioningly as her father met her gaze.

He swallowed hard and said with a deadpan voice, "Rodney Devereaux."

A shriek loosened her tongue. "William's father?" Sarah's stomach lurched threatening to empty itself. Her hands began to shake and her eyes burned as fresh tears trickled across her cheeks. The room began to swirl when she heard her mother's voice whisper, "take a deep breath, hold it for a count of five, release..."

Sarah followed her mother's instructions until she regained her focus, her emotions dipping and soaring like one of those supersonic roller coasters.

"Are you telling me William Devereaux is my half-brother?"

"Yes," her father replied.

The meal she'd eaten hours earlier refused to stay put sending Sarah rushing to the half bath by the kitchen. Once her stomach was emptied, she splashed cold water on her face and gazed in the mirror. The person she'd always believed herself to be wasn't who she was at all.

Her mom and dad weren't her birth parents, her biological mother was haunting her, and now she understood why William always made her skin crawl. The filthy creature was her half-brother. Her stomach heaved again as her mother rapped on the door.

"Sarah my dear, are you alright?"

Before she could answer, a thought popped into Sarah's head. William doesn't know. He'd lose his mind when he learned he'd been hitting on his half-sister all these years. A laugh erupted from her lips like lava from a volcano. Her mother's knocking intensified when Sarah opened the door, a weak smile lifting her flushed cheeks.

"I've got to call Danni," she blurted out.

"Whatever for? We already spoke with her and she said the estate will rightfully go to you."

Except that wasn't why Sarah wanted to talk to Danni. The missing pieces of the mystery had finally come together and she wanted to share it with her best friend, the only one who'd ever accepted Sarah's unique abilities without judgment.

Sarah laughed again hugging her mother close, the tension draining from her body. She didn't understand it but for the first time in her life things made sense. She knew what Edie was trying to tell her, that her haunted dreams were some sort of strange gift, and why William was so repulsive. Amidst the insanity was sanity.

"So, you forgive us?" her mother asked, holding her daughter at arm's length.

"There's nothing to forgive. You did what you thought was best for me. You're my parents and I love you. Everything is a bit overwhelming right now. I just need some time to process it."

Her mother smiled, the same glowing smile she always gave when Sarah did something extraordinary. "And now you know why I've worked so hard to shield you from the gossip in this town," she said, her manicured hand cupping Sarah's cheek.

Sarah embraced her mother again. "Love you, Mom."

"Love you too."

Sarah scooped her father into a long embrace. "Love you bunches Dad."

"I'm proud of you baby girl," he replied as Sarah stepped away and grabbed her keys. "Where are you going?"

"I've got to see a ghost about a house."

Sarah drove straight to the manse, a renewed sense of belonging pervading her spirit. The old familiar crunch of oyster shells sang out as if welcoming her home. She still had the house key and used it to let herself in. Stepping through the front door, she was greeted by newly polished wood floors and gleaming windows. She closed the door and leaned against it taking a moment to relish the scene before her, a smile raising her cheeks when the scent of Chanel No. 5 tickled her nose.

Danni sat at the fire pit in Sarah's backyard with a beer in one hand and her cell phone in the other.

"Are you ready?" Sarah asked.

"Yup. Hitting record now," Danni replied, holding up her phone.

"Here's to being debt free!" Sarah declared, tossing a copy of the mortgage papers to her cottage into the flames. Danni recorded the event as the corners of the papers curled into dust.

When it vanished from sight, they hollered "Hoorah!" and toasted Sarah's newfound independence from her mortgage.

Apparently, Edie had accumulated a nice little sum of cash over the years, just enough to pay off the mortgage on Sarah's cottage. She'd finally achieved her goal. Sarah was officially debt free.

46

SARAH MEANDERED through the gardens wearing her grandmother's straw hat while deadheading the heirloom roses behind the mansion. In only a few months, she had managed to reform the overgrown boxwoods exposing the original English maze design. Crepe myrtles were trimmed, weeds pulled, and colorful petals once again highlighted the flowerbeds. Freshly manicured gardens breathed life back into the tabby mansion, softening the dismal feel that had shrouded it for more than a century. Sarah was thankful to have her family, her best friend, and a career she truly loved. It seemed as if life was finally falling into place.

Following the announcement of her ancestral ties, Sarah managed to survive the onslaught of gossip after a lifetime of being protected from it. Local headlines reported the windfall of the multimillion-dollar estate going to Edie's illegitimate child, thus answering many of the lingering questions about Edie's plummet from debutante to nudist to free spirited drunken protester.

The coroner's report ruled Nora's death a murder due to strangulation although the person responsible remained a mystery. Only Sarah and Danni would ever know the truth.

Armed with the new knowledge about her biological mother, Sarah's affection for Edie grew and with it her confidence. She'd never felt as if she'd fit in anywhere and now she understood the reason. She held no animosity towards her parents for keeping their secret; after all they'd given her an amazing life. Her only regret was not getting to know Edie, especially after the emotions revealed in the letter she'd written decades before.

Best of all, William had avoided her after learning he'd been trying to pick up his half-sister for years. Rodney Devereaux refused contact with her for which she was thankful, as she wanted nothing to do with him. He was as disgusting as every other Devereaux she'd ever encountered.

Absorbed in her gardening, Sarah startled when the Batman theme blared from her pocket.

"Hey Danni."

"Where are you?"

"Working in the garden," Sarah said, wiping sweat from her brow.

"Who's running the store?"

"Manny's there."

"Did she get moved into the cottage?" Danni asked.

"Yup. She's thrilled with the place," Sarah replied.

"Of course, she is. You're letting her live there free of charge while she finishes her Master's degree. Anyone would be exuberant with an offer like that."

"Now that it's paid for it seemed like the right thing to do," Sarah said.

"I still can't believe you didn't sell it."

"I put my sweat and tears into renovating that place. It's part of me." Sarah chuckled. "By the way, why are you calling?"

"I need you to swing by my office."

Sarah's heartbeat quickened. "Did you learn something new from the *Dreamist* book?"

"A few things but that's not what I need to discuss."

Sarah recognized Danni's serious tone and decided not to delay. "Let me clean up and I'll be right over."

Spring breezes flowed through the open windows of the Beast as Sarah drove to Danni's office. She parked in the gravel lot, the ramshackle engine blustering for a few moments as she removed the key. Sarah entered the office surprised to find Anita there on a Saturday.

"Hello Ms. Holden, Ms. Cook is waiting for you."

"Thanks Anita," she said on her way to Danni's office, grabbing the cup of tea waiting next to the coffee pot as she went.

"Hey, what's up?" Sarah asked, taking a seat in front of Danni's desk.

"I got a phone call from an attorney friend of mine in Edgefield. He has a situation he can't handle due to a conflict of interest, so he asked for my help."

"Edgefield? Haven't been there since I was a kid."

"They need someone to handle the liquidation of an estate. You up for it?"

"I suppose. Business is slow right now, so I have the time."

"I can't believe you're still working. And when are you going to buy a new truck? I could hear the Beast two blocks before you arrived."

"I like what I do," Sarah replied defensively. "And as for my truck, it gets me where I need to go so there's no need to spend money on another one."

"If you say so," Danni smirked.

"Tell me more about this job."

"It shouldn't take more than a few weeks. We'll be staying at a house near the square downtown. But before you agree, there's something you need to know."

"Go ahead."

"The house we'll be staying at is supposedly haunted. Are you OK with that?"

Sarah shrugged her shoulders. "Why not? What's the worst that can happen?"

ABOUT THE AUTHOR

Kim Poovey is an author, storyteller, and living historian. She has traveled the Southeast for more than 20 years performing in period attire on 19th century fashion, mourning practices, and other Victorian era topics. In 2011 she portrayed Mrs. Stanton, wife of Secretary of War Stanton (Kevin Kline), in the Robert Redford film, *The Conspirator*. Her published works include *Truer Words, Through Button Eyes; Memoirs of an Edwardian Teddy Bear,* and *Dickens' Mice, The Tails Behind the Tale.* In addition, Kim has written for several magazines to include Beaufort Lifestyles, Bluffton Breeze, Citizen's Companion, and the Civil War Times. Kim lives in a haunted 1890s Victorian cottage in the South Carolina Lowcountry with her husband, Darryl, and their furry children.

For more about upcoming releases, giveaways, and ghostly tales, sign up for Kim's newsletter at:

kimpoovey.com

ALSO BY KIM POOVEY

<u>Dreamist Series:</u>

The Haunting of Monroe Manse

The Haunting of Edgefield Manor

The Haunting of Borden House

The Haunting of Intermont Hall, a Novella

The Haunting of Hayden Place

<u>Shadows Trilogy</u>

Shadows of the Moss

Shadows of the War

<u>Other Titles</u>

Truer Words

Recipe for Writing

www.ingramcontent.com/pod-product-compliance
Lightning Source LLC
Chambersburg PA
CBHW021807110726
47902CB00006B/1689